"Do you... you ma...

Obviously, he didn't because he simply stared at her. Shaking his head, Brave leaned against the railing, turning his body toward her.

"Most women would have proclaimed to be outraged by my behavior. Some would even have demanded I marry them, and most would have demanded an apology whether they believed I meant it or not. You, all you want is for me to say I'm *not* sorry."

Rachel glanced away. "It's hurtful to a woman's confidence to hear a man say he regrets kissing her."

Brave nodded. "Then I should be honest with you, Rachel. I shouldn't have kissed you."

Rachel's heart fell.

"But," he continued, "I'm not sorry for it at all."

Avon Books by
Kathryn Smith

ELUSIVE PASSION
A SEDUCTIVE OFFER

Coming Soon

A GAME OF SCANDAL

KATHRYN SMITH

A SEDUCTIVE OFFER

AVON BOOKS
An Imprint of HarperCollinsPublishers

This is a work of fiction. Names, characters, places, and incidents are products of the author's imagination or are used fictitiously and are not to be construed as real. Any resemblance to actual events, locales, organizations, or persons, living or dead, is entirely coincidental.

AVON BOOKS
An Imprint of HarperCollins*Publishers*
10 East 53rd Street
New York, New York 10022-5299

First Avon Books paperback printing: January 2002

Avon Trademark Reg. U.S. Pat. Off. and in Other Countries, Marca Registrada, Hecho en U.S.A.
HarperCollins® is a trademark of HarperCollins Publishers Inc.

Printed in the U.S.A.

10 9 8 7 6 5 4 3 2

For Heather

For allowing your little sister to play with your typewriter,
for all the clothes and makeup over the years,
for always laughing at my jokes,
and for providing calm waters to float my armada.
I nub nu, Albalfa.

Chapter 1

Yorkshire, 1816

A scream pierced the darkness.

Balthazar Wycherley, seventh Earl Braven—known to his intimates as "Brave"—froze as the earsplitting shriek turned his blood to ice. He'd never heard anything like it before. There was something unholy about such a sound on a cold damp night like this.

The banshee's wail echoed off the wall of trees surrounding him, fading into an eerie whisper as the cold October wind swept it away. He looked up at the clouds, indistinguishable against the black sky, save for where the frosty touch of the moon turned them into puffs of luminescent silver. Perhaps it wasn't a banshee bringing news of his demise. Perhaps it was a ghost from the past. Or more likely, the one of his guilty conscience. The forest was now perfectly silent. No specters slipped from the darkness to claim his soul. His heart still beat in his chest—with uncomfortable determination, in fact.

He stood there for a moment, listening for the rattle of ghostly chains, before chuckling bitterly. So this was what he'd become—a coward quivering in the woods, waiting for the dead to claim their—*her*—revenge.

Another scream tore through the night, raising the hair on the back of his neck and sending his heart pounding against his ribs. If it was a ghost, it was a terrified one.

Brave didn't think. He simply reacted. He ran in the direction of the scream, crashing through the trees and dodging roots that would pull him to the ground with the agility of one who knew the land like he knew his own face. Anxiety swelled within him, drove him. He had to find the woman whose fear shivered down his spine. Whether it was out of a sense of heroism, or the hope of coming face-to-face with the ghost that haunted him, he couldn't say.

Or wouldn't.

Seconds later, he stood on the bank of the Wyck. Recent rains had swollen the river so that it tumbled and roared in its bed. Moonlight spilled across its path, turning foaming whitecaps to silver against the inky water. He shivered, knowing how cold it would be at this time of year.

An arm rose from the raging flow, and Brave's eyes widened as he realized it belonged to a young woman clinging tenaciously to a large rock in the roughest part of the river. He watched in dry-mouthed horror as she struggled to hang on to the slick stone as the current pushed against her. If she lost her grip, the river would kill her for certain.

Dear God.

"Miranda?"

"Please, help me!"

No, not Miranda. This voice was far too low and far too alive to be Miranda.

Which meant it was up to him to keep it that way.

"Hang on!" he yelled, cupping his hands around his mouth in an effort to be heard above the raging river. There was a bridge just a few yards upstream. He could cross it and attempt to rescue her from the opposite shore—although he had no idea how such a feat was to be accomplished.

An eternity passed as he raced along the bank to the bridge. As he ran toward her, he could see the girl struggling to keep her head above water as the belligerent current tossed wave after wave into her face. Gasping, she pulled herself farther up onto the rock. Her face was strained with the effort.

As he came to a halt beside a towering old tree, Brave realized just how difficult rescuing her would be. He might very well risk his own life in the process. He tossed his gloves to the ground.

She watched him intently in the frosty moonlight, her expression both relieved and fearful. Her eyes, round and black with panic were almost too big for her stark white face. Lord only knew how long she had been hanging off that rock, and if the cold didn't soon conquer her, the strain in her shoulders just might.

As if to prove just how cold the water was, frothy droplets sprayed his face as a large wave smashed against the bank. Icy pinpricks stung his cheeks.

Damn chivalry.

"Braven?"

Surprise coursed through him. She knew him. Startled, and more than a little wary, he took a good look at her.

Long blond hair that shone like tarnished silver in the moonlight obscured some of her face. But there was no mistaking the owner of those huge, waiflike eyes and strong nose. It was Rachel Ashton—the daughter of one of his father's closest friends. All the more reason why he *had* to save her. Rachel was in serious danger of drowning, not to mention freezing to death, and only he could save her.

It had been a long time since he'd saved someone. Wishing he had didn't count.

Pushing all thought except the present from his mind, Brave yanked off his coat and rolled up his sleeves. The autumn air bit through the thin lawn of his shirt, and he shivered, knowing the river would be much colder.

"What are you d . . . doing?" Rachel cried.

"Rescuing you—if all goes according to plan." Eyeing the branches hanging just above his shoulder, Brave hesitated. What he was contemplating was madness—the servants would have a fit when they found out. Odd, but as crazy as his plan was, he hadn't felt so right about anything in a long time.

And perhaps saving her would take away some of the pain for the one he hadn't saved.

Grasping a low branch, Brave pulled his weight upward, swinging himself into the yawning embrace of the tree with surprising ease. Bits of bark clung to his reddened palms, and he brushed them against his trousers before easing himself into a horizontal position on the branch.

He inched forward, the muscles of his fingers and thighs clenched tight around the limb for balance and leverage. As the bark tore the buttons from his waistcoat, he moved his large frame cautiously forward. The tree was old and sturdy, but he hadn't tested its strength since he was a lad and he was much larger now than he had been then. It would do neither of them any good if he tumbled into the water with her. He could swim, but he doubted he could carry their combined bulk against the current.

The branch didn't budge under his weight. Satisfied that it would hold him, he crept farther until he was suspended directly over Rachel. She stared up at him, mute and wide-eyed. It was a look he had seen before—an expression of desperation that only women seemed capable of. Miranda had given him the same look.

Thrusting haunting visions of tear-filled eyes to the back of his mind, he turned his attention back to the task at hand. He was Rachel's only chance, and he wasn't about to let her down.

"I hope this works," he muttered, before taking a deep breath and throwing himself over the side of the branch. The world tipped and fell. How did he get himself into these situations?

Because he went looking for them. Ever since he was a child he'd gone out of his way to rescue whatever pitiful creature needed it. He hadn't always been successful.

Please God, don't let me fail this time.

Beneath him Rachel gasped at his daring move. He would have laughed were it not for the fact that he was hanging upside down like a bat above an irate river. With his legs wrapped securely around the tree, the momentum of his action had him swinging like a lazy pendulum above the raging water. He knew his legs could easily support his weight.

He just didn't know if his legs and the branch could support her weight as well.

The river washed over her, alternately pushing and pulling her into its frigid bosom. She came up gasping for the breath stolen from her.

"Grab my hand!" he yelled above the crashing water. His fingers brushed the side of her face as he reached down for her. Her chilled flesh was soft—silky. The shock of it almost made him yank his hand away. How long had it been since he had touched a woman?

Despite her obvious fear, she didn't have to tell her twice. She gripped his arm with one hand, then the other, crying out softly as the current lifted her.

"It's all right," he told her once he was certain the branch wasn't going to break—yet. "I've got you."

Yes, but what was he going to do with her? He had no idea how to get her to shore other than trying to lift her, and trying to lift something that probably weighed between eight and nine stone while hanging upside down was not going to be easy, doubly so when that nine-stone weight was also waterlogged.

"Damn." He gazed down at her, painfully aware that the blood was rushing to his head and making him dizzy. "Hang on. Whatever you do, don't let go." Fuzzy warmth swam behind his eyes.

"Don't worry," she yelled above the rush of the river. "I won't."

With determination that came from knowing he had to do something or let her die, Brave clenched his jaw, took a deep breath, and began to curl himself up at the waist. His shoulder groaned, his stomach muscles burned, and it felt as though his eyes might burst right out of their sockets, but he lifted his upper body until he was able to grasp the branch with his free hand.

Her weight threatened to pull him back down. She was a good-sized, healthy girl. Lucky for him the fashion was for flimsy gowns. If she had been wearing anything heavier than her waterlogged muslin gown and pelisse, he never would have been able to lift her this way.

Clutching the branch in a death grip, he strained every muscle in his body to hoist himself facedown onto the limb, grasping the rough bark tightly as the world suddenly dimmed before him. His head swam with prickling dizziness, and pretty colors danced before his eyes.

"Oh God, p . . . please don't faint!" Rachel cried, as she slowly separated his arm from his shoulder.

He smirked down at her, even though he wasn't sure which image undulating before him was truly her. "I'll try to refrain from swooning until my arm is completely wrenched free of its socket." His vision began to clear and he gave his head a quick shake. "I'm going to pull you up. When I get you up here I want you to try to pull yourself onto the branch."

She nodded, and Brave clenched his jaw against the task at hand.

The pain in his shoulder was almost intolerable, but he was no stranger to pain. Reaching around with his free hand, he grabbed her other arm and began pulling her up.

By the time he helped her down the tree to the ground, he was ready to collapse on the grass alongside her. Brave's teeth were chattering and he sagged weakly against the thick trunk. The bark poked through to his skin, but he didn't care. He would be in bad shape come morning.

"Oh, Braven. Thank you." Wrapping her arms around her shivering form, Rachel weaved on her feet. "I s . . . surely would have died if you hadn't c . . . come along. I w . . . would have hated to d . . . die like that."

He laughed humorlessly. There was a certain irony to being allowed to rescue the girl who hadn't wanted to die. Maybe there was a grand plan to the world after all.

Or maybe he'd just gotten lucky this time.

"I am glad . . ." Words failed him as he looked up at her. Right-side up and not neck deep in water, she was definitely a sight to behold.

An angel, actually. Had she always been so lovely?

Pale ribbons of hair clung to her face and slender neck. Her thin coat and gown clung to her curvaceous form like second skin. Her wide eyes seemed to glow with an ethereal light. Her lips . . .

"Oh Lord, your lips are turning blue!" He staggered over to where he had thrown his coat and returned with it, wrapping it around her shivering shoulders. He couldn't bring himself to look at her. Not until the color returned to her face. It was too much. That frigid pallor brought back too many memories.

Rachel trembled against him. "Th-thank you."

"Come, we must get you dry."

She didn't argue, as he helped her to her feet. Nor did she

ask where he was taking her. He supposed she was too numb to care, or just assumed he would take her Wyck's End.

Holding her frigid hand in his own, he tried to concentrate on warming her fingers, not on how delicate her bones were, or how much larger his own hand was. It had been a long time since he'd held a woman's hand. And only a man out of his wits could be so aware of a half-drowned chit.

Half-drowned. Oh yes. There was irony there.

There was a path from the river to his estate, and he made for it. It was different from the route he'd taken to the river, and much shorter.

Eager to get both himself and his icy angel warm, he practically dragged her through the woods toward Wyck's End. She stumbled behind him like a newborn colt after its mother. With luck, the movement would warm her limbs.

He tried not to think about her limbs. He'd seen the curve of her thighs outlined by her sodden gown, the soft roundness of her calves. It wasn't as though she was out of the common way. But his reaction to her was. He'd believed that part of him dead these last two years. It was both comforting and alarming that it hadn't completely given up the ghost.

When she fell to her knees on the edge of the back lawn, he scooped her up into his arms with a muffled curse and, despite his protesting muscles, staggered the rest of the way carrying her. She snuggled against him, her chattering teeth the only sound in the otherwise silent night.

With his arms incapacitated by his waterlogged bundle, Brave gave the back door of Wyck's End a resounding *thwump* with the sole of his scuffed Hessian.

Reynolds, his butler, looked only mildly surprised to see his master stumble in the servant's entrance with a soaking-wet woman in his arms.

"Do you require some assistance, my lord?" he intoned, arching a thin gray brow. He had been part of the household ever since Brave was an infant and was more like family than a mere servant. He was also one of the few servants who didn't treat him as if he could snap at any moment.

"Some hot tea, Reynolds," Brave grunted decisively, lurching down the corridor. "And some blankets and fetch one of my robes."

"Yes, my lord."

"Tea would be l-lovely," the bundle in his arms agreed through clattering teeth. "Thank you."

"You may thank me when I finally put you down." Brave groaned, maneuvering around a sharp corner into the main body of the house. "I might be more appreciative of it then."

He carried her down the dimly lit hall. Portraits of his ancestors watched with haughty disapproval at the dribbles of water left behind him on the carpet. Brave stared straight ahead, ignoring their criticizing gazes along with the pain in his back and shoulders.

It became harder to lift his feet as he crossed the front hall. Each step echoed heavily on the polished marble floor. Grecian statues cast monstrous shadows in the lamplight, their features cast in sharp relief. Brave felt like a villain out of one of those popular novels as he moved among them, carrying the endangered heroine deeper into his lair.

What a fitting analogy.

The housekeeper, Mrs. Bugley, and two maids carrying blankets followed them into the library, where a blazing fire flickered in the hearth and danced along the curves of gilded furniture and ornate picture frames. For once Brave was happy that his servants had acquired the somewhat parental habit of waiting up for him. The pale blue chaise would be the perfect spot for the villain to ravish the heroine, and he would really much prefer to be the hero of this tale.

He set Rachel on her feet. He didn't immediately move away for fear she might fall without his support. She didn't.

Oddly disappointed, and not quite sure whether he should leave the room or not, Brave waited just outside the door, longing for a warming snifter of brandy while the servants divested the girl of her clothes and wrapped her up in his robe and several thick blankets.

"All done, my lord," Mrs. Bugley informed him, casting a suspicious glance over her shoulder. Brave almost smiled. His housekeeper acted as though she believed Rachel was a threat to his safety.

Their arms filled with wet garments, the two maids exited the room, each casting a warm smile in his direction as though he was a knight in a fairy tale. Despite all that had happened to him, his servants still believed him to be some-thing other than he was. They saw him as some kind of hero, and he hated it.

Brave returned their smiles with an awkward one of his own and stepped inside the library. He would have laughed at the sight of her were it not for the fact that his damsel still looked so wretched.

She was bundled up enough to survive a winter in Siberia. All he could see peeking out of her mountain of blankets were the biggest, most unusual blue eyes he had ever seen. They were the color of ripe blueberries. As a child those eyes had seemed almost too large for her face. He was glad to see she'd grown into them.

"Are you any warmer?"

"A little, thank you," She sniffled. Remembering his man-ners, Brave handed her his handkerchief as he seated himself across from her. Only the tips of her fingers appeared above the blankets.

The tea arrived and Brave poured them each a full, steam-ing cup. That he managed the task without spilling any was a wonder. Not only was his arm stiff and awkward from having lifted her, but his hands were much bigger than the delicate china pot.

"Cream and sugar?"

She nodded, a bobbing face in an unmoving cocoon. A

long, shapely arm suddenly appeared from the mountain of cloth, a delicate hand accepting the cup and saucer. Her hands were just as lovely as he had imagined.

Brave still would have preferred the brandy, but as he had no idea what effect it might have on him, he drank the tea. It was surprisingly satisfying, and just as warming.

Rachel sat across from him, holding herself like a duchess despite her absurd appearance. She was the first woman in two years, other than his mother and his servants, to step foot within Wyck's End.

And with that realization the walls closed in on him, and Brave suddenly, desperately, needed her to be gone.

But he couldn't toss her out, not until he'd done his duty and made certain she would be all right. And he certainly couldn't send her home in nothing but a few blankets.

Nothing but a few blankets . . .

"Rachel," he said setting his cup on his saucer with a loud clink, "what the devil were you doing near the river? You of all people should know how dangerous it can be after a rain."

She raised a brow at his harsh tone. "It's good to see you again too, my lord."

Brave sighed. Still a brat. He hadn't known her well as a child, there being a good four or five years between their ages, but he remembered her being difficult even then. His father had adored her, though. "Of course it's a pleasure to see you again, Rachel. It's been too long. Now, will you please tell me what you were doing at the river?"

Her eyes glittered with a hint of mischief. "What do you think I was doing at the river?"

Trying to drown yourself.

For a split second, Brave feared he'd said the words out loud. "I can't imagine."

"I often go there to be by myself," she admitted. "I didn't even know you were still in residence. Had I known you were here, I never would have trespassed." Her full pink mouth came fully into view as she lifted the cup to her lips with trembling hand.

No, she wouldn't have known he was there. Hardly anyone did. He was like a ghost in his own house, in his own village. "You may wander on my property all you want, Rachel, you know that. I'm just glad I happened to be out tonight as well."

"As am I, my lord," she replied with just a trace of defensiveness. "Although I may live to curse you and your heroism."

Brave arched both brows at this cryptic remark. He really shouldn't care about her or her problems. He had enough of his own. "Oh? Why?"

She shook her head, the blanket falling back to reveal a glimpse of pale blond hair.

"Rachel," he teased with a lightness he hadn't felt in some time. "You cannot tell a man you may curse him and not explain why." Leaning back in his chair, he crossed one leg haphazardly over the other; his thighs were still a little shaky from climbing the tree.

Rolling her eyes, Rachel lowered her cup to its saucer. "Sir Henry is planning to see me married."

Brave didn't see the problem. And he certainly didn't understand why the thought of her married should be so disturbing. "Isn't that a stepfather's job?"

"Perhaps if he were a little better at it, I would be more appreciative of his efforts." Her tone was light, amused, but her eyes were dark and bitter.

"I take it you are opposed to the match?" He raised his cup.

Rachel nodded. "My stepfather is very enthusiastic about it, however, and will brook no refusal. Unfortunately, that's just what I plan to do—refuse. He will not like to have his plans disrupted, nor will his chosen son-in-law."

And Sir Henry Westhaver had never struck him as the kind

of man who would take disappointment lightly. In fact, he'd never struck Brave as much of a man at all. Brave supposed he was lucky. His mother had stopped trying to toss him into the marriage mart a long time ago. He doubted that she would bring up the subject again for quite some time. If ever.

"Who is the lucky bridegroom?" he asked, lifting his cup to his lips.

"Today it is Viscount Charlton."

Luckily he had not drunk or he would have choked. "But he's fifty if he's a day!" *And fat. And lecherous.*

She nodded, her smile grim. "So, you see why I may see fit to curse your good deed."

What kind of father—even a stepfather—would marry his daughter off to such a man? A greedy one, no doubt. The idea of an old man like Charlton laying a finger on Rachel's curvaceous form made Brave angry in a way he did not want to admit.

He dropped his cup and saucer on the table between them and laid his palms flat against his thighs. It was what he had been told to do when the urge to break something came upon him. He hadn't had to do that in quite some time.

"If there is anything I can do . . ." He forced his voice to remain calm. What the devil was he doing? He didn't care whom she married, didn't care what happened to her at all as long as it didn't happen on his property.

Rachel glanced up, smiling tightly. "Short of marrying me in his stead, my lord, I don't see that there is much you could do. Are you in need of a countess?"

For one split second he believed she was serious, and then he realized she was merely joking. Or was she? A smile curved her lips, but there was little humor in her gaze.

His hands clenched into fists—not with violence, but with the sudden, stabbing pain the revelation of her obvious despair brought to his chest. He knew that feeling—that certain knowledge that the battle being fought could never be won. Everything in his nature told him he should help her, but the voices in his head told him it was insanity even to consider it.

"I am afraid I am not such a good catch," he replied softly, hoping it sounded lighter than it felt. He had been a good catch at one time, or at least he'd thought he was. But then he'd been told otherwise.

And then he'd proven otherwise.

"Oh well," she said with a breezy wave of her hand. "It was just a thought."

The silence was both awkward and welcome. Brave sipped his tea and stared at the dancing flames in the fireplace. He had no idea what to say. How soon before she would leave? He glanced toward the door, hoping to see a maid there with dry clothes.

"I cannot feel my feet," she announced with something that sounded like a hiccup, staring down at the motionless lump of blankets closest the fire.

Muffling an oath, Brave leapt to his feet. He stomped across the brief expanse of floor that separated them and knelt before her, his hands diving under the blankets. Cold flesh brushed his fingertips.

"Braven!" she gasped, jerking back from his touch.

He rolled his eyes. "I appreciate your maidenly reserve, Rachel, but if you do not allow me to attend to your feet, you may very well lose them."

Beneath the cold-heightened ruddiness, her face turned white. "Truly? I could lose my feet?"

Brave dipped his head in a curt nod. "I've seen it in happen in extreme cases of prolonged exposure to cold. There's a chance you'll be fine, but do you want to take the risk?"

Eyeing him warily, she extended her legs cautiously toward him. "Will it hurt?"

He sat back on his haunches. "Is pain not preferable to

nothing at all?" God knew he would rather suffer the fires of hell than the numbness that permeated his soul.

"I wouldn't know," she replied, her expression one of bewilderment, her eyes searching his face.

"Then I envy you." Jerking his gaze away from her inquisitive one, he peeled back layer after layer of blanket until he reached the frigid flesh beneath.

"Good lord, they're huge!" he exclaimed, unable to hide his astonishment. The rest of her seemed so ethereal, so otherworldly. Who would have though such a delicate creature could be possessed of feet so long?

She leaned forward so that their faces were almost touching. "All the better to kick you with, my lord," she warned with a sardonic smile.

Holding up his hands in mock surrender, Brave sat back on his haunches. "I beg you will not kick me, madam. I fear you might give me a concussion."

Rachel laughed, her dark eyes sparkling. "You're impertinent, Lord Braven."

He wrapped his fingers around her chilled foot, his lips curving into the shadow that now passed as a smile. True, her feet were long for a woman, but they were slender and fine-boned.

He could almost imagine running his tongue along the high arch of her instep. He forced himself to massage it instead. Lord, what was he about having such thoughts about a girl he'd known since they were both children?

"Your hands are so warm." Her voice was low and sighing, sending a shiver down his spine. The blankets parted as she leaned back in the chair, revealing her legs to just above the knees. She had donned his dressing gown as well and the wine-colored silk brocade was a stark contrast against her pale, shapely calves as it slipped open around them.

Against his better judgment, Brave's gaze traveled up the leg he held in his hands, past the gentle curve behind her knee to the soft, round thigh peeking through the folds of the robe. Little Rachel Ashton had grown into quite the voluptuous beauty. His hands stilled in their ministrations as he imagined what he might see if she spread her legs just a little bit wider . . .

"Is there something wrong?" she inquired innocently, leaning forward again.

The movement caused the robe to slip even farther. Heat suffused his cheeks as he stared at her naked flesh. He felt like a schoolboy trying to peer up a young girl's skirts. Too long. It had been far too long.

Swallowing hard, Brave took a deep, shuddering breath. Oh God, he could smell her. The scent was faint, but sweet, musky, and decidedly feminine.

"No," he rasped, tearing his gaze away from the dark apex that concealed her succulent flesh. His groin was tight and throbbing with desire. His hardened flesh strained against the front of his snug buckskin breeches. Damnation, what had come over him?

It was the shock of the evening. It had to be. That was the only explanation for the heatedness of his blood and his startling reaction to her. It was the euphoria of having saved her life. Nothing more.

He grabbed a corner of one of the blankets and placed it strategically over his lap. Staring at her toes he stammered, "I . . . I thought perhaps I was hurting you?"

"Oh no," Rachel assured him, resuming her former relaxed pose. "I'm actually starting to feel some warmth in that one." She wiggled the toes of the foot he held.

"Good." He rubbed briskly, her foot turning pink as the blood and his palms warmed it. He did not allow his gaze to move from his hands. He tried to keep his mind blank, but he could not keep her scent from tantalizing his nostrils.

He rubbed her other foot as well—quickly—then rose to turn her chair closer to the fire.

"There. You should be fine now." He kept his hands folded in front of him to hide the stubborn evidence of his body's reaction to her.

She smiled at him, her big eyes crinkling at the corners.

"That's twice that you've saved me, my lord. I'm afraid I may soon have to declare you my hero." There was laughter in her voice.

Brave's throat tightened so close he almost choked on his breath. Most men would kill to be thought a hero by a beautiful woman, but not him. The mere mention of the word almost turned his rod as limp as a used cravat.

"I'd rather you didn't. I wouldn't want such praise to go to my head—or yours." Now he was just being stupid.

Rachel nodded, her smile fading. "You're right," she said, staring somewhere over his shoulder. Her gaze was shuttered, but the slump of her shoulders spoke volumes. "I might expect you—the handsome young knight—to save me all the time rather than save myself."

Brave wasn't certain how to take her bluntness. "Quite right," he replied softly, keeping his tone light.

She leaned forward in the chair, the blanket fell back from her head, revealing the mass of damp, silver-streaked hair that framed her face like a halo. The line of one calf was also still visible, and Brave was certain he had never seen anything quite so seductive.

"I don't expect you to rescue me again, Brave. You've done enough already. I shall always be in your debt."

Part of him wanted to run. Another wanted to laugh, while a third part of him wanted to go to her and yank her to her big feet. He wanted to feel her breasts crushed against his chest, plunder her mouth with his tongue until all either of them could taste was each other. He wanted to lose himself in her luscious body, bruise that softness until he felt human again.

She said he would be her hero.

God, what was he thinking? He had to put an end to this

situation before it became even more like a child's fairy tale. He had rescued the princess once—twice if he listened to her—but there was a limit to his knightly powers, especially when he knew all too well what a sham they were.

She watched him intently as he stood. A small frown wrinkled her otherwise smooth brow.

"No doubt your family is quite concerned about you." He turned toward the door. "My mother always leaves clothes here for her visits. I will find you something to wear and see that you are taken safely home."

"That is not nec—"

"No!"

She stared up at him, startled by his vehemence. Her eyes were huge and dark against the pallor of her face. He couldn't blame her. He sounded like a lunatic.

"I insist," he went on in a much softer tone of voice. "I would not rest easy knowing you were out alone." With that said, he bowed briefly and strode from the room.

Every fiber of his being strained with the effort it took to walk away from her even though his mind told him it was the right thing to do. The sooner she was out of his house, the sooner his life could return to the closeted loneliness he'd come to find safety in. A woman like Rachel Ashton was anything but safe.

As soon as the door closed behind him he broke into a dead run.

Chapter 2

～◦◦◦～

Softly closing the door behind her, Rachel held her still damp clothes at arm's length and tiptoed across the polished oak floor. Two wall sconces were lit, bathing the hall in mellow light. Hopefully, that meant Sir Henry was either not home or passed out drunk in his study.

"Where the devil have you been?"

Rachel stiffened. So much for sneaking in. Straightening her shoulders, she turned to face her stepfather.

"I couldn't sleep and I went for a walk." It was on the tip of her tongue to add that it was all his fault, but she was in no mood to argue with him. Besides, he would only take pleasure in her discomfort, and she didn't want him to know that she'd uncovered his latest plans for her.

His eyes narrow, her stocky stepfather moved forward. The dim light darkened the creases of his face, making them appear deeper and the rest of his fleshy features all the more bloated. He looked just like a troll in a child's bedtime story.

"What happened to your hair and your clothes?" he demanded, jerking his chins at the bundle in her arms.

Rachel's jaw tightened. "I got too close to the river and fell in."

Sir Henry circled her as he might a horse at auction. His close appraisal made the hair on Rachel's neck rise. "Lucky for you that you didn't drown."

"Lucky for you as well." She stared at a point over his shoulder, not even wanting to meet his loathsome gaze. "Otherwise, you wouldn't be able to sell me to the highest bidder."

Sir Henry swore, but otherwise ignored her barb. "Where'd you get those clothes? You look like a strumpet."

Rachel looked down at the tight bodice of the gray-silk gown she wore beneath a soft cashmere shawl. Even though it displayed a shocking amount of bosom, it was the most exquisite gown she had ever seen, let alone worn.

Ignorant old goat. You wouldn't know fashion if it bit you on your gout-ridden foot.

"Lord Braven loaned them to me," she replied tauntingly. She raised her chin to meet her stepfather's pale, narrow gaze. "They belong to his mother." There was no way he could find fault now unless he wanted to insult the earl or the countess.

"Braven? I thought he was dead."

Smiling in self-satisfaction, Rachel shrugged. "He is very much alive, and I'm afraid you not only owe my present wardrobe to his generosity, for 'twas he who pulled me from the river."

From the edge of his receding hairline to the rounded paunch of his double chin, Sir Henry Westhaver flushed a dull red. "Well, just so you know, your poor mother's been worried sick," he said gruffly. "Now go to bed."

"Yes, Sir Henry." Obediently, Rachel turned on her heel and left the salon. She doubted her mother even knew she had been out. Henry just wanted to make her feel guilty. Oh, she knew she shouldn't think such thoughts of her father, and she wouldn't—were Henry Westhaver her father.

Rachel was the product of her mother's first marriage to a wealthy Yorkshire landowner. When William Ashton died in a carriage accident, leaving his estate entailed to a distant relative and his daughter's dowry tied up until Rachel turned twenty-five, Marion Ashton had no choice but to seek a new life for herself and her child. Sir Henry Westhaver made the first offer.

Rachel never quite forgave her father for dying as he had, for leaving them.

It quickly became apparent that Sir Henry was far from the answer to their prayers. By the time his true nature revealed itself it was too late, and Rachel was powerless to protect her mother. She swore at a very young age that someday she would get them both out from under her stepfather's roof. And then no one would ever hurt her mother again.

Opening the door to her room just enough to avoid making the top hinge squeak, Rachel slipped inside. The fire dying in the grate cast low shadows on the faded flowered wallpaper, but the room was warm and cozy regardless. No doubt Sir Henry had little idea how comfortable her room was, or he'd have her moved to the attic just for spite.

She did not remove the lovely gown upon reaching her room. Instead, she stretched out upon the faded rose-and-ivory counterpane and stroked the soft silk that stretched across her chest.

Judging from the tightness of the bodice and the fact that the skirts ended well above her ankle, Rachel judged the countess to be a tiny little bit of a woman.

Her son, however, certainly wasn't a little man.

Lord, Rachel had thought her eyes were going to pop right out of her head when she looked up from her nest of blankets and saw him standing there in the firelight. In her panic at the river, she hadn't noticed how much bigger he was than the last time she had seen him.

Lord Braven was a tall man, with broad shoulders and narrow hips. During his daring rescue, the buttons had come off his waistcoat, leaving the torn garment completely open in the front. His shirtfront was damp where he carried her against him, and the thin lawn clung and conformed to the muscles of his chest and abdomen.

Being accustomed to the soft form of her stepfather, she had been completely enthralled by the hard planes and ridges that made up the earl's torso.

And that face! In the moonlight he'd look positively fierce—like something straight out of a myth. With those slashing brows, Romanesque nose, and grim mouth he'd been the perfect warrior sent to save her. Those puppy-dog eyes had been the only softness on his face, and even then they were so solemn she couldn't bear to look at them for long.

Oh no, there wasn't a woman in England who wouldn't be content to go limp in the Earl of Braven's strong arms and let him carry her wherever he wanted.

It was odd, calling him by his father's title, even though it wasn't that different from the nickname he'd earned years before. Some silly girl had apparently commented on how brave the future Earl of Braven was, and the appellation "Brave" stuck. Rachel had always thought it rather silly, but now she thought he rather deserved it. No doubt his father—the old earl—would be proud of the man he had become.

She remembered the old earl from her childhood. He had been a big man with sparkling eyes and big hands. He always had sweets for her whenever Rachel's father took her with him on one of his visits to Wyck's End. How kind he had always been. Rachel had actually wept at the old man's funeral.

The present earl looked little like his father—except perhaps for his chocolate brown eyes and the size of his hands. He had sat with them on his thighs as if he had no idea what to do with them. Strong hands, obviously, because he had hauled her out of the river as though she was nothing more than a piece of laundry. How awkward they looked holding the delicate china cup he had sipped his tea from. How warm they had been as they massaged her icy feet. The mere thought of those long fingers against her flesh was enough to make her feel hot all over.

Had David ever made her feel that way? Once maybe, but now all she felt when she thought of him was a strange mix of sorrow and relief. Sorrow that he hadn't been the man she thought him to be. And relief that he'd chose to abandon rather than marry her. He would have made her miserable.

And she had enough misery in her life without a husband adding to it.

There was a sadness about Brave that she found utterly intriguing. There was something holding him back from life, she could sense it. The young earl had scars and secrets buried deep within him that made a woman want to open him up and look inside his soul.

"Stop thinking about him," she muttered to herself crossly. "Remember how far beneath him you are."

As if she could ever forget.

There was a soft tap at her door and she called out for whoever was there to enter, grateful that thoughts of her savior could be put aside.

The door opened. "May I come in?" asked a soft voice.

Rising into a sitting position on the soft mattress, Rachel frowned. "Mama, what are you doing up?"

Marion Westhaver shuffled into the room. Her long brown hair was unbound and hung heavily around her slender shoulders. The voluminous nightgown she wore hung off her thin frame. She looked like a child playing in her mother's wardrobe, but her walk was that of a woman—a woman in pain. Every step was slow and agonizing—for both Rachel and her mother.

He mother closed the door. "I wanted to wait until Henry was in his chamber before coming to yours."

A familiar, frigid rage curdled in the pit of Rachel's stomach, sending tendrils of ice shooting throughout her limbs. "What did he do to you?"

Marion shook her head and wearily waved a thin hand.

"Nothing that he hasn't done before." She eased herself into a pink-cushioned chair and sighed.

Rachel fought to stifle her temper. She had long ago learned that Henry Westhaver was a coward. He would belittle and beat her mother, but whenever Rachel confronted him, he refused to act against her.

Whenever she retaliated on behalf of her mother, Sir Henry made life all the harder for Marion. Rachel had given up trying to fight her mother's battles. Instead, she plotted for the day she could take her mother away from there—the day she turned twenty-five.

Only a few months away in January, Rachel's birthday meant she would get the money her father had set aside for her—the money neither she nor her mother had been able to touch when they needed it. Once she had it, Rachel could afford to pay for a divorce on the grounds of brutality. And if that didn't work, she would at least be able to take her mother away where Sir Henry could never find her.

So, it was important that Rachel avoid her stepfather's efforts to marry her off at all costs, since a husband would automatically gain control of her money. Taking care of her mother meant that she would probably never marry a man she could love, at least not until her mother was safe, but she didn't care. She cared only that she and her mother would soon be free of Henry Westhaver.

If Sir Henry didn't succeed in killing her mother first.

"I thought we should have a talk since your stepfather wants to see you married soon."

Rachel jumped at the sound of her mother's tired voice.

For a moment, she thought the other woman had fallen asleep in her tiny, uncomfortable seat.

"Talk about what?" she asked, drawing herself up into a sitting position on the bed.

"About wifely duties."

Rachel felt as though she had just been hit in the face with a snowball.

She already knew what "wifely duties" entailed. A few years ago Rachel had stumbled upon Sabine, a chambermaid, having *relations* with one of the footmen. Later, Sabine had come to her room and, sensing how much the discovery would distress a "virginal miss," had explained the process in detail.

It was more detail than Rachel had wanted at the time, but it came in handy during her older years when scant few young men tried to lure her into dark gardens and secret alcoves. And it had kept her from making an irreparable mistake with David.

The idea of allowing Viscount Charlton to touch her as David had tried to touch her was somewhat sickening. Rachel didn't even want to *think* of performing her "wifely duties" with Charlton.

"Rachel dear? Are you unwell?"

"I already know what is expected of me in the marriage bed, Mama," she replied, rubbing her throbbing forehead with the heel of her hand. "Not that I entertain any idea of having to go through with the experience anytime soon, no matter what Sir Henry wants."

Marion's face took on the expression of fear that Rachel had become accustomed to since they had come to live with Henry Westhaver. Anxiety, despair, and a tiredness Rachel despised were reflected in the pale depths of her mother's blue eyes and etched in the lines of her face.

"Don't fight him, Rachel. I've tried fighting him for years, and I've yet to win."

"I'm not you, Mama." No, she wasn't. She didn't have a young daughter to think about and no one to go to for help.

She understood the fact that her mother had only Sir Henry and the poorhouse to choose from, but that didn't stop her from sometimes wishing her mother had chosen the poorhouse. Ten years of watching her stepfather beat her mother into the ground had taken its toll. As had ten years of being pitied by the rest of the townspeople.

There had been times when she had just wanted to run away, leaving her mother to her own devices, but she couldn't bring herself to actually go. After all her mother had done for her, she couldn't just leave her. Not when it was her fault her mother had made such a disastrous marriage in the first place.

Marion flushed, but her gaze never wavered from her daughter's. "No. You're not."

Rachel knew all too well there was a chance that life on their own would be no easier than life with Henry Westhaver, but at least they would be free. They would be left to their own devices, but they would have a little money left once the divorce was settled and they would answer to no one but themselves. Even if Rachel had to look after her mother for the rest of her life, she would have the satisfaction of defeating Sir Henry.

Patting her mother's thin hand, Rachel managed a slight smile. "I appreciate your concern, Mama, but I really do know all I need to know. And if Sir Henry finds me an agreeable husband, perhaps we can come to an agreement." She hated lying to her mother, but she didn't want to risk her mother ruining her plans by confessing to Henry out of fear, either.

Her smile grew. "Although I don't imagine even Sir Henry could find a man I wouldn't drive to distraction with my stubbornness anyway."

Her mother's pale, nervous gaze met hers. "A wife shouldn't provoke her husband, Rachel."

Rachel's face tightened. "And a husband shouldn't beat his wife, Mama. Now why don't you stop worrying and leave everything to me?"

In a rare show of humor, her mother smiled, reminding Rachel of the happy woman she used to be.

"*That* is what worries me," she joked, lifting herself out of the chair with an agonizing stiffness that made Rachel ache just from watching her. Slowly, Marion crossed the floor to her daughter.

Rachel didn't have to force a smile as her mother stood before her. Carefully, she wrapped her arms around her mother's waist. From her seat on the bed, she could rest her head against her mother's bosom as she had as a child. It still gave her comfort even though the woman who had once seemed so round and solid now felt little and frail. Rachel wasn't certain if it was because she was now the larger of the two or if her mother had actually lost weight along with her spirit over the years with Henry.

Gentle hands stroked her hair. "Do what's best for you, dearest. You don't have to worry about me."

Rachel's throat constricted painfully as tears filled her eyes. Part of her wanted to accept her mother's offer, but then she thought of all the bruises, all the insults and broken bones this woman had endured in order to give her a comfortable life, and her rage gave her strength.

"Yes, I do," she replied, pulling free of the warm embrace with a sniff. "And I will until you're free of that man."

Marion did not respond, but her smile was one of sad gratitude. She squeezed Rachel's hand and slowly drifted toward the door. Rachel watched, her heart breaking, as her mother took every painful step with quiet dignity.

Left alone again, Rachel was immediately filled with that

old familiar sense of guilt that these talks with her mother always inspired.

How could she not feel somewhat responsible for her mother's fate? Had it not been for her, her mother might have been able to make it on her own. She could have started a new life somewhere, but that had been impossible with a child to support. She had sold herself to Henry Westhaver, just as Rachel was now being sold to Viscount Charlton.

Well, there was one subtle difference between Rachel and her mother. Rachel would allow no man to degrade her as Sir Henry had degraded her mother. The first man who ever struck her would soon find himself regretting it—if he lived that long.

She wagered the Earl of Braven had never struck a woman. His hands were warm and gentle, not brutal like Sir Henry's or cold and damp like Charlton's. If only Sir Henry would find someone like that to be her husband. Even if he could find someone like Brave willing to have her, it would be too kind of Sir Henry to sell her to someone even remotely close to her own age, let alone someone handsome and kind. No, he wanted her to suffer.

She would not give him the satisfaction. She would persevere. She would take her mother away from him and she would do everything within her power to give her the life she deserved.

She slid off the bed and went to the window. Her gaze traveled the moonlit length of the well-groomed grounds to the edge of the garden. Her stepfather's house and garden were among the finest in the county. Sir Henry believed in keeping up appearances—or at least some appearances.

Sir Henry believed money spent on Rachel and her mother to be a waste. He'd much rather spend it on horses he rarely rode, but could show off to his cronies as having cost him "a fair portion." He also liked to gamble, drink, and keep himself in the pink of fashion while Rachel and her mother remodeled old dresses until the fabric was too thin to wear.

In a few more months, she would never have to look at Sir Henry's ugly face again. She would never have to look at those awful meticulous grounds again.

Her gaze moved westward. There, beyond a great copse of evergreens she could barely make out the shadowy smoke drifting from the chimneys at Wyck's End.

Rachel placed one hand against the pane, conscious of the cold glass against her palm. It was almost as though she could just reach out and touch his house, and touch him in the process.

If she closed her eyes she could see him standing before her in his drawing room. His dark, honey-streaked hair damp and wild around his head, his eyes so dark and intense beneath straight brows—and his mouth, so somber in a face that had no business being as enticing as it was.

The heat of his hands had warmed not only her skin but her blood as well. How grateful she was that when his fingers touched her foot he mistook her gasp of sensual shock as maidenly reserve!

She had wanted him to touch her, had wanted to feel his fingers stroke the ticklish valley behind her knee, the tender flesh of her inner thigh and more, so much more. The wanton in her had wanted to throw off the constrictive blankets and let him have his way with her.

No man had ever affected her in such a manner. She had always prided herself on the fact that she'd never lost her reason where the opposite sex was concerned. But now she knew what Sabine had meant when she had told her that one day she would "burn" for a man.

The Earl of Braven had lit a torch inside her.

Briefly, she wondered if the Earl of Braven was looking for a wife.

What am I thinking?

Giving herself a mental shake, Rachel opened her eyes. Even if he was looking for a wife, he could certainly do better than Henry Westhaver's stepdaughter.

Her gaze dropped for an instant to the bodice of the exquisite silk gown she wore. It wasn't the cost of the gown that made her smile. It wasn't the fact that her bosom threatened to spill out of it either. It was the fact that the gown provided a reason to see him again.

And she would see him again.

Brave hadn't planned to attend the ball that evening at Lord Westwood's estate. He hadn't been out in society much in the last two years, and he wished he hadn't decided to come out this night. The lights, the crush of hot bodies pressed together, mingling sweat and perfume until the smell became overpowering, was more than he could stomach. It was like being locked in a whore's closet and twice as suffocating.

It wasn't that his shoulder still bothered him. He rather liked the dull ache in his muscles. He had earned it.

And it wasn't that he didn't like people or felt the society beneath him. He just didn't want to have to answer questions as to why he kept to himself, or what had happened to change him from social animal to near recluse. And then there might actually be someone who would bring up "that poor girl's death," and then see the guilt on his face. He didn't want to lie any more than he wanted to tell the truth.

He also didn't relish the idea of being looked at like a prime cut of meat at market. Every mama present was eyeing him as a potential son-in-law. There was no way he could convince them he didn't want to marry—that he could *never* marry.

If anyone knew of his involvement in Miranda's death, no one would want him anywhere near their daughters. Or hardly anyone. There was always someone who cared more about money and titles than blood and responsibility and madness—oh yes, *temporary* madness. Perhaps he should tell them that his friends and family had begged him to seek the care of a physician for the sake of his sanity. And maybe he should tell them how little help that physician had been able to give him.

But *that* was something he didn't want to admit.

And he certainly didn't want to admit that his reason for accepting this invitation had anything to do with the hope of seeing Rachel Ashton again. For the past three days he'd played their dramatic meeting over and over in his head until he knew every detail by heart. He didn't know how, he only knew that deep, deep inside saving Rachel Ashton had made a difference.

The thought of what would have happened if he hadn't come along filled him with panic. She would have died, alone and scared.

Had Miranda been scared?

"Champagne, Lord Braven?"

Automatically, Brave accepted the glass offered him. "Thank you, Lady Westwood." He smiled down at the plump matron. "You look lovely this evening."

The elderly woman seemed not to notice that his smile was broken, and tapped him lightly on the arm with her fan. "You're a sweet boy to say so." She gazed up at him with a shrewd yet pleasant expression. "Why aren't you dancing?"

Because the last time I danced was with Miranda. "I would be honored to take a turn with you if you wish it."

Lady Westwood unfurled her Chinese silk fan and waved it violently in front of her face. Brave had to take a step to the right just to avoid being stabbed by the lacquered sticks. He watched as the brightly colored feathers in her hair bobbed in the breeze she created. It was as though they longed to fly again but couldn't because they were fastened to a woman instead of a bird.

"Oh Lord, bless you." She sighed. "My husband, however, does not approve of the waltz, the prudish old buzzard." She cast him a sidelong glance. "Why would you dance with an old thing like me when there are younger and prettier partners to be found?"

He decided to be equally as blunt. "Perhaps because I can be reasonably certain *your* mama won't take it as an intention of marriage."

Lady Westwood grinned. "So that's why you've been hiding in the corner all evening! I might have known they'd be on you like flies on sugar." She patted his hand in a maternal gesture. "Drink your champagne, dear boy. That will give you strength."

Brave stared at the glass of sparkling liquid. His mouth watered for a taste of the tart sweetness its scent promised. Surely one little glass of champagne couldn't hurt, could it? One glass wouldn't make him lose control.

Cautiously, he lifted the glass to his lips, offered up a brief prayer that he wouldn't humiliate himself in any way, and drank. It was cool and crisp against his tongue, filling his mouth with a most delightful sensation. He managed to stop himself before he drained the glass in one gulp.

No demons came screaming from the balcony to carry away his soul following his rash action. And it certainly didn't make him want to drink until he couldn't think.

"There now!" Lady Westwood cried. "Don't you feel better? Now, let's see if we can find you a decent dance partner."

Brave's fingers tightened around his glass. "No. Lady Westwood, I beg of you—"

"Sssht! Here she comes."

Following her stare, Brave almost groaned out loud. Duped. He had been neatly and utterly ensnared. Gliding across the floor toward them in a decidedly ungraceful manner was Lady Westwood's only granddaughter.

"Et tu, Brute?" he demanded with a wince.

The old woman stared up at him with eyes that seemed to peer into the very soul of him. He started at the pleading in their faded depths.

"She was a failure this Season, Lord Braven," she whispered quickly. "Too shy to do anything more than fade farther into the woodwork every time someone even looked at her." She turned her head to watch the young woman approach. "I daresay a turn about the floor with a handsome, sought-after earl who rarely comes out into society would do wonders for her popularity and confidence."

It was the love in her voice that was Brave's undoing. That and the picture of a shy young girl standing alone, waiting for someone to ask her to dance. He knew how it felt to be rejected and how easy it was to withdraw into oneself. He also knew of the bitterness it could breed.

"I would be honored," he replied softly, just as the girl reached them.

Lady Westwood did not reply, but seized his hand and squeezed.

Introductions were made, and Brave requested the honor of being Lady Victoria's next dance partner.

"That is, if you are not already spoken for?" he inquired with what he hoped was a charming smile.

Blushing furiously, the young woman smiled, her pale lashes fluttering. "I would be honored, Lord Braven."

Brave couldn't remember the last time he felt so good about himself. The smile on his partner's cherubic face warmed his heart. She was surprisingly light on her feet, and he found himself enjoying the dance—and the disdain of many of the mamas present. No doubt they were incensed that he had asked the local wallflower to dance over their more-deserving daughters. And as long as he kept Lady Victoria talking, he couldn't think about the past.

It wasn't until much later, as the Allemande ended and he

escorted a giggling Lady Victoria back to her grandmother, that Brave realized Rachel Ashton had arrived.

She stood, silent and vibrant in a simple gown of muted violet, near, but not part of, a gaggle of laughing pastel-clad young women, seemingly oblivious to their mirth. There was little doubt in Brave's mind that Rachel herself was what the girls were giggling at. Her gown was obviously old and out-dated, her hairstyle too simple to have been created by an experienced abigail. William Ashton would roll over in his grave if he knew his daughter was at an assembly dressed like someone's poor relative.

It was common in the country to invite every young person of good birth to such a gathering, as young people were often scarce. Rachel's father had been well thought of in the community, and even though Sir Henry wasn't, his title made it difficult to totally ignore him or his family.

Despite the fact that she was sorely out of place, Rachel held herself as elegantly as a queen. And she was watching him so intently that his mouth went dry. Her expression was unreadable, but something in her eyes called out to him. All his instincts told him to turn around and walk away from her, but he could no more do that than pretend he hadn't hoped she would appear.

Vaguely aware of the curious gazes following him, Brave moved toward her. One by one, the young ladies around her caught notice of his approach and began nudging and whispering to each other.

He was not so daft that he didn't realize they were all hoping to be the one who had caught his attention. In the country a young man with a good fortune was considered a prime catch, and a young earl with a large fortune was open game. They'd been stalking him all evening.

Like ducks bobbing on a pond, the curtsies began, each delving deeper than the one before in an effort to garner his notice. Brave smiled blindly at them all, his gaze darting back to the woman who had bewitched him simply by allowing him to save her life. A woman so proud that she would risk ridicule rather than stay at home, where others believed she belonged.

"Miss Ashton," he said, surprising himself with the confident tone of his voice. He bowed and took her hand. "How lovely it is to see you again."

Out of the corner of his eye, Brave watched as half a dozen mouths dropped open. He smiled.

Rachel curtsied. "Lord Braven. It is indeed a pleasure to find you here at our little assembly. Are you enjoying yourself?" Her voice was steady, her tone polite, but Brave detected the slightest hint of a tremor in her honey-smooth voice. Obviously it was harder for her to face the gossipmongers than he initially believed.

"I am, thank you." He stared into her wide eyes, searching the purple-blue depths for some hint that this tension he felt between them wasn't just madness. He found nothing but uncertainty.

"My evening would be all the more enjoyable if you would condescend to dance with me." What was he doing? He hadn't danced for two years and now he was going to do it twice in one evening? The gossips would be wagging their tongues for a week. He would become known as a man who only danced with those no one else would dance with, and Rachel, once their jealousy wore off, would be laughed at for being another one of his charity cases.

Though his reasons for wanting to hold her were far, far from charitable.

"Lord Braven, I—" His grip on her fingers tightened. She faltered, her mouth working silently. "I would be delighted."

It was all he could do not to sigh in relief. He led her to the dance floor and, lifting their entwined fingers high, placed his other hand lightly on the small of her back. The urge to haul her against him, pressing his hips deep into hers, was overpowering. As it was he held her closer than what was proper.

"I am pleased to see that you have not suffered any ill effects from your accident the other night," he commented as they twirled around the floor. She was extremely graceful.

"None," she replied, gazing earnestly at him. "I think I have your quick thinking to thank for that."

Brave smiled ruefully. "Then perhaps I should apologize."

Rachel frowned, puckering the skin between her delicately winged brows. "Apologize?"

He nodded. "I would think a case of ague would be most beneficial in avoiding attending this evening."

The instant the words left his mouth he regretted them. The color drained from her face and her eyes become flat and expressionless.

"And deny them the pleasure of laughing behind my back?" Her voice was laced with bitter humor. "I quite thrive on their pity, Lord Braven. I assure you it is the one thing in my life I've come to take for granted. In fact, a day just doesn't feel right if I have to go without."

He felt the full sting of her words. He'd angered her, shamed her by bringing it up. It was badly done.

"You've done nothing to deserve their pity." It was as close as he could bring himself to an apology. An apology would take away from her resentment, and she had every right to it.

A wry smile curved her wide lips. "No, but my mother did by marrying a man as worthless as Westhaver, and that makes my situation all the more pitiable because I had no control over it." She shrugged, causing the fabric of her gown to slide against his hand. "It does have its advantages when the whole village feels sorry for you. That's why you asked me to dance, isn't it?"

Her gaze challenged him to deny it. By lumping him in with the rest of the town she could continue on with this strange self-punishment. She could continue to believe she was alone, friendless. She didn't strike him as a martyr, but she seemed to feed off the very social exile he feared. It gave her strength.

"Actually, I asked you to dance because you were the only woman in the room that didn't look at me as though she'd like to cosh me over the head and carry me off to the parson."

There was a moment's silence, and then she burst out laughing as though he'd just said the funniest thing she'd ever heard. The deep, body-shaking resonance of her laughter was contagious, and Brave was shocked when a hesitant, awkward smile curved his own lips. It had been so long since he'd made someone laugh—so long since he'd felt like laughing himself.

Lost in the wonder that he had created that sparkle in her eyes, it took a few seconds for Brave to realize when she stopped laughing. When he finally did, it was to find her regarding him with an expression so warm and open it thrilled him straight to his toes.

Oh yes, she was dangerous.

Aware that they were under the scrutiny of all those watching the dancing, Brave steered her farther into the protective circle of the other dancers. This dance had suddenly become a very private, intimate moment for him, and he didn't want to share it with the gossips.

She smiled at him. "Thank you for reminding me that I shouldn't feel so sorry for myself. I'd forgotten that everyone has their own problems."

Brave whirled her around. "Just so long as you don't now feel sorry for me, you're welcome."

Chuckling, she tilted her head to one side and regarded him through impossibly thick eyelashes. "You're not the kind of man who inspires sorriness, Brave. Sympathy, perhaps, but never pity."

He wasn't sure how to respond to that—and especially not to her use of his nickname—and so he said nothing.

When the music ended, they were poised beside the balcony doors, and, as a handful of other couples made their way out into the crisp night air, Brave suggested they do the same. He hadn't taken a young woman out onto a balcony since Miranda, and he wasn't quite sure why he was doing it now. He only knew he didn't want this moment to end so soon.

"I feel compelled to warn you," Rachel said as she laid her hand on his arm, "that our going outside is only going to fan the flames of gossip."

"What flames?"

She smiled coyly. "Rumor has it that the reason you attended tonight was to begin a search for a bride."

"Damn," he muttered between clenched teeth. Just his luck. If he'd remained a recluse, they'd gossip about that, too.

Rachel laughed at his ungentlemanly outburst. "Relax, my lord. No one would even dare entertain the idea that you might consider me a candidate for countess."

"You'd make a better countess than any of those . . . those *children* I've had thrown in my path this evening." They stepped up to the balustrade, and Brave realized that they were, in effect, completely alone. Many of the other couples had gone down into the garden, or had gone off to darker corners. If he pushed her into the potted plants behind them, they'd be completely hidden. He could kiss her, and no one would be the wiser.

Now, where in the name of God had that thought come from?

Bracing her arms on the railing, Rachel smiled like a fairy queen in the moon-silvered darkness. "I imagine you are quite popular with the single ladies now that you have entered back into society."

Brave rolled his eyes. "Unfortunately. It does have a tendency to make one feel like a fox being chased by hounds."

"A decidedly unkind analogy, my lord," she chastised with a grin. "No matter how accurate it might be."

He looked down. "You called me Brave earlier. I liked it."

Silence as his heart drummed out the seconds.

"All right."

Turning to face her, Brave leaned against the cool stone and folded his arms across his chest. "How accurate do you think?"

She raised a pale brow and flashed him a teasing grin. He didn't need to explain. "Very. They all believe you'll find a bride in London during the Autumn Season, so they're hoping to catch your eye before you fall prey to all those town ladies."

Brave snorted. "I don't want a town lady."

"A country bride then?" Again that teasing smile that made him want to kiss her until he'd filled himself with her. What did she have to be so lighthearted about?

"I'm not looking for a bride at all."

"No?" She seemed surprised by his confession. "How extraordinary. We're in exactly the same predicament. You don't want a wife, I don't want a husband, and no one seems to care."

She'd summed it up quite succinctly.

"Then there is only one logical conclusion," he announced.

Her face glowed with humor. "Oh? And what is that?"

"Our only escape is to marry each other and enjoy a marriage of convenience." He was only half joking, a realization that gripped him with sudden horror. No marriage was convenient, especially not for him. Was he that desperate for the promise of female flesh he'd marry for it?

Mad. He was truly mad.

Rachel didn't look at him as though he were mad. She looked at him as though he'd said something hilarious. Brave allowed himself a chuckle of relief as she started laughing. He ignored the strange sense of disappointment her amusement brought with it.

"Oh, Brave, thank you!" She wiped tears from her eyes with her gloved fingertips.

"For what?" He wasn't certain he wanted to know.

She sniffed and smiled at him. The urge to kiss her was overpowering. "For saving my life. For asking me to dance when few others would, and for making me laugh. I needed that."

Her open gaze unnerved him and he shrugged. "It becomes you. You should laugh more often."

"Odd. I was just thinking the same thing about you."

His heart twisted suddenly beneath his ribs, and he stepped away as she lifted her hand to his cheek. He'd toss what control he had left to the wind if she touched him.

Disappointment clouded her features as she dropped her arm. "I'm sorry."

Knowing he was responsible for that expression cut Brave to the quick. He shook his head and took another step back. If he were smart, he'd leave her there. Now.

"I'm the one who should be sorry, Rachel."

A tiny frown creased her brow, and she stepped toward him. "For what?" Her lips parted in confusion, and Brave could only imagine how he must look to her. If half of what he felt showed on his face, she had a right to look confused.

And every reason to run screaming.

But she didn't run, and Brave reached out and grabbed her little hand in his own. "For this," he growled. He pulled her into the blackness behind the plants.

And then he kissed her.

Chapter 3

Cool, hard stone pressed against her back.

Warm, hard man pressed against her front.

With her arms held high above her head, and her body pinned by Brave's, Rachel was completely powerless against the knee-weakening power of his kiss. It was perhaps the first time in her life that she didn't mind not being in control.

His lips were firm and warm yet undeniably soft as they moved against hers. Rachel followed his lead, breathless as his mouth teased her lips apart. Anticipation pebbled her flesh in the chill night air. She shivered as parts of her body tightened in response and others melted into wanton submission. A hardness pressed against her hip, and lifting herself on her toes, Rachel pressed back, gasping as her movements heightened the throbbing low in her pelvis and brought an answering groan from Brave.

Music from the ballroom, muted and faint against the sounds of their breathing, drifted around them. It was as though the rest of the world had faded into the background, leaving only the two of them and this wondrous heady kiss!

The pressure of his mouth increased with the pressure of his hips. Rachel's lips had no choice but to open beneath his, tasting champagne on the dampness of his breath.

Oh dear God! Was that his tongue? Opening her mouth to his exploration, Rachel sank deeper and deeper into a world where nothing existed but sense and sensation. A place where it was becoming more and more difficult to ascertain where her body stopped and Brave's began, so desperately were the two trying to become one. The pressure between her thighs intensified, blocking out all reason until only instinct ruled—and instinct demanded to be satisfied.

She used to scoff at those young women who'd been stupid enough to give themselves up to temptation, and allowed themselves to be ruined by a man. Now, she found herself all too willing to risk sharing their fate if it meant following this moment to its inevitable conclusion. She'd be all too willing to let this man ruin her.

And she didn't think being ruined would be such a horrible experience. Not with Brave.

And then he was gone, and where there had been heat there was only chill, and where there had been the sweet coercion of his body there was nothing but bewildered loss.

Still against the wall, Rachel felt as though she'd been thrust through a portal into another time and place. Gone was the beautiful world she and Brave had created, replaced by the cold reality they had left. A spell had been broken, and its magic left her wanting more.

Lowering her arms, she winced at the pain in her shoulders and took a hesitant step toward the man who had promised her so much and then taken it all away.

"Well," she said, her voice strained in an attempt at humor. "That was . . . *interesting.*"

He raised his head to meet her gaze. She'd been prepared

to see regret in his eyes, perhaps even embarrassment, but she wasn't prepared for the sheer horror—or was it anguish?—she saw in the depths of his dark eyes.

"Rachel, I'm . . . I'm very sorry."

It was like a slap with a cold hand. Quickly, the fire of desire was replaced with cold indignation. That was it? He made her insides melt and he was *sorry*?

"Sorry for what, Brave? For kissing me? Or for making me like it? Or maybe you're sorry for liking it yourself?"

He stared at her, confusion replacing the wretchedness in his expression. "Well . . . all three I suppose."

Clenching her hands into fists, Rachel fought the urge to clock him with one. "What a gentleman you are, Brave. I suppose I'm expected to thank you for your remorse?"

He obviously hadn't been expecting sarcasm. "I stopped, didn't I? I didn't have to. *You* certainly weren't offering any resistance."

Rachel's face flamed with embarrassment at his reminder of her abandoned behavior. "So you do want me to thank you then."

Tossing his hands into the air, Brave laughed humorlessly. "No, I don't want you to thank me! Damn it, Rachel, I said I was sorry. What more do you want?"

"What I *want*," she ground out, moving toward him, "is for you to tell me you were caught up in the moment, or that you were overcome by the moonlight reflected in my eyes, or perhaps that you just couldn't resist me any longer." She stopped in front of him and poked a finger in his chest hard enough to make him grunt.

"What I *don't* want, you big lout, is to be told you're sorry! God! Do you have an idea how that makes a woman feel?"

Obviously he didn't, because he stood there staring at her as if she was totally insane. Then something that sounded very much like strangled laughter burst from his lips.

"What?"

Shaking his head, Brave leaned against the railing, turning his body toward her. Rachel had to keep her eyes focused on his face to keep from sneaking a peek at that part of him that had, just minutes ago, been pressed so intimately against her.

"Most women would have proclaimed to be outraged by my behavior. Some would have even demanded I marry them, and most would have demanded an apology whether they believed I meant it or not. You, all you want is for me to say that I'm *not* sorry."

It did sound like bizarre reasoning when he put it that way. She glanced away. "It's hurtful to a woman's confidence to hear a man say he regrets kissing her."

Brave nodded. "Then I have to be honest with you, Rachel. I shouldn't have kissed you."

Rachel's heart fell against her ribs.

"But I'm not sorry for it at all."

Unable to totally suppress the urge to grin like an idiot in relief, Rachel smiled. "See, that wasn't so hard, was it?"

Oh, but the rest of him had been.

He gave one of those half smiles of his. It was like his smile had been broken and he hadn't been able to fix it. She wasn't sure why it struck her that way, but it did. What had broken his smile? A woman, perhaps? The idea of any woman having the power to hurt him like that was something Rachel didn't want to think about. It made her angry in ways she couldn't explain.

"Let's just put it behind us," she suggested.

He raised a brow. "Say we were overcome by the moon and stars?"

Her grin grew. "And the magic of the moment."

"Sounds good to me." He held out his arm. "Shall we go back in?"

Rachel shook her head. "I don't think we should go back inside together. People might talk." And Rachel didn't want the gossips to link her with Brave. Everyone knew how shabbily Sir Henry treated her mother and herself. She didn't want them thinking she was setting her cap at Brave and his fortune. And, she certainly didn't want to hear them pitying her for being fool enough to do so.

And more importantly, she didn't want *him* to hear them pity her.

He nodded in consent. "You're right, of course. I'll see you inside?"

"Of course." But the minute he was gone, Rachel turned and leaned her forehead against a tall, stone post in the balustrade.

She'd just been thoroughly kissed by one of the most stunning examples of manly perfection she'd ever known, and now that she knew he *wasn't* sorry for kissing her, she had to keep herself from making too much of it, or wondering why he'd done it.

So much of her wanted to believe he was attracted to her. What normal woman wouldn't? But Rachel knew too much about men to allow herself such a fantasy. Weren't men the sex that frequented brothels and *paid* to bed women they didn't even know, let alone love? Certainly if a man could do something like that, he was capable of kissing a woman he didn't even like.

David had claimed to love her, and that hadn't stopped him from leaving.

Not that Brave didn't like her. He seemed to like her well enough, but Rachel wasn't foolish or naive enough to believe he'd fallen in love with her. And she certainly wasn't in love with him. Despite what the poets said, there was no such thing as falling instantly in love with a person. True that ever since the night Brave had rescued her Rachel had thought of little else but him, but wasn't that normal? He was an attractive man, and he had saved her life. It was very easy, and only natural, to have romantic fantasies about him. It might even be natural to suspect that he would have fantasies about her in return, but it wasn't natural, blast it all, to dwell on it as though she didn't have more important things to worry about!

She should be ashamed of herself for daydreaming about a man when she should be concentrating on finding a way to keep Sir Henry from marrying her off to one of his cronies. In only a few months she would have her money, and if worse came to worst, she would do whatever was necessary to get her mother out of that house and away from the monster she'd married. It was the least Rachel could do after all her mother had done for her.

With that thought firmly entrenched in her mind, Rachel squared her shoulders, took a deep breath and tried to ignore the faint throb still echoing low in her abdomen. As she moved toward the balcony door, she couldn't help but wonder if women were as capable of sharing their bodies without love as men were.

"I have something for you."

Sprawled on her stomach on her bed, Rachel looked up from her reading. She hadn't heard her mother come in. "What is it?" she asked with a grin as she set the book aside. Her mother's surprises never disappointed.

Stepping into the bedroom, Marion Westhaver pulled several swatches of fabric from behind her back. She smiled proudly.

"What's that?" Rachel didn't see how several scraps of cloth—no matter how pretty they were—could possibly be thought of as a good surprise.

"Fabric, obviously," her mother replied teasingly. "These are just samples. The rest of the bolts are at Mrs. Ford's."

Mrs. Ford owned a dress shop in town. Her husband did quite well in trade and imported all the beautiful fabrics she used in her gowns. Rachel and her mother hadn't been able to afford to have a gown made by her in years.

Anticipation and unease uncoiled in Rachel's stomach. She had no doubt her mother was going to tell her she could have a new gown. The question was, how had she managed to pay for it?

"What's going on, Mama?"

Sighing, her mother plopped down on the bed beside her. "You remember that quilt I made? The patchwork."

"Yes." It had taken her mother a year to make that quilt.

"Well, Mrs. Ford asked if she could buy it." Smiling, Marion whispered conspiratorially, "I asked a ridiculous sum for it, Rachel."

The idea of her mother asking a "ridiculous sum" for anything was enough to make Rachel laugh. "And she agreed?"

"She did, even more so when I asked if she'd be willing to pay in trade. She gave me my choice of any three fabrics—at her own price, mind you! And offered to have her girls make the dresses as well. Isn't that a wonderful bargain? All you have to do is go in town for a fitting."

The sinking feeling returned. Rachel had no doubt her mother had been the unwitting receiver of one of Mrs. Ford's random acts of charity. No quilt was worth that kind of money. Part of Rachel wanted to refuse the gowns, but it wasn't worth the blow to her mother's pride.

"Why am I to get new gowns and not you?"

Her mother shrugged and looked away. "I'm an old woman, and you're a young one."

"You're also a pitiful liar."

Her mother still didn't look at her. "Sir Henry already bought me a new gown. Now I want you to have one."

Which meant Sir Henry hadn't offered to buy one for Rachel. It was just one more example of his rotten business sense. How did he expect to get a good price for her if she looked like a ragamuffin?

Rachel sighed. Her mother was just as eager to see her married, although for less mercenary reasons. "You want to dress me up like a debutante and see if I can't snag myself a husband."

Blushing, Marion swatted her with the pieces of fabric. "If you were a dutiful daughter, you'd go along with my plans."

Rachel rolled onto her back and into a sitting position. "I thought I was being a dutiful daughter by trying to get you away from your husband."

The look her mother shot her was tired. "I was hoping you'd give up on that."

Rachel shook her head. "Not a chance."

"I was afraid of that." Her mother sighed. "Will you at least go have the gowns made?"

"Yes," Rachel conceded, but only because it would make her mother happy. "Although I don't know how you think a new gown is going to make any difference as to how the gentlemen around here think of me."

Marion smiled knowingly. "Change the way a man sees you, and you change the way he feels about you. Besides, I heard you already captured the interest of one young man."

Rachel froze. "And who might that be?"

"Who do you think? Other than Lady Westwood's granddaughter, you were the only girl he danced with."

It didn't take long for the rumors to start.

"Mama, Lord Braven danced with Lady Westwood's granddaughter because no one else would. The same reason he danced with me."

But he hadn't kissed Lady Westwood's granddaughter, had he?

Her mother gazed at her, seeing her as only a mother could. Her mother saw her as a diamond of the first water, an incomparable, not some penniless ape leader. Rachel would love to see herself the same way, but she was far too practical. No man would marry her because she was poor and because no man was foolish enough to tie himself to Sir Henry

Westhaver. Such embarrassing connections were to be avoided at all cost, and that cost was Rachel's chance at marital happiness. Besides, a husband would only get in the way of her plans. No man would want the scandal of a divorce to touch them, and certainly no man would want to part with her dowry in order to do it.

"He's been asking about you."

"What?"

Marion stroked a piece of sapphire-blue silk, barely containing her smug smile. This teasing side of her was one Rachel hadn't seen in some time. Sir Henry must be in one of his loving phases. He always treated her mother like a queen after a beating. "Lord Braven. Apparently, he's been talking to some of your mutual childhood friends. I wonder why?"

So did Rachel. Why would he be asking about her?

"What's he been asking?" She tried to keep from sounding too eager.

"Why you've never married, for one."

Any hopes Rachel might have had fell like stone. "That's not a good thing, Mama. Everyone will tell him that I've got no prospects, no connections, nothing to make me worth marrying."

"You get over ten thousand pounds when you turn five-and-twenty."

The thought of Brave wanting her for her money hurt more than the thought that he might not want her at all, and Rachel wished she would just stop thinking altogether.

"The Earl of Braven does not need ten thousand pounds."

"But it would make his interest in you a mercenary one rather than one of affection, and that's easier for you to accept, isn't it?"

How had the conversation gone from dresses to this?

"He's not interested in me, Mama." Rachel's jaw was beginning to ache, she was clenching it so hard.

"No?" her mother asked in that tone only mothers could

use. That singsong voice that meant that she knew everything and her poor little girl still had so much to learn.

"No offense, Mama, but you're hardly an expert on men."

If she'd expected her mother to flinch, she'd thought wrong. Marion's expression lost much of its humor, but the smile still remained.

"I know more about them than you do, my dear. I had the good sense to marry your father and the practicality to marry Sir Henry. I've never once mistook the character of either for anything other than what it was. Perhaps if you thought a little more of yourself and stopped being so distrustful of anything male, you'd be able to see things more clearly."

Stunned, Rachel could only stare as her mother rose to her feet.

"Now," Marion said, tossing her the scraps of fabric on the bed, "do be a good girl and pick out what fabric you'd like to have your dresses made from."

Brave returned from his morning ride with his cheeks flushed with cold and his head full of thoughts of Rachel Ashton. He'd been talking to some of the townspeople about her—people who had grown up and played with them both as children, back when social class meant nothing to any of them.

Gravel crunched beneath his feet as he walked from the stables to the house, the only sound on this clear, cold morning. Twirling his riding crop in one hand, he allowed his gaze to drag lazily across the serene beauty of his estate as he pondered what he'd learned over the last few days.

Everyone he spoke to said the same things. Very few men had found Rachel's charms ample enough to risk aligning themselves with Sir Henry Westhaver. The man was a leech. There had been one young man who had paid particular attention to her but nothing came of it. And of the few who had tried to court Rachel since, they'd been dismissed by her stepfather as not rich enough—or by Rachel herself for being too forward in their attentions.

Brave had to wonder just how forward the gentlemen had tried to get, because she certainly hadn't told *him* to sod off.

He almost smiled at how she'd demanded he not apologize for kissing her the other night at Lady Westwood's party. He had no business kissing her, no business at all, but it had felt so good, so *right* to press his body against hers.

He was right. Rachel Ashton was dangerous—a danger to herself. He was as drawn to her as a moth to a flame, but it wasn't the possibility of his getting burned that worried him. It was the thought of how easy it would be for him to extinguish the fire within her. He had to stay away from her, and if she was as smart as he believed her to be, she'd stay clear of him as well. Nothing good could come of this strange attraction he felt toward her. Nothing at all.

Yanking open the door, Brave stepped inside the house. He knew some men who would have made the servants open the door for them, but it seemed so pretentious, especially when he was capable of opening it himself.

"Dr. Phelps is awaiting you in the green drawing room, my lord," Reynolds told him as he took his coat and gloves.

Brave groaned inwardly. Not again. "Thank you, Reynolds. Be so good as to have a bottle of brandy brought to me after the doctor leaves, will you? I've a feeling I'm going to need it."

The butler bowed, no reaction whatsoever to the request. After all, Brave had only asked for one bottle, and that was a pittance compared to what he'd drunk after Miranda's death. "Yes, my lord."

Straightening his cuffs, Brave strode down the corridor toward the green drawing room. Busts and statues of legendary gods and heroes lined the walls. Hades stood just outside the drawing room door. Now that was irony. The god of the Underworld standing at the portal to hell—or at least fifteen minutes' worth.

He paused in the doorway.

"What shall it be today, Phelps? Would you like to feel the bumps on my head again or would you prefer to check the color of my urine?"

The physician, standing at one of the east-facing windows, whirled toward him. "Lord Braven! Forgive me, I didn't hear you approach."

Douglas Phelps had been Brave's physician for the past year and a half—ever since the breakdown that followed Miranda's death. Brave had entered into his care at the urging of his mother and his friends. Not so much because he wanted help, but because he wanted them just to leave him the hell alone.

Phelps had helped him stop the pattern of self-destruction he'd started, and he'd convinced Brave to stop drowning his grief in a bottle, but Brave had a suspicion that had more to do with common sense and waking up too many mornings with a head that felt as though it had been kicked by a mule than any "treatment" the doctor had tried.

He'd removed himself from the doctor's care months ago, when he'd become convinced that these treatments, while for the most part harmless, were not doing anything to ease his guilt or make him feel better about Miranda's death. Still, Phelps showed up every fortnight or so, wanting to check up on him.

Brave gestured to another chair as he seated himself. "So what sort of treatment have you prepared for me today then?"

Phelps smiled, the corners of his pale eyes crinkling like the pleats of a lady's fan. "Oh, no treatment today, my lord. I've simply come to talk."

"Pity. I'd rather hoped to persuade you to rub my head again."

"It's called 'phrenology,' my lord. Many in the field swear by it."

Brave wanted to ask just what field that was exactly—
medical, or the one out back dotted with sheep manure—but
he kept his opinions to himself. Dr. Phelps was a good man
and he had no wish to insult him when he so obviously
wanted to be of help.

"What exactly did you want to talk about, Doctor?"

Phelps's weathered cheeks reddened. "I've heard some
rumors, my lord, and I wanted to come to you directly to ascertain whether or not there's any truth to them."

Brave raised a brow. "You hardly seem the type to put
much stock in gossip, Phelps."

"I'm not, my lord, unless that is, it involves one of my patients." The older man's chin rose a notch, as if defying
Brave to deny the nature of their relationship.

Lord but he could use that brandy. "What's gotten you so
riled up, Phelps?"

Again the doctor flushed. "They say, my lord, that you
plan to marry."

Oh do they? Brave shrugged. "I suppose I'll have to
someday."

Phelps seemed pleased by this. "But not in the near future?"

Brave shook his head. "No, not in the near future. Marriage is not a step I'm prepared to take right now."

Rising to his feet, the doctor smiled. "I agree. Such decisions are best made at a leisurely pace—especially when one
is . . . apprehensive."

"I beg your pardon?" Brave's head snapped up so fast
pain shot up the side of his neck. "Apprehensive of what?"
And where the devil was the man going? Normally, Phelps's
visits lasted longer than this.

Phelps started for the door. His smile was one of patient
amusement.

"Of many things, I should think. Of failure for a start.
Maybe that you've changed somehow, been permanently

damaged. Perhaps of being hurt by life again, of somehow disappointing those you care about." He turned. "Shall I continue?"

"No," Brave decided, also rising from his chair. There was a bitter taste in his mouth. "You've said enough, thank you."

Phelps shrugged. "You ask me to talk, then tell me not to. By Jove, you sound like a normal aristocrat to me."

Realization tickled the back of Brave's mind. "You said you hadn't come here to play with my head anymore."

"What can I say?" Phelps asked as they both walked into the corridor. "I lied."

Brave couldn't help but chuckle. The doctor was smarter than he gave him credit for. And Brave honestly didn't mind his visits. It was nice to have someone to talk to—even if that person was trying to climb inside his head.

"Does the widow Hershel appreciate your wiliness?" he asked as they stepped out into the foyer.

"She seems to. Now if I could just get her to marry me, I'd be all set." He took his hat and gloves from Reynolds and nodded his thanks.

"I can't believe she's still saying no."

"Nor can I." Phelps plunked his hat on his head. "Can't say that I like it either, but I'd rather have her than not, so I'll go along with whatever she wants."

"Spoken like a man in love," Brave replied, walking the doctor to the door.

"Aye, that I am. And you needn't make fun of me, young man. It'll happen to you soon enough."

It had happened. Once. Brave smiled indulgently as the older man drew on his gloves. "I doubt that, Phelps." But even as he said the words, an image of Rachel drifted through his mind. Brave pushed it aside. She was the first woman he'd found attractive since Miranda's death. It was no wonder he was a little infatuated with her. It was normal.

That in itself was frightening. How long had it been since

he'd behaved in a normal fashion? He didn't even know what normal was anymore.

After bidding good day to the doctor, Brave retired to his study, where Reynolds had left the bottle of brandy he requested. Sitting on his desk in a crystal decanter, it looked as harmless as water. But Brave knew differently. He knew all too well how addictive it could be. That sweet euphoria had been the only thing that kept him from sinking deep into depression, and yes, madness. He never thought he'd prefer feeling guilt over that blissful peace.

Other than the champagne at Lady Westwood's soiree, he hadn't had a drop of liquor since he'd become so utterly dependent on it to relieve his guilt and despair after Miranda's death. The champagne hadn't sent him over the edge, but would brandy?

Phelps had told him that an addiction to spirits was a dangerous thing, but that Brave didn't show any symptoms of having such an addiction. True, he'd spent a good many months drunk, but he hadn't *needed* to drink; he'd chosen to.

Praying his decision was the right one, Brave opened the decanter. He poured a conservative amount into the snifter and put the bottle away in the nearby cabinet. Leaving it out might prove too much temptation.

Warming the glass in his hands out of habit, he strode over to his favorite chair—an old armchair his father used to sit in when Brave would crawl up on his knee as a child. He settled into the worn blue velvet, propped his feet up close to the fire, picked up the book he had been reading the night before, and took a drink.

The brandy hit his tongue in an explosion of flavor, and Brave swirled it around in his mouth before swallowing.

Nothing.

Other than appreciation for the taste of fine brandy, Brave felt nothing. Not the urge to drain the glass, not the urge to drain the bottle. He took another sip.

When Reynolds knocked sometime later, there was still brandy in the glass and Brave was thirty pages into his novel.

"I beg your pardon, m'lord, but there are two gentlemen here to see you."

Brave set the book aside. "Gentlemen? I—"

"He doesn't know any gentlemen!" boomed a familiar voice, and Gabriel Warren, Earl of Angelwood and school friend of Brave's, sauntered into the room, a huge grin on his face and his black hair mussed by riding through the wind.

Behind him was Julian Rexley, Earl of Wolfram, and the man who should have been Brave's brother-in-law. It didn't hurt to see Julian now, but it was still hard. His chestnut hair and golden complexion were much like his sister's, only Miranda had been frivolous and fun while Julian was quiet and serious. Brave knew his friend didn't blame him for Miranda's death, but that was hard to accept when Brave still blamed himself.

Still, he was pleased to see them and didn't bother to hide it. He went to them, clapping them both on the back and being embraced in return. It wasn't until they were all seated with a drink that Brave asked what they were doing there.

"We're on our way to Jules's property up north," Gabriel replied, his gray eyes bright. "We couldn't go on without imposing upon you for a few days."

"We're going to be doing some hunting," Julian added in his softer tone. "You're welcome to join us, Brave."

Brave shook his head. "Thank you for the invitation, Jules, but I'm afraid business here will prevent me from taking you up on it." That was a lie. There was nothing going on at Wyck's End that couldn't wait a few days, but Brave had no intention of ever visiting that particular property of Julian's again, and his friend knew it. That was where Miranda had died. In fact, he was surprised that Julian still used it.

"I go every year," his friend reminded him. "The whole

family would pack up and come up here 'til after Christmas. Do you remember that?"

Brave did indeed. When he and Julian had discovered they lived in such close proximity for part of the year, the young men wasted no time in spending much of their time home from school at one property or the other during the colder months. Gabriel, who hadn't much of a happy home life, would often join them.

"I'm the only one to go now." Julian's voice was low. "Letitia would rather stay in London or the Lakes. She's never felt for Yorkshire the way Miranda and I did." He drifted into silence, staring into his glass.

Letitia was Julian's younger sister, and the only family he had left. Like Julian and Gabe, he'd lost his father at a young age. In fact, Julian had been the first to come into his title. Gabriel had been the second. Julian lost his mother and father at the same time, becoming both parents to two young girls. Brave couldn't imagine the responsibility, but he knew that Julian had also been overcome by grief at Miranda's death, blaming himself for not raising her as his parents would have wanted. Did he still carry that guilt?

The silence was short-lived. Gabriel's gaze went from Julian to Brave. "Not this again. If the two of you get maudlin on me, I'm leaving."

Brave flashed him a crooked smile. Gabe would leave, too. The toughest of the three of them, Gabe had been brought up by parents who cared more about parties than their son.

He didn't know all the details, nor did he want to, but Eloise Warren had been known for her promiscuity and Gabe's father had been a notorious gambler. And then there had been Lilith. Brave didn't know what had happened between Gabe and the girl he loved. He only knew that one day Gabe had wanted to marry her and the next he never spoke of her again. That had been the day Gabriel became hard and cynical, caring only about his two school chums and little else.

Julian raised his head, also smiling. "Maudlin? My dear friend, I get paid for being maudlin."

Gabriel rolled his eyes. "You get paid for making young ladies titter and fan themselves, Julian. It's dem fortunate that you don't need the money to live because that fool Murray doesn't pay you half of what you're worth. He doesn't even buy your good work."

Brave and Julian exchanged glaces. Julian's topaz gaze twinkled. It was an old argument. John Murray was Julian's publisher, the very same who published Byron. Julian seemed very pleased with his arrangement with Murray. It was only Gabriel who believed he could do better.

"I don't need the money." Julian took a drink of his brandy. "My poetry is a lark. Nothing more."

Gabriel shot him a dark look. "It could be more."

Brave smiled. That was Gabriel. He had to be the best at everything. There was no point to a venture if one didn't want to be the best or make a success of it. For him, there was no such thing as doing something simply for the pleasure of having done it.

Julian sighed and shook his head, sending a thick chunk of reddish brown hair over his brow. "I'm not having this discussion with you again, Gabe. Why don't you tell Brave about the strange invitation you received."

Arching a brow in an expression of surprise, Brave turned to his friend. "An invitation? Surely it was a mistake. No hostess in her right mind would invite a critic like you anywhere."

Gabriel shrugged. "One doesn't have to be a recluse to be sought after, my friend. Not even my scandalous mama keeps my name from the guest lists. In fact, this time I believe she might be the cause of it."

Brave was too intrigued to be bothered by his friend's offensive remark. Besides, it was true, so what point would there be in being insulted?

"So what kind of invitation was it?" He demanded when Gabriel offered no further information.

The dark-haired man sipped his drink and smiled—it didn't reach his eyes. "I've been invited to an orgy."

Now *that* did surprise Brave. No one who knew Gabriel would ever dream of inviting him to such a thing. Anyone close to him knew that he was as far from promiscuous as a normal man could get.

"An orgy." Brave turned to Julian for verification.

Julian nodded, barely hiding his mirth. "Is it not the most laughable thing you've ever heard?"

"Obviously the host is not a close acquaintance."

Gabriel grimaced. "Not bloody likely."

"So where is this den of licentiousness anyway?" Brave asked, taking a drink. He'd almost forgotten about his brandy.

Gabriel set his empty glass aside. "Viscount Charlton's."

Brave's gut clenched. "Charlton?" Did Sir Henry know the man he wanted his stepdaughter to marry held orgies in his home? He wasn't sure he wanted to know the answer. He already felt a surge of unaccountable hatred for the man. The idea that he'd willingly sell Rachel to such a degenerate made him see red.

"That's the one. His estate's a few miles north of here." Gabe shook his head. "Never liked the man much myself. This just proves what an excellent judge of character I am." This was said with just a hint of sarcasm. That was a habit that had started when the relationship with Lilith ended.

"Naturally your good judgment made you decline," Julian added, smiling at Brave.

Gabriel snorted. "I never even bothered to acknowledge him with a reply. The cretin."

Brave managed a smile. It was good to see his friends. Very good. In fact, it felt just like old times. Too much like old times, because for the first time in two years, Brave had the overwhelming urge to stick his nose in where it didn't belong—namely preventing Rachel from marrying a man who was little more than a whoremonger.

"I find it odd that Charlton didn't invite me to his gathering. Don't you find that odd?"

"What I find odd," Gabriel replied, fixing him with a curious expression and eyes that looked too deep. "Is that you even care. I wouldn't have thought this the kind of party you would care to attend."

A falsely bright smile lit Brave's face. "But like you said, Gabe, I don't get out enough. This might be a good place to start."

Gabriel and Julian exchanged puzzled glances.

"Well, if you think so . . ." Julian's bewildered tone trailed off into a shrug.

"Excellent," Brave enthused. Clapping his hands together, he wondered just how much of an impact on his quiet life Rachel Ashton was truly going to have. "When is it?"

Chapter 4

"It's a little daring, don't you think?" Rachel turned to the woman on her right.

Belinda Mayhew, Rachel's dearest—and only—friend, leaned in closer to study the fashion plate on the page before them. The thick mass of black ringlets circling her head obstructed Rachel's view. "I think it's lovely. Don't you agree, Mrs. Ford?"

Bending in from the left, Mrs. Ford nodded with great enthusiasm. "I think that dress in a shade of dark blue would be most becoming."

Unconvinced, Rachel peered between their heads at the print. It certainly was a lovely gown, even if the V-shaped neckline was lower than what she was accustomed to. Its style was simple and elegant, and most importantly, plain enough that Rachel could easily make it over with a few well-placed ruffles and ribbons. But . . .

"Do I really need an evening gown?" She turned to Belinda.

Belinda's brown eyes widened. "Dearest, *everyone* needs at least one evening gown."

Rachel smiled, but she couldn't help but wonder if Belinda didn't know there were more important things in life than gowns and fashion. They'd been friends since childhood, having grown up just two miles from each other. They would have gone on to the local ladies' academy together had Rachel's circumstances not changed so drastically. Funny how her mother had actually married *up* but her consequences went *down*.

While they had been born into similar situations, Belinda's father was still alive and supporting his family. Belinda had a beautiful wardrobe filled with up-to-the minute fashions, and several successful London seasons spent studying what was fashionable. The fact that she was now engaged to a wealthy landowner from Derbyshire was the reason Rachel's mother had suggested Rachel invite her friend to accompany her to Mrs. Ford's.

Glancing from Belinda's encouraging countenance to Mrs. Ford's hopeful one, Rachel knew she was outnumbered. It seemed like such a frivolous expense, but she had to admit, she *really* would like to own such a beautiful gown.

"All right," she said. "I'll take it."

Belinda and Mrs. Ford beamed.

Rachel had chosen her three gowns. All that was left was to choose the fabric. Bottle green muslin for one day gown, lightweight plum merino for another, and a sapphire-blue silk for the evening gown. By the time the material had been chosen, Rachel felt positively decadent—and tired.

"What do you want to do now?" Belinda asked as they stepped out into the gray and chilly afternoon. "Shall we go buy you a new bonnet at the milliner's?"

"Lord no!" Rachel stifled a yawn. "Even if I could afford a new bonnet, I haven't the energy to shop anymore today."

Linking her arm through Rachel's, Belinda pulled her down the street. "Then you can come and watch me shop instead."

Rachel wondered if that hadn't been the plan all along.

"All right, but then I have to go home." Rachel didn't like leaving her mother alone for very long. Even though Sir Henry was out hunting with some of his cronies, there was always the chance he wouldn't have killed anything that day and would decide that beating her mother was just as satisfying, especially if he'd been drinking.

"I promise not to stay very long."

Rolling her eyes, Rachel allowed herself to be led. Asking Belinda to shop quickly was like asking the sun not to rise. She knew she had at least a few hours before Sir Henry would return home as it was still early afternoon. Besides, she was enjoying this time with her friend.

Inside the shop, Rachel planned to sit quietly and wait, but Belinda wouldn't stand for it.

"Try this one."

The bonnet was rose velvet and perfectly matched the cape Rachel wore. She'd made it out of a pair of drapes she'd found in the attic, purchased when Sir Henry had decided to redecorate her mother's bedchamber three years ago. Her mother hated the color, and for once, Sir Henry had caved in to her wishes. Wearing the cape always made Rachel feel stronger, more confident.

She shook her head. The bonnet was lovely, and if she tried it on, she'd only want it.

"Try it on." The tone of Belinda's voice brooked no refusal.

"All right," Rachel gave in. "But only because you look so ridiculous in that hat."

Belinda adjusted the befeathered turban so that it sat straight on her head. "Whatever you do mean?" she demanded with a grin.

The bonnet did suit, and Rachel took it off as quickly as she had put it on. She couldn't afford it, but she didn't want Belinda to see how bothered she was by the fact. Maybe if there was any money left over after she paid for her mother's divorce and once they were resettled, she'd buy herself a new hat, but for now she had go without.

"How about this one?" She asked, cramming a chipped-straw bonnet loaded with faux fruit down on her head. The brim stuck out a good four inches around her face, and the fruit was so heavy, her head tilted to the left.

Belinda clapped her hands together in mock enthusiasm. "I love it!"

"Personally, I preferred the pink one."

Rachel's stomach fell at the sound of that rich voice. Slowly, she reached up and removed the foolish fruit bonnet from her head. Smoothing her hair with the palm of her hand, she turned.

"Rose," was all she could think of to say, as the shop suddenly seemed to shrink around her. How could one person's presence make a room so much smaller?

He shook his head, as though he hadn't heard her right. "I beg your pardon?"

"The bonnet. It's rose, not pink." Clutching a handful of wooden cherries, she curtsied. "Good day, Lord Braven."

He raised a brow.

My, aren't we the expressive one today. So maybe she wasn't quite herself. What did he expect after that kiss? Maybe he could pretend it meant nothing, pretend it didn't happen, but Rachel couldn't, not when practically every waking moment since had been spent dwelling on it!

"Good day, Miss Ashton—or do you go by Westhaver now?"

She'd sooner cut off her own arm. "No. I've kept my father's name."

He nodded, as though he should have known. "And good day to you as well, Miss Mayhew." He bowed his head in greeting. "Might I introduce you ladies to my friends? Lords Angelwood and Wolfram."

More curtsies, more bows. More niceties. Rachel felt as though they were at court.

"And might I inquire what brings you in here today, Lord Braven?" She didn't fool herself that he had come in specifically to see her, even though it would have been nice. But there was no way for him to have known she was there, unless he saw her through the window.

"Lord Angelwood"—he pointed to the black-haired man now browsing a rack of gentlemen's hats—"has a nasty habit of losing hats. We've come in search of a new one."

Rachel smiled, a little too brightly perhaps, but at least she wouldn't look disappointed. Perhaps he wasn't pretending. Perhaps the kiss really had meant nothing to him. Of course, he really couldn't say anything about it with all these people around, could he?

"And of course seeing you makes the trip all the more worthwhile."

Nicely said, she thought as her heart floundered in her chest. Was it just her or had his voice lowered just the slightest bit? He sounded almost . . . seductive.

Then again, the Earl of Braven could recite a grocery list and make it sound erotic. It was that low voice of his, that melancholy lilt that made every word sound almost like a sigh. But his expression was unchanged, and there was nothing in his gaze—his oh-so-intent gaze—that would lead her to believe he was nearly as affected by her presence as she was by his. She was making far too much of the situation. They were both adults. There was no need to be uncomfortable.

Rachel's smile was more natural now. "Indeed," she quipped, "I shudder to think how deplorable the afternoon might have been had we not met."

He gave her one of those half smiles of his. "A deplorable thought."

His other friend, the tall brunette, interrupted their banter. Blushing lightly, Rachel realized she'd forgotten all about him. "Please excuse me, Miss Ashton, Brave, but I want to purchase a new pair of gloves for tonight." With a bow, he left them.

His exclusion of Belinda, made Rachel look for her friend. She found her at the counter, having her purchases wrapped. She and Brave were completely alone—or as alone as they could be in a busy shop.

"And what mischief are you boys up to this evening?" she teased, in an effort to conceal her own sudden shyness.

The humor faded from his eyes. "Viscount Charlton has invited us to a party at his estate."

"Viscount Charlton? I did not think you knew him." The very idea of Brave and Charlton together disgusted and alarmed her. She didn't want to put him in the same category as Charlton, and she was distinctly uncomfortable that he was going to spend at least one evening with the man Sir Henry wanted her to marry.

"I don't." From his expression she thought he wanted to say something else, but he didn't. He just stared at her. She stared back, her gaze drawn to his mouth, the firm lips that had been so soft, so demanding on hers. He'd tasted of champagne, and the taste had stayed with her long after he left her on the balcony. What, she wondered, would he taste like if she kissed him now?

Her gaze flickered to his. He was staring at her mouth, and for a moment Rachel thought she saw something hot and urgent in the dark depths of his eyes. Then he caught her gaze, and all the warmth vanished, replaced by an unreadable wall.

"Ah, well," she said after a few minutes of uncomfortable silence. "I hope you have a good time."

"Thank you, although I can assure you there will be little pleasure in the evening."

She frowned, and although she knew it was impertinent, she couldn't help but ask, "Then why are you going?"

"For a friend." He gave her that same strange look, and understanding dawned.

"Ohhh." She nodded. Obviously one of his friends had asked him to go for some personal reason. Perhaps a gaming debt or something. Charlton was a reputed gambler. "That's very good of you."

"Thank you."

His expression gave her pause. Was it possible that *she* was the friend? It was almost too much even to dare entertain.

She caught a movement out of the corner of her eye, interrupting her foolish thoughts. Belinda was standing by the door, her packages in her arms. She studied a straw gypsy hat with all the interest of someone enthralled, but Rachel knew her friend was just being polite.

"I see my friend is ready to leave." She placed the rather battered fruit bonnet back on its rack. "I should take my leave."

"It was good to see you again."

He meant it. Of that she was certain, but his expression was so solemn, so utterly remote, she couldn't tell how much he meant it, or in what manner. "I agree." And with that, she walked away.

Fortunately, Belinda waited until they were outside and in her awaiting carriage before opening her mouth.

"What was that all about?" Tossing her packages on the seat, she turned to face Rachel with an eager expression.

Rachel leaned back against the squabs, glad to be out of the shop and glad that her first meeting with Brave since their kiss was behind her.

"What was what all about?"

Belinda nudged her leg. "Lord Braven was flirting with you!"

"Don't be ridiculous. I don't think the man knows how to flirt." He *had* said that seeing her made the trip worthwhile. Of course, any well-bred gentleman would have said the same thing. Wasn't a change of expression required while flirting? Or did flirting have its own countenance? Regardless, she was fairly certain Brave's face hadn't looked flirtatious at all.

Belinda stripped off her gloves. "Do you have any idea how sought-after he is? How wonderful that you caught his eye."

"I haven't caught his eye," Rachel replied with some exasperation. Between her mother and Belinda she suddenly felt like an old maid everyone was trying to marry off to any man who looked at her. She wasn't that old yet, and everyone seemed to forget that she had no plans to get married.

"That's not what they're saying in town."

The hair on the back of Rachel's neck stood on end. Gossip ran rampant in a small town, but talk of her and Brave was becoming far too common. "What are they saying?"

Belinda smiled coyly, oblivious to Rachel's distress. "Only that he rescued you from certain death and gave you one of the countess's gowns."

Oh God. Closing her eyes, Rachel allowed the fluttering in her stomach to wash over her in time with the swaying carriage. Her blood shivered in her veins. The servants had been talking. They were the only ones who could have known about the dress—except for Sir Henry, and he had too much at stake to risk letting such a thing become general knowledge. Thank God no one had seen her and Brave on the balcony that night, or they would have been forced into marriage.

If she wasn't more careful, the rumors could do just as much damage to her reputation as that kiss. And as the stepdaughter of Henry Westhaver, her virtue was all she had.

"Just think. You could be a countess!" Belinda giggled.

Groaning, Rachel dropped her head back on the cushions—and realized she'd left her bonnet in the milliner's. She had no intention of going back after it now. It would look completely contrived if Brave was still there. She would fetch the bonnet tomorrow.

"Then you could have all the gowns you could ever want." Belinda's own fashionable bonnet was tossed into the corner, with its brim bent against the seat. Rachel frowned. Did Belinda take wealth so for granted that she'd treat bonnets like old rags?

"Gowns have never been at the top of my priority list," Rachel reminded her, rubbing her eyes. "Not because I don't like them, but because I have other things to worry about. Remember my mother? The woman who married a totally despicable man just to put a roof over our heads? I vowed to free her from him, remember?"

Belinda frowned, marring her perfect white brow. "You wouldn't risk your own chance at marriage just to—" She slumped against the seat. "You would, wouldn't you?"

Rachel nodded. "Of course I would. Even if Braven was interested in me—and I don't know what makes you think he is—I would never sacrifice my mother's well-being."

"Rachel . . ."

Bolting upright, Rachel grabbed her friend's hand in a grip so tight Belinda gasped. She'd never told Belinda just how awful Sir Henry could be, or how greatly she feared for her mother.

"Belinda, I'm afraid he's going to kill her someday."

Belinda's dark eyes were round with shock. "My God."

"I have to get her away from him." Releasing her friend's hand, Rachel dropped her head into both her own. "I just don't know how much longer we can wait. If we can make it until my birthday, then I'll have enough money to pay for a divorce and take her somewhere that he'll never hurt her again."

"Rachel"—Belinda's voice was filled with concern—"your mother's safety is just one more reason to get married."

"Married?" Rachel's head snapped up. "Why is it reason to get married? It's just one more obstacle in my path. How can I take my mother away if I'm leg shackled to some man?"

Sighing, Belinda reached out and took one of her hands. "A rich and powerful husband can help you protect your mother—especially if he's titled."

It was an idea Rachel had thought of before—back when she was younger and still could dream of being swept off her feet by a handsome prince, one who didn't care that she had no connections or that she was the stepdaughter of one of the most despised men in the county. Long before David had taught her that young men didn't exactly have marriage on their mind when they tried to shove their hands down a lady's bodice.

She thought maybe word of her inheritance would get around and that she would go to London and men would fall at her feet. Sir Henry never allowed her to go to London, and he let it be known that *he* would have the deciding say in whomever she married.

There weren't many princes to choose from in Yorkshire.

Except one who was attending Viscount Charlton's party for a friend. Did he plan on spying on Charlton for her?

Nonsense. It was foolish to think he would go to such lengths for her. It wasn't as though they'd been close as children, despite the friendship between their fathers. And it wasn't as though *he* was the sheltered virgin who'd only been kissed three times in her life. He'd probably kissed hundreds of women.

Reason took hold again. "Belinda, even if I could manage to find a rich and powerful husband, which I'm not likely to do, he would have to be very powerful to keep Sir Henry from my mother. She is his wife, and as you know, therefore his property. He is *allowed* to beat her, and I seriously doubt there is a magistrate in the county that would side against him if he tried to take her back. Divorce is the only option."

"But—"

"And there's not a man alive who'd want his mother-in-law living under his roof, I don't care what you say. And there's no saying that such a marriage wouldn't land me in exactly the same kind of predicament my mother is in. No. I would only contemplate marriage as a last resort." She gave a sharp nod. End of subject.

"You're the only woman I know who has ever referred to marriage as a 'last resort.'"

Rachel shrugged. "Most women judge marriage by what they stand to gain. I judge it by what I stand to lose."

Smiling, Belinda shook her head. "And what do I stand to gain by my marriage?"

An answering smile curved Rachel's own lips. "A vast fortune, a beautiful estate, and a man who cannot live without you."

"Now you make marriage sound very appealing," her friend remarked in an arch tone.

"It is." Before her friend could interrupt, Rachel continued, "For you. You were lucky enough to fall in love with the man who asked for your hand."

"And wasn't it scandalous of me, too," Belinda drawled, rolling her eyes, and Rachel laughed.

Belinda's love affair with her Mr. Winchelsea had set London society on its ear, it not being used to such matches among the monied masses. It was an odd society that didn't even blink when couples married for fortune or rank, but thought it absolutely absurd that two people might actually *love* one another.

Her laughter fading, Rachel smiled warmly at her friend. "I shall miss you when you're gone."

"I shall miss you, too." Belinda's expression turned hopeful. "You must come to visit."

Rachel nodded. "I will." Even though she knew she wouldn't—couldn't—not while she and her mother still lived under Sir Henry's roof, and even then Belinda's house would be the first place he'd think to look for them once they did escape.

"I bought you a little something to remember me by," Belinda told her, picking up one of her packages and setting it in Rachel's lap.

"You shouldn't have." Half-embarrassed, half-pleased, Rachel plucked at the cover of the bandbox.

"Consider it a thank-you gift for being such a good friend."

Rachel loved surprises. It was one thing she'd never grown out of. In fact, the older she became the more she appreciated the random acts of kindness and generosity that went into a surprise.

She removed the cover. It was the rose-velvet bonnet.

"Oh, Belinda." Touched beyond words, Rachel's eyes burned and her throat ached. "I don't know what to say. Thank you."

"You can thank me," her friend replied with a calculating smile, "by wearing it."

"Oh, I will. I promise."

Belinda's grin grew. "The next time you see Lord Braven."

Glancing around at the many scenes of debauchery being played out before him, Brave wondered for the eighth time that evening if perhaps he shouldn't have just stayed home. Everywhere he looked men and women were strewn about in various stages of undress, openly fondling one another. Some had enough courtesy to retire to their chambers, but few others seemed concerned that they were putting on a show for everyone else.

Or perhaps providing entertainment was their object. It

was really quite embarrassing. He didn't want to be caught watching, but he couldn't seem to help himself. It was like a terrible accident. One didn't want to see the wreckage, but couldn't help but look. What else was there to do? He certainly didn't want to join in, no matter how many invitations he'd received from the women present. The idea of lying with a woman who might have already been with at least one man that evening made his skin crawl.

"You look just like you did that time Letitia made us those hideous lemon tarts," Julian remarked, falling into the chair beside him.

Brave smiled. Five years ago, Julian's youngest sister had wanted to impress her older brother's friends with her culinary skills. The results had become a long-standing joke between the friends.

"They would have been delicious if she'd remembered the sugar."

Julian shrugged. "She got it right eventually."

A soft chuckle escaped Brave's lips. "If she's half as stubborn as she used to be, I've no doubt she now makes better tarts than your cook."

Julian stared at him, his expression one of open curiosity. "Why are you here, Brave?"

"I was wondering when you were going to get to the point." Brave took a sip of his port. It was excellent. Charlton certainly knew how to entertain.

"I do not have the patience for hedging that Gabriel has."

It was on the tip of Brave's tongue to tell Julian that Gabriel wasn't any better at wiggling information than he was, but decided against delaying the inevitable any longer.

"I could tell you that I'm here because it's been too long since I've had a woman—"

"It has been too long since you've had a woman."

Brave ignored him. "But in truth, I'm here because of a friend."

Stretching his long legs out in front of him, Julian watched the near orgy before them with artistic indifference. "Would this friend be Miss Ashton, by any chance?"

Brave started. "What makes you ask that?"

Julian pinned him with a knowing stare. "Only that you've talked of little but her since we ran into her earlier today. And you took the bonnet she forgot home with you."

A frisson of discomfort ran between Brave's shoulder blades, making him squirm in his chair.

"I was worried that if I left it at the shop, it might get misplaced."

Julian rolled his eyes. "Please, there's no way on this earth that anyone would mistake that shabby thing for a new hat, and I can hardly imagine any lady mourning its loss."

"Ra— Miss Ashton is not like most ladies of your acquaintance, Jules, and I have no doubt that she will miss the bonnet. I doubt she has many others." He thought of how fetching Rachel had looked in that pink—*rose*—velvet bonnet and wished he could have found a good excuse to buy it for her, but such a gesture would have been highly inappropriate, no matter what his motives.

Especially since even he didn't quite understand his motives.

"Yes," Julian agreed, a shrewd gleam in his eyes. "I can see that Miss Ashton is quite extraordinary indeed."

Brave frowned. "Whatever you're thinking, it's wrong."

"It doesn't matter what I think," Julian replied diplomatically. "But may I ask what your being here has to do with Miss Ashton?"

Normally, Brave would not share a confidence with someone else, but he knew that Julian would not repeat what he heard. Perhaps his old friend might give him some insight, or at least help him figure out why a woman he had not seen in years, and who had never been within his intimate circles, should suddenly mean so much to him now.

"Miss Ashton's stepfather, Sir Henry Westhaver, wants her to marry Charlton."

Julian's jaw dropped. "He what?" Leaning over the arm of his chair, he whispered, "Does he know what kind of man Charlton is?"

With a grimace, Brave pointed to the far corner, where a heavyset man had his hand down a courtesan's bodice. "That's Sir Henry there."

The poet made a moue of bad taste. "Charming. So you're here to find out exactly what kind of man Charlton is, or to try talking sense to the stepfather?"

"I'm not sure," Brave replied. "I don't imagine either will do much good. Sir Henry obviously knows what he's dealing with, and since he appears to be cut from the same cloth, I doubt there is much chance of changing his mind."

"Miss Ashton can always refuse to marry Charlton."

Brave nodded. "For all the good it might do her." He was fairly certain refusing would get Rachel nowhere.

Julian's expression was one of polite disinterest, but Brave knew better than to accept it as such. "And what help can you possibly be to Miss Ashton if Sir Henry does try to force the marriage?"

"I don't know," Brave's voice was wrought with frustration. "But I will do all that I can to help her."

"Why?"

Brave thought for a moment. "Because it is the right thing to do."

"For whom? Is it the right thing to do for Miss Ashton because you'll save her from marrying a degenerate, or right for you because you'll feel better for not having been able to save my sister?"

Scowling, Brave leaned toward his friend. "What the hell are you talking about?"

"Oh stop scowling." Julian took a drink. "And don't pretend you don't know what I'm talking about."

"Perhaps you should explain so I don't hit you for the wrong reason."

Julian laughed at that. "You've never hit me in your life."

Brave's anger faded a bit. "I could start."

Meeting his gaze evenly, Julian's smile was sympathetic. "Brave, I know your . . . problems after Miranda's death stem from the fact that you were unable to prevent it."

He made it sound so pathetic. "And just how do you know that?"

Julian's smile faded. "Because I felt the same way. Only as her brother, I was able to see my way clear of it."

"I loved her," Brave announced bitterly. "I should have been able to help her. Instead, I turned my back on her."

"Brave, she didn't want your love, and she didn't want your help. There was nothing you could have done."

But she had wanted Brave's help. She'd begged for it, in fact. And he hadn't given it to her.

It was the first time they'd spoken of Miranda's death since he and Gabriel had talked him into seeing Phelps. Talking about it didn't hurt like it used to, and Brave wasn't sure how he felt about that. It should hurt. He deserved to hurt.

He had loved Miranda and wanted to marry her, but she was in love with someone else—a groom on her parents' estate. The young man was dismissed, and when Miranda realized she was carrying her lover's child, she came to Brave for help, and he, too caught up in his own hurt, had refused. Miranda killed herself rather than face disgrace.

Brave could accept that she hadn't loved him; what he couldn't accept was that he had been responsible for her death. He could have married her so the child could have a name, but he'd been so hurt by her earlier refusal that he'd lashed out and rejected her. Instead of giving her his help, he'd helped fish her body out of the pond she'd drowned herself in.

He could have prevented the whole thing.

And if he could do anything to prevent Rachel from having to marry Charlton, he would.

"Would you let a young woman marry something like *that*"—he pointed to where Charlton was sprawled on a sofa with his face buried in one woman's bosom, his hand up the skirts of another—"if you could possibly stop it?"

"Of course not, but I would also make certain I was clear as to my reasons for doing it."

"Protecting her from a lecher isn't good enough for you?" Brave demanded mockingly.

Julian rose to his feet. "If I'm protecting her from a lecher out of the kindness of my heart, that's one thing, but if I'm protecting her because I have a personal interest in her, that's quite another. I would want to be very certain of what I was doing before someone else decided she needed to be protected from me. Now, I'm going to fetch another drink. Care to join me?"

Brave glanced up. "Will you stop talking?" He didn't even want to think about what his friend had just said, because then he'd have to question himself and his motives toward Rachel, and that was something he just wasn't prepared to do.

"No," Julian replied with a smile. "But I do promise not to say another word about Rachel Ashton."

"Good enough." Brave stood and followed his friend across the room to the bar. They were stopped by several female "guests" along the way, and though Brave managed to fend off their advances with flattering kindness, Julian, who was so much better at putting words on paper than in his own mouth where women were concerned, muttered some lame excuse and went off in search of Gabriel, leaving Brave alone again.

"Frailty," Brave muttered, pouring himself another glass of port. "Thy name is Wolfram."

He shouldn't be there, and he certainly shouldn't have

brought his friends, but he'd brought them because he wouldn't have been able to go on his own, and not just because he hadn't been invited. He hadn't known how he would react to the temptation to drink himself blind and take what the women present offered.

He should have known neither would prove much of a temptation. The port was adequate, but the women . . . Well, it had been a long time since he'd been tempted.

And Rachel Ashton didn't count. His reaction to her was the reaction of any normal man who'd been too long removed from the world.

So why didn't he react the same way to any of the women around him now? There were women there who were prettier than Rachel Ashton, albeit without those striking lavender-blue eyes of hers. There were women there whose bosoms were bigger, smaller, higher, lower, even creamier, and he'd be willing to bet that most of the women there had smaller feet, but that didn't make him want them. Meanwhile, the memory of Rachel's bosom straining against the neckline of his mother's gown was enough to make him start to harden.

Maybe Julian was right. Maybe it was *him* Rachel needed protection from.

"Good evening, Braven."

Or maybe not.

Turning to face Viscount Charlton, Brave plastered his best and least sincere smile on his face. "And good evening to you as well, Charlton. This is quite the . . . soiree you've got here."

Charlton smiled. He wasn't really a bad- or evil-looking man. He was a little stocky and could stand to bathe a bit more often, but it was his personality that made him so revolting, not his looks or smell.

"Well, I'm glad to hear it. I must confess, I was beginning to wonder if you were enjoying yourself or not. Are the ladies not to your *liking*?"

Something in his tone of voice made Brave's hackles rise. No man liked having his sexual preferences questioned.

"I prefer to watch," he replied, and then realized how that sounded.

Charlton clapped him on the back so hard Brave thought he might have knocked one of his lungs loose. "So, that's the way of it, eh? Well, I've enjoyed being a spectator once or twice in my day as well. You should have told me, old man. There's a room upstairs with a peephole that allows a person to spy on the room next door. I could have put you up there instead of Hathaway."

Brave tried to keep his expression polite. "That's very kind of you, *old man*, but I'm quite content where I'm at. I like to browse a bit, see what mares are available before I choose a suitable mount." His father would slap his mouth if he could hear him now. Charles Wycherley had not raised his son to be a libertine, and Brave did not approve of using women solely for pleasure and then casting them aside.

Another reason he could never figure out why Miranda had chosen a roguish stableboy over him. Maybe *that* was why.

Charlton laughed and gave him another slap on the back. "Quite right, Braven, quite right! I've never cared whether she be filly or nag, just as long as she gets me where I want to go!"

Brave hid a grimace behind his glass and drank deeply. He didn't know how much longer he could stand to witness this debacle that would make even a Roman emperor blush.

Charlton leaned closer, so close that Brave could smell him. He held the glass of port under his nose to try and mask the odor. Sex and sweaty feet did not mix.

"Although, I've discovered it is time to buy a new mare, Braven."

Brave stiffened, his heart racing. "Really? Did you have to put your old one out to pasture?"

Chuckling, Charlton shook his head. "I've decided to marry."

Brave nodded in mock sympathy. "Decided to start your nursery, have you? Well, never fear Charlton, it happens to us all eventually."

Charlton sighed. "Aye, 'tis time for that as well, but it's not just for an heir that I've decided to marry."

"Oh? And what is the other reason."

"A bird in hand is worth two in the bush," Charlton replied as though the old saying held some secret, mystical meaning.

Brave shook his head. "I'm afraid I don't follow."

Charlton stepped even closer and Brave was forced to take a step back to keep his eyes from watering. The *old man* was ripe tonight.

"You see these women, Braven? I had to have them sent up from London, and even then it was hard to get enough of them to come."

"They don't like the country?" His tone was dry.

"They don't like *me*."

Can you blame them? "Oh, now I don't believe—"

"It's true. Word's gotten around that I sometimes have . . . peculiar tastes."

"Well, you're scarcely alone there," Brave replied honestly. "Seems half of England has peculiar tastes."

"Be that as it may, there's only one bawdy house in London that'll allow me within its doors, and even then there's only a few of the girls that'll have me. And since they know no one else will have me, they've begun charging me a king's ransom for my pleasure."

The pieces fell together in Brave's head like a child's puzzle, leaving him cold inside. "And you don't have to pay a wife."

Charlton nodded. "And a wife can't refuse her husband."

Brave swallowed the bile at the back of his throat. Sir

Henry was knowingly selling his stepdaughter—Rachel—to this man. No doubt he thought he was getting a pretty good price, and no doubt Charlton was all too happy to pay it.

He took a swallow of port to wash the bad taste out of his mouth. "When is the happy occasion to take place?"

Charlton shrugged. "Not sure. As soon as I can secure it. I don't mind telling you I'm looking forward to saving the blunt."

"I'm sure you are," Brave replied, barely hiding his rancor.

Charlton blinked. "Yes, well, feel free to watch all you want, Braven. Join in if you wish. There's plenty to go around."

The only physical activity Brave was interested in at that moment was beating both Charlton and Sir Henry into bloody pulps.

"Thank you, Charlton, but I think I've seen enough for one evening." Setting his glass on the bar, Brave turned his back on the confused viscount and strode toward the door. His jaw was clenched so tight it ached and his hands were balled into tight fists at his sides.

One way or another, he was going to protect Rachel from Charlton's sick and twisted desires.

And he wasn't doing it out of the kindness of his heart either.

Chapter 5

What was Brave doing with her bonnet?

Strolling up the lane to Tullywood, Rachel silently asked herself the question for the hundredth time since leaving the milliner's shop. The owner hadn't found any unfamiliar bonnets in his store after she and Belinda left the day before, but the Earl of Braven had been carrying a lady's bonnet when he and his friends departed shortly after. Obviously it was hers.

Well, he could have at least returned it to her. Perhaps attending Viscount Charlton's party was more important?

Or, she thought with less bitterness, it hadn't occurred to Brave that it might be the only one she owned—other than the rose-velvet one she hadn't yet been able to bring herself to wear. Certainly he was used to ladies with extensive wardrobes, but Rachel owned only one bonnet that was fit for wear. She borrowed one of her mother's for the walk into town—she hadn't wanted to walk into the milliner's wearing the bonnet Belinda had purchased the day before. Then they'd know of Belinda's generosity, and that made Rachel uncomfortable.

So, she thought, returning to the matter at hand, when did he plan to return it? Just the idea of seeing him again was enough to make Rachel's stomach knot with anxiety. Brave was an appealing man, despite his brooding appearance, and Rachel was well aware she owed him a debt of gratitude for saving her life. But he made her nervous.

Ever since that kiss on the Westwoods' balcony things had been different. She'd even had a servant return his mother's gown so she wouldn't have to face him again.

She'd been so aware of him in the hat shop. His scent, the sound of his voice, the somber set of his features, even when he smiled—if that's what one could call that sad twist of his lips. She'd been completely overwhelmed by all of it.

Rachel wasn't so naive that she didn't understand what it meant. She was attracted to Brave. Very attracted, and for that reason alone it was best that she stay away from him. She could never give herself to a man who wasn't her husband—it went against everything she had been raised to believe. At the very best she would end up making a fool of herself, for a woman in her position—even if she wanted to marry—had no hope of ever marrying an earl, especially when that earl hadn't given her any indication that he returned her attraction.

Rachel didn't know what would be worse—having her feelings returned, or not having them returned. If they weren't returned, only her pride would be bruised, but if they were . . .

There was no point thinking of that. As long as Sir Henry was a threat to her mother, Rachel couldn't stay in Yorkshire and couldn't even entertain the idea of marriage. Her mother's safety came first. What kind of daughter would put her own wants before the needs of the woman who raised her? Especially a woman who had aligned herself with a man like Sir Henry just so her daughter would have food in her belly. No, Rachel would just have to get past this foolish attraction to Brave. And she would.

"There's a gentleman waiting for you in the parlor, Miss," Potts, the butler, informed her when she entered the house.

Rachel gaped at the round-faced elderly man.

"A gentleman? For me?" Was it Brave? Despite her resolution of only moments before, Rachel's heart thrilled at the prospect of seeing him, even if he was there only to return her hat.

Handing Potts her bonnet and cloak, Rachel smoothed her hands over her hair and skirts and hurried across the foyer to the front parlor.

Her smile of greeting froze as her gaze fell upon her visitor. *Viscount Charlton.*

He rose to his feet and started toward her as she entered the room. "Miss Ashton, how lovely to see you."

"Good morning, Lord Charlton." Etiquette dictated that Rachel offer him her hand, and as she did so, the odors of cologne, stale sweat, and hair pomade struck her full force.

The viscount had decided to pretty himself up for her. Charming.

"To what do I owe the pleasure of this visit?" she asked, pulling her hand free of his before he could kiss it. She made no move to sit, and therefore the viscount couldn't either. His gaze darted around in bewilderment before coming back to hers.

"Er . . . no doubt you are aware that your stepfather and I have come to an agreement."

"No."

The viscount looked even more confused. "I beg your pardon?"

Calm. She had to be calm. If she went into hysterics now, it would ruin whatever chance she had of getting herself out of this mess. She would refuse him, and she would do it calmly and as haughtily as any highborn lady.

Schooling her features into a polite mask, Rachel shrugged. "I am not aware of any agreement between my stepfather and you, Lord Charlton."

"Oh." Now clearly befuddled, the viscount ran a hand over his hair, wiping the smear of pomade that came off it onto his breeches. *Lovely.*

"Ahem . . . yes, well . . . you see, my dear, I have asked your stepfather for your hand in marriage, and he has given his consent." The viscount smiled, revealing teeth that were in need of a good cleaning.

"I see." Still wearing her mask of tranquillity, Rachel continued, "And why was I not consulted on this matter?"

Charlton frowned. "Why should you've been? The marriage settlements are between Sir Henry and me. As a woman, they do not concern you."

Rachel had a hard time keeping her disbelief from showing. "Yes, but I'm the one being bought and sold."

"From father to husband, as it has always been done. There was no need to consult you. An agreement has been reached, and we are to be married in one month's time." He stomped past her. Rachel added an extremely short temper to the growing list of the viscount's faults.

Suddenly much calmer than she had been all day, Rachel kept her gaze fixed on the far wall, not even bothering to turn toward him as she gathered her courage. She drew a deep breath. "No."

This time there was no mistaking her meaning. There was a clomping of boots, and the viscount was in front of her again. "What did you say?"

Rachel met his gaze evenly. "I said no, Lord Charlton. I will not marry you."

Charlton's face flushed crimson. "You're sorely misguided if you think you have any say in the matter, missy. I paid good money to have you and have you I will, by whatever means necessary."

Her blood turned to ice water in her veins. How could she have ever thought she could just simply refuse someone Sir Henry chose? Of course he would not make it that easy for her. He despised her as much as she hated him, and his choice of bridegroom proved that.

A shaky smiled curved Rachel's lips. "By 'have' I assume you mean to bed me, Lord Charlton?"

The viscount's gaze traveled the length of her body and back up again, making Rachel feel as dirty as a roll in a pigsty. "It includes bedding, yes," he replied, his tone low and hoarse.

Rachel shuddered, but went through with her plan. "Then I'm afraid you've purchased damaged goods." It was a lie, but Charlton didn't know that.

Pomade-stained fingers reached out to touch the swell of her bosom above the neckline of her gown.

"I don't care that you're not a virgin, Sweetness. In fact, I'd prefer it if you weren't."

What man wanted a wife who wasn't pure? Hysteria threatened again, and Rachel mentally reached for the first lie she could think of. "And you don't mind that I have the pox?"

Charlton froze. "You *what*?"

To be honest, Rachel wasn't even certain what having the pox entailed, but she knew from the expression on the viscount's face that it was bad. Very bad.

Rachel almost smiled at his horrified expression. "I have the pox. Did Sir Henry not tell you?"

"No," Charlton ground out. "He most certainly did *not* tell me."

"Hmm." Rachel shrugged. "Perhaps he forgot. Anyway, Lord Charlton, I'm sure you understand now why I cannot marry you in good conscience. It would be very wrong of me." She hoped she didn't look as insincere as she sounded.

The viscount looked so angry, Rachel thought he might have a seizure right there in front of her. "Miss Ashton, are you being quite honest with me?"

Rachel put on her best innocent face. "Lord Charlton, the pox is not the kind of thing a young woman would ever want to lay claim to, especially if she did not have it."

He seemed to believe that, even though anyone with half a brain would know that a desperate young woman would say almost anything to avoid marrying a man she found disgusting. Obviously, the viscount saw himself as quite the catch.

"Yes, of course," he agreed, his face still tight with anger. "I am sorry for wasting your time, Miss Ashton, and I thank you for your candor. You may rest assured your . . . condition is safe with me."

Rachel didn't doubt that for a second. Charlton wouldn't want anyone to know of his humiliation.

"Thank you, Lord Charlton. I appreciate your confidence. Now, I am certain you will wish to be on your way . . ."

Minutes later, Rachel watched Viscount Charlton's horse gallop down the lane, with the viscount bent over its neck as though Satan himself were on his heels.

Sagging onto the window seat, she congratulated herself on a job well-done. She had successfully managed to avoid marriage to Lord Charlton. She'd made him doubt Sir Henry, and, because of that, Charlton would never believe Sir Henry hadn't lied to him. She was safe from Charlton—for now.

Which led Rachel to wonder what Sir Henry's reaction would be when he found out what she'd done.

Her stepfather was *not* going to be pleased.

"What the hell did you tell Charlton?"

Looking up from her sewing, Rachel ignored the worried

glance her mother shot her and greeted her stepfather with what she hoped was a bland expression. It had been almost six hours since Charlton's departure. She had expected Sir Henry before this.

Standing in the doorway, his clothes wrinkled and his hair standing on end, he looked pathetically out of place in the neat parlor.

"Good evening, Sir Henry," Rachel replied, ignoring his anger. "I believe cook saved some dinner for you."

Sir Henry's round face reddened with rage, but Rachel felt no fear for her own safety. Her stepfather had never struck her, but she wouldn't put it past him to take his anger out on her mother.

She met her mother's worried gaze. "Mama, perhaps you should allow Sir Henry and me to talk in private."

"Good idea," Sir Henry agreed, his jowls quivering. "Better she not hear what a wicked wretch her daughter is for refusing to marry a peer of the realm!"

One look at her husband's face and Marion knew better than to argue. Casting one last worried glance at her daughter, she put aside her needlework and hurried from the room.

Rachel rose to her feet as her stepfather approached. "I assume you've talked to Lord Charlton." There was no need to delay the inevitable.

Sir Henry nodded, his dark eyes narrow and bright. "He had a very interesting story to tell me—after demanding that I return the gold he paid me to marry you. He said you told him you had the pox."

Rachel smiled. "I did."

Crack!

The blow was staggering, the back of Sir Henry's hand struck Rachel's face with a force that almost drove her to her knees and brought tears to her eyes. She would have fallen had she not grabbed the arm of the chair for support.

Her stepfather grabbed her by the shawl, hauling her toward him until they were almost nose to nose. Fear—real fear—clutched at Rachel's chest.

He shook her, his eyes black and cold in the firelight. "I told him you were lying, a case of maidenly nerves, that the marriage would go ahead as planned."

Rachel could taste blood inside her mouth, but she forced her gaze to his. Her arms dangled helplessly at her sides, pinned by the shawl. Physically, she was unable to defend herself, but she would not back down from him. Even if he beat her black-and-blue, she would not consent to marry Charlton.

"I hope you haven't spent any of that gold, Sir Henry, because you're going to end up having to repay it all." How cool and controlled she sounded! No one would know she was terrified. "Even if you can convince Charlton that I don't have the pox, I'll find another way to avoid marrying him. You cannot control me."

He flung her backward. She hit the mantel with a crash, the hard oak gouging her shoulder blades with a force that made her cry out. Pain shot down her back, and her shawl fell to her feet as she sank to the floor. If he'd pushed her a bit more to the left, she would have ended up in the fire.

She wasn't so sure that hadn't been his intention.

With bleary vision she watched him move toward her and she groped for a weapon, anything to keep him from hurting her again. Her hands closed around the poker near the grate.

Dragging herself to her feet, Rachel delved deep within herself, past the fear and pain to the rage she felt whenever Sir Henry hurt her mother. Calling on that anger, she raised the poker like a sword.

"Put that down," he demanded, poised like an animal ready to pounce. Rachel had never seen him look so energetic, so anxious.

Good Lord, he was enjoying this! It pleased him to see her bleed. Until that moment she'd never quite realized just how much he hated her.

"Get away from me." She swung the poker at him when he tried to advance. Pain shot through her shoulders. "You come near me again, and I'll kill you."

Sir Henry smiled, sending a shiver down Rachel's bruised spine. "You can't fight me forever, Rachel. Sooner or later I will break you, and you will do as I say."

Anger, fear, and pride brought Rachel's chin up a notch. "Once I turn twenty-five, you can't touch me, you bastard. I can certainly fight you 'til then."

Confusion furrowed his brow. "Twenty-five? What happens when you're twenty-five?" Then, he laughed, as though he'd just gotten the gist of a joke. "Oh, your inheritance! Is that what you're talking about? You're planning to take your little nest egg and fly the coop, are you?"

"That's right. And you can't stop me."

Still chuckling, Sir Henry relaxed his stance. Unease wormed through Rachel's veins. What did he find so amusing?

"But, Rachel"—he chuckled—"I already have stopped you."

That unease curdled into full-fledged dread. Raising the poker, Rachel assumed a more defensive stance, hoping he couldn't see the length of iron quiver in her grasp. "What do you mean?"

"You have no inheritance." He wiped his eyes with the back of his hands. "Well you did, but it's long gone now."

Rachel's muscles began to shake. "Gone?"

Grinning, Sir Henry nodded. "I made sure I had my hands on that shortly after I married your mother. Wasn't difficult either since I'd been declared your guardian until you reached your majority."

She had to grab the mantel with one hand to keep from falling down. The poker drooped in the other. "You're lying," she rasped, but one look at the triumphant expression on his face told her the just as ugly and twisted truth. He had robbed her of her future, her independence.

Her one chance to save her mother.

He laughed again as her desolation brought her literally to her knees. Gone. It was gone, and with it all her hopes.

"So, it seems, my dear, that I've won after all." Rachel didn't even look up as his voice drifted toward the door. "You'll marry Charlton in one month. I'm so going to enjoy giving you away—especially to a man with Charlton's . . . tastes."

The door clicked shut behind him, leaving nothing but the crackle of the fire and Sir Henry's mocking laughter ringing in her ears.

Rachel stared blindly at the drops of blood splattering onto her skirts. What was she going to do? Neither she nor her mother was safe from Sir Henry now. Whatever power she had held had disappeared the moment he realized he'd foiled her plan. If she wanted to keep her mother—and herself—alive, she'd have to think of another way. How were they ever to be free of him?

She didn't know what to do, didn't know if there was any way she and her mother could lawfully escape Sir Henry, but she did know that this situation had spiraled out of her control. Short of murder, she was powerless to stop Sir Henry on her own.

But she knew someone who might be able to.

Hauling herself up on trembling legs, Rachel retrieved her shawl and tossed it over the chair before carefully picking her way across the carpet to the door. The hall outside was quiet as she crept toward the stairs. She hurried toward the ground floor, peering as far ahead of her as she could to make certain Sir Henry didn't catch her.

Potts was in the foyer when she staggered into it. "Miss Rachel!" he cried, his eyes round and his cheeks as pale as his hair. "Are you all right?"

"Yes, Potts," Rachel assured him, "I'm fine. Has Sir Henry left the house?"

The aging butler nodded. "Yes, Miss. He rode out just a moment ago."

"Good." Ignoring the pain in her face and back, Rachel instructed Potts to fetch her cloak and gloves. Slipping into her cloak was pure agony, but she managed to do it with the butler's help. A sheen of perspiration dotted her brow as she pulled on her gloves.

"When my stepfather returns, Potts, I want you to have at least one bottle of brandy waiting for him in his study."

If the request surprised Potts, he didn't show it. "Of course, Miss. Might I inquire as to where you're going?"

"No, Potts. It's perhaps best that you don't." Wrenching open the door, Rachel stepped out into the chilly, damp night air and hurried toward Sir Henry's precious stables.

Moments later, clenching her teeth against the bone-jarring agony of every stride, she galloped down the lane on a quicksilver-fast gelding bound for Wyck's End.

And Brave.

Brave returned from a late-afternoon ride feeling better than he had in months. It had been so long since he had allowed himself the pleasure of permitting his mount to run at full speed. He'd forgotten how it felt to have the wind sting his face as a horse with legs like lightning carried him across ground that was nothing more than a blur. He'd forgotten just what freedom truly was.

Oh, it would take more than a ride across the moors to wipe his soul clean of its burden. The weight of Miranda's death and the effects of the self-destruction that followed could not be lifted so easily, but instead of turning in circles, a path was beginning to emerge before him—a path that could lead him to redemption.

That path started with Rachel Ashton.

Not that helping her could change what happened with Miranda. He knew that, but he hoped that helping Rachel might somehow allow him to atone for his sins by evening the balance, allowing him to make a difference in one life even though he hadn't been able to in another. It might not work, but he owed it to himself to try. And regardless of how it might benefit him, he couldn't knowingly watch as Rachel was sold to a man like Charlton.

It was this vow that gave him a purpose. It might not sound like much to some—then again others might find it a tad melodramatic—but if the end result kept Rachel out of Charlton's hands, if it could show just how sorry he was for Miranda's death, he didn't care what anyone else thought. Pulling Rachel from the river wasn't good enough.

Gabriel and Julian joined him later for dinner. It was nice to sit at that huge table and see other faces.

"When do you leave for Heatherington Park?" Brave asked.

"Tomorrow," Julian replied, slicing into a piece of roast beef in wine broth. "We'll be there for a few weeks before returning here and then back to London. Letitia has a birthday coming up, and she is quite insistent that I be there for it." He lifted his fork to his mouth and closed his eyes in pleasure. "Exquisite. Your chef is divine."

"He's French," Gabriel remarked with a glint in his eye. "All things French are divine."

"Would that statement have been influenced by the fact that your mistress is French?" Julian asked, taking a sip of wine.

Gabriel grinned.

It was odd to hear Nanette referred to as Gabriel's mistress. The two of them had been together for several years. Brave was surprised the relationship had lasted as long as it had. Nanette was a lovely woman, but she was too docile, too quiet for a man like Gabe.

Gabriel needed someone vivacious and strong-willed—like Lilith. Perhaps that was why he avoided women of that temperament now.

Brave could relate. Since Miranda he'd avoided women like the plague. Even if his heart were capable of feeling those gentler feelings again, he was not in any hurry to offer it up. He never wanted to be in the position to be hurt—or to hurt another ever again.

As with most things these days, his mind turned to Rachel Ashton. He wondered what she would think of him if she knew the truth about him. Would she question his mental state? Or would she try to be understanding and sympathetic? Perhaps she'd be disappointed. He seemed to have a habit of disappointing people.

He didn't know which would be worse. One thing he did know, however, was that even if Rachel was only half as drawn to him as he was to her, there could be no denying that kiss. Oh, he could avoid discussing it, but he could never pretend it hadn't happened. Not when it had shaken him right to the very center of his being.

His gaze fell on Gabriel and Julian. The cynic and the romantic. Gabriel had chosen Nanette because of her beauty, her innocence, and their common interests. Julian's current amour was an older widow who appreciated poetry and art. Feelings weren't a consideration. They certainly cared about one another, but had either of his friends ever been tempted to throw all caution to the wind for the sake of one kiss?

Gabriel had. That Brave knew, but it hadn't been Nanette's kiss that inspired him.

The touch of Rachel's lips had been so inspirational it had almost been a religious experience. Brave chuckled. Perhaps he'd found his salvation.

"What's so amusing?" Julian asked, a curious smile curving his lips.

Brave shook his head. "Nothing. I was just thinking about religion."

Julian arched a brow. "Nothing like thoughts of judgment and all that to put a smile on your face, eh?"

His smile fading, Brave nodded. "Something like that." Would Rachel judge him? For some reason, the idea of disappointing her filled him with a deeper anxiety than even Miranda's death could inspire. Perhaps because he was putting so much hope into saving her—and in return hoping she would save him.

After dinner they retired to the billiards room for brandy and some good-natured competition. They were laughing at one of Julian's stories—and Gabriel's losing streak—when Reynolds knocked on the door.

"I beg your pardon, Lord Braven, but there is a young lady here to see you."

Brave frowned, not only at the butler's words, but at the discomfited expression on his narrow face.

"A young lady," Gabriel echoed in a singsong voice. "Were you expecting company, Brave?"

Shaking his head, Brave started to walk toward the door. "I was not. Where is she, Reynolds?"

"I put her in the green drawing room, my lord."

Brave paused long enough to turn to his friends. "I won't be long."

"Take your time" Julian replied, lifting his glass. "We'll continue to enjoy your excellent brandy."

Brave had no doubt his friends would do just that. No doubt they'd both be half-drunk and laughing at their loss of coordination when he returned.

A fresh fire burned in the grate, and Reynolds had lit almost every candle in the room. He doubted his mysterious lady caller had anything illicit on her mind with the room lit up like a ballroom. So if his visitor wasn't looking to seduce the "hermit earl," why was she there?

She sat near the fire, with her back to him. One look at the bright blond hair gleaming in the firelight and Brave knew instantly who she was.

"Rachel," he said, stepping into the room. "What are you doing here?"

She rose to her feet like someone in great pain, and when she turned to face him, Brave knew why.

Her hair was a mess, several strands having slipped from their pins. Her eyes were wide and dark in a snow-white face. Blood had dried in a thin trail from her mouth to her chin, and the right side of her face was swollen and red.

"My God," he whispered, crossing the carpet to stand directly in front of her. "What happened?" His first—and most horrifying—thought was that Charlton had forced himself upon her, violated her in order to force her to marry him. If that were the case, then Charlton would be dead by morning.

"He hit me," came the hoarse reply. "It's all gone, and he hit me."

Sharp relief flooded Brave's veins, but he forced it aside. Her distant expression told him something awful had happened, and just because she hadn't mentioned a more intimate assault, it didn't mean it hadn't happened.

He led her to the sofa and made her sit. She winced. "What is it? Where do you hurt?" he demanded.

"My back," her voice was still so matter-of-fact. "He threw me against the mantel."

Visibly trembling with rage, Brave went to the small cabinet in the corner and poured her a glass of sherry—the strongest spirit his mother kept in this room, which was primarily meant for ladies.

He gave Rachel the sherry and seated himself on the sofa beside her. He waited until she took a drink to speak. "Start at the beginning and tell me what happened." It was hard to sound calm and detached when what he truly wanted was to strangle whoever had hurt her.

Rachel didn't look at him. She stared at the little crystal

glass in her hands, twirling it so it glimmered and glowed in the firelight.

"Charlton came to see me this afternoon—"

Charlton. He knew it! His fingers tightened into fists.

"He told me that he and Sir Henry had arranged for me to marry him. I refused. He wouldn't hear it, so I lied to him to make him not want to marry me." She gazed up at him, a faint smile curving the side of her mouth that wasn't swollen. "I told him I had the pox."

Brave was stunned by her nerve. He could kiss her for being so inventive—or strangle her for taking such a chance with a man of Charlton's temperament. "And he believed you?"

She nodded, looking away again. "He did—until Sir Henry told him the truth."

Brave listened in stunned silence as she told him about Sir Henry's violence toward her mother, how he had struck her when she refused to marry Charlton, his robbing her of her inheritance, and his final threat that he would see her married regardless of her wishes.

He had known the baronet to be a low kind of man, but he never would have guessed he was so utterly despicable. His blood boiled with the knowledge of what Sir Henry had put Rachel and her mother through.

He was going to have a little talk with Sir Henry Westhaver.

"Rachel, you must leave his house."

She shook her head. "I cannot leave my mother."

"But Rachel, if you continue to fight him . . ." He didn't even want to think of what Sir Henry might do to her if she remained under his roof. Brave would not stand for it.

"No!" Rachel cried, leaping to her feet and gasping in pain as she did so. "I *will* fight him. I will not let him beat me into submission as he has my mother, and I *will* get her out of his house!" She whirled to face him, wincing as she did so. "Surely there is *something* we can do, some way to stop him."

We? Did she mean herself and her mother, or did she include him in her equation? Did it matter? He'd already decided to do whatever he could to help her.

Brave wasn't as familiar with British law as he would like to be, but he knew that it was more in Sir Henry's favor than Rachel's or her mother's. Somewhere along the way, some barbarian had decided that a man's wife was his property and therefore his to do with as he wanted, and that included violence. Supposedly, a man wasn't allowed to beat his wife with a stick bigger around than his thumb, and abject cruelty was considered the basis for a divorce, but it was terribly hard to prove, and since divorce was considered so horribly scandalous, most women opted to endure the abuse.

However, Brave himself was now a witness to the kind of brutality Westhaver was capable of. He had also witnessed the baronet's adultery at Charlton's party the night before.

"Has anyone other than you ever seen the results of his attacks on your mother?"

Rachel shook her head, her expression glum. "The servants know what a monster he is, but I'm not sure they know everything. Mama has always been very careful to mask as much of the bruises as she could. She's even gotten me to help her dress so the maid wouldn't see the marks. She was ashamed of them—as though they were her own fault."

Brave knew all to well what if felt like to believe you deserved whatever punishment you got. Obviously, Rachel's mother had been made to feel that way as well. "I might be able to use my position to help."

Rachel's eyes lit up.

"I can help you go through the proper channels if a divorce is what your mother wants, but it would be a long and drawn-out process, and she would have to be willing to testify against Sir Henry. It would mean airing all the cruelty you and your mother have suffered to the world, and Sir Henry might very well terrify your mother into dropping the suit."

From the crestfallen expression on her bruised face, he knew that was exactly what her stepfather would do. God, but he had never hated anyone like he hated Sir Henry at that moment.

"Then there is nothing," she whispered.

Brave's heart broke. "If you had someone of social import—someone titled within your family, then perhaps they could take up the cause and offer you their protection. At least then you and your mother would be safe until your case could be heard."

"There is no one." The gaze that met his was resigned. "Short of killing him, there's nothing I can do, is there?"

Her words struck fear deep into his heart, for he heard the determination in them. He had no doubt that if pushed hard enough, Rachel Ashton would not break, she would explode, and she would put an end to Sir Henry without so much as a blink.

The courts would not be kind to Rachel for killing a baronet, no matter how much a favor his death would be to the world. She would be taken to Newgate, and then she would be hanged for murder.

He could not let that happen.

Wrapping his arms around her, he pulled her against his chest, careful not to hurt her back and shoulders. He pressed his cheek to the softness of her hair.

"I will help you in whatever way I can."

Rachel's arms came up around his ribs, seizing him as though he was all she had left to cling to in the world. Instead of terrifying him as it should have, the idea filled him with a strange, buoyant warmth.

"Why would you do that for me?" She lifted her gaze to his, her eyes bright with hope.

Why *would* he do that for her? Looking down into those wide, scared eyes, Brave could think of only one answer, and it had nothing to do with Miranda. Was it out of the kindness of his heart, as Julian had asked, or because of his own agenda.

Because he wanted to. Whether or not helping Rachel would assuage his guilt didn't matter. He simply could not allow her to return to Westhaver knowing what he did without offering whatever assistance he could give.

He stared at her. She stared back, and before he knew what he was about, his head lowered to hers. His lips contented themselves by brushing feathery kisses along her temple and cheek, as her poor mouth would be too sore to kiss as he wanted.

This was how Gabriel and Julian found them not seconds later. Brave had forgotten to shut the door tight behind him, and his nosy friends had been unable to squelch their curiosity any longer. He should have known they'd come spying, but he hadn't known Rachel was his mysterious visitor when he'd left them, and when he had discovered his visitor's identity, all thoughts of his friends had gone right out the window.

Brave didn't know what made him raise his head. He only knew that Julian, Miranda's brother, stood staring at him from the doorway as he held another woman in his arms. A woman who was beaten and obviously scared and clinging to him like ivy to stone.

And he knew there was no turning back. His path was set. No matter what Julian thought, no matter what he expected Brave to do, Brave *knew* there was only one course of action to take if he was going to save Rachel and himself in the process.

Quietly, Gabriel and Julian backed out of the room, but not before Rachel caught sight of them. Hiding her bloody lip and flushed cheeks, she pulled free of Brave's embrace.

"I believe I know how to solve your problem."

Her expression was wary. "How?"

Swallowing hard, Brave met her gaze. What he was about to suggest could be the salvation or ruination of them both.

The kindness of his heart? No, not that.

"Marry me."

Chapter 6

❧⟶∾⟨⟩∿⟵❧

Was he mad?

Just in case he was mentally unstable, Rachel took another step back. "You can't be serious." But his expression was serious—*too* serious for her liking.

He moved toward her, stopping when she stepped back again. "What other choice do you have?"

What other choice did she have? Her situation might be bad, even bleak, but all hope wasn't lost just yet. Was it?

"I'm not sure," she replied, hugging her arms around her at the chill that had permeated deep into her bones. "But I'm fairly certain that marriage will lessen what control I have over my life, not improve it."

She'd shocked him. His eyes widened with it. "You don't trust me."

"Should I? Would you trust me with your future?"

Something flared in his gaze, something that told Rachel he was prepared to do just that. She shivered.

"I mean no offense, my lord, but experience has taught me

that the only person I can trust is myself. Your sex has done nothing but leave me to my own devices—whether by fate or by choice."

Her father had lost his life due to his own irresponsibility—he'd been driving too fast. Sir Henry certainly hadn't been a father to her. And anyone who'd ever tried to court her gave up when faced with her stepfather.

Those who did get past Sir Henry—such as David—certainly hadn't been the type with marriage in mind, with the exception of Charlton, and he only wanted to marry her so he'd have a body to use whenever he wanted.

Was it any wonder she wasn't prepared to put herself—and her mother—into another man's hands?

"I'm afraid you may not have a choice now either, Rachel. In fact, I'm afraid neither of us has."

Rachel's eyes narrowed as her spine went rigid with anger. "What do you mean I don't have a choice?"

Sighing, he pinched the bridge of his nose. "I mean people are already talking." He dropped his hand. "I've heard the rumors, I know the whole town is abuzz with gossip about us. They all know about the river—and my mother's dress."

For a man who rarely left his house, he was certainly up on his scandalbroth.

He moved toward her, and this time she didn't step away. There was nowhere to go; the small of her back was pressed up against a writing desk.

"I also know that by tomorrow morning the entire town will know that you came here this evening. *Alone*. As loyal as my servants are, people still gossip, and eventually the whole village will know about the state of your clothing and your hair. And if any of my servants are half as nosy as my friends, they'll also know that you and I were alone in this room and that I held you in my arms."

Rachel closed her eyes, blotting out his face but not his words as a shudder wracked her body. He was right, blast it all! She'd been so scared of her stepfather that she hadn't given a thought to her reputation, which would surely be ruined if—*when*—word got out about her visit to Wyck's End and her embrace with its lord.

She'd really gone and done it this time. Her decision to come to him had been an impulsive one. She hadn't thought of the consequences. And what consequences they were!

"Rachel." Warm hands cupped her shoulders. She opened her eyes, lifting her gaze to the somber face above hers.

"This isn't exactly how I wanted things either."

For some reason his words didn't make her feel better. In fact, she suspected they only made her feel worse. This ranked right up there with apologizing for kissing her.

"But I like you," he continued, and she raised a brow. Did he expect her to thank him for admitting it? "And I won't deny I find you attractive. I think that's fairly obvious, as is the fact that you're attracted to me."

She should deny it. She should tell him exactly what he could do with his arrogant assumptions, but he was right, and, quite frankly, she was still too stunned by the fact that he was attracted to her to speak.

His lips curved into that broken smile of his. "I may not be what you'd hoped for in a husband—"

He really was mad if he didn't think he was what any woman would want in a husband.

"—but I'm better than Charlton. And I want to help you and your mother."

"In return for what?"

His hands fell from her shoulders. "What do you mean?"

Did he think her so naive that she wouldn't know there was a catch? There was always a catch, even with the handsome ones—especially with the handsome ones. "What do you get out of this marriage, Brave? I have a hard time believing you'd do this out of the goodness of your heart."

He paled, and she knew she'd been right. He did want something. She shouldn't be so disappointed by the revelation.

"I want what most men of my station want. If I'm going to enter into this marriage and spend the rest of my life with you, I want a real marriage."

Rachel's throat went dry. "You want an heir."

"I want more than one."

Oh dear lord, he wanted to . . . to . . . he *wanted to!* With her! Heat suffused her cheeks, but that wasn't why she jerked her gaze away from his. It was so he couldn't see the desire in her eyes. The very idea of continuing that kiss to its logical conclusion sent a hot thrill blossoming between her legs and made her nipples tighten with longing.

Wanton, that's what it was, but if the Earl of Braven thought sharing her bed was equal payment for what he was offering to do for her, he was completely out of his wits. Did he not realize that any sane woman would be more than happy to give him all the fat, healthy babies he wanted? If he got her mother away from Sir Henry, Rachel would give him enough heirs to start his own cricket team.

He gazed at her expectantly, awaiting her answer. Rachel's heart thumped heavily against her ribs. It was madness even to consider his proposal, but what other choice did she have? She needed to get her mother—and herself—away from Sir Henry as quickly as possible. There was no other way, not if they were truly going to be free of him. And Brave had said he'd help her anyway he could . . .

"Will you sign a promise to help my mother? Sign that you'll testify against Sir Henry?"

If he was surprised by her request, he didn't show it. He simply puffed his cheeks out as he exhaled. Had he been holding his breath?

"I'll sign."

She smiled, pushing all doubts far, far from her mind. "Then yes. I'll marry you."

Slipping her key into the front door, Rachel turned it and opened the door. It swung open with a faint creak. She stood silent on the step, half-expecting, half-terrified that Sir Henry's fist would come flying at her.

Nothing. She stepped inside.

The hall was dark save for the flames from two candles. Tiptoeing to keep from making any noise, Rachel closed the door behind her and locked it again. It was well after midnight, and the house was as silent as a church. All the servants were long since abed.

"Good evening, Miss."

Rachel started, but managed to keep from screaming as her heart jumped out of her chest and up into her throat.

"Potts," she hissed, pressing a hand to her chest. "What are you still doing up at this hour?" As it was, the old man was in his nightgown and cap.

A rueful smile tilted Potts's thin lips, making rosy apples out of his full cheeks as he helped her out of her pelisse. "Sorry to frighten you, Miss Rachel, but we drew straws below stairs to see who would wait up for you. I won." He folded her coat over his arm.

Rachel was touched by the servants' concern. "Given the time and the heaviness of your eyes, Potts, I'd say you lost." She squeezed his shoulders in a brief hug. "Off to bed with you now." She began to turn toward the stairs.

"Yes, Miss Rachel." He gave a small bow. "I thought you might like to know that the baronet has been in the library ever since he arrived home quite some time ago."

Rachel paused on the first step and turned. "Is he asleep?" She cursed her heart as it dropped heavily in her chest. She would not fear Sir Henry. She wouldn't.

"I have no idea. I took the liberty of leaving him two bottles of brandy rather than just the one you suggested, Miss. He has been rather quiet." His eyes sparkled with mischief.

Rachel flashed the elderly man a bright grin despite the pain that shot through her face. "Potts, I love you."

"I don't blame you at all, Miss," he replied in a deadpan voice. "If you have no further need of me, I believe I will head off to bed now."

"Pleasant dreams, Potts." She watched until he rounded a corner and disappeared from sight.

Squaring her shoulders, she stepped back onto the floor, picked up the candle Potts had left her, and turned down the hall toward the library. She hoped that her stepfather was indeed unconscious. She had promised Brave she wouldn't mention their impending marriage to Sir Henry until he had a chance to talk to the baronet. She didn't know if she would be able to keep from gloating.

Even now she had trouble believing what had happened at Wyck's End that evening. Brave had offered to marry her! Offered her and her mother his protection until they could take their case against her stepfather to court! She patted the paper he'd signed to that effect nestled in her bodice. He'd given her back her hope, and for that she would be eternally grateful.

She refused to think of anything other than that hope, and that included all the hesitations her mind had tried to force on her during the ride home from Wyck's End. She would not allow second thoughts—and her foolish fears—to ruin her one chance to save her mother.

Sir Henry was snoring loudly when Rachel peeked around the door. Using his greatcoat for a blanket, her stepfather slept slumped in his favorite chair by the dying fire. His fleshy chin rested on his chest, rising and falling with every breath. An empty decanter lay on its side on the floor, just inches from his mud-encrusted boots. Another lay a few feet away.

A satisfied smile curved her lips. Obviously, he couldn't refuse the bait Potts left for him. She took comfort in that fact. It meant he probably hadn't gone up to her mother's room, and therefore hadn't had a chance to take his anger at her out on her mother.

"Soon we'll be free of you," she whispered defiantly, her words drowned out by a cacophony of snorts and sighs.

Still smiling, Rachel closed the door and drifted back toward the stairs. Hiking her skirts up around her calves, she hurried as quietly as she could up to the first floor, where the family rooms were. Her footfalls seemed to echo through the darkness, emphasizing the tomblike stillness of the house. She'd spent her childhood in a house that had always seemed full of laughter, and the quietness of Tullywood had always frightened her even though she was not a person who believed in ghosts and spirits.

Wyck's End was a quiet house as well, but that was nothing a little celebration couldn't remedy. Brave had already agreed to throw an impromptu engagement party in a week's time, once the first of the banns had been read. Some would panic at the short notice, but no one would refuse the earl, and no one would miss the chance to gossip about their hasty engagement. No doubt the whole parish would think it either a scandal or a love match.

Rachel paused at the top of the stairs. Wouldn't it be wonderful if they were? What would it be like to marry for love rather than a sense of responsibility? She wanted to get her mother away from Sir Henry and Brave wanted to help her, but wouldn't it be wonderful to marry for love?

But maybe she wasn't meant to marry for love, and she certainly didn't want to die a lonely old woman. On the other hand, she didn't want to die a lonely young woman either, which would be the case if Sir Henry realized what she was up to.

"*I won't let Sir Henry hurt either you or your mother*

again," a phantom voice whispered in her ear. Brave had promised them a safe haven and his protection. The only thing he hadn't promised her was the moon.

Which was good, because she was a practical creature, not a romantic one. She would do well to remember that he had made no mention of any feelings for her other than attraction. Neither had she for that matter. What else could the tingling she felt whenever he was near be? There was no other explanation for how her heart thrilled at the sight of his eyes.

With a resigned sigh, she pushed the image of her betrothed—*her betrothed!*—from her mind and turned down the corridor toward her mother's chamber. She hated to wake her, but she needed to tell her what she and Brave had decided.

The door was unlocked—Sir Henry didn't allow locks on any doors except his own private rooms. She stepped inside to find her mother sitting up in bed, reading by the light of a single candle.

She looked so small in that great big bed, but at least she looked better than she had the last time Rachel returned home from Wyck's End. Sir Henry must be in one of his apologetic phases.

"You'll ruin your eyes doing that," Rachel chastised with a smile. The cut in her lip pulled sharply.

Marion set the book down on the quilt that covered her. "I did not want to go to sleep until you came home."

Shutting the door behind her, Rachel moved toward the ancient, canopied bed. Her mother looked like a little doll in the middle of the large, square frame.

"How did you even know I was gone?"

Marion's thin fingers plucked at a loose thread. "Potts told me." She stared at her daughter's bruised and swollen face, her pale gaze grave. "This house is no longer safe for you, Rachel."

Seating herself on the edge of the mattress, Rachel covered her mother's hand with her own. "We won't be here much longer, Mama."

Marion's eyes widened in dismay. "What did you tell him?"

She feigned surprise. "Tell who?"

Anyone but her mother would have believed her innocent tone. "You know very well who—Braven."

"Nothing that he didn't figure out on his own." She picked up the book her mother had been reading. "*Pride and Prejudice*. Is it good?"

"I'm enjoying it, yes. Now what did you tell Braven?"

Rachel met her mother's gaze evenly. "I told him how Sir Henry beats you, how he tried to force me to marry Lord Charlton."

"You didn't!" Marion's face was stricken. "Rachel, how could you?"

Damn her mother's ridiculous pride!

"What else would you have me do? Sit back and allow Sir Henry to beat both of us whenever he chooses? To sell me to the first lecher who offers the most money? Maybe you're content with the current situation, Mama, but I assure you I am not!"

As soon as the words had left her mouth, she regretted them. Taking her mother's hand in her own, Rachel softened her voice again. "He's going to help us be free of Sir Henry."

"How?" She asked the question as if it were impossible, and Rachel wanted to tell her everything they had planned, but she didn't dare in case Sir Henry became suspicious and tried to beat the truth out of her. She would tell her only what she needed to know.

"He's asked me to marry him." She waited for the words to sink in.

Marion pulled herself farther up on the pillows behind her shoulders. "He did what?"

Rachel scooted closer. "He offered us the protection of his name, Mama. A marriage of convenience."

Her mother shook her head, her graying hair waving about her shoulders. "Rachel, marriage is not a game."

"Do not lecture me now!" Her sharp tone surprised even herself. "Mama, I know you hoped I would eventually marry for love, but Sir Henry is determined to sell me to Viscount Charlton before the month is out."

Marion gasped, yanking free of her daughter's grip. "He wouldn't!"

"He's already taken the money Charlton offered him. Mama"—Rachel took her mother by her thin shoulders—"he took the inheritance my father left me."

Her mother stared at her in stunned silence.

Rachel fought the urge to shake her. "We can leave him. We have to."

Her mother's gaze was downcast, and Rachel's fingers tightened. Frustration throbbed in her veins. Didn't her mother understand what this meant?

"I am going to marry Braven, Mama. I'm going to make a new life for myself—and for you too, if you'll let me." She drew a deep breath. "I've already spent ten years watching my mother die. I refuse to watch any longer." She swallowed, hoping she sounded more convincing than she felt. There was no way she'd leave her mother alone—not even for her own freedom.

Marion's quivering chin lifted. Her eyes were bright with tears. Rachel gritted her teeth against the hot wetness that threatened to spill from her own.

"Henry wasn't always like this," her mother whispered. "He was very attentive the first few years. Do you remember? He used to be so sweet. I didn't know what he was. I would never have married him if I knew."

Rachel did remember. He hadn't been a great catch for a husband or a father, but at least he'd pretended to be kind to Rachel while courting her mother. That had stopped right after the wedding. He'd lasted longer with Marion.

"Let me do this for you," Rachel pleaded hoarsely, relaxing her hold. "Let me save *you*." Her father had left them, and Rachel had been too young to save her mother from marrying a man she didn't love. She would not fail this time.

Cool fingers stroked her cheek lovingly. "You're so much like your father," Marion murmured, her voice choked with emotion.

Rachel's eyes burned with unshed tears. It was a statement she'd heard more and more frequently as the years went on. Sometimes it was a compliment, other times it hadn't been. "How so?"

"You have his strength," came the quiet reply. "His determination. There was nothing he couldn't do once he'd set his mind to it."

The old bitterness that Rachel tried to hide flowed to the surface. "Obviously he never set his mind to providing for you after his death. If he had, we wouldn't be in this situation in the first place."

Her mother looked away. "Don't talk about him like that."

"Why not? I loved Papa as much as you did, but if it hadn't been for his thoughtlessness, his recklessness, you wouldn't have had to marry Sir Henry in the first place. We could have survived on our own." She'd never forgiven her father for not providing for her mother, and that wound was all the more raw now that she knew he hadn't taken sufficient steps to protect what he'd left for her either.

Marion's eyes were hard as her gaze met her daughter's. "Your father was as far from thoughtless as any man could be. He doted on you, cherished you. He loved us both more than his own life. How dare you forget that!"

Her lower lip trembled and her vision blurred, but Rachel's anger drove her on. "Then why didn't he leave anything for you? Why did he leave you penniless with a child to support so that you had to sacrifice yourself to Henry Westhaver? Why were you not able to use the money he left for me?"

"Because we thought we would be together forever!" her mother exploded. "He was only forty. He wasn't supposed to die so young! We were supposed to grow old together. We used to talk about what your children would look like—" Her voice broke off into great gulping sobs.

Ashamed and astounded, Rachel gathered her mother into her arms. She had never realized how painful it must have been for her. She had thought only of her own grief and anger. Her mother had lost everything, and yet she continued on—for her.

"I'm sorry, Mama. I'm sorry." She made shushing noises to quiet her mother's tears, rocking her back and forth like an infant.

Looking up, she saw their reflection in the mirror above her mother's dressing table. Her face was drawn and tired, her eyes red from tears, but beyond that she could see bits of her father in her features—around the eyes and mouth. She could see bits of her mother as well.

At one time she would have ignored how her face was a composite of the two people who gave her life, but now she found a certain kind of comfort in it.

She found *strength*.

Brave was already dining when Gabriel and Julian joined him for breakfast the next morning. Neither of them made any mention of Rachel's presence the night before, and Brave knew neither of them would. Rachel was not the kind of woman one trifled with, and his friends would make no mention of Brave's relationship with her until he gave them leave.

"I'm getting married."

Gabriel froze. Marmalade dripped from his spoon onto the limp slice of toasted bread in his hand. "I beg your pardon?"

Julian looked up. He said nothing, but stared at Brave with a questioning gaze laced with concern over the rim of his cup of coffee.

"You may leave us now, Charles," Brave told the footman, pointedly ignoring his friends as he settled a napkin in his lap. He didn't want to tell them about Rachel's situation with a servant present. Servants gossiped, and he didn't want anything about his reasons for marrying Rachel getting back to Sir Henry.

He speared a bite of ham with his fork and neatly piled a load of eggs on top, dumping the whole thing into his mouth with a groan of satisfaction.

"Lord, this is good." His friends still stared. He decided to not keep them in suspense any longer. "I will be marrying Rachel Ashton as soon as the banns have been read."

The satisfaction he should have experienced as their faces paled and their mouths dropped open was dimmed by his guilt. He was marrying Rachel Ashton.

He had no business marrying anyone.

"Why?"

Brave's head snapped up. For a split second he thought he might have spoken out loud.

"Why are you marrying her?" Gabriel demanded. "If it's physical companionship you crave, you certainly don't have to marry someone for it."

Pushing his plate out of the way, Brave leaned his forearms on the polished tabletop. "You think I'm marrying her because I'm randy?" He would have laughed if his entire body didn't ache at the idea of Rachel in his bed. A man would have to be dead not to desire a woman like Rachel. She had a body made for a man's, and a fierceness for life that couldn't help but spill over into everything she did—including lovemaking. Being with her would be like plunging into the eye of a hurricane.

Gabriel met his gaze with a shrug. "Am I wrong?"

"I would think you would be used to it by now," Julian commented drily. "Honestly, Gabe, sometimes I think you not only have the manners of a goat, but the brain of one, too."

Gabriel smiled. "Now that you mention it, I have been likened to a *ram*."

"Probably because you smelled like one." Julian took another sip of coffee. "Brave, you know Gabe and I would never reveal having seen you with Miss Ashton last night, so would you please explain why you've decided to marry her?"

Rachel's pride wouldn't like him airing her problems to his friends, but Brave trusted Gabriel and Julian with his life. He knew they wouldn't repeat what he was about to tell them. "She came here last night because she had nowhere else to go. Sir Henry had hit her."

Julian's eyes narrowed; Gabriel's jaw tightened. Despite their sometimes differing opinions on women, both agreed where violence toward them was concerned.

"Apparently he's even worse toward her mother." Brave ran a finger along the rim of his cup. "I told her I would help her mother petition for a divorce."

"And by marrying her you give her not only financial support, but the power and protection of your title," Julian added.

Brave nodded. "Yes." His gaze went from Julian to Gabriel. "I won't lie to either of you. My reasons for the marriage aren't completely noble. I'm attracted to Rachel. I like her. And I'd rather have the mother of my children be someone whom I can respect." He couldn't bring himself to admit that helping Rachel might somehow atone for Miranda's death. That was something he wasn't ready to share.

"How romantic," Julian commented.

Brave's smile was bitter. "I was in love once before, Julian. The results were devastating for all involved. Rachel has made no such demands of me, and I have no expectations toward her other than she supply me with the required heir."

Gabriel arched a brow. "And if she does someday make such 'demands' of you?"

Brave started. He hadn't thought of that. What if Rachel fell in love with him? He couldn't imagine it. It was not a responsibility he wanted, not when he wouldn't be able to return the emotion. He was a disappointment to everyone he loved. He would not make the mistake again.

"She won't. She understands our arrangement."

His friends just stared at him.

"My God," Julian breathed, his cup hitting the saucer with a loud clank. "You're actually going through with this."

Brave didn't expect him to understand. Nothing but the deepest love would ever induce Julian to marry.

"Yes," he replied, meeting the poet's gaze. "I am."

Julian shook his head. "I can't say I agree with your decision, Brave. But if it's what you want, then I support it."

"Mmm." Gabriel's stare made Brave uncomfortable. It was as though his friend could see past his cavalier attitude and saw all the fear and hope inside him. "What can we do to help?"

Their loyalty was touching—even if they did think he was out of his mind.

"I would like the two of you to accompany me this morning when I go to speak to Sir Henry." He forked another bit of egg into his mouth and grimaced. They were cold.

"You're not actually going to ask his permission, are you?" Gabriel demanded.

"Hardly," Brave replied. "He's not very likely to refuse me."

Julian tossed his napkin on the table. "Certainly we'll come with you if you want our support."

Brave's smile was brittle. "I don't need your support. I want you to make sure I don't kill him."

"Lord Braven." Sir Henry set aside his book with apparent reluctance and glanced up with red and puffy eyes. "To what do I owe the pleasure of this visit?"

Brave smiled coolly at the obvious dislike in the baronet's

tone as he entered the library. His gaze skimmed over the opulent furnishings as he introduced his friends. The man himself was dressed at the height of fashion, drinking expensive liquor while Rachel and her mother dressed in near rags.

"I've come to discuss a matter of great importance to both of us, Sir Henry." Since he was not asked to sit, he leaned his shoulder against the mantel while Julian and Gabriel stood closer to the door. Setting his hat and gloves on the polished oak, he turned to face his adversary.

The older man regarded him distastefully over the rim of his glass of port. "And that would be?"

"That my offer of marriage to your stepdaughter has been accepted."

Sir Henry choked on his wine. Tiny red rivulets ran down his fleshy chin and onto his dove gray waistcoat.

"Damnation!" he cried, leaping up from his chair. He swiped at his face with the back of his hand, his eyes darting about for something more substantial.

Brave offered him his handkerchief with theatrical flourish. "Does that mean we have your consent?"

The baronet snatched the linen from his hand without so much as a thank-you and swiped it across his mouth and chin.

"No," he grumbled. "I want an explanation, damnit! Just how did the two of you come to this *arrangement*?"

Brave couldn't very well tell him that Rachel had arrived at Wyck's End battered and bloody, and that he'd offered his help. The baronet might try to force Rachel to tell him the whole story, and Brave really would kill Sir Henry if he harmed Rachel again.

"Rachel and I have been meeting secretly for some time now," he replied, thinking that it wasn't a complete lie.

Sir Henry's narrow eyes shrank even farther into his round face. A glimmer of understanding shone in their swampy depths.

"Caught up in her skirts are you, Braven?" The baronet chuckled and slurped up the remainder of his port. "Well, I admire your honor, man, but don't feel like you *have* to marry the chit."

Brave's face flamed with the insinuation. "I'm sure I don't know what you mean, Sir Henry," he replied, his jaw clenched.

Sir Henry waggled a thick finger at him. "Oh, I'm sure you *do,* Braven. Why buy the cow when you can have free milk, eh? Besides, Rachel's already been promised to another. A man who doesn't necessarily want an inexperienced bride. You'd actually be doing me a favor."

It was difficult for Brave to breathe with the rage building inside him. The conversation would be absurd if he didn't know Rachel, but being as drawn to her as he was, respecting her as he did, it was damn near impossible not to want to pummel the slimy baronet within an inch of his life.

"Now, a man like you wants a pure wife," Sir Henry continued with an engaging smile. "That don't mean I'll stop you from having your fun with Rachel, no, my lord, but I certainly won't hold you to your offer of marriage."

"Just what are you getting at, Sir Henry?" His eyes felt so hot he was certain flames must be dancing across his irises.

The stocky man shrugged. "Just that why marry her and be saddled with her for life, when you can have her for as long as you want—for a fee."

Brave's heart pounded with the effort to keep from killing Sir Henry. His vision blurred, and for a split second he thought he had burst something in his brain. This . . . this . . . *bastard* would sell him Rachel's body, her innocence, and then sell her again to Charlton.

Understanding came with a rush of dizziness. Sir Henry wasn't just a despicable bastard, but he hated Rachel with a passion. He didn't just want to profit from her, he wanted to destroy her.

Why?

Head swimming, he looked for something to grab on to. Sir Henry's throat was tempting.

Julian came to the rescue.

"Sir Henry, I do believe you misunderstand my friend's intentions."

The baronet scowled. "Oh?"

Julian smiled, even though Brave could see the muscle ticking in his jaw. Perhaps Julian would save him the trouble of killing Sir Henry by doing the job himself.

"There have been no nefarious relations between Brave and your stepdaughter. Her honor is quite intact."

His anger ebbing, Brave almost laughed. *Nefarious?*

Sir Henry snorted like the pig he was. "He seriously wants to wed the baggage?"

Julian nodded.

His gaze trailing between the three men, Sir Henry appeared to be looking for some manner of deceit about them. Let him look. At that moment Brave knew there was nothing more honest than his desire to marry Rachel and get her out of this house.

The baronet's chin jerked up defiantly. "I don't know if I want to just *give* her away," he remarked sullenly. "I've already been offered a substantial bride-price."

Every muscle in Brave's body knotted with barely restrained tension. Now he knew how people could commit murder in a fit of rage.

Julian tried his best to be congenial. "Surely the two of you can—"

"How much?" Brave growled. Every muscle in his body tightened.

Both Sir Henry and Julian jumped at the barked question. Brave relaxed a bit as Gabriel came up beside him, laying a calming hand on his shoulder. He didn't care if Sir Henry saw how badly he wanted to tear him apart; he didn't care what the consequences would be if he decided to do so.

"W . . . well, there is the cost of the wedding to c . . . consider." Sir Henry stuck a finger under his cravat to loosen it and swallowed. "And she'll need new clothes, and I have my own expenses—"

"I'll pay for the wedding and anything Rachel needs," Brave informed him, moving toward him like a cat on a fat mouse. "How much do you want for her?"

Sir Henry stared at Brave's chin for a few courage-gathering moments before raising his gaze. His eyes were hard, shining with greed and the mistaken idea that *he* held the balance of power between them.

"Ten thousand," he declared with a smug smile.

Julian gasped. Brave nodded. "Done. I shall have my solicitor draw up the agreement." He looked down at the baronet. "You realize that you will never get another cent out of me?"

Sir Henry seemed momentarily disappointed, but was too swelled up with his own gluttony for riches to let it last. "Yes, yes. Of course."

Brave's eyes narrowed. "And you realize should anything happen to Rachel or her mother between now and the ceremony, I will consider this arrangement null and void."

"What could possibly happen to them?"

Brave shrugged. "Accidents happen all the time. One of them could fall down the stairs, run into a door . . . You know how clumsy women can be?" He arched a brow.

Sir Henry flushed a dull red, but nothing else betrayed his guilt. "Indeed I do, Lord Braven."

"Good. Now that I'm certain my future countess is in safe hands, I will bid you good day. Let us go, Angelwood, Wolfram."

Gabriel and Julian bowed to Sir Henry. Brave turned on

his heel without extending the same courtesy. He didn't think he'd ever been so happy to leave a place in all his life.

"I hope you know what you're getting yourself into, Braven," Sir Henry called after him. "But better the chit under your roof than mine."

Brave flashed a cold smile over his shoulder. "Sir Henry, I couldn't agree with you more."

Chapter 7

"**Y**ou look so beautiful."

Lifting her gaze to the mirror, Rachel looked first at her mother's beaming reflection before settling on her own more sedate countenance.

She did look nice, but *beautiful*?

Annie had piled her hair artfully up onto the back of her head. A fine dusting of powder took the shine from her nose and added a touch of pearl to her cleavage. A heavier mixture worked to disguise the discoloration on her cheek. The bruise hadn't turned ugly, and was fading, but it was still noticeable. Annie had done an excellent job of concealing it. Her eyelashes had been darkened just a touch to offset the pale powder, her lips—now healed—touched by the softest of pink creams.

The Wycherley sapphires had arrived by footman earlier that afternoon. A brief note from Brave stating that he believed the stones came close to matching the brilliance of her eyes accompanied the heavy oak box. Rachel had gasped when she opened the lid. She'd never seen so many gems in her life. She shivered as the cool necklace, set in platinum, settled against her skin. The earbobs were heavy on her lobes and dangled against her neck in a way that made her want to swing her head, just to watch them sparkle.

Mrs. Ford had made certain her evening gown was ready in time for that evening. She and Belinda had been right about the color. The rich, dark blue silk brought out the darkness of her eyes and made her skin seem as pale as alabaster. It completed her transformation from plain Rachel Ashton to elegant stranger. She could scarcely believe her eyes.

Would Brave find her beautiful? She stared at her reflection with a growing sense of hope. Surely a man who took notice of a woman's eyes took more than a passing interest in her appearance? She'd only seen him once since his proposal—in church the morning the first of the banns was read. Everyone had stared at them as their names floated out above the congregation. Rachel had flushed scarlet under the scrutiny, the scratchy, incoherent whispers buzzing around her. But Brave had smiled that little smile of his and gazed upon her as though their marriage was more than just a sham. He'd given her strength to face the gossips.

"It was very thoughtful of the earl to have the jewelry sent over for you." Marion smoothed the front of her chocolate-velvet gown. She looked lovely—the mother Rachel liked to remember from her childhood.

Rachel shrugged. She didn't want to believe Brave might actually care about her feelings. She shouldn't wonder if he would be affected by her appearance. To do so might lead to thinking that he cared about *her*, and she couldn't allow herself to forget just why he was marrying her. Even if he did think her eyes were more vibrant than the beautiful sapphires that glittered against her skin.

"It was a nice gesture, but I'm afraid it's going to give our guests the impression that the marriage is more than what it is. People might think it's a love match." Indeed, she was having trouble herself remembering that it wasn't.

Her mother regarded her strangely. "Of course," she replied softly before looking away.

Rachel shot her a sidelong glance. "What?"

Marion's face was pulled tight with concern. "Would it really be so horrible if you fell in love?"

"If he wasn't in love with me, yes." She stood, the rustle of silk like music to her ears as she moved toward her mother.

"What if he loved you, too?" Her expression was as hopeful as a child arguing the existence of unicorns.

Picking a speck of lint off her mother's shoulder, Rachel smiled ruefully. "What if he did? Who would look after you? The whole idea behind this marriage is to get you away from Sir Henry. We can't do that from a mile away."

Her hand was brushed away with an impatient frown. "Am I so frail and weak that I need to be taken care of?"

"Mama—"

"Do not try to cajole me as though *I* were the child and you the parent, Rachel." Marion glided toward the window, giving Rachel a clear view of her squared shoulders.

"That is not what I meant—"

Her mother whirled around. "I have enough guilt in my life without you adding to it by sacrificing the chance to have a life of your own." Her hand sliced through the air like a blade. "I'll go through the scandal of divorce if it comes to that, but I'll not have you martyring yourself in the process!"

Rachel smiled. "Yes, Mama." But there was a hard lump in her throat, for despite her mother's impassioned speech, Rachel knew she would never be able to pursue her own life until she knew her mother was safe from Sir Henry.

Before Marion could reply, the bedroom door came banging open, revealing Sir Henry's corpulent form. Rachel placed herself in front of her mother and met her stepfather's dark gaze with challenge in her own.

"I thought I'd find you two in here," he boomed, looking them both over from head to toe. "We're going to be late if you two don't get yourselves downstairs in the next two minutes!"

Collecting their wraps and reticules, Rachel and her mother strode toward the door. Rachel guided Marion to her husband. Her mother's expression was guarded, but Rachel regarded her stepfather with a mixture of amusement and defiance. "How colorful," she commented drily.

He puffed up like a peacock. "Yes, it is rather splendid, isn't it?"

Rachel curved her lips into a sweet smile that didn't reach her eyes. "Indeed."

Despite his penny-pinching when it came to his family, Sir Henry had no trouble spending money on himself. His clothes were beautifully tailored, if not better suited for a much younger, much more flamboyant gentleman. His cravat was intricately tied, his shirt points so high on his cheeks that he could scarce move his head. His coat was dark blue velvet, paired with a silver-and-green-striped waistcoat. His pantaloons were custard yellow, and so snug they revealed every nook and cranny of his lower body. There were some things, Rachel thought with a shudder, that were better left to the imagination.

"Well, we'd better not keep the earl and his guests waiting any longer," Marion remarked, taking her husband's arm.

"Just a minute," Sir Henry barked, shaking free of her grip. "I want a word with Rachel."

Marion's worried glance darted between Sir Henry and her daughter. Rachel waved her on her way.

"We'll be down in a minute, Mama." She gave her a reassuring smile.

Her mother hesitated, but turned and left the room. Sir Henry closed the door behind her.

"What do you want, Sir Henry?" she demanded, folding her arms across her chest. "I assume this isn't going to be a touching father-to-daughter talk?"

He shook a finger at her. "One day that smart mouth is going to get you in some serious trouble, missy."

Rachel shrugged. "But not today. What do you want?"

Straightening his waistcoat, Sir Henry didn't even glance in her direction.

"I wanted to tell you to be a good wife to Lord Braven." He tugged on his cuffs. "He paid a lot of money for you—"

It felt as though someone just dropped a bucket of ice water down her back. "He what?"

Her stepfather finally looked up, a confused expression on his full face. "You didn't think I'd let you go for nothing, did you?"

Rachel couldn't believe her ears. Brave had paid for her? Of course. Charlton would have always been there with a "loan" whenever Sir Henry wanted it, but Brave wouldn't feed her stepfather's greed. Sir Henry had seized the chance to get whatever he could from the earl now. How was she ever going to repay Brave for his kindness? She had nothing to offer him, and so far he had already given her so much.

"You know, coming from some fathers, that statement would have almost been sweet, but not from a greedy bastard like you."

Sir Henry's face darkened with rage. His nostrils flared as he raised his hand to strike her. "You ungrateful little bitch!" Then he flinched, as though he remembered something and lowered his fist.

"How much did he pay you?"

He glanced at her in disgust. "More than your true worth, that's for certain."

Despite her alarm at being placed even further in debt to Brave, Rachel couldn't help but smile wryly. "That little?" She took a step forward. "Have you always hated me, Sir Henry?"

He didn't even seem surprised by her question. In fact, his expression indicated that he believed she already knew the answer.

"Yes," he replied gruffly. "I thought it would pass, but you were a reminder of your father. Your mother went on constantly about how much you resembled him. She doted on you—more than she ever doted on me, and it was all because you were *his* daughter."

His gaze met hers with a blazing hate that frightened her. His hands clenched into tight fists. "She could never love me while you were around, reminding her of him. Once you're gone, she'll love me again." The way he said it made it sound like a warning.

Rachel could have felt sorry for him if he hadn't made her mother's life such a living hell. She shook her head at him. "She'll never love you again, Sir Henry. You beat that out of her."

He blanched as she spoke. "I'll make her love me again," he insisted. "I don't care if it kills me."

Rachel strode past him to the door, yanking it open in an effort to burn off some of her anger. She glanced at him over her shoulder.

"If only it would, Sir Henry. It would make all our lives so much happier."

"Having second thoughts?"

Brave rubbed his hand. Sir Hugh had nearly crushed his fingers with his enthusiastic congratulations.

"Would you be more at ease if I were, Gabe?" he asked with a smile, turning to face his friend.

"I would worry less." The darker man tugged at his cuff. "Christ, Brave, you're getting married, and you act like it means nothing. Nothing."

Oh it meant a lot more than nothing. Brave realized that in church the morning the banns were read. All those speculative gazes, Rachel's blush, and the whispers—some of which were far from kind—had made him want to wrap his arms around his betrothed and protect her from those who would dare slight her in any way. She'd suffered enough at their hands by coming to church with her lip swollen and bruised. She hadn't needed any more indignity added to injury.

Brave took his friend's arm and steered him away from the heavy traffic of the ballroom to a darkened corner near the top of the stairs. The house hadn't originally been built with a ballroom, so Brave's father had renovated several rooms on the first floor to suit the purpose. From where they stood, they could watch as guests strolled through the great hall and keep an eye out for Rachel when she arrived, but remain relatively unnoticed themselves.

The servants had gone above and beyond their duties with the preparations for tonight's festivities. They'd wanted to show him how much they supported him, how pleased they were he'd decided to wed. It had worked. Brave was touched by their efforts.

He was also touched that Gabriel and Julian had changed their plans in order to attend the party. They'd postponed their trip to Julian's property, deciding to return to Yorkshire for their hunting trip after Letitia's birthday. They would remain at Wyck's End until the day of the wedding.

"I'm aware of the impact my wedding to Rachel will have, my friend," Brave replied in a hushed voice as they stepped into the shadows. "It means that soon Sir Henry will never strike Rachel or her mother again. I'd hardly call that 'nothing.' "

"But is that noble cause truly your reason for wanting to

marry her?" Gabriel crossed his arms over his chest. His expression dared Brave to argue.

Brave met his friend's gaze evenly despite the erratic pounding of his heart. "What other reason would I possibly have?"

"How long has it been since you've bedded a woman?" Gabriel countered. "Eighteen months?"

Thankful that his friend couldn't see his face flush in the dim light, Brave averted his gaze. "A little more."

"Your cause is a noble one, my friend, but can you honestly tell me you have not thought of Rachel Ashton in your bed?"

"Yes." His voice was a harsh whisper. On the floor, against a wall, in the dirt even, but not yet in his bed.

In his mind he had dug his fingers into her soft flesh, tasted the sweat on her skin, driven himself into her until they were both sore and exhausted. But such fantasies served nothing but to make him frustrated and irritable. The idea that he would soon have her only made the ache worse.

"You lie."

Brave's head whipped around at the soft accusation. "It's none of your business," he snapped, angry that he had been so transparent.

"So I see." Gabriel's tone was nonchalant, but his gaze was scrutinizing. "Obviously I have overstepped my bounds. My apologies."

Brave nodded curtly. If Gabe was the one apologizing, why did he feel so foolish?

The silence between them was strained. Brave gazed into the shadows behind them while Gabriel studied the toe of his shoe.

"This is ridiculous!" Brave sighed and massaged his forehead with his right hand. The other rested on his hip beneath his jacket.

"Gabe, why are we arguing?"

"Because I accused you of being too cavalier about your

wedding," his friend replied, leaning his shoulder against the staircase. "I realize now that you are not as unaffected as I believed. Quite the opposite, really."

Chuckling humorlessly, Brave met his gaze. "Trust me, I am not immune to Rachel's charms; but I know what I'm doing, Gabe. I'm not going to make a mess of things this time."

Strong fingers gripped his shoulders as Gabriel stepped forward. "My friend, you have often taken on more responsibility than your share, and I have seen you carry more guilt than was rational, but I've never seen you make a mess of anything you set out to do. In fact, you often take it to the opposite extreme."

Brave smiled wearily. "I hope you are right."

A cocky grin lit up Gabriel's face. "I usually am."

The sound of another arrival caught their attention. Brave's heart began to pound in his chest. She was here.

Sir Henry and Marion came up the stairs first. Sir Henry was dressed like a dandy while Rachel's mother was the picture of understated elegance. She was a frail-looking little woman, but Brave detected a resemblance between mother and daughter around the eyes and mouth.

Rachel was behind them, one gloved hand on the banister as she kept her gaze fastened on her mother's back. She looked nervous.

Brave was glad for the darkness surrounding him, enabling him to feast his eyes on her without her being aware. Otherwise, she would catch him gaping at her like a silly schoolboy.

Lord, but she was beautiful! In the golden light, her bare shoulders glowed like ivory, her hair like the palest gold. Her eyes were dark and fathomless in her angelic face.

The gown fit her to perfection, emphasizing every curve of her figure without flaunting her luscious shape. The color was perfect for her, almost perfectly matching the stones around her neck. He'd chosen well. The fashionably low neckline revealed the tops of her creamy breasts, while the high waist pushed them against the shimmering silk. The narrow skirt fell past her ankles and brushed against her legs as she moved. From where he stood, he could make out the outline of her long thighs, the curve of her generous hips and gently rounded belly . . .

"For God's sake, breathe man!" hissed a voice in his ear.

Brave did. His lungs expanded greedily. He hadn't been aware that he had been holding his breath as he watched his fiancée ascend.

"Have you ever seen anything so beautiful?" Brave asked, stepping out of the shadows as she neared the landing where he and Gabriel were hidden.

"She's a very pretty girl," Gabriel allowed.

Brave frowned at him. "You think I'm too excessive in my compliments?"

The darker man shook his head. "I have no doubt that you find her as incredible as you say."

Shrugging, Brave stepped out to meet her. "Beauty is in the eye of the beholder, they say."

"Yes," Gabriel murmured, trailing behind him with a worried frown. "And in the heart."

"Sir Henry, Lady Marion, good evening."

Rachel's breath caught in her throat when Brave stepped out of the shadows to greet them. She'd been so intent on placing one foot in front of the other and not stepping on her hem that she hadn't noticed him standing at the top of the stairs.

Had there ever been a man more magnificent than he? Tall and long-limbed, with wide shoulders and slender hips, he looked like a Greek sculptor's ideal. Only his stark black evening clothes—no different from what most men of his station wore—belied his mortal status. Even then, Rachel was convinced that there was no other man in attendance who did as much justice to those evening clothes as Brave did.

His chocolate brown eyes were void of their usual sobriety; instead they shone with something that set her insides fluttering with anticipation. Something warm and erotic.

"Good evening, Rachel." His voice was just as seductive as his gaze.

Insides fluttering, Rachel managed a smile. "Good evening, my lord."

He offered her his arm. "May I?"

There were many layers of fabric between them, but Rachel could have sworn she could feel the heat and muscled hardness of his forearm beneath her palm. What would it feel like without all that clothing between them?

Her cheeks flushed, she glanced over at her fiancé, hoping he would not be able to discern the shameful nature of her thoughts.

Lord, but he was looking at her as though he'd like to devour her right there on the carpet! A shiver raced through her, tightening her nipples and pooling between her legs with an aching throb. She was less embarrassed by her reaction to him now and more anxious to do something about it. One of the few consequences of this marriage she even allowed herself to think about was the wedding night. She wanted him, and there was no point in lying to herself about it.

They stepped into the ballroom and suddenly a deafening chorus of applause and cheers rose up around them. The sensual spell Brave had woven around her was broken as Rachel's gaze fell upon at least a hundred familiar smiling faces.

Now she knew how a bride-to-be should feel. Under the watchful stares, she felt nervous, special, and yes, even beautiful. But the most beautiful part of the evening had to be the fairyland spread out before her.

Brave had obviously spared no expense, despite the fact that their marriage was a sham. Thousands of flowers in shades of white, pink, and lilac filled the ballroom. Delicate blue-and-lavender shades had been fashioned around several of the chandeliers, bathing the people beneath in a soft pastel glow. Shimmering silks draped the walls and ceiling, and dozens of footmen dressed in the Wycherley livery of pale blue and gold carried trays laden with champagne as they threaded their way through the sea of guests.

Rachel was struck speechless. She'd never seen anything quite so grand.

The orchestra immediately began to play, and Brave pulled away. For a moment, Rachel panicked. He couldn't just leave her there to face all those people! But then he held out his hand.

"May I have the honor of this dance?" His dark gaze enveloped her, drawing her into its fathomless depths.

Rachel could not have resisted even if she wanted to. She placed her hand in his. Could he feel the dampness of her palm through her glove? Would he instinctively know about the moist heat swirling low in her belly?

What was it about this man that made her want to toss everything she had been taught, everything she had worked for, to the wind? At that moment she was certain she would forsake even her own mother to feel those long fingers on her naked flesh.

He led her out onto the middle of the floor. All eyes watched as he took her into his arms. Did they notice her start when his hand settled on the small of her back? Did they wonder why her lips parted in a silent exclamation as her hand slid up his chest to his shoulder?

Rachel stopped caring what they thought the moment her gaze locked with his. For that matter, her heart stopped too.

"Rachel," he said softly, holding her so close she could feel the heat of his thighs against hers through the cool silk of her gown. "I do believe you are the most beautiful woman here tonight. And before you accuse me of playing to your ego, let me assure you that I would think that even if you were not my fiancée."

His teasing smile—the closest she'd seen him come to a real smile—was infectious, and Rachel found herself smiling back, relieved that the tension between them had eased.

"Thank you, Brave. Allow me to return the compliment and say that you are without a doubt the most extraordinary gentleman I have seen this evening."

He quirked a brow. "With the possible exception of your stepfather, of course."

Rachel laughed. "Of course. Sir Henry is quite the Incomparable." Her expression sobered. "I hear you are to be thanked for the money to purchase his latest ensemble."

He shook his head, but did not attempt to deny it. Rachel wasn't certain how to react to his honesty. One part of her didn't like being sold like a mare at auction. Another part of her warmed at the thought of Brave paying to marry her. After all, he was helping her gain her mother's freedom. All he was getting out of the bargain was an agreeable wife.

"I'd prefer to take no blame for his latest shopping spree, although I may very well be responsible. He made it very clear he would not let you go without payment."

The bastard. "How much did you give him?"

His gaze darkened. "You need not concern yourself with that."

Indignation coursed through her veins. "Don't tell me such nonsense!" she hissed, gazing about to make certain no one had heard. "I have every reason to concern myself with it."

"And are you going to stomp your foot and pout if I refuse?" he inquired, his voice low with amusement.

Rachel could not prevent the smile that crossed her face. Nor could she stop herself from chuckling at her own behavior. "Quite possibly, yes."

He whirled her around, causing her to squeal with delight. "Then we will discuss it—but not here. Not tonight, and I shall be certain to wear a pair of thick boots." He smiled at her. It was still one of those little half smiles, but different.

This one actually reached his eyes. Rachel could not help but beam back.

"How can I ever thank you for your kindness?" She didn't even know if such a thing was possible. Had he any idea just what he had done for her and her mother? Any idea how much it meant to her?

"Helping you get out from underneath Sir Henry's control is payment enough as far as I am concerned," he replied. "Besides, I'm not totally without something to gain."

She ignored that, knowing that he could have had his pick of any woman in the village. "You have no idea how much it means to me that my mother may be able to start a new life without my stepfather in it." Gratitude burned the back of her eyes with hot tears. "Indeed, I don't even want to think about what might have become of her if you hadn't made your generous offer."

His gaze locked with hers, and there was a tenderness there she hadn't seen before. A tenderness that both thrilled and frightened her.

"Rachel, I must confess that when I made my offer, I was thinking of you and you alone. I wouldn't have been able to face myself in the mornings if I'd stood by and watched Sir Henry marry you off to a man like Charlton, knowing what both he and Sir Henry are capable of."

Rachel didn't know what to say. This man hardly knew her, and yet it was if they were bound by something much bigger than either of them. Some force had drawn her to seek his help just as something drove him to give it.

"I know how proud you are," he continued. "The fact that you trusted me with your problem, and accepted my help, means more to me than I can say."

Rachel could only stare at him. He had given her a glimpse inside him, through the sadness that wrapped around him like a cloak, to the pain at the very center of it all. He'd been hurt in the past, dreadfully so. No woman, no matter how strong her resolve, or how desperate her mission, could ignore wanting to touch a man's heart when it was so bared.

She was very much in danger of losing her own heart to him if she was not careful. Would that be sufficient payment for all that he had done for her?

And would she ever be able to get it back?

Where the devil was she?

More than a little annoyed, and a touch worried, Brave crossed the floor toward the balcony doors. He had searched everywhere he could think of for his fiancée but to no avail. The last time he had seen her she'd been dancing with Gabriel, but that was at least half an hour ago. Had he forgotten that she had promised him the next waltz?

Stepping out into the night air, he wondered why he hadn't checked the balcony sooner. The breeze was chilly, but much welcome after the stifling atmosphere of the ballroom, and the air was sweet and crisp, without a trace of wax, sweat or heavy perfume.

He leaned his forearms against the marble balustrade, closing his eyes in pleasure as the breeze lifted the moisture from his brow. This reprieve was just what he needed after the stress of the evening.

Too bad he hadn't been out there during his meeting with Rachel. The cold air would have combated the fire that swept through him as he met her lavender-blue gaze. He could have sworn that she had eyed him just as hungrily as he had her. He even thought he saw her nipples tighten beneath the thin silk of her gown.

He took a deep breath as his groin began to tighten. He shouldn't be thinking about it. He didn't want to dwell on how tempting it had been to slide his hand down toward her buttocks while they danced, to press himself against her ripe softness . . .

"I thought we were supposed to have the next dance?"

He smiled at the annoyance in her voice. It was decidedly an indignant-lover voice, and it warmed him to hear her use it. Why, he didn't want to consider.

"We were," he replied, turning to face her. "But I couldn't find you."

"Obviously not since I was inside and you were out here shirking your responsibilities as host."

"Shirking?" She was teasing, the smile on her face was proof enough of that.

She moved to stand directly in front of him. In the moonlight, she was Titania, the fairy queen, and he was awed by the cool and ethereal beauty of her.

"I can hear the music," she said softly. "Could we not dance out here?"

"Perhaps we should go inside," he replied, not sure of the wisdom of dancing in the dark with her. It would be far, far too easy to lose sight of things. "You must be cold."

She reached out, took his hand in hers and placed it on her waist. Stepping closer, she clasped his other hand in hers. They were in the waltz position.

She smiled. "The dancing will keep me warm."

He arched a brow at her bold behavior. "And would you like to lead as well?"

Rachel laughed, tilting her head back and exposing the long column of her throat and the swell of her breasts to his hungry gaze. He could lower his head and fasten his mouth to her white flesh, and she would be in no position to fight him.

"Spin me," she commanded, her head still thrown back.

He did. "How much have you had to drink?"

Stumbling to a stop, Rachel lifted her head and swayed unsteadily in his arms. "A lot. I'm afraid."

"Perhaps you should sit down." The last thing he wanted was her casting her accounts all over his shoes.

She stepped closer, tightening her hold on his hand and

shoulder as though she thought he would thrust her away. "You promised me a dance."

Had she been any other woman, Brave would have pushed her away. He would have steered her toward the nearest chair and left her there to come to her senses, but this was Rachel and the feel of her body pressed against his was every bit as intoxicating as it was dangerous.

It was either dance with her or make love to her, so Brave began to dance. Rachel laughed in pleasure. The sound of it tugged viciously at his heart. Joy. He had given her joy, and the knowledge of it seemed to lift the weight of a thousand guilty consciences off his shoulders.

She kept asking how she could thank him. How could he thank her? Since she'd entered his life, he'd felt like he had a purpose. Every day with her gave him part of his old life back, gave him back part of himself. Even Phelps and all his theories and books hadn't been able to do that.

He led her into a twirl, and she stumbled. He caught and lifted her so that she fell against him, rather than twisting her ankle or getting stepped on. When he set her back on her feet, she was staring at him strangely.

"What?"

"You're always rescuing me." Did she actually sigh when she said that?

Brave smiled. She was definitely well on her way to a hangover the next morning. "I seem to, don't I?"

Rachel nodded. "I think you must be quite the knight-errant."

"Oh do you?" He couldn't keep the chuckle from his voice.

"I do. I think you like rescuing me." Her eyes sparkled with mischief and inhibition as she stared up at him.

Did she know how she teased him with those eyes? Did she even realize that he could feel every inch of her delectable body through the flimsy silk of her gown? Could she feel how hard he was getting just from holding her and breathing in her scent?

"Well, I do prefer rescuing you over the alternative, Rachel." For the sake of his sanity, Brave tried to step back and put some distance between them.

She followed him, her body still maddeningly close to his. "Have many women come to you looking to be saved, my lord?"

"A few." His breeches were becoming increasingly uncomfortable.

"And have you rescued them all?" Her tone was light-hearted, but he detected the slightest tremor in her voice. Despite their arrangement, she obviously wanted to feel like she was special in some way. If he lived to be a hundred, he would never understand women, but he could honestly admit that no woman had ever affected him as she did.

"Not all, no." He would not think of Miranda. He would not ruin this moment.

"And what do you hope to gain from those you do?"

Brave stared at her, at the uncertainty in her gaze, the raw vulnerability in her expression. She deserved nothing less than his complete honesty.

"That one of them might be able to rescue me," he replied, his chest clenching with the admission.

Wide eyes locked with his as her fingers came up to touch his cheek. He flinched at the gentle contact.

"Show me how," she whispered.

His heart stopped. She understood. Of course she understood, she had been trying to save her mother for years.

Desperately, he hauled her against him. She didn't even gasp in surprise. It was as though she had anticipated his move.

"Please."

They seemed to be making quite a habit of kissing on balconies, Brave thought with a groan as he brought his mouth down on hers. Her lips parted, eagerly welcoming his tongue as he plundered the sweet recesses of her mouth. She tasted of champagne and caviar and life. He couldn't seem to get enough of her.

Her tongue met his, not with virginal tentativeness, but with womanly assurance. Matching him stroke for stroke, she wrapped her arms around his neck, pressing her breasts and hips against him. He held to her as though he were drowning and she was the only thing keeping him afloat.

The only thing that could save him.

Chapter 8

❝ **I** now pronounce you husband and wife."

The cool brush of Brave's lips against her own was nothing like what Rachel had experienced on the balcony the night of their engagement party. And this stiff impartial kiss was certainly nothing like the blazing embrace she had spent the last fortnight fantasizing about.

She understood that he could hardly thrust his tongue into her mouth in front of half the village, but couldn't he show a little warmth? There was no indication, not even the slightest bit of pressure, that he remembered the kiss they had shared that night. It was as though he had forgotten.

Or *wanted* to forget.

Was that it? Did he regret the kiss and wish to discourage her from believing it meant anything to him? But that made no sense. He'd told her he wanted their marriage to be more than in name only. He wanted an heir. He'd shown her that he wasn't indifferent to her.

Looking up, she could see nothing in his dark gaze that

told her otherwise. Concern, relief, yes, but no passion, no remembrance. Strange for a man who claimed to be attracted to her.

And it certainly wouldn't dispel the rumors that he'd been tricked into marrying her. She knew she wasn't much of a marriage prize where many of the townsfolk were concerned, but she would like to think that she wouldn't have to stoop to trickery to capture a man's interest. Of course, this wasn't just any man. This was the Earl of Braven, and he was a catch indeed.

It really shouldn't matter. She hadn't entered into their agreement in order to gain an attentive husband. She'd done it to save her mother. Nothing could get in the way of that.

She would have to be more careful in the future. Acting on this attraction she felt for him was trouble with a capital T. She knew that, but whenever she was around him, all her common sense seemed to go right out the window.

She would not allow such flights of fancy to happen again. No matter what happened between them she would not fool herself into believing it meant anything. Theirs was a marriage based on mutual benefit. If she hadn't been foolish enough to go rushing off to his house alone, they wouldn't be in the mess right now.

Somehow she couldn't bring herself to regret it—not when it might mean her mother's freedom.

Hooking her arm around his, she allowed him to guide her down the aisle. She stared straight ahead, concentrating not on the solid warmth of his forearm beneath her hand but on the one visible wheel of the Braven carriage.

"Are you feeling ill?"

She started at the sound of his voice and almost tripped over the hem of her gown. Blushing furiously, she mumbled, "I'm fine, thank you."

Outside, the sun was shining high in the late-October sky, but there was a definite chill in the air. Brave handed her up

into the open carriage where thick woolly robes were laid out
for them to bundle up in.

Rachel smiled vacantly at the well-wishers as Brave,
dressed splendidly in a blue coat and ivory breeches, threw
handfuls of silver coins into their festive midst. How easily he
smiled and joked with them all, his teeth flashing in the sun.

She found some satisfaction that the smile didn't quite
reach his eyes. For all her wanting to get a reaction out of
him, the idea that he might be truly pleased to wed her would
be too much for her to handle. She didn't know what had
happened to him to make him so sad. Part of her wanted desperately to find out. Another part wanted them to remain as
distant as possible. She didn't want to fall in love with him,
not when she had the feeling his heart wasn't available.

Finally, he dropped onto the seat beside her, hastily wrapping both of them in the warm blankets as the carriage rolled
out onto the long lane that led to Wyck's End.

"Well, that is done," Brave remarked brightly. "Now we
only have to make it through the breakfast, and then we can
relax."

"I'm sorry to put you through such bother," she replied
with more tartness than she intended.

His head turned, his eyes narrowing against the sun in his
face. "What makes you think you've been a bother?"

Rachel arched a brow, and he chuckled. "I can't say the
situation has been entirely enjoyable, but I can honestly say
that *you* have not been a bother at all." He reached over and
gave her hand a gentle squeeze. She hoped the blush that
surged to her cheeks would simply be mistaken for cold.

The rest of the morning passed in a blur. Many of the
wedding guests joined them for breakfast at Wyck's End, and
the eating and festivities went on for hours. Even the servants
joined in the celebration, and Rachel was touched by how
kind they were to her.

Rachel couldn't remember the last time she had eaten or

talked quite so much. Nor could she remember a time when she'd felt so hopeful—and the implications of that joy were more than she wanted to face.

Finally, her stomach full to bursting and her jaw tired from so much talking and eating, she escaped from the banqueting hall, finding refuge in the two-story library.

The heavy door muffled the sounds of laughter and loud conversation. Closing it behind her, Rachel crossed the gold-and-blue carpet to the window with a grateful sigh. She was unused to spending so much time in society—not just because of Sir Henry's frugality, but because of the pity, and sometimes censure, she saw in so many eyes.

An instant calm washed over her as she stared at the majestic scene spread out before her. The sloping lawn spread out along the front of the house was still green despite the time of year, and was spotted with sunshine and half a dozen ducks. A stone bridge arched over this lazy section of the Wyck. It was serene here, not like the spot where she had almost drowned, and reflected shades of amber and blue on its calm surface. Its glassy surface was rippled only by the bobbing of birds and the flurry of harried fish. Beyond that were rows of brightly colored trees and rolling hills dotted with tiny sheep.

She was mistress of it all. This house and these grounds that she had so adored as a child would be hers to explore at her leisure. A genuine smile spread across her face as she thanked fate for tossing her into the river the night she met Brave.

She had no right wishing for more than he had already given her. Where would she be if he had not found her that night? Dead? Married to Viscount Charleton? Both?

So what if Braven didn't feel the same attraction, the same emotional pull toward her? She already owed him her life, and so far he had asked for nothing in return but children. Most women would be satisfied with that. It might not be a marriage like the one her parents had enjoyed, but it was better than most.

The thought did not lift her spirits as she hoped it might.

"I thought I saw you sneak in here."

Rachel did not turn to face her mother, but smiled over her shoulder at the welcome intrusion.

"The crowd was beginning to give me the headache." Her gaze returned to the sheep on the far hillside. "This was all I needed to cure it."

"It is a lovely prospect," Marion agreed, coming up to stand beside her. "You're a very fortunate young woman."

Rachel's brow puckered as she turned her head. "The fortune is not mine alone. You'll soon benefit from my marriage as well."

Her mother blushed as she cast a sidelong glance in her daughter's direction. "Seeing you happy is benefit enough for me. Besides, I may soon benefit from my own marriage."

This time her entire body turned. Hands on her hips, Rachel stared at her mother with dawning horror. "What the in the name of God are you trying to tell me?"

Marion's flush deepened to the roots of her hair. She stared down at the carpet and traced its pattern with the toe of her slipper.

"I didn't see any of the maids preparing a chamber for you," Rachel continued, her voice beginning to rise. "You are staying for a *visit*, aren't you, Mama?" Her mother had agreed to stay with them for as long as she could—hopefully as long as it took to begin the divorce.

Marion lifted her chin, but her gaze remained averted. "Sir Henry thought it missish of you to want your mother to stay with you on your wedding night. He said a few days apart will do neither of us any harm and that I might come visit in a few days' time."

"And you *agreed*?" Rachel whirled away. Facing the window again she was overcome by the sudden urge to put her fist—or her head—through it. Instead, she pressed her knuckles to her temples to ease the pounding there.

"He was so reasonable," her mother explained. "He says he just wants us to have some time to ourselves." A soft hand came down on her shoulder. "Rachel, I do believe he's trying to change."

Surely something snapped inside her brain. "Change?" The flat of her hand crashed into the window sash, reverberating all the way up her arm. It hurt, and the pain numbed her anger.

Her mother, who had been the victim of so much violence during the past ten years, blanched and backed away.

Oh, so she was the villain now, was she? *She* was the one who'd suffered a split lip, not Sir Henry.

"He's going to kill you," Rachel seethed. "And you're going to let him." Blast it! And there would be nothing she could do to stop it.

Marion's head jerked back and forth. "No, he promised things would be different now that—" She looked away.

"What? Now that I'm gone?" She flung her arm wide in an effort to burn off some of her frustration. "Certainly things will be different. There will be no one in that house to keep him from doing exactly what he wants to you!"

Marion wrung her hands. "The two of you never liked one another. Perhaps things will be better now that you have left the house."

Rachel couldn't believe that her usually intelligent mother was spouting such drivel. She didn't honestly believe what she was saying, did she? What if she did? Trying to convince her that Sir Henry meant her harm might just achieve the opposite.

Sighing, Rachel pushed her anger and frustration deep down within herself. She relaxed her shoulders, not surprised to find them hunched up almost to her ears.

It took every ounce of her strength to keep her voice level.

"Promise me you'll come stay with us if he so much as raises his voice to you."

Her mother nodded, a relieved smile curving her thin lips.

"You'd better get back." Rachel tilted her head toward the door. Spots danced before her eyes. Her headache was back in full force. "Sir Henry will no doubt have noticed your absence."

She was embraced in a cloud of jasmine and roses as her mother wrapped her arms about her shoulders. Rachel bit her lip in an effort to not burst into tears of helplessness. Foreboding swirled within her. She knew her stepfather too well to think he could have possibly changed so quickly. And unless Sir Henry seriously injured her mother, Rachel was powerless to remove her from his home. The law was on his side.

"I promise to come in a few days," Marion said with a smile as she opened the door.

Rachel only nodded in reply, managing a weak smile as her mother slipped outside.

Alone again, Rachel sank into a generously padded armchair and ground the heel of her hand into her forehead. Her plans were crumbling around her. What would Brave think when he discovered her mother had returned home with Sir Henry? Would he think she really had tricked him into marriage as the gossips hinted? Or would he realize just how Sir Henry had tricked her mother?

What if her mother decided to stay with Sir Henry for good? What would happen then? Would Brave cast her aside? She couldn't—*wouldn't*—go back to Tullywood. Perhaps he would still want her to stay and fulfill her part of their bargain. Or perhaps he'd give her enough money to get to London and she could spend the rest of her days working in a dress shop sewing until her fingers bled.

She didn't even want to think about it.

Instead, she leaned back against the plush velvet and closed her eyes. She thought about the way he had kissed her at the engagement party. Over and over again she relived the sweet pressure of his mouth against hers until the pain went away.

And darkness claimed her.

She was curled up sound asleep in his father's favorite chair when Brave found her. A happy smile curved her lips.

What was she smiling for, he wondered as he stood watching, unwilling to disturb her just yet. Surely it wasn't because her mother had left with Sir Henry more than an hour ago.

In fact, all the guests were gone. Marion had informed him immediately of his wife's—his *wife's*—headache, and Brave had made all the necessary excuses. Out of consideration to the clearly overwhelmed bride, the well-wishers had begun to leave shortly thereafter.

Julian and Gabriel had been the last to leave, with the promise that they would both be back after their trip to London. Brave was sorry to have disrupted their plans, but he was glad to have had them with him. No doubt they would have left sooner if it weren't for the fact that they wanted to make sure Brave hadn't completely lost his wits.

His friends' concern aside, it had been hours since Brave had seen or touched his wife, and the need to do so now was more important than whether or not he'd done the right thing by marrying her.

It had taken all his resolve in the church not to kiss her the way he wanted. The kiss they had shared the night of the engagement party haunted him. The desire in it tortured him. For those brief moments he had allowed himself to believe that she might actually want him as he wanted her. But she had shown no other signs of it, and he could only assume that he had mistaken her drunken passion for something more. Something he had no right to hope for.

It had been a mistake to kiss her. Just as it was a mistake

now to drop to his knees beside her chair. Her lips were so close he need only lean forward . . .

Her eyelashes fluttered just inches from his own. Brave froze, his heart thudding heavily in his chest. His breath caught and held, waiting for her to open her eyes and see him so close.

"Aghh!" she cried, her eyes and arms flying wide.

Not the reaction he had been hoping for.

Brave smiled sheepishly at her from where he had landed on the carpet. He pressed his fingers against the stinging spot on his forehead where her flailing hand had hit it, and was surprised that it wasn't bleeding. She had certainly hit him hard enough when she bolted from the chair.

She stood several feet away, one hand pressed to her heart, the other to her head. She did not look happy to see him.

"What were you trying to do, kill me?" she demanded. The hand on her head moved down to her hip.

Brave hauled himself to his feet with the aid of her abandoned chair.

"That's it," he replied in a dry tone. "I only married you for your fortune and good name, and now that I have those you must die." He rubbed his forehead again. "I haven't seen you for hours. I was concerned."

"Hours?" Rachel's brow puckered as she turned her head toward the window. Brave's gaze followed, drinking in the cameo perfection of her profile against the pink-orange splendor of the setting sun.

"You've slept through your own wedding celebration," he reminded her, trying to keep his tone light. He had wanted her by his side, had wished her to at least pretend she wanted to be his wife.

She turned to him with pink-stained cheeks and wide eyes. She looked absolutely mortified.

Good.

"I am so sorry," she said haltingly, shaking her head. "I

came in here for some peace and quiet and then Mama came in . . ."

"And told you she was leaving with Sir Henry," he finished for her. "I thought you would be displeased to hear that."

Her lips tightened. "That's an understatement. I thought I was going to suffer apoplexy. I couldn't go back out there"— she gestured toward the door—"with a huge vein throbbing in my head, now could I?"

Smiling sympathetically, Brave strode toward her. "Certainly not. All our guests would have run screaming." He stopped, leaving only inches between them. "How do you feel now?"

"Like I've been put through a clothespress," she muttered, bringing a hand up to massage the back of her neck.

"Let me." Grasping her by the shoulders, he turned her to face the nearest wall of books and began massaging the tight muscles beneath his fingers.

"Oh, Lord!" she groaned, clutching one of the shelves for support.

A warm tremor shot through Brave's groin at her husky cry. The creamy flesh of her shoulders was soft and warm against his hands. What would she do if he pushed the flimsy silk of her gown down her arms, baring her breasts? Would she try to cover herself and slap him, or would she lean back against his chest so that he could caress their fullness?

Drawing a shaky breath, he tried not to think such hopeless thoughts. The aching flesh stirring in his trousers was an embarrassing reminder of how long it had been since he had made love to a woman.

"My father's book."

The mention of the word "father" was enough to dampen anyone's sexual appetite. "What's that?" Brave asked, tearing his gaze away from her pale flesh.

Smiling, Rachel plucked a leather-bound volume off the

shelf and turned to face him. Mere inches and several hundred sheets of paper and ink was all that separated them.

Brave glanced down at the book. *A Treatise on the Rights and Obligations of Man.* He remembered the book now. He'd been a boy when his father received it as a gift from Edward Ashton. How odd that their fathers had been such good friends and that Brave and Rachel had been little more than passing acquaintances. Brave's father had respected Edward Ashton greatly. What would his father think of the fact that Brave had married his good friend's daughter?

Rachel's smiled was poignant in its sweet sadness. "My father fancied himself quite the philosopher."

Brave nodded, his attention focused solely on her face. Her expression reminded him very much of how he felt when he thought of his own father, dead these five years.

She stroked the spine. "He died when I was fourteen."

"A carriage accident, wasn't it?"

"Yes," she whispered, her face clouding. She stared down at the book. "Mama couldn't even honor a full year of mourning. We were so poor she had to marry Sir Henry within months of my father's death."

What could he say to that? Nothing he could do or say would change the past—he had tried it often enough himself to know better.

"May I?"

After a second's hesitation, she placed the book in his hands. It was thick and heavy, the smooth leather cool against his palms.

Aware of her watchful gaze, Brave reverently thumbed the well-worn pages. Obviously his father had been a great fan of the book, for not only did it show signs of having been much read, but notes had been scribbled in almost every margin.

"I think I would like to read it."

"You don't have to just because my father wrote it." She tried to take it out of his hands.

"I'm not," he replied. He could have left it at that, but he could not let this moment pass between them without baring his own grief as she had bared hers.

"I want to read it because it obviously meant a lot to my father."

Understanding flashed in her gaze. "Of course. They were very good friends. Did you ever meet my father?"

Nodding, Brave set the heavy book on a nearby table. "I believe so. Papa often spoke of him. His opinion was one of the few my father actually respected." He smiled in an effort to lighten the mood. A sudden melancholy had settled over her, and he had no idea how to lift it.

Rachel chuckled. "My father was not one who kept his opinions to himself. I'm afraid he was something of a radical."

"Ah, so that's where you came by it."

Her eyes regained some of their normal sparkle, and a sigh of relief filled Brave's lungs.

"I suppose I inherited some of his traits, yes." She glanced away. "I'm sorry I left you to contend with the mob by yourself."

He shrugged as he walked along the book-lined wall. She didn't want to talk about her father anymore. He could understand that. It hurt to talk about his as well.

"They were very sympathetic to your bridal delicacy." Was it his imagination or did she just turn pink at his words? "Not one left without wishing you a speedy recovery." And at least several of the gentlemen wished him good luck in the wedding bed, but he wouldn't mention that.

"That was very kind." She clasped her hands behind her back as she stared down at her slippers. He followed her gaze, smiling as he noticed the clenching and uncurling of her toes through the thin satin.

"It isn't anything to worry yourself over."

Her head snapped up so quickly they both winced at the sharp *crack*.

"I . . . I beg your pardon?" She rubbed her neck.

"You're as tight as a miser's purse strings," he said with a chuckle and a shake of his head.

Three long strides brought him before her. He pushed her hands out of the way and resumed his earlier massage. He regretted it as soon as the first flicker of pleasure slackened her features. He'd never seen such pleasure in a woman's face without the benefit of being deep inside her at the same time.

"Honestly, no one thought anything of your absence." Except for himself and her stepfather. Sir Henry had raged about her poor manners while Brave had wondered if she was truly ill or just regretting marrying him. "It's hardly worth all this tension."

Her eyes flew open, wild swirls of hope and trust that robbed him of all reason.

"Tension? Who said I'm tense?"

He smiled mockingly and gave her shoulders a gentle squeeze.

"Aughhh," she moaned.

Brave loosened his grip and raised a brow. She scowled at him. "All right, you've made your point, but it's not because I missed most of the reception."

He frowned, kneading her knotted muscles just to see the joy on her face. "Then whatever is the matter?"

"My mother left with the man I've been trying to get her away from, remember?"

How could he forget?

"Do you think he'll harm her?"

Her head dropping forward so he could better massage the back of her shoulders, Rachel shrugged. "I honestly don't know. He could beat her senseless or shower her with rose petals. She certainly seems to think she's safe with him."

Brave pressed his thumbs into the soft flesh where her neck met her shoulders and resisted the urge to bend and smell the shiny golden hair just inches away from his face. "You're not so readily convinced."

"Of course I'm not," she replied with a moan. "I don't trust Sir Henry. He may *want* to be different, but people like him cannot change overnight. His kind of cruelty is like a madness. I'm not sure that it can be cured."

What would she think of his madness? He'd certainly felt mad for a while after Miranda's death. Would she believe him capable of being cured? What would she think of his belief that she was that cure? Perhaps she would laugh at his foolishness. Or perhaps she would pity him or find him weak. Regardless, it was not something he was prepared to admit to her, not now, not ever.

The thought of disappointing her sent a wave of unease rippling through his chest. He hadn't realized how lonely he'd been before meeting her. Wallowing in self-pity had rendered him incapable of thinking about anything else. The night he pulled her from the river, it was as though a veil had been lifted from his eyes.

Her eyes were closed as he massaged her neck and shoulders. The flesh beneath his hands grew warm and pink from his manipulations. Lord, but she had lovely skin. So soft and white, with just a hint of rose. Not a blemish could be seen marring the perfection of her breast save for the faint blue trace of a vein beneath the surface.

Standing this close, Brave could feel just the barest pressure of her breasts against his chest, could smell the perfume she'd dabbed in the deep valley of her cleavage. Her scent, heightened by the warmth of her flesh, tantalized his nostrils; sweet cinnamon and a hint of something floral swam together like an opiate in his head. A man could drown in a woman who smelled like that.

He drew closer, so that her breasts were flush against his chest. Her hips brushed against his upper thighs. Bending his neck, he placed his cheek against her temple and breathed the fragrance of her deep into his starving lungs. She shivered under his fingers.

Velvet. Her skin was like velvet beneath his cheek. He rubbed his face against hers, feeling the stubble of his beard abrade her flesh. He wanted to rub his face all over and watch that exquisite paleness flush pink and hot, knowing he had done it to her.

Her eyes opened. Petal-soft lashes fluttered against his temple. Brave did not lift his head, but instead, slid his hands down from her shoulders to the gentle mounds of her bosom, rising above the neck of her gown. Beneath his palms her breathing became more rapid, pushing her flesh into the cup of his hands. Warm, damp breath hitched softly against his ear.

He lifted his head—just enough to see her clearly. Wide blue eyes stared at him, dazed with desire. How was it they could believe they could survive this impulsive marriage unscathed when they both obviously wanted each other? The first kiss he could rationalize, even the second, but this . . . *This* would not be denied by either of them.

A flush crept up her chest, toward her neck. Brave followed the trail with his thumbs, bring them together beneath the jut of her chin. His fingers splayed across her jaw and throat as he silently drank in every feature of her beautiful, beautiful face.

She didn't move, didn't fight him as his mouth claimed hers. A low growl soared up from the depths of his soul. God, her lips were so soft, so sweet! They opened without resistance as he probed with his impatient tongue. A hint of champagne, sharp and tangy. The growl became a groan, and he lost himself in the taste of her.

Her fingers gripped the lapels of his jacket, her knuckles pressing against the wool. Could she feel the pounding of his heart through the layers of fabric? She must, for it pounded against the wall of his chest like a prisoner intent on freedom from his cell.

God help him this wasn't supposed to happen, he thought as his hands slid down her shoulders and spine to cup her buttocks. He pulled her tight against him so she could feel just what she did to him. Tight and hot, his body burned for her, yearned for her. Threatened to tear him apart to get to her.

The sound of their tortured breathing echoed throughout the library until there was nothing but breath and the feel of their bodies pressed together. Nothing else existed, and Brave clung to her so that they might tumble into the sensual void together.

He pushed her back, moving her across the room until her back was pressed against a wall of books and they were as close as they could be with their clothes still on. Breathing hard, he tore his mouth from hers.

Their gazes locked. Did his eyes seem to glow with the same fire as hers? Was his breath as hot as it caressed her face? Her lips were red and moist, and her chest rose and fell as rapidly as his own. Her breasts, pushed up by her gown and flattened against his chest were dangerously close to popping out of her bodice. A tiny crescent of pale pink peeked at him from the top of her neckline.

Driven by desire, he lifted his hands to her shoulders, yanking the delicate sleeves so forcefully that one snapped in his hand. Heedless, he shoved the other down her arm, tugging at the snug bodice until both breasts were bare.

Rachel did not try to stop him, even though his roughness must have caused her some discomfort. She shivered and pushed herself against him. Age-old body signals for *yes*.

His mouth captured hers again, his tongue thrusting into the hot wetness as his fingers found her nipples. They were hard, the aureolas puckering tightly at his touch. He squeezed them, feeling her gasp against his mouth. He jerked his hips against her, certain that the force of his desire would soon send them crashing through the book case.

He had never wanted a woman as he wanted her. The need

to bury himself within her was more powerful, more intense than any other lust he had felt before. It terrified him, and yet it drove him to continue.

He planted a hasty trail of kisses along her jaw and neck in his journey to her breasts. Dropping to his knees before her, he pulled her down so that her gown rode her hips as she straddled his thighs, her breasts level with his mouth. He lowered his head, his hands impatiently pushing at her skirts to find their way to the delicate flesh underneath.

His hands found the ties of her garters as his mouth closed around the hard sweetness of her nipple. He felt her dig her shoulders into the books behind her, arching her back. The thigh beneath his hand flexed as she dug her heels into the carpet, tilting her hips in an instinctual rhythm. Her hands tangled in his hair, pulling with every suckle. The harder he sucked, the more fierce her tugs and whimpers became until he could not tell if either of them knew a division between pleasure and pain.

The juncture between her legs radiated heat. Beneath her skirts, his fingers crept past a frilly garter to the dampness spreading onto the soft flesh of her inner thigh. His cock leapt at the contact, aching to sink itself into the searing moisture his fingers now parted and stroked.

She was keening now, her sharp cries music to his ears as she pushed against his hand. Under his thumb, a tiny mound of flesh grew taut and slick as he slowly drew it back and forth.

Rachel moaned.

Her breast slid from his mouth as he pulled back. He continued to stroke her, staring up at her flushed face while his other hand pushed her gown up around her thighs. He wanted to taste her on his tongue. Wanted to devour her as if she were a succulent morsel and he a starving animal.

But more than that, he wanted to feel her muscles tense around him, wanted to feel that hot wetness take him to oblivion.

Continuing to stroke her with one hand, he fumbled with the falls of his breeches with the other. His hard flesh sprang forward and he arched his hips, pressing the blunt head against the moist lips of her sex. One thrust and he would be inside her. He probed her gently.

Rachel tensed. "Brave, no!"

The blood froze in his veins as her words washed over him. *No?* That close and she told him no? The urge to shove himself inside her regardless was overpowering, but Brave had never defiled a woman in his life and wasn't about to start now—even if he was legally entitled to take her whenever and however he wanted.

Brave drew back, fastening his trousers around rock-hard flesh that did not want to be put away unsatisfied. He was angry. Angry at himself, angry at his cock, and so very, very angry at her. What the hell was wrong with him? He'd never wanted sex so badly that he was tempted to take it by force.

It wasn't sex. It was her. He wanted Rachel so badly he'd almost taken her on the floor like a common whore. The knowledge was terrifying.

"We can't do this," she was saying, tugging at the neck of her gown. "Not here. Not like this." She nodded toward the room entrance and Brave tore his gaze away from her lovely gown, which he had ruined, to the door, which was partially open.

Mortification hit him like a punch in the groin. She was a virgin, innocent, and he'd been about to take that innocence on the floor of a room where anyone could have walked in and found them!

He'd promised to protect her, to help her—not to help himself to her. Rachel deserved better than that.

"Brave?"

He jerked his head around to meet her stare. She looked so little and timid sitting there on the floor in her torn dress, her lips puffy and her face red with whisker burn. He was going to have to learn to close the door when he was alone with her.

"Aren't you going to say anything?" she asked.

I'll save you if you promise to save me. What was he thinking? Even if he felt it, he would never admit it. He swore never to make himself vulnerable to a woman again. He could pursue, he could even fall in love, but until he was sure of her feelings, he would not lay his out to be trampled upon.

"I forgot myself," he replied, his voice harsh in his own ears. "It's very fortunate for both of us that you managed to regain your senses in time." Did she blanch at that? Shouldn't that make him happy?

"We must be very careful to ensure this kind of . . . abandonment doesn't happen again." The words were like dirt in his mouth.

"No," she whispered, averting her gaze. "We wouldn't want that."

Brave smiled. It felt more like a snarl. "Good. Perhaps it would be best then if you retired for the evening. I will ask cook to send a tray up to your room if you like."

Rachel nodded and rose to her feet. Brave's heart twisted at the humiliation on her face, but he couldn't go to her, couldn't offer her any comfort. There had to be some distance between them if they were going to survive this marriage unscathed.

"Good night, Brave."

His throat constricted as she opened the library door. "Good night."

She walked out the door, and Brave's heart went with her.

Chapter 9

◦~◦◦◦~◦

Rachel rose with the sun the following morning. It seemed the most sensible thing to do considering she hadn't slept all night and wouldn't be likely to now that it was light.

She'd spent the entire night reliving that awful, awful scene with Brave in the library. A scene made all the more awful by the sheer fact that it hadn't been awful at all. It had been wondrous, intoxicating . . . intense.

So why had she stopped him? Her body certainly hadn't wanted to stop. Her body had wanted to take him inside and experience all that he had to offer. But then she'd remembered where they were and the circumstances surrounding their marriage, and she'd frozen. It wasn't so much the fact that a servant could have walked in on them, it was the fact that the only emotion Brave felt for her was lust and that she had been about to give him her virginity on the floor. She didn't want it to happen that way.

And she'd been scared. Scared of the need that bubbled

inside her. Because until that awareness hit her, it hadn't mattered that they were on the floor or that she was a virgin or that Brave was more feverish than gentle. She'd wanted him—any way he was willing to give himself to her, and that frightened her almost as much as leaving her mother under Sir Henry's roof.

It had been a long time since she'd needed anyone. She was the one who was always in control.

Brave had proven to her that she was not in control where he was concerned. He made her feel things she'd never felt before—hot and wanton. Society taught that these were not ladylike feelings. Sabine had told her otherwise. And while Rachel was a little embarrassed by such urges, were they not very similar to a man's? Surely it was only natural for a woman to want a man as he wanted her? Although perhaps not on an Aubusson carpet.

So why did she still feel that stopping had been a mistake? As long as she lived, she would never forget the expression on Brave's face. Disappointment, anger, even a little disgust. Whether that disgust had been directed at her or at himself, Rachel wasn't certain, but she knew that while her actions might not have pleased him, the rest of her had certainly seemed to.

For all the good it did either of them.

Swinging her feet over the side of the enormous four-poster bed, she sighed and stepped down onto the plush carpet. She'd been installed in the countess's bedchamber, and found she could become very accustomed to the pale green and gold elegance of the room were it not for the fact that it was separated from Brave's by nothing more than a small sitting room.

Was he still abed? Had he slept as ill as she? Was he naked . . . ?

"Oh!" Shaking her head in frustration, Rachel stomped over to the wardrobe and pulled out one of her old gowns. It wasn't as fine as the new ones she'd ordered from Mrs. Ford, but it was in good repair and closed in the front, making it easier to get into by herself.

She washed, dressed and pinned her hair up into a sleek and simple knot high on the back of her head.

Her mother was always up this early, even though it was Sir Henry's habit to sleep 'til afternoon, so Rachel bundled up in a heavy cloak and her warmest gloves and set off on foot for Tullywood.

The sun was already heating the earth, drawing a fine mist low to the ground, and Rachel hurried down the lane, eager to climb the next hill and see all the village laid out as though arising from a cloud.

The mist had lost its appeal by the time Rachel reached Tullywood. After stubbing her toes on too many unseen rocks, Rachel began to curse the knee-high fog that kept her from seeing her path as clearly as she should.

Smoke rose from several of Tullywood's chimneys, and the scent of coal and wood clung to the frosty air like a warm embrace. From the outside the manor house gave every appearance of being an inviting country home, but Rachel, of course, knew better.

Potts answered her knock. His blue eyes sparkled with pleasure as he took her outer garments from her. Rachel couldn't remember ever seeing him so happy. It warmed her to think her presence might be the cause of it. He insisted upon bowing and calling her "Lady Braven." Even though it was her title now, Rachel felt like a fraud for using it.

She limped into the dining room and was relieved to find her mother indeed alone.

"Rachel, dearest," her mother greeted her. "Whatever are you doing here?"

"Breakfast?" Rachel suggested weakly.

Marion smiled as if she knew exactly what was wrong and why she was there. "Of course. Sit down."

Moments later, sans her outer garments, Rachel was seated at the table, picking at a plate full of ham, coddled eggs, and steaming bread, dripping in butter.

"Don't tell me you and Braven have fought already." Her mother peered at her over a cup of tea.

Rachel chewed and swallowed, even though food was the last thing she wanted. "We haven't fought, no." Unless one counted the cold tone in Brave's voice when he dismissed her last night as fighting.

Her mother raised a brow. Rachel twitched under her stare. "Did you make love?"

"Not exactly," Rachel replied, her face flaming.

"Not exactly? My darling, it's one of those things that is either done or it isn't."

Was her mother laughing at her? Rachel searched her face for amusement, but found nothing but motherly concern.

"We—" Lord, but she couldn't believe she was having this conversation with her mother. Her mother! "We almost did."

Marion calmly buttered a slice of bread as though talking about marital relations was nothing out of the ordinary. "So what happened?" She didn't look up.

"He stopped." Her cheeks blushed even hotter. "*I* stopped."

Her mother popped a piece of the bread into her mouth. "Why?" she asked around it.

"I'm not sure." Almost as an afterthought, she looked over her shoulder to make certain Sir Henry wasn't standing there listening. "I was frightened."

"It is a little intimidating the first time." Then, as though a nasty thought occurred to her, Marion looked up. "He didn't hurt you, did he?"

Not physically, no, but the look on his face . . . "No. It was nothing like that. It just didn't feel right." Her cheeks flamed as she revealed to her mother what she hadn't even truly revealed to herself. "It would have felt like a business transaction—like we were fulfilling a contract."

Marion's gaze snapped to hers. There was nothing but affection in her pale gaze. "You would have been. It's called consummation for a reason."

Rachel now knew where she got her penchant for flippant remarks. "I don't want—" She lowered her voice. "I don't want the first time I make love with my husband to be like signing a contract. It makes me feel like his property."

She expected her mother to remind her that she was indeed now Brave's property. He owned her, just as Sir Henry owned her mother. Before she could panic, Rachel reminded herself that Brave was nothing like her stepfather.

Marion shrugged and tore off another chunk of bread. "Braven isn't a boy; he knows the consequences of bedding you, just as you do. A man might be ruled by his . . . loins, but you may rest assured that those loins aren't about to do anything that will put them someplace they don't want to be."

"I beg your pardon?" What the devil was her mother talking about? Ruling loins?

Marion sighed. "I'm saying that Braven knows that a physical relationship between you would truly make you man and wife. Perhaps that is what he intended—to put you at ease, not seal the arrangement or however you want to put it."

Now Rachel knew her mother was insane. When she said "man and wife" she meant it in the same sense that she and Rachel's father had been joined—the way God intended, not like some financial arrangement as the *ton* preferred.

"Mama, that is just nonsense. Of course Braven doesn't want us to truly be husband and wife. He can't."

Her mother slathered a spoon full of jam on her bread. "Why can't he?"

Because he just wants me for heirs.

"Because he doesn't even know me." Rachel didn't know him either, but that didn't stop her from fantasizing what it would be like to spend the rest of her life with him. Or stop her from wanting to turn those sad little smiles of his into the real thing.

"You don't have to know all there is to know about a person to love them," her mother replied. "I was married to your father for three years before I found out what his favorite color was. Five before I discovered he was afraid of cows."

Rachel rolled her eyes. "Those things aren't important, Mama."

Marion grinned—something Rachel hadn't seen in a long time. "They are if you're standing in the middle of a field with your husband up a tree because some farmer's cow got loose and decided to come graze beside you."

Rachel didn't know whether to laugh or cry, so she plopped her head into her hands and sighed.

A gentle hand curved around her wrist and she looked up. Her mother smiled. "What I'm trying to say is that neither you nor Braven can control how you feel about each other. When the time is right for you to give yourself to him, you will. And if you're going to fall in love, then you'll fall in love, and neither of you will be able to stop it. It's frightening, yes, but it's worth it."

A shiver ran down Rachel's spine. Was her mother still talking about her and Brave, or was she talking about something else?

"Are you . . ." She swallowed against the revulsion rising from deep within her. Clenching her jaw, she fought to keep her voice even. "Are you falling in love with Sir Henry?" Just the very idea made her want to vomit.

Marion blushed. Rachel's stomach lurched. "He's been very sweet lately," her mother replied softly.

Now it was Rachel's turn to grab her. She was dangerously close to hysterics. This could *not* be happening.

"Do not tell me you've changed your mind about the divorce."

Marion looked at her, her expression open. "I'm not saying any such thing. But even if I had, would it be so bad?"

"Yes!" Then lowering her voice, "You cannot stay here."

Her mother's gaze was sympathetic. "Rachel, what I decide is for me alone to decide." She must have seen the horror in Rachel's eyes because she continued, "I have not changed my mind about leaving. Not yet. But there's nothing saying you have to take care of the arrangements or me when I do go. I can take care of myself."

Rachel almost laughed out loud.

"Besides, Sir Henry has promised me that he is a changed man. The least I can do is give him the benefit of the doubt."

The laughter died in Rachel's throat. "You don't believe him!"

Her mother's brow puckered. "I don't know what to believe, but he asked me to give him a chance to prove himself, and I told him I would. Wouldn't you rather see me happy in my marriage than spend the rest of my life watching over my shoulder?"

"Of course I would—just not with Sir Henry!" Her appetite completely gone, Rachel shoved the plate away. "I can't believe you actually intend to stay with him after all he's done to you!"

"I am not an idiot," her mother retorted peevishly. "Do not speak to me as if I were. I didn't say I was going to stay with Sir Henry. I said I was going to give him a chance to prove himself."

Oh, Rachel had no doubt that her stepfather would prove himself. He could be very charming when he wanted to be. No doubt he'd say all the appropriate things and do all the appropriate things and then one day her mother would style her hair in a manner Sir Henry didn't like and he'd beat her black-and-blue.

Grinding the heel of her hand into her forehead, Rachel fought to keep the top of her head from exploding. She had to remain calm if she was going to maintain control of the situation. One way or another, her mother was going to leave Tullywood, even if Rachel had to drag her out by the heels screaming. Better that than in a box.

"How long did you give him?"

Her mother shifted in her chair. "We didn't fix upon a specific amount of time."

Rachel nodded. There was nothing she could do short of forcing her mother to leave, and although she was close enough to panic to seriously consider it, Rachel knew Sir Henry would come to collect her and that her mother would willingly go back. She was too damn trusting, even after all he had done to her. She wanted to believe he was a good man underneath it all.

It hurt to think that her mother might actually believe that Rachel was to blame for his cruelty. His sudden change of demeanor certainly brought credence to his claim. Surely her mother wasn't foolish enough to believe that. Was she? She couldn't stop it from niggling in the back of her mind.

"You're angry." It was a statement rather than a question.

Shaking her head, Rachel looked her mother straight in the eye and lied. "No, I'm not. I'm just confused."

Her mother patted her hand. "Don't worry, dear. It will all work out in the end. It always does."

Rachel was very tempted to remind her mother just how often it *never* worked out for either one of them, but thought against it. She just wanted to leave. She needed to be alone so she could think. If her mother refused to leave Sir Henry, there would be no divorce and that would mean Rachel had married Brave for nothing and that would lead to a whole new batch of consequences that she didn't even want to think about.

"I have to go now," she told her mother as she rose to her feet. "Brave will no doubt be wondering where I am." In truth, she doubted her husband would even care where she was. He would probably be glad to find her gone.

"Will you be all right?"

Rachel nodded. She was so tired. "I'll be fine. I think I'll go home and take a nap." With any luck she'd sleep for the next year and wake up to find Sir Henry dead and her mother run off with a stableboy.

She kissed her mother's cheek. "I'll see you soon."

Marion smiled. It was so hard to stay frustrated at her mother when she looked at her with so much love in her eyes. "Take care of yourself, dearest. You worry too much."

Rachel didn't respond, just squeezed her mother's shoulder, collected her things and left.

She took her time walking back to Wyck's End. What was the point in hurrying when there was only humiliation to hurry back to?

Instead she wandered down to the Wyck and sat down on one of the huge roots at the base of the tree Brave had hung from the night he rescued her. It was hard to believe this gently babbling river had almost killed her almost a month ago.

A month. It felt like years since Brave had swept her up into his arms like a knight out of a fairy tale. Had he any idea of the mess Rachel would drag him into, he would have no doubt tossed her back in the river.

When had her life become so complicated? It used to be so simple—get her mother away from Sir Henry. That had been her one and only goal. Now that she had finally done the one thing that could practically guarantee success, everything else had started falling apart around her. The situation she had thought she had perfect control over was crumbling beneath her feet.

She would save her mother. She would, and nothing, not even her attraction to Brave would stop her. Not even her mother's foolish belief that Sir Henry could change would stop her. She'd spent almost the last ten years of her life waiting for this opportunity, plotting for it. She was *not* going to give up so easily. Sir Henry would not win. She was not powerless. She was not!

She didn't even realize she was crying until one fat tear slid down the tip of her nose and dripped onto her lip. Startled, she wiped at her face with her gloves, but the tears kept coming. Finally, she gave up, buried her face in her hands, and wept—little hiccuping sobs that mixed with the burbling of the river to sound like ghostly laughter.

It was because of her that her mother married Sir Henry in the first place. It was up to Rachel to fix it, but every time she tried to fix it things just got worse. When she was younger she used to wish an angel from Heaven would swoop down and make everything better and take her and her mother away. The angel never came.

"Rachel? Rachel, why are you crying?"

She looked up, and wiped at her eyes. Through her blurred vision, she saw Brave striding toward her, looking strong and beautiful in his buff breeches and greatcoat. It wasn't until he knelt before her that she saw the concern on his face. She sniffed.

"Rachel, sweetheart," he murmured, yanking off a glove to wipe away her tears with his fingers. "Whatever is the matter?"

She shook her head, puckering up her face in an effort to hold the torrent at bay.

His fingers brushed her cheek, so soft and gentle. "Tell me what I can do to make it better."

His words were her undoing, and she flung herself into his arms, her little hiccups becoming huge racking sobs.

Brave hadn't much experience with sobbing women in his lifetime. No doubt that was the reason his heart broke at the sight of Rachel's tears.

And he had obviously said the wrong thing by offering to

make it better because that had just made her cry all the harder, so he resolved to remain silent and allow her to cry it out.

He hadn't slept for most of the night because of her. Even half a bottle of brandy hadn't helped. All it did was make his mouth dry and his head fuzzy. In fact, he believed the liquor had only made his situation worse because his mind had conjured up all kinds of carnal images involving himself and Rachel—things he'd never even done before but certainly wouldn't mind trying now that he'd pictured them.

When he tapped on her bedroom door that morning and entered to find her gone, his first thought was that she was simply an early riser. When he went downstairs and she wasn't there—and he looked everywhere—he panicked, certain that last night had driven her back to Tullywood.

Then his senses returned and he realized that Rachel was not the kind of woman to turn tail and run—certainly not back to Sir Henry. No, she would be off somewhere trying to sort out how to act around him and how to get her mother out of Sir Henry's house, because no matter what else happened, Rachel was obsessed with saving her mother.

Did she even know how she was saving him? She thought he was saving her. How would she react to the fact that he'd married her not just to help her but to help himself? Would she feel used or would she simply throw herself into the task?

And when it was all over, who was going to save her from him? Or him from her? After last night, Brave was smart enough to know that neither Sir Henry nor his own guilt were as dangerous as the way he felt when his wife was near.

The muffled sobs against his shoulder were quieting. He couldn't see her face because the brim of her bonnet was shoved up under his chin, but he could feel her body grow still. Keeping one hand pressed against her back, he reached into his pocket and withdrew his handkerchief with the other. Still blinded by the bonnet, he offered it to her.

"Use this."

She took it with muttered thanks and pulled free of his embrace to wipe her face and blow her nose. She'd left a huge wet spot on his coat, but Brave lamented the loss of her in his arms more than any damage done to his clothing.

His knees were beginning to ache, and dampness seeped through his trousers from the grass, so he moved onto the root beside her. They were so close their shoulders touched. He half expected her to pull away. She didn't

"Would you like to tell me what has you so distraught?" he asked once all the sniffing and blowing had stopped.

She didn't look at him, but he caught a glimpse of swollen eyes and a red nose as she gazed out over the river. Odd that he had known she would come here, to this place where both their lives had been irrevocably changed. He'd been drawn back there more than once in the last few weeks himself.

"I feel so foolish." Her voice was thick and heavy from her tears. He hadn't heard anything so utterly pathetic sounding in all his life—excluding his own self-pity, of course.

He turned his own gaze to the river. "About what?" As if he didn't have a good idea. He felt rather foolish himself.

Rachel was very still beside him. "Many things. Are we pretending last night never happened? Because I don't want to talk about it if we are."

He laughed. Dear sweet, blunt Rachel! "I don't think either one of us is a good enough actor to pretend it didn't happen."

"No," she agreed, a hint of a chuckle in her voice. "We neither of us are that."

Clasping his hands between his knees, Brave looked down at the grass between his feet. "So do you feel foolish because it went as far as it did, or foolish because we stopped from going any further?" Why was he torturing himself like this?

"Both." She still did not look at him as she laughed humorlessly. "I feel foolish for both, and I can't believe I'm telling you this."

Something Brave couldn't identify bloomed hot and giddy in his chest at her words. "I feel foolish, too," he admitted.

Now she looked at him. Her nose was as pink—*rose*—as her cloak. "You do?"

He met her gaze. "I do. I should have handled things differently." Such as the location. He should have at least taken her to bed. And no doubt he'd frightened her with intensity of his desire.

Reaching over, he took one of her hands in his own. Hers was so small compared to his. His gloves were cleaner, too. He couldn't believe they were having this conversation. "It's been a long time since I've been with a woman, and you're very beautiful and attractive."

She smiled at that.

"It's only natural that I would be drawn to you, just as your natural curiosity about . . . what happens between a man and a woman would draw you to me." He didn't dare allow himself to believe it to be more than that. "We were swept up in the moment. It's nothing to be embarrassed about."

"I know what happens between a man and a woman," she informed him defensively.

Brave stared at her, amused by the defiant angle of her jaw. "Do you?"

"I've been told the basics, and I've got an imagination, Brave. I'm not completely witless."

Oh, but he was. He definitely was when it came to her. Clearing his throat, he nodded. She knew in theory, but there weren't enough words to describe what she did to him. "The fact that you've never experienced it makes you curious, and the fact that I have experienced it makes me want it." *Badly*. So much in fact he was growing hard just talking about it.

"I'm sorry if I frightened you. I hope you know I would never intentionally hurt you."

How neat and tidy it sounded—how simple! He didn't believe it for a minute. How could he have lost his control so completely; after all the months of trying to keep everything inside, he'd almost unleashed it all on Rachel.

"You didn't frighten me." She glanced around the brim of her bonnet. "The act itself is a little intimidating, but not you."

He squeezed her hand. "Then we'll take things slowly until you're more comfortable."

Rachel nodded, like a woman committed to her fate. "You are right. We are adults, not children. Surely we can deal with this in a mature manner. And after all, the marriage must be consummated."

She said it as though the word left a bad taste in her mouth. Did the idea of making love with him disturb her that much?

"Quite right," Brave agreed. "You must let me know when you're ready."

Rachel looked so alarmed that the decision would be hers that Brave found her expression strangely heartwarming. He wanted her, knew that he'd give anything to have her and could easily imagine waking up beside her for the next fifty years or more. But truly having her as his wife would mean being completely honest with her about his past and he wasn't certain he wanted to risk her reaction. Perhaps giving them both a little time to get used to each other would be a good idea, despite how much every inch of him railed against it.

"Surely our . . . indiscretion of last night isn't the sole reason for all these tears?" He tried to make his tone light.

She shook her head. "I went to visit my mother this morning."

"Ah." Thank God his lack of control hadn't been entirely to blame. "And things were . . . good?"

She made a disgusted scoffing sound. "He's promised to be good, and she wants to give him a chance. I can't believe she's being so foolish. She told me that she doesn't know if she wants to leave him or not. She wants to wait."

If Lady Marion didn't leave Sir Henry, how was Brave going to help Rachel? How was he going to make amends for Miranda's death? Brave shook his head. It was those kinds of selfish thoughts that had led to the tragedy in the first place. Rachel was what mattered right now. Why was she so upset?

Was it because she was worried Sir Henry might seriously injure her mother in the meantime? Or was she upset because things weren't going the way she'd planned them? Or did she feel as though she'd married him for nothing?

Deciding it was perhaps better not to ask, Brave tried another tact. "Rachel, men like Sir Henry don't change overnight. You and I both know that. Your mother knows it as well. Sooner or later he will revert to his old ways, and she will leave. In the meantime all you and I can do is wait and start preparing our case."

She turned to him, her gaze so full of cautious hope it hurt to look at her. "What if he really hurts her next time? I fear he's going to kill her, and that by staying there she's giving him permission."

Brave slipped his arm around her shoulders and pulled her close in a firm hug. "I don't think Sir Henry wants to kill your mother. His kind usually just wants to keep women under their control. I don't want to frighten you, but your mother is in less danger now than she will be once she is removed from the house. Lulling Sir Henry into a false sense of security is probably the best course of action we can take at the moment."

"Do you really think she's safer with him right now?"

He nodded. "So long as Sir Henry believes he is in control, yes. Trust your mother, Rachel. Do you really think she'll stay with him if he beats her again, especially knowing that she can come to us?"

"I . . . I don't know. I'd like to think she'd come to me at the first sign of trouble." Her eyes filled again. "I just don't know what to do!"

"Listen to me." He gave her a little shake. He hated to see her tearing herself apart over this. "You can't do anything but carry on with your life and wait for your mother to make her decision. In the meantime you are free from your stepfather and can start living your own life. And when Sir Henry falters, we'll be ready for him."

She dried her eyes. "We?"

He smiled at the sight of her damp lashes and pink-rimmed eyes. She looked like a wet rabbit. "We. You didn't think I married you just for your looks, did you? I promised to help you in any way I could, and I meant it. Now, why don't we go back to Wyck's End and have Cook make us some chocolate? We can play at cards if you like."

He stood and helped her to her feet. With a hearty sniff, she flashed him a tremulous smile. "How about billiards?"

"Done." Smiling, he tucked her arm around his and steered her down the path toward his home.

Things were almost normal between them by the time they arrived back at the house. Brave doubted that they could ever return to the relaxed friendship they'd started to build before their marriage. Their relationship had been forever altered by the passion they'd shared in the library, but somehow he didn't think it had been altered for the worse. Talking about their attraction—even if they had both downplayed it—had made it easier to deal with one another and had deepened a bond between them. There was a closeness between them that hadn't been there before, and he had no intention of giving it up.

A black-lacquered carriage was parked in the drive when they rounded the corner. Footmen unloaded trunks and boxes in a steady stream of traffic that could mean only one thing.

"My mother," Brave replied when Rachel asked who their visitor was.

Could the woman possibly have worse timing? He'd seen her maybe a handful of times in the last two years—the ma-

jority of those while he'd been under Phelps's care. She'd
never really come out and said it, but Brave knew he'd disappointed her with his illness.

Rachel froze. "Your mother?"

He glanced at her horrified face and summoned a small
smile. "I do have one, you know."

She ignored his teasing. "It looks as though she packed
for a long stay." Brave had to agree. "Brave, I cannot meet
your mother looking as I do."

He was about to suggest she run around to the servants'
entrance when a clear voice split the chilly air.

"Balthazar!"

Too late.

"I don't think you have much choice but to meet her,
Rachel. I'm sorry."

Beside him, Rachel sighed and smiled. It looked so decidedly false when her eyes were still red and puffy from crying.

Annabelle Wycherley looked every inch the dowager
countess as she glided toward them, a beaming smile on her
lovely face. Despite everything else, Brave was happy to see
her. He'd just wished he'd had time to prepare for her.

There was silver in the perfectly coiffed blond hair. Not a
wrinkle could be seen in her immaculate peacock blue traveling costume. In fact, there was nary a line or wrinkle on her
face. Perhaps a few around the eyes, but those were smile
lines and didn't count—or so she always told her son.

She stood directly before him, arms outstretched, waiting
for him to embrace her. He did. She felt so little in his arms,
but she smelled of fresh air and roses, a smell that never
failed to make him smile.

"Hello, Mama. Why are you here?"

His mother stepped back, holding him at arm's length.
She still smiled. "I'm sorry I didn't send word first. It was a
spur-of-the-moment decision." She peered around him at
Rachel. "Who's your friend?"

To her credit, Rachel didn't hesitate to step forward. She was a half head taller than his mother, but Annabelle had been known to make even Wellington quake in his boots. Rachel met the older woman's gaze evenly.

"Rachel, this is my mother, Annabelle, Dowager Countess Braven. Mama, this is Rachel, my wife."

If his mother was shocked, she hid it remarkably well. Taking Rachel's hand, she smiled serenely. "I'm very sorry to have missed the ceremony, my dear."

Brave felt Rachel's questioning gaze but kept his own fastened on his mother. "I thought you were still in France, Mama." To be honest, he hadn't thought of it. If Gabriel and Julian hadn't been there, he wouldn't have invited them either. His only thought had been of Rachel—her saving him, him saving her, having her . . .

"I think I'll go inside," Rachel said, gesturing toward the house. Dipping a slight curtsy, she pivoted on her heel and took off toward the house.

Out of the corner of his eye Brave watched her practically run up the steps and inside. He couldn't help but smile.

"Balthazar, what's going on? Are you truly married to that girl? And why does she look as though she's been crying?"

Brave turned to his mother, his smile fading. He supposed he owed her a bit of an explanation. He would just omit his true reasons for marrying Rachel. Those were no one's business but his own.

"Come inside, Mama, and I'll explain." As she took his arm, he drew her up the steps to the door.

Staring straight ahead, Brave kept his voice low so no one but his mother could hear. "By the way, Mama, Rachel doesn't know about Miranda or Phelps." He patted her hand. "I'd like to keep it that way."

Chapter 10

❧ ❦❧ ❧

Rachel delayed meeting her mother-in-law until after luncheon. Taking a tray in her room allowed her to bathe and don a nicer gown. It also gave her eyes time to regain their natural size and color. She refused to meet the dowager countess looking anything less than her best.

What had Brave told his mother about their marriage? About her? Did Lady Braven know the mother of her future grandchildren was little more than a charity case? She doubted that's how Brave would describe her. He was far too kind, but what else would a mother think given the circumstances? No doubt the dowager would believe she married Brave for his title.

Better to tell her own side of the story before someone else did. At least Rachel could trust herself to be reasonably truthful. There were some aspects of her marriage that Rachel didn't plan to discuss with anyone—particularly Brave's mother. Rachel didn't care how intimidating the older woman was.

With that resolution—and her new gown—giving her strength, Rachel went in search of her mama-in-law late that afternoon. She couldn't find the dowager anywhere. Her confidence beginning to wilt, she'd almost given up hope when she spotted her quarry standing in the door of Brave's study talking with an older gentleman not known to her.

Hiding behind the corner of the intricately carved staircase, Rachel was too far away to hear their discussion. Then the two of them entered the study and closed the door behind them.

Curious. Who was the gentleman? If Rachel's guess was right, he was of the same age as the countess, and his clothing gave him away as a gentleman, albeit a country one. He lacked the inborn arrogance of an aristocrat, so it was unlikely he was a particular friend.

She was just about to go back up stairs when she spotted Reynolds approaching the staircase as well.

"Reynolds?"

The little man looked up. "Yes, Lady Braven? Did you require something?"

Smiling self-consciously, Rachel glanced toward the study door. "You're going to think I'm terribly nosy, Reynolds, but who is that gentleman with the dowager countess?"

Reynolds seemed surprised that she did not already know the answer. "Why that is Dr. Phelps, Lady Braven. His lordship's physician."

Rachel's brow puckered. "Is the countess ill?"

Something flickered across the butler's face, something that immediately made Rachel suspicious. It was a look that said he'd said something he shouldn't have. Perhaps it wasn't the dowager Dr. Phelps was here to see.

Putting on her best lady-of-the-manor face, Rachel took another approach. "Who is he here to see, Reynolds?"

"Lord Braven, my lady," Reynolds replied, looking as

though he'd just bitten into something decidedly unpleasant. "I was just on my way to fetch the earl."

"Is Lord Braven ill then?" Simple nosiness had given way to genuine concern.

His narrow face was void of any emotion. "You would know better of that than I, Lady Braven. I have no idea whatsoever as to the nature of Dr. Phelps's visit."

Rachel wasn't certain if he was telling the truth or not. One thing was for certain; he was loyal to his master and was not going to tell her anything.

"Thank you, Reynolds. You may go about your business. *I* shall inform Lord Braven of Dr. Phelps's arrival."

From the expression on the butler's face, that was the last thing he wanted, but he couldn't very well defy his mistress, could he? Bowing stiffly, he acknowledged his defeat. "Very well, my lady. I shall be in my office going over the household accounts if you need me."

As he walked away, Rachel was left with the feeling that Reynolds didn't know who he was more disappointed with— himself or her. She felt a little bit guilty regardless. Perhaps it was a private matter between Brave and his physician. Perhaps they were simply friends. Either way it was really none of her business, but as his wife didn't she have the right to know if he suffered from poor health? After all, it might affect their children.

If they ever got around to creating any. He didn't really expect her to be so forward as to seduce him, did he?

She found Brave in the library. For a moment, she simply stood in the doorway and admired the perfection of him. Seduction didn't seem like much of a hardship at that moment.

He'd removed his coat and lay sprawled across a sofa like a big lazy tomcat. His shirt was pulled taut across his back beneath his waistcoat. How had he gotten so big? He was built like a farmer, or someone accustomed to hard labor. She didn't remember him being that big when they were younger.

Even his legs were big, and hard with muscle beneath his snug buckskin breeches. She remembered how those thighs had felt between hers.

Against her own volition, her gaze turned to the left wall, to the bookcase in front of which they'd almost made love the night of before. It seemed like forever ago, but her cheeks still flamed and her knees trembled with the memory.

He was so engrossed in his book he didn't even hear her enter.

"What are you reading?"

Brave glanced up, a smile—an almost whole smile— lighting his face. "A book by someone named Edward Ashton. I doubt you've ever heard of it."

Smiling at his teasing, Rachel stepped into the room. "Sounds horribly dull."

He set the book on a low table, but made no move to sit up. To Rachel, his languid pose now seemed sensual and seductive, as if he were offering himself to her and inviting her to take whatever she wanted.

A dangerous proposal, that.

"Have you sought me out for a reason, or did you just miss me?"

She smiled. "If I say I had a reason, you'll be disappointed. If I say I didn't, your arrogance will be impossible to live with, so I shall simply say, both."

Brave chuckled. "I married a diplomat. Very well, what can I do for you?"

"There's a Dr. Phelps here to see you. He's in your study with your mother."

His easiness disappeared as his entire body went taut at her words.

"Why didn't Reynolds announce him?" he asked, his tone careful as he rose to his feet.

Rachel stared at him. Why was he acting so strangely?

"He was on his way to tell you when I ran into him. I told

him I would deliver the message." Her natural curiosity and concern won out over trepidation. "Brave, are you ill?"

His head lifted. His expression was completely blank. "Why do you ask that?"

She shrugged. "Well, Dr. Phelps is your physician, is he not?"

He was so still Rachel couldn't even tell whether or not he was breathing. "Who told you that? My mother?"

"Reynolds did," she replied, stepping back from the cold blackness of his eyes. She'd never seen someone look so hollow. It was if Brave had buried himself somewhere deep inside the shell of his body.

"Reynolds is most accommodating isn't he?" He spoke as though they were strangers—as though she was someone he didn't want to know. It scared her and angered her at the same time.

"What the devil is the matter with you?" Rachel demanded, hands on her hips. "All I did was ask if you were ill."

His expression didn't change. "Why?"

Now she was just plain baffled. "Because I care about your welfare."

He seemed genuinely shocked by her reply. The color rushed from his cheeks, leaving his eyes unnaturally dark against the pallor of his skin. He opened his mouth as though to speak and closed it again, turning his back to her as he did so.

"Your concern is appreciated, madam, but it is neither wanted nor needed. Please do not trouble yourself by wasting such sentiment on me in the future."

He could have slapped her and done less harm. In silence, she stared at him, her heart cold in her chest. Why was he being so callous, so cruel? What had she done that would warrant him shutting her out like this? Whatever his reasons, his method had certainly been effective. At that moment, Rachel felt every inch the fool for thinking he returned her feelings.

Still avoiding her gaze, Brave turned toward the door. "Now if you will excuse me, I have kept Dr. Phelps waiting long enough."

"Yes, go," Rachel muttered under her breath as he left the room. Tears burned the back of her eyes and trembled in her breast. "I don't care."

A little while later, Rachel left the house dressed in her old riding habit. It was several years out of fashion but would serve the purpose.

Her anger had dissipated somewhat by the time she slipped her foot in the stirrup, but she was still hurt by Brave's strange behavior. He'd been cold, not the man she thought he was at all. What had she done to deserve such treatment?

True, perhaps she shouldn't have been so curious about Dr. Phelps, but her curiosity certainly hadn't warranted such a bizarre reaction, she thought, as she and her mount sped across the field. He'd closed a door on her and refused to let her in. Why?

Unless Brave really was sick.

She slowed the honey-colored mare to a walk as they entered a path through the woods. It was such a simple explanation. Why hadn't she thought of it sooner?

Because she'd been angry, as he'd intended her to be. It was all so clear now. Brave had intentionally been cold so she wouldn't realize there really was something wrong with him.

It was a serious error on his part. If he'd really wanted to keep his condition a secret, he should have pretended Dr. Phelps was simply an old friend come to call. Rachel wouldn't have given it another thought if he hadn't made such a drama out of it.

But he had, and now her anger gave way to an even more worrisome emotion. Fear. What could possibly be wrong with a man so young and obviously healthy as Brave? It had to be something serious for him to want to guard it so closely. Was he dying?

Rachel's stomach clenched at the thought. She couldn't even bring herself to entertain such a notion, even though it made the most sense. Was that why he had agreed to help her? Is that why he asked for children in return? So he'd have an heir to leave behind? Then why was he letting her decide when they would finally make love?

Because he was a gentleman. Because he wasn't as selfish as she was, thinking only of her own problems.

Tears threatened, and she pushed them aside. If Brave was truly suffering from a deadly illness, he would not want her bawling over it. He would need her strength and her support, and he would get it, whether he wanted it or not.

She just needed to find out what she was dealing with— and how she could help him.

The path she'd taken came out farther upstream than she normally traveled along the Wyck. The grass was thick and damp beneath the mare's hooves, and the air smelled of crisp cold and rich earth. A small waterfall tumbled from rocks high above her head, splashing into the river with a gentle roar.

The vibrant shades of the foliage contrasted sharply with the cool silver-grays of water and rocks and the darker shades of dirt and tree bark. It was nature at its most beautiful—a little piece of Heaven on earth.

It was also already occupied.

Of all the places Rachel could have expected to run into her mother-in-law, this was not one of them.

"I was wondering when you'd notice me," Annabelle Wycherley called with a smile from her perch on a large rock near the river. "It's beautiful, isn't it?"

"Yes," Rachel replied. If this wasn't fate, she didn't know what was. What a perfect opportunity to find out what was wrong with Brave. Surely his mother would know.

She slid to the ground and walked her mare toward the same tree where the dowager had tethered hers. She looped the reins around a branch, gave the horse a pat on the neck, and turned to the older woman with a smile.

"I do hope I'm not intruding upon a solitary moment?"

Annabelle gestured to a boulder next to her own. "Of course not. I am glad for the company."

It was the invitation Rachel had been hoping for.

"You know, I grew up not far from here, but this is the first time I've ever seen this waterfall." She sat down on the rock, the light wool of her skirts protecting her from the cold surface.

"I'm not surprised," the countess replied warmly. "My husband and I did our best to keep it a secret. It was our special place." She smiled as she gazed around her, as though every blade of grass held a lifetime of memories. "Every couple should have a special place."

Rachel instantly felt like an intruder. She'd been so caught up in her own concerns that it hadn't even occurred to her that the countess might have a reason for being there.

"Now I am truly sorry," she admitted. "Had I known, I never would have dreamed of disturbing you."

Annabelle patted her leg. "Nonsense, dear girl. As I said, I'm glad for the company. It keeps the blue devils at bay. You said you grew up near here. Where was that?"

Rachel was almost embarrassed to say. "I've spent the last ten years at Tullywood with my mother and her husband, Sir Henry Westhaver, but before that, my parents and I lived at a little manor called Windfleur."

Annabelle clapped her hands together. "Then you must be Edward's daughter! I thought you looked familiar."

Blushing, Rachel nodded. Obviously she and the countess had met years ago, but she didn't remember. "I'm sorry for my behavior earlier, Lady Braven. I'd had some unsettling news and wasn't quite myself. I hope I didn't offended you with my lack of manners."

"Oh, not at all, my dear. And please, call me Annabelle. After all, we're family now."

Rachel's blush deepened at her mother-in-law's knowing gaze. "I am very sorry you were not invited to the wedding, Annabelle."

Annabelle waved one elegantly gloved hand. "Balthazar didn't even know I was back in the country." Her green gaze was sly as it met Rachel's. "He refused to tell me anything about how the marriage came about until you could join us."

No doubt so they could get their stories straight, Rachel thought in relief. She wasn't sure how much she wanted to reveal to his mother.

Drawing a deep breath, Rachel kept her voice even. "Perhaps after Dr. Phelps has left, the three of us could sit down to tea."

Annabelle's gaze was guarded. "Do you know Dr. Phelps?"

Rachel shook her head. "Only by sight. I saw you talking to him when he arrived. Reynolds told me who he was. Is he a friend of the family?"

Her mother-in-law nodded. "Yes. My husband often suffered from megrims. Dr. Phelps treated him."

Rachel frowned. Surely megrims wouldn't be reason enough for Brave to get so upset? Regardless, she'd had enough of skirting the issue. "And is he treating Brave for something as well?"

Annabelle lifted shoulders in a delicate shrug, making the tassels on her epaulets wave back and forth. "To the best of my knowledge, my son is in excellent health."

There was something much like relief in her voice that made Rachel wonder if she shouldn't have phrased the question differently, but she was too relieved to question her further. A mother couldn't lie so easily about such a thing. There was no doubt that Annabelle was hiding something, but Rachel didn't think it was that Brave was dying.

"But you are right," the older woman remarked, rising to her feet. "Dr. Phelps's departure would be an excellent time to corner my son. Would you care to ride back with me?"

Rachel also stood. "I would love to accompany you. It will give us more time to get to know one another better."

"Wonderful. I should like to find out how you and Balthazar met."

And I should like to find out more about Balthazar. Returning Annabelle's sunny smile, Rachel untied her mare and led her over by a rock so she could mount. Returning to Wyck's End with Brave's mother was the best course of action for her to take, especially if she managed to catch Dr. Phelps as he was leaving. Perhaps he would tell her what the devil was going on. After all, she was a countess now, and that title ought to be good for something, shouldn't it?

"So, how did the two of you meet?" Annabelle asked as they picked their way side by side through the forest.

"He pulled me from the Wyck and saved my life." Rachel smiled at the memory. "I thought for sure we were both going to drown."

The older woman looked aghast, and again Rachel wondered what she was missing. "That must have been very traumatic for both of you."

Rachel glanced at the path. "It was very frightening at the time, yes."

"And was it love at first sight?" The lightness of her tone didn't quite ring true.

With a sigh, Rachel realized that instead of solving the mystery of Brave's welfare, she just seemed to be falling deeper into more intrigue. Not only was she now curious as to what was wrong with Brave, but she wondered why his mother was acting so strangely over the fact that Brave had saved her life.

"He was like a knight in silver armor," Rachel replied

truthfully, avoiding a more direct answer. She'd always found Brave attractive—the pain on his face had broken her heart at his father's funeral. But love? The only example of that she had to draw upon was her parents and their sweetly affectionate relationship. She and Brave were nothing like that.

The rest of the ride back to the house was quiet except for the sound of the horses' breathing and their hooves striking the soft earth.

When they rode up to the stables, Dr. Phelps's horse was still there.

"They must have a lot to talk about," Rachel remarked, as a groom helped her dismount.

Annabelle smiled. "I'm certain they do."

Rachel tried not to scowl as she dismounted. "But Brave isn't sick."

Slipping gracefully to the ground, her mother-in-law sighed. "Rachel, as I've already told you, to the best of my knowledge my son is in perfect health. The only person who can tell you otherwise is Balthazar. If you're so concerned, perhaps you should talk to him."

"I did. He told me not to concern myself."

Annabelle's mouth tightened slightly before smoothing into a wide smile. "Then I'd say you have nothing to worry about. Now, if you'll excuse me, I wish to freshen up before tea."

Rachel watched her walk away with a growing sense of determination. Didn't concern her? Did Brave and his mother think that just because she wasn't truly his wife, his welfare didn't concern her? She'd confided her fear of Sir Henry to him. She'd even started to talk about her father with him—something she rarely discussed with anyone, not even her mother or Belinda—and he was just going to cut her out of his life like a stranger?

Not bloody likely. Brave had gone above and beyond her expectations by offering her his help. The least she could do was offer hers in return. But first she had to find out what his problem was.

And find out she would.

"So why haven't you told your wife about what happened to you after Miranda's death?"

Brave lifted his head, the fingers of his right hand twirling the white queen from the chessboard by the window where he stood. "Because it's none of her business." He was very tempted to tell Phelps it was none of his either.

Dr. Phelps's smile said he had expected that answer. "But she is your wife."

Brave stopped twirling the queen and studied her cool ivory features.

"She is my wife in name only." The words tasted bitter in his mouth. "There is no reason to tell her anything." He set the queen and her assessing gaze upon the chessboard, and turned her so he couldn't see her face.

"You don't think she'd understand?" The physician's voice drifted over his shoulder. Brave didn't have to see the man's face to know that Phelps already knew the answer.

He didn't turn. Instead, Brave clasped his hands behind his back and fixed his attention out the window. Staring at the village roofs in the distance, he replied, "No."

Rachel would understand all too well his desire to save Miranda. It had been much like her own desire to save her mother. She would probably even understand how that affected his desire to help her. What she might not understand was his failure. A woman as determined as she might have trouble understanding how Brave had let Miranda slip through his fingers.

And he did not want her to know that he'd refused Miranda his help when she did ask for it. He would rather almost anything than that.

"Tell me again how you think helping her get her mother away from this abusive husband will make you feel better about your own life."

Behind him, Brave heard Phelps scratch his quill on a sheet of paper. He must have a whole book of notes on him now.

"Balance." A cloud of smoke rose from one of the distant chimneys, reaching for Heaven even though it would fade into nothingness long before it made it that high.

The scratching stopped. "Balance?"

Brave glanced over his shoulder. All he could see were the other man's boots. "I couldn't save Miranda, but if I save Rachel, then maybe I'll be even."

More scratching. "And what happens if you are not able to help your wife?"

Yes, what then? Staring out at darkening sky, Brave shrugged. "I don't know. The scales might tip farther, or perhaps just the fact that I tried will be enough."

"But you don't want her to know?"

"No." His shoulders were tensing again.

"And you don't think she'll make any further attempts to discover the nature of our relationship?"

Remembering the hurt expression on Rachel's face when he told her not to waste her concern on him, Brave shook his head. The image would not leave him.

"No. I don't think she'll ask any more questions." Lord knew he was good at putting distance between himself and others.

"Let's talk about something we haven't discussed in a while."

Brave turned. Phelps sat in an armchair, his legs crossed, ink on the table beside him. He'd been humoring the physician when he'd agreed to sit and talk to him. In fact, he'd been too preoccupied with Rachel to turn the older man away. He'd wanted the company to keep from thinking of his wife. Now, he'd wished he'd gotten drunk instead.

"What's that?"

Phelps's lips curved on one side. "Miranda."

Brave frowned. "We've discussed little else in the last year."

"We've discussed her death and how it affected you, but we haven't discussed her as a person in quite some time. Why don't you start by telling me how you felt about her."

"I don't understand what difference this is going to make." It was hard to hide his frustration. What good did it do to discuss a girl who had been dead for almost two years? "Talking about her won't change a thing."

"Things may have changed themselves," Phelps replied cryptically. "What I'm trying to gauge here, Brave is how your feelings and perceptions have changed since we last discussed Miranda. I'll be able to see what kind of progress you've made when I check these notes against the last time we spoke of her."

It still seemed like a waste of time. Brave didn't see how his "perception" of Miranda could have changed when she was dead, but if it made Phelps feel as though they were getting somewhere, what could it hurt?

"What do you want to know?"

Quill poised above his paper, Phelps didn't raise his head. "When you think of Miranda now, how do you see her?"

Brave thought for a moment, picturing Julian's younger sister in his mind. He smiled. "Willful, a little spoiled. Pretty."

"Describe your feelings for her at that time."

"I suppose I fancied myself in love with her. She was the prettiest girl I'd ever seen, and we'd known each other for years. Marrying her would have linked our families permanently. She was the perfect choice."

"How does it make you feel now when you think about her falling in love with her father's employee?"

Shaking his head in sorrow, Brave replied, "I feel sorry for her. She fell in love with a man who didn't love her in return, and she believed all his lies because of it."

"And how do you feel about the fact that she killed herself?"

"I feel guilt," he confessed. "She asked for my help, and I refused her. I didn't know she'd take her own life, and it makes me mad as hell to think that she preferred death over the scandal. I don't think she even thought of her family—or of me for that matter. She was just so scared."

Phelps gazed at him. "And yet, you still carry a large amount of guilt for a situation that was beyond your control."

"I should have done something."

"You tried."

Brave looked away. "Not enough."

"What could you have possibly done?"

Shrugging, Brave glanced away. "I should have married her."

Expressionless, Phelps stared at him. "And whom would that have served? Miranda or yourself?"

Brave didn't reply. He didn't need to.

Sighing, Phelps put aside his quill and lifted his satchel from the floor by his feet. "I think that's enough for today. I don't know about you, but it comes to a point where I can't stand the sound of my own voice anymore. Once I've compared today's notes with our last discussion of Miranda I'll send you a copy of my findings." He paused. "I don't know why you're holding on to this."

Brave's lips twitched. "Next thing you're going tell me is that it's all in my head."

The doctor chuckled as he hoisted his bag. "Might I offer some advice?"

"Certainly."

"Talk to your wife. I've a feeling she won't be as condemning as you suspect."

Opening the door, Brave fought the urge to close it on the doctor as he walked through it. "I'll think about it," he replied. Think about it and forget it.

Phelps shook his head. "I'll be in touch soon."

After saying farewell, Brave shut the door and threw himself into a nearby chair. Phelps's visits often left him feeling as though he'd been fed through a clothespress.

Maybe the physician was right. Maybe he should confess all to Rachel and let her draw whatever conclusions she would about him, but she had enough on her plate without adding his problems to it. And even if he could be certain she wouldn't look at him with pity or think him a failure, it probably wasn't a good idea to tell someone you were trying to help how you'd failed someone else.

Marrying Rachel had been a huge mistake. It made him want what he couldn't have. He wanted a real marriage. He wanted her to give him as much of herself as she gave everything else she did, but he couldn't have it, not when he was incapable of giving anything in return.

He knew all this already, so why did he insist on dwelling upon it? He never used to feel this sorry for himself all the time. Before Miranda's death, he dreamed of the future, of someday being the kind of man his father would be proud of. Now it seemed he spent all his time lamenting what he couldn't have rather than concentrating on finding something he could.

A knock on the door interrupted his thoughts. It was his mother and Rachel wanting him to join them for tea. He was amazed Rachel would want to join him for anything, but when he looked into her lovely face, all he saw was concern. No condemnation, no anger.

How would she feel if he told her he'd refused the woman he loved because she'd hurt his feelings, and that she'd killed herself because of his rejection? Would she grant him the forgiveness he sought, or would she see him as a monster like Sir Henry? And why did it matter so damn much what she thought of him. Why did he so desperately want her approval?

Because for the first time since Miranda's death, he felt as though he had a chance to set things right.

Helping Rachel was still the best way of regaining something of his old self. Surely he would begin to feel that balance he told Phelps about. Yes, that was it. And once he had achieved that, he would be better able to put his feelings for her in the right perspective. This tenderness he felt for her was nothing more than his own cursed vulnerability—something else he had to conquer. His father had never been a weak man; Brave was determined not to be one either.

Not anymore.

Chapter 11

After a surprisingly comfortable dinner with Brave and his mother, Rachel retired early to her room. She had hoped to speak to Brave privately to let him know that he could depend on her, trust her—no matter what the problem was. She couldn't do that in front of his mother, however.

Upon reaching her room, she changed into her nightgown and wrapper and spent the remainder of the evening at her desk, outlining as much of Sir Henry's cruelty toward her mother over the years as she could remember. It was an emotionally painful task, but would be well worth it if it persuaded the crown to grant her mother a divorce.

And it took her mind off Brave, which was a blessing in itself. Lately, it seemed she was incapable of thinking of anything else.

She went to bed early and rose the next morning refreshed and with a purpose. She bathed and dressed, and while sipping a cup of chocolate, penned a note to her mother inviting her to tea that afternoon. She didn't trust this newfound amiability of Sir Henry's and wanted to keep as close an eye on her mother as she could. If that meant making up excuses to see her every other day so be it.

She went down to the dining room prepared to meet her husband for breakfast and was both disappointed and relieved to discover he had already eaten.

"Lord Braven had business to attend to in town, my lady," Reynolds informed her. "But he asked me to give you this." He offered her a sealed letter.

Intrigued and more than a little anxious, Rachel took the letter. "Thank you, Reynolds. You may go now."

The diminutive butler bowed and departed, leaving Rachel all alone in the large room.

She broke the seal before her backside hit the chair. Was it an apology, or did he want her out of his house?

You were missed at breakfast. I would like to speak with you. I will await you in my study later this morning. Brave.

Well, it wasn't exactly an apology, but it wasn't an eviction notice either. And the fact that he'd missed her that morning was a good sign. If he was still upset, he wouldn't have mentioned her absence.

After a leisurely breakfast of buttered eggs, toast, and sausage, Rachel had her note sent off to her mother and had a carriage brought 'round to take her to Belinda's. She hadn't seen her friend since the wedding, and since Belinda would soon be marrying herself, Rachel wanted to see her as often as she could.

Plus, Belinda had an ear for gossip. If anyone in the village was going to know anything about Brave and his secrets, it was she, and as Rachel's friend she would divulge all that she had heard.

The carriage rolled and thumped along the worn country road. It hadn't rained in a few days, but the damage was done. The road was little more than a series of ruts and bumps in some places.

Staring out the window at the passing landscape, Rachel realized just how much her life had changed over the last month. When was the last time she'd actually had the luxury of having a carriage at her disposal? Never. They'd had one when she was a child, but she'd never been allowed to go anywhere alone. Now here she was in a fine, well-padded carriage, driven by a coachman in the Wycherley livery. She wore a fine new gown with her rose cape and the bonnet Belinda had given her.

All of her shabbiest gowns were gone, replaced by ones so exquisite and lovely that Rachel's eyes had watered when Mrs. Ford delivered them. Courtesy of Brave, she had an entire new wardrobe. Of course he couldn't have his countess dressing like a ragamuffin, but Rachel was touched by the gesture all the same. Such generosity was overwhelming.

She was in a position of power now, socially and politically. Her rank placed her above Sir Henry. Marriage to Brave had taken her out of the humiliation of her former life and made her someone of importance. Not only was her stepfather forced to defer to her, but the whole town was as well. Any whispering the other young women wanted to do about her would have to be done behind her back now. No one would dare cut her.

Rachel almost laughed aloud at the irony of it. She had everything she'd ever wanted, and none of it would matter if her husband didn't let her into his life, or she couldn't use this new power to help her mother.

As it was, her mother could very well choose to stay with the apparently reformed Sir Henry. And what then?

No. She refused even to entertain the idea. It wouldn't happen. It couldn't.

That just left Brave. When she'd first accepted his proposal, she'd allowed herself to believe it was solely to help her mother. True, she'd had few other options—marriage to Charlton was *not* one of them—but Brave's noble offer hadn't been the only reason to marry him, it had simply been the best.

Obviously, she would have been an idiot to refuse him. He was a dream come true. She hadn't lied when she told his mother she'd believed him to be a knight. His daring rescue of her had proven that.

He was handsome and rich, and for the most part he'd been nothing but kind, his reaction to her questions about Dr. Phelps the one exception. He was the most-sought-after gentleman in Yorkshire, but his looks and fortune—even his kindness—were superficial compared to the real reason Rachel had committed the rest of her life to him.

It was the way he made her feel. He looked at her in a way no one else ever had, as though he were truly seeing her. He looked at her as though she was the one who had saved him and not the other way around. And then there was the way that sad smile of his tugged at her heart, or the way the slightest touch of his hand could turn her knees to jelly . . .

She had the awful feeling that she was falling in love with him. Normally, falling in love with one's husband would be a good thing, but not if he didn't return that love, and not if there was something wrong with him that might make a life together impossible.

As the carriage rolled past the lane leading to Tullywood, Rachel peered through the glass toward the house. Her thoughts turned from anxiety over Brave to other concerns.

A steady cloud of smoke rose from the chimneys, adding yet more gray to an already dark sky. There was something almost picturesque about Tullywood's redbrick Tudor style set amongst the gentle hills. Horses grazed in the field, and the lane that led to the house was smooth and free of ruts.

For a house of nightmares, it looked damn near inviting.

Was her mother up yet? Was she giggling at something Sir Henry said over breakfast? Or was she lying in her bed, battered and broken and unable even to get up for a glass of water?

Rachel leaned back against the squabs so she couldn't see

the house any longer. Upsetting herself would not do her mother any good. Until she heard from either her mother or Potts, she would have to trust that Sir Henry was still behaving himself. Her mother might not tell her if he hit her or not, depending on how sincere Sir Henry sounded when he apologized—and he always apologized—but Potts would send word to her. This she knew.

She sat like that until they reached the village, then pulled herself up straight so no one would see her slouching as if she had no backbone.

The blacksmith was at his forge, a coach prepared to leave the inn, its passengers practically sitting on top of each other it was so full. The dour look on one lady's face as she was crushed between a portly old man and a woman with a small dog was enough to make Rachel laugh out loud, and she was again very thankful for the Earl of Braven's roomy carriage.

People turned to stare as they drove by. The coat of arms on the door told everyone to whom the coach belonged, and they were no doubt curious for a glimpse at the quiet earl or his new countess—probably to see how she cleaned up. Rachel smiled and waved to those she knew and ignored those she didn't.

A few moments later, the carriage rolled up the drive to Belinda's father's house. Mr. Mayhew had often voiced his concern about Rachel's unfortunate connection to Sir Henry and the scandalous way her mother had married before going through a proper mourning period. It was easy for people in better circumstances to pass judgment on others.

But Belinda's father had continued to allow the girls to be friends because it meant so much to Belinda. Rachel wondered if Mr. Mayhew would find her a more suitable friend for his daughter now that she had married a peer of the realm.

But that wasn't something she was destined to find out during her visit. Belinda's father was nowhere to be found, and as Belinda herself had just barely woken up, Rachel went directly to her friend's bedroom rather than one of the parlors.

Belinda was in bed, propped up against a mountain of pillows when Rachel entered the room. Her dark hair and pale skin were complemented perfectly by the simple pink-and-white color scheme of the chamber. She looked like a little doll.

"What are you doing still in bed?" Rachel demanded with a smile as she untied her bonnet. Absently, she realized she matched the flowers in the wallpaper.

Belinda raised a delicate china cup to her lips and sipped. "Rachel, it's only ten o'clock."

She tossed her bonnet on the chest at the foot of the bed and unfastened her cloak. "I've been up since seven."

"Yes, well you're unnatural." Belinda grinned. "If I had a husband like yours, I'd stay in bed all day—provided he was with me."

Rachel's cheeks flushed hotly as she laid her cloak beside her bonnet. "You know our marriage isn't like that." And it never would be, because she'd never find the courage to tell Brave she wanted him!

"Hmm. Pity." She took another drink and patted the bed beside her. "Well, come on."

Careful not to put her shoes on the bedclothes, Rachel climbed up on the bed beside her friend. It was as though they were girls again.

Belinda yawned. "Forgive me. We were out late last night—a card party at the Coles's."

"I'm sorry. If I'd known, I never would have called on you this morning."

Her friend shot her a look of disbelief. "If you'd known, you would have come at nine!"

Laughing, Rachel leaned back against the pillows. "You know me too well."

"Indeed." Setting her cup on the beside table, Belinda turned her torso to face Rachel. As she propped herself up on her elbow, her expression turned serious. "And since I know you so well, I know that this is not merely a social call. What's the matter?"

How did she ask without sounding like an idiot? "I need some information."

Now Belinda looked curious. A tiny pucker appeared between her arched brows. "About what?"

"About Braven."

Those brows shot up. "I take it you're not looking for details such as height, hair color, et cetera?"

Rachel ignored her glib remark. "I need something much more specific, things I can't come right out and ask him—not if I want an answer."

Blowing out a deep breath, Belinda scratched her head. "I'm not sure I can be of much help. You're married to him; I'm sure you know more about him than I would."

She shifted position, turning so that they faced each other. "Not about his past, I don't. After my father's death I rarely saw him, except at his father's funeral. You traveled in the same circles as he did, attended the same parties. Weren't your mothers acquainted?"

Belinda's expression was shrewd. "So you want gossip."

Rachel blushed. Belinda made it sound so tawdry.

"I want to know what changed him from a rakish young man to someone who can't seem to remember how to smile. I want to know if he's ever been ill or had an accident. Anything." *Is it something I can fix or do I have to lose yet another person I care about?*

"Why?"

Sighing, Rachel thumped her head against the headboard. She'd lost her father. She was in danger of losing her mother. She would not lose Brave as well.

"Because I want to help him remember how to smile if I

can." What was she saying? How could she admit that out loud, even to Belinda?

"And I'm nosy," she added lamely.

Belinda nodded, a smug little smile curving her cupid's bow lips. "I understand. Well, let me see. What can I remember hearing about Braven . . . Oh! I remember overhearing Lady Easterly tell Lady Pembroke that he was equipped like a stallion. Does that count?"

Rachel's entire face burned as her friend burst into gales of laughter. "No," she growled. "It does not count!" Lord, she wouldn't even be able to look at Brave without wondering . . . *it* had certainly felt rather large in the library that night, but then she had nothing to compare him to.

Belinda was watching her closely. "Hmm. Something in your expression wants me to ask you if Lady Easterly was correct, but you wouldn't tell me anyway, would you?"

"I have no idea what you're talking about." Her tone was unconvincing.

"Of course you don't." Her friend gave her hand a patronizing pat. "I do remember that he was rather taken with the Earl of Wolfram's younger sister, Miranda. I remember hearing that he'd proposed to her and she refused. Idiot."

Rachel had to agree. She couldn't imagine any woman refusing Brave.

"Whatever became of her?" The only sister Julian had spoken of during any of the brief time Rachel had spent in his presence was Letitia. Surely Miranda's family hadn't deserted her?

Belinda's expression softened. "Poor thing took her own life."

Gasping, Rachel pressed a hand her mouth. "Why?"

"No one's quite certain. There was all manner of speculation, of course. Rumor was that Braven found the body. He grieved over her like a husband."

Rachel wasn't sure she wanted to hear this. "And then what?"

Belinda shrugged. "He seemed hell-bent on joining her. He started building quite a reputation for himself, drinking and fighting." Her gazed locked with Rachel's. "With women. Then he just disappeared."

She definitely didn't want to hear about the women. "Where did he disappear to?"

"I believe he just locked himself up in that great big house of his. Although some of the more romantic types like to believe he murdered the man who seduced Miranda and fled to the continent to escape persecution."

Brave, a murderer? "I don't believe that for a moment."

Another shrug. "Few people do, since Lady Easterly claims to have hired the blackguard for her own stables. Her own *private* stables."

The aristocracy were sometimes the most disgusting creatures. "And that's all you know about Braven?"

Belinda nodded. "I can't think of anything else, except that he apparently fell into the Thames one night whilst deep in his cups. He would have drowned if the Earl of Angelwood hadn't been with him, although Angelwood wasn't in much better condition. Of course there were those who believed Braven tried to commit suicide."

Rachel couldn't imagine Brave doing something so drastic.

Belinda's information only served to deepen the mystery about Brave, not help her solve it. The death of the woman he loved would certainly account for the perpetual aura of sadness around him, but it hardly explained why he was seeing a physician.

She slammed her fist down upon the bed. "This is so blasted maddening!"

Obviously surprised by her outburst, Belinda could only stare at her, her mouth agape. "What's maddening?" she eventually asked.

"Braven!" Rachel cried, waving her fingers in the air. "Lord of Secrets. What?"

Being laughed at by her one and only friend did nothing to improve her mood.

"What do you care about his secrets?"

Folding her arms across her chest, Rachel tucked in her lower lip, which was in danger of falling onto her bosom she was so churlish. "I just don't understand why he won't tell me what's going on."

Belinda smiled teasingly. "Perhaps it's none of your business?"

"I'm his wife!" Rachel yelled, scowling so deeply she could see her own eyebrows.

Most people would have probably shied away from her right then, but not Belinda. No, she just sat there laughing as though Rachel was a rambunctious kitten rather than a full-grown woman.

"Stop that!"

Much to her surprise, Belinda did. Dabbing at her eyes with a corner of a coverlet, Belinda drew a deep breath and turned to face her with a smile.

"And you're certainly acting like a wife as well but, dearest, I didn't think you were interested in being his wife? I thought all you wanted was to get your mother a divorce."

"That is what I want." Then why did she sound so utterly pathetic and pouty?

This time Belinda's smile was gentle, and perhaps even a little sad. "Then his secrets are none of your business. Why should he confide in a woman who's only using him to get what she wants?"

That stung. "You make it sound so mercenary." She plucked at the lace ruffle on one of the pillows.

The smile drooped a little, became sadder. "It is. Rachel, he offered to marry you to help you. You accepted for the same reason. You can't expect him to treat you like a real wife in some ways and then not allow him to in others."

Cheeks burning, Rachel averted her gaze. Her friend's

meaning was perfectly clear. "It doesn't matter. I've got more important things to worry about."

"We both know that's a load of hogwash." Flinging back the covers, Belinda scooted off the bed.

Rachel's head snapped up. Dejection was replaced by annoyance. "What's that supposed to mean? You know I have to look after my mother!"

Belinda padded across the floor and shrugged into a white dressing gown that matched her nightrail. The expression on her face was unimpressed. "From what I saw last night, your mother is perfectly capable of looking after herself."

"L-last night?"

Her countenance softening, Belinda walked back toward the bed. Lifting one leg on to it, she plopped down onto the mattress. "Sir Henry and your mother were at the party last night." She reached over and took one of Rachel's hands in her own. Her palm was warm against Rachel's icy fingers.

"I'm not sure how Sir Henry managed an invitation, but the two of them were the very picture of domestic bliss. Your mother did not look like a woman who wanted to be rescued from her husband. In fact, she was quite the opposite."

A flock of birds seemed to take flight in Rachel's chest. She was going to be ill, but first, she was going to scream.

"I can't believe it," she whispered.

The warm hand squeezed. "Rachel, as your friend, I'm begging you, give up this foolish obsession with getting your mother away from Sir Henry and get on with your own life. If there's any part of you at all that wants to be a real wife to Braven, don't push it aside."

Looking into her friend's pleading gaze, Rachel couldn't even speak. What was wrong with everyone? How could both Belinda and her mother possibly believe Sir Henry had changed? And how could either of them expect her to walk away? Not when it would be her fault if her stepfather seriously harmed her mother. Didn't they see that? Didn't they know it was all her fault?

"I have to go." Jerkily, she climbed off the bed, her stiff limbs tangling in the blankets.

Belinda reached for her. "Rachel, I'm sorry. Don't leave."

Scooping up her cloak and bonnet, Rachel shook her head. She was cold, bone-cold. "No. I have to go." She turned toward the door. "Good-bye."

Belinda called out after her as she ran out of the room, but Rachel didn't stop. She ran down the stairs, through the foyer, and past the puzzled footman who held the door for her.

"Take me home," she instructed the driver before clamoring into the carriage. "Quickly!"

Yes, home. Home to Wyck's End. Home to Brave, who despite all his secrets, seemed to be the only person still on her side.

Standing in front of the row of windows that lined the wall of his study, Brave watched the carriage as it sped up the drive. A few seconds later, he heard the front door open and shut, followed by voices in the entrance hall.

Rachel was home.

Where had she been? He'd arrived home shortly after ten to discover she'd gone out. Had she gone to her mother's so they could commiserate on what awful husbands they had? Or perhaps she'd simply gone into town to purchase herself some more new clothes. Lord knew she needed them. He'd purchased a few things for her, but not enough. Maybe she'd forgive him for being such an ass if he bought her more.

"Did you get my note?"

Brave jumped. She hadn't even knocked. Perhaps he would make a wife of her yet. Turning to face her, he schooled his expression into one of careful neutrality.

The sight of her was still like a rock to the gut. She was wearing one of the gowns Mrs. Ford had made her, some purply, fruity color he didn't know the name of. It made her eyes seem bluer and her skin seem brighter. Or perhaps it was just the fact that he had missed her that made her appearance today seem all the more lovely.

"About your mother and Sir Henry?" he asked when he finally found his voice.

She nodded.

"Yes, I've read it. You were very detailed in your descriptions. Even the most stoic of men would have to be moved by your mother's plight." He didn't plan on telling how horrified he'd been to read about some of her mother's injuries. He understood why she was so desperate to free her mother from Sir Henry's rule. The man was a monster.

Or should he say, had been a monster? From what he'd heard the last few days Sir Henry had been conducting himself as the model husband.

"Good. I would like to begin proceedings as soon as possible. Today." She swept around to his desk, perching herself on the edge of one of the chairs in front of it.

Brows raised, Brave clasped his hands behind his back and strode toward her. Her back was to him and he could see just how rigid her shoulders were. She was pulled tighter than a spinster's topknot.

He leaned against the side of the desk and faced her, folding his arms across his chest. "Would you care to tell me what has happened to make you so upset?"

She met his gaze. "Would you care to tell me why you're seeing a physician?"

Oh, she was good. "Back to that, are we? Dr. Phelps has been a friend of my family for years, Rachel. He occasionally comes to call, especially when my mother is in residence. It's nothing to concern yourself with." At least he wasn't lying—not outright anyway.

She didn't look completely convinced. Lord, but she could be annoying! She was like a dog worrying a bone.

Still, her interest warmed him. It had been a long time since anyone had cared so deeply about his welfare. However, he couldn't afford to have her snooping around. He didn't want her to uncover the truth—not before he was prepared to tell her himself.

"I occasionally visit with Mrs. Johnson, the midwife as well," he told her, his tone mocking. "Would you care to ask whether or not I'm with child?"

Rachel blushed—not the delicate pink of debutantes and gently bred girls, but a hot, impossible-to-hide red. She never did anything halfway, his Rachel. She was constantly full speed ahead and damn the consequences. She gave her all or nothing.

She would give her all in bed. The very thought of it sent a surge of longing straight to his loins, causing them to stir and tighten.

God, was he to lose all his dignity where she was concerned?

Thankfully she didn't seem to notice his growing erection. In fact, she kept her attention focused on his boots. Her stare was so intent Brave wondered if she could see her reflection in the shine.

He clasped his hands in front of his groin. He seemed to do that a lot these days. No one would ever know he'd been practically impotent—devoid of all sexual interest—for months. Rachel had brought all those long-dead urges back with a vengeance.

"What happened?" Perhaps this time she would answer rather than counter with a question of her own.

She lifted her chin and her face regained something of its normal color. "Sir Henry took my mother to a party last night."

Brave shook his head. Had he heard her correctly? "I beg your pardon?"

"He took her to a party!" Her throaty voice was hoarse

with indignation as she flopped back in the chair. She gazed at him as though she expected him to understand why this revelation was so horrifying.

"And that's a bad thing?" Yes, if it had been one of Charlton's. His gut tightened at the thought.

"Yes, it's a bad thing!" She leaned forward, pressing her face into her hands. "He took her to the Coles's."

Brave's forehead constricted and relaxed in a brief frown. Tilting his head thoughtfully, he tried to wrap his mind around her distress. "Rachel, I understand your suspicion, and you're right to have it, but I would think you would be glad Sir Henry is treating your mother with some kindness."

Rachel looked up. "Why? So it can be all that much more of a shock when he stops making the effort?"

"No—"

Her laughter was humorless. "When a man's made a habit out of a certain kind of behavior, he doesn't just give it up overnight, Brave."

Something in her words struck a chord deep within him. Was that what he had done? Fallen into a habit he didn't know how to break?

"You don't think he can make a habit out of the right behavior?"

"Do you? If you'd spent most of your life being picked on by a bully, wouldn't you wonder what he was up to if he suddenly announced he wanted to be your best friend?"

She had a point.

"Even if Sir Henry is sincere in his efforts, what do you think will happen when the glow wears off?" Her face was taut with emotion. "What will happen when my mother displeases him in some way? Do you think his first instinct is going to be to talk about it? No. His first instinct is going to be to hit, and my mother will be his target."

"And there's nothing you can do about it."

She shook her head and pressed a hand to her face.

Brave knew how powerless she felt. He'd felt much the same way when Miranda died. As much as he believed he should have stopped it—that he *could* have stopped it, he had no way of knowing that it would have made a difference. There was no proof that he could have made her happy.

"And the worst part is that Sir Henry's good behavior will damage our case." Rubbing her forehead, she continued, "People will ignore his violence and concentrate on the good because he is a man and a baronet. Everyone will think it really was my fault he abused her."

"Your fault?" Was she deranged? "How could anyone possibly believe that you were to blame?"

Rachel's gaze was weary as it met his. "Because he told me it was. And that's what he'll tell everyone else. He'll tell them that I was a reminder of my father, that I provoked him, that I tried to come between him and my mother, and people will believe it."

"People who don't know him might believe it, but—"

"Do the men who'll be hearing our case know him?"

For a woman who had spent most of her life in rural Yorkshire, she certainly knew the way of things. Sir Henry would no doubt play upon the number of unhappy marriages among the upper ranks. Without evidence of violence—especially with testimony that Sir Henry had changed once Rachel left his house—Sir Henry would end up inspiring the sympathy of his self-indulgent, arrogant peers, and Rachel would become the villain.

But the men who would be hearing their case were Brave's peers as well. "They also knew my father," he informed her, and if his erratic behavior after Miranda's death hadn't convinced them he had lost his mind, they also knew him. He had more respectability behind him, more money and prestige than Sir Henry Westhaver could ever hope for.

"I'm not certain how much good it will do us, but it might keep them from being completely swayed by Sir Henry.

Plus, if he does injure your mother before then, it will look very bad for him."

Her hopeful expression faded. "He's going to have to hurt her. She won't leave him unless he does. And if she doesn't leave him, then we have nothing."

Brave's heart went out to her. "Then we have no choice but to wait for your mother to come to a decision."

"I'm afraid that could take some time." She sighed. "I'm so sorry I had to drag you into this. No doubt you were hoping this mess wouldn't last more than a couple of months."

He didn't care if it lasted a lifetime as long as he could help her, but he couldn't tell her that. He shrugged. "My calendar is free. Will you be all right?"

"I don't have much choice." She was slouched so far down into the chair now her knees almost touched the armrests. "Do you ever feel like so much is expected of you, and you just don't know if you can ever do it?"

Brave chuckled drily. "Sometimes I feel as though I've spent my entire life trying to be something I'm not."

"Truly?" She sounded genuinely surprised.

He met her gaze. "I've grown up under the shadow of my father—a remarkable man as you know."

She didn't look as though they were in complete agreement. "Well, he was a good friend of my father's and always treated me well."

"He treated everyone well. Ever since I was a child I tried to live my life in a way that would make him proud." He thought about his behavior after Miranda's death, the drinking and the whoring. His father would not have been impressed with him then. He would have been very disappointed.

"I think you've succeeded."

"Do you?" At her nod, he shook his head. "I don't know. I've tried to emulate him so much since his death. I wanted to prove I could fill his shoes. People loved my father. They respected him."

Her expression was dubious. "And you don't think you're loved and respected?"

"I know my servants, tenants, and employees harbor a certain respect for me, but sometimes I wonder if it's as deep as the esteem they had for my father." He couldn't believe he was telling her this. He'd never spoken to anyone about his insecurities, not even Gabriel or Julian.

"What about love? Surely you've known that."

"I know my friends and mother care about me very much."

The look she gave him made him uneasy. It was as though she could look right through him to his very soul and read his deepest fear—that he just wasn't worthy of true love, that somehow he couldn't be what everyone expected him to be. That he was a disappointment.

The silence stretched between them and still she sat there staring. Finally, Brave straightened and moved away from the desk.

Clearing his throat, he turned his back to her. "I owe you an apology for my behavior yesterday. I was in a foul mood and I shouldn't have taken it out on you when you were merely being curious and concerned for my welfare." It had sounded much smoother when he'd practiced before.

"Apology accepted."

It was an effort to keep his shoulders from sagging in relief.

"And I am sorry as well for prying. I overstepped my bounds."

Bounds? He met her gaze over his shoulder. "Rachel, I would like to think that we are on intimate enough terms for there not to be boundaries between us." Perhaps *intimate* hadn't been the right word. It conjured up images of that night in the library, when he'd felt the damp heat of her against the head of his cock.

She smiled, but it was sad, as though she didn't believe him, and he realized that he'd just lied to her. He wanted her to feel like she could tell him anything, but he didn't plan to let his own walls crumble. And she knew it.

Trust. It had to go both ways.

"I think I'm going to have a drink," he announced, already halfway across the room. "Would you like one?"

"Brave."

He stopped. Something in her voice made him reluctant to face her. It took every ounce of strength he had to turn and face the unabashed concern and trust in those blueberry eyes of hers.

"I just want you to know that you can talk to me. About anything. I'm here if you need me."

If he needed her? He'd never needed anything in his entire life like he needed her! Physically she drove him insane. Emotionally, she made him want to be whole again, to toss all of his fears to the wind and take a chance. She was his salvation. And she had no idea.

But before Brave could reply, the door to the study came flying open. A harried Reynolds stood in the frame.

"Reynolds." More surprised than angry at the intrusion, Brave could only stare at his butler. "What the devil is the matter with you?"

The little man's anxious gaze darted between Brave and Rachel. "Forgive my impertinence, Lord Braven, Lady Braven, but there's something of an emergency out front, my lord."

"An emergency?" Rachel echoed, rising to her feet.

"Well, spit it out, man!" Brave cried as she came to his side.

"It's Lady Westhaver, my lord, she's—"

But Brave didn't give him a chance to finish. He raced from the room and down the hall as fast as his legs would carry him.

Behind him, he could hear Rachel's panicked shouts, demanding that he wait for her. He ignored her cries. He had to get outside. He'd only seen that horrified look on Reynolds's face once before.

The night his father died.

Chapter 12

Rachel ran.

Skirts hiked up around her knees, heart hammering in her chest, she chased Brave into the entrance hall with Reynolds hot on her heels.

Ohgodohgodohgodpleaseletherbeallrightpleaseplease please . . .

Her legs felt as though they were asleep—heavy and weak. Each step seemed to take forever and yet the walls streamed past her and the floor blurred beneath her feet. Every inch of her filled and tingled with fear.

Sir Henry had reverted to his violent nature. She knew it. What else would bring her mother to Wyck's End? What else could fill Reynolds's face with revulsion and terror? She knew the feeling. She'd felt it herself the first time her stepfather beat her mother.

It was different from the way she'd felt when she'd seen her father's body after his death. A dead person—particularly one hit by a carriage—was expected to have marks upon him. One did not expect to see a body that battered get up and move about. One did not expect to hear the voice of a loved one coming out of a face so battered they didn't recognize it. That was real horror, the knowledge that beneath all that awfulness lived a real person—a person who must suffer greatly. A person you could barely bring yourself to touch because just the sight of him brought the bitter taste of bile to your mouth.

That, Rachel knew, was what she would find when she saw her mother.

At least a dozen servants clustered together in the foyer. The dowager stood on the stairs, one hand pressed to her mouth in horror. One footman knelt beside the body of a woman lying facedown on the marble floor. He was checking her wrist for a pulse.

Rachel ran faster.

Brave fell to his knees beside the body—beside her mother. He yelled something, and the footman helped him turn her mother over.

Rachel collapsed beside him, banging her knees on the hard stone. It didn't hurt as much as it should have. Brave tried to block her view, and she shoved him aside with all the panicked strength in her body. "Get out of my way!"

She looked down.

Oh sweet God.

"That's not her." Turning, she met Brave's stricken gaze. The scream bubbling inside her came tearing out of her throat. *"That's not her!"*

Warm hands cupped her trembling shoulders. "Rachel, it is her." His voice was low and calm, but his eyes . . . his eyes were black with despair.

"No!" she cried, pulling free of his grip. "It's not her! It's not!" She knew her own mother, knew her face like the back of her hand, and the face of the woman on the floor looked nothing like her mother's.

It looked like nothing she'd ever seen before. And it was *not* her mother.

Brave turned to say something to one of the footmen, and Rachel's gaze went back to the woman on the floor. She didn't want to look, but she couldn't help herself.

Something awful had happened to this woman. She must have been in a horrible accident. No one human could possibly be capable of such evil. No one could possibly inflict so much pain, so much . . . *damage* upon another person.

Perhaps her carriage had overturned, and she had been thrown from it. That would explain all the blood and bruises and the dirt on her clothes. That's what had to have happened because Rachel couldn't think of any other explanation— *wouldn't* think of any other explanation. And somewhere this woman's family was waiting for her to return. They would be so worried.

Rachel turned to tell Brave that they should contact the woman's family when something brushed her knee. She froze, cold stabbing through her veins like shards of ice. It shivered up her spine, along the back of her neck to dance along her scalp.

Don't look down. Don't look down.

She looked. A dirty and bloodstained hand rested heavily on her leg. The woman had put it there.

"R-Rach . . . el."

She knew that voice. It was her mother's voice and it was coming out of this . . . this thing! And then realization came crashing down around her, hot and stifling as it broke through the layer of denial she'd built in her head.

Blackness swam before her eyes. Bile rose in her throat as she jerked away from the bloody fingers. She looked up to see Brave and the servants staring at her. Brave spoke, but she couldn't hear him above the roaring in her ears. He reached for her, and she fell to her side to keep him from touching her. The movement put her face inches away from her mother's.

Her mother.

She just managed to roll to the other side and lift herself up onto her hands and knees before her stomach rejected its contents and heaved them onto the floor.

"Drink this." A tiny splash of liquid spilled over the rim of the glass onto Brave's fingers as he thrust it toward her.

Rachel's red-rimmed gaze narrowed suspiciously as she eyed the snifter in his hand. "What is it?"

They were in his study waiting for Dr. Phelps to finish with Rachel's mother. Rachel sat in one of the chairs near the window. The heavy green-velvet drapes were tied back with gold cord, letting in what was left of the day. The fading afternoon sun cut a bright, unsympathetic slash across her ravaged features.

"It's brandy. It will help calm your nerves." He waited for her to take it.

She didn't. Instead, she fixed him with a gaze that was almost mutinous. "I don't want to be calm. This is not the kind of thing one should be calm about."

"I beg to differ," he replied, not so calm himself. "This is exactly the kind of thing one should deal with in a calm and rational manner. Heightened emotions lead only to rash decisions and more heartbreak." Something he was all too familiar with.

Rachel raised her chin. Her eyes were dark with anger, not at him but at the situation. "I am her daughter. Do you expect me to be *rational* about what that . . . that . . . *animal* did to her?"

"I am your husband," he told her in a matter-of-fact tone. "I imagine I shall expect a lot of you over the next forty years. Right now, I expect you to drink this." This time, he seized one of her hands in his and forcibly wrapped her fingers around the bowl.

She held it stiffly, but didn't drop it to the carpet as some women he knew would have. Rachel was willful, but not spoiled.

Miranda would have dropped it.

The comparison gave Brave a bit of a jolt. He supposed given the fact that he'd decided to help Rachel because of the mistake he made with Miranda that it was normal to compare the two women. The fact that the comparison had been unfavorable to Miranda came as a bit of a surprise.

Miranda had faults, this he knew, but he'd always overlooked them as a man in love was wont to do. His guilt over her death only intensified his perception of her as an innocent victim in his memory. Now, to hold Miranda up against Rachel and find that memory wanting . . . Well, it wasn't something he was certain he wanted to think about.

Especially when the woman he'd compared Miranda to was being so obstinate. "I don't want to be foxed when Dr. Phelps comes down from examining my mother."

Brave rubbed his eyes with the heels of his hands. His head was beginning to ache. "You don't have to drink the whole thing." He lowered his arms. Blinking to straighten his vision, he turned to her. "Just sip it. Please."

It was the "please" that got to her. He could see it in her face. Raising the glass to her lips, she took a drink. He smiled as she swallowed.

"What?" he asked when he caught her staring.

Rachel shook her head. "Nothing." Another drink. "Do you think she'll be all right?"

He caught his breath, not sure how to respond. He'd seen men beaten as badly as Marion Westhaver that had lived to tell—brag even—about their injuries. But he'd never seen a woman so brutalized before. He didn't know if women were built to recover from such violence as men seemed to be.

Men were by nature the more violent sex, and Rachel's mother was such a tiny little thing.

"Yes," he lied, because he couldn't bear the fear on her face. "I think she'll be fine."

She looked up. Her gaze was bright with hope. So bright that it broke Brave's heart just to look at her.

But it was better than the stark terror he'd seen there when she'd first seen her mother's battered countenance. Her fear had struck deep into his soul, because he knew exactly how she felt. He'd felt the exact same helplessness when he'd pulled Miranda from the pond—that same denial. In his heart he'd known she was dead, but his mind kept screaming over and over that it couldn't be true, that it wasn't her, that there had been some kind of horrible mistake.

At least Rachel still had hope that her mother would recover. He hadn't been given that. Miranda was dead when he found her. She'd been dressed in the same clothes she'd worn to visit him. Which meant that she'd killed herself immediately after his rejection.

"It's all my fault."

His head snapped up at the sound of her voice echoing the thoughts in his head. "I beg your pardon?"

Her mouth trembled as her gaze met his. "It's all my fault that he—" Her voice broke. "That she's hurt."

"Rachel—"

"I'm to blame for it all."

An expert in self-punishment, Brave couldn't see how she could possibly blame herself for her mother's injuries—or for anything for that matter. Ever since she'd walked into his life, she'd done nothing but plan to free her mother from Sir Henry's cruelty. She was the last person who could claim responsibility for any of this.

"You're not to blame for any of it." It came out harsher than he intended.

She laughed—a hard sound that made him wince. She

took a long swallow of the brandy and Brave regretted giving it to her. He hoped to calm her with it. Now he realized she wanted the numbness it would bring. She wanted a respite from the guilt that threatened to consume her.

But at least that was a mistake that he could fix.

He snatched the brandy from her hands before she could take another drink. He was tempted to finish the remainder of it himself, but he walked over to the mahogany mantel and placed the snifter there, far from her reach. And his own.

"If I'm not to blame, then who is?" She demanded as he walked toward her.

He paused for a moment in mock contemplation. "Oh, I don't know. Sir Henry, perhaps?" He didn't like this self-deprecating talk coming from her. Rachel was a doer. She didn't wallow or waste time lamenting the past.

Not like he did.

But that was different. He truly was to blame for Miranda's death. The only thing Rachel was guilty of was trying too hard.

She laughed again. It sounded more like a sob.

"Oh no. You can't put all the blame on Sir Henry. My mother knew what he was when she married him. Of course she had no idea just how bad he could be, but she knew." Her eyes brightened with tears. "And you can't blame my mother, because she didn't have a choice but to marry him."

Brave raised a brow at that, but wisely said nothing.

"But—" A tear slid down her cheek and she wiped it away with her sleeve. "You can blame me because if it hadn't been for me, she would have had a choice. She wouldn't have had to marry him just to put a roof over my head. She married him because she wanted to provide for me!" Her face crumpled. "And look what it got her in return!"

She buried her face in her hands as great sobs wracked her shoulders. Despite this being the second time in their short marriage that Brave had seen his wife burst into tears, he couldn't help but feel that this was not something she did often.

Years of watching her mother be horribly abused had taken their toll on her. The guilt and helplessness were becoming too much for her to carry. Again, he understood how she felt, except he hadn't allowed himself the pleasure of weeping. Instead, he'd allowed Phelps to poke him, bleed him, douse him with ice water until he was too tired to do anything but sleep.

Crossing the short expanse of space between them, Brave knelt on the wine-and-green carpet. Carefully, he pried her fingers from her face.

"Rachel, how old were you when your father died? Thirteen?"

"Fourteen," she said with a sniff, as he wiped her tears away with the pads of his thumbs.

"And was there anything you could have done to help support yourself and your mother?"

She stared at him, her tears giving way to bewilderment. "What do you mean?"

"Could you have gone to work at a seamstress shop or become a lady's maid?"

Frowning, Rachel shook her head. "I didn't know how to do anything."

Brave heard the guilt creeping back into her voice, but he continued anyway. "You were a gently raised young girl. The only labor that was expected of you was learning how to run a household. If you had been older or raised differently, you might have been able to do something to prevent your mother having to marry Westhaver, but you couldn't. And your mother wouldn't have wanted you to even if you could. She *chose* to marry so you would have a chance to maintain the kind of life to which you were accustomed. She did it *for* you, not because of you."

"It's the same thing," she insisted, her eyes filling again.

"If it hadn't been for me, she wouldn't have had to make that choice!"

She tried to push his hands away from her face but he held fast. "It was her choice!" he cried, tilting her head so she was forced to meet his gaze. "And she chose what she thought was the best course of action."

"But—"

Lord, but she was infuriating! "Listen to me!" He stared into her eyes, trying to make her see the reason in his. "It is not your fault. You had no control over your mother or Sir Henry."

No more control than you had over Miranda.

It was almost enough to make him fall backwards, but he didn't. Instead, he kept his fingers firmly locked around her head. A hairpin bit into one of his palms. "You were a child, and you cannot be blamed for anything your mother—or anyone else—did. Have you not tried for years to get her to leave? Haven't you planned and plotted for a divorce—a divorce that just a few days ago she told you she might not want?"

She nodded as much as his hold on her would allow.

"Then why—*why*—do you insist upon blaming yourself for the fact that your mother—who for all her sweetness and goodness—was naive enough to believe in a man who has done nothing but hurt her?"

Her eyes widened, and she stared at him as though seeing him for the very first time. Brave didn't blame her. He rather felt the same way. What the devil had gotten into him?

"Other people are to blame." Softening his tone, he traced the curve of her cheekbones with his thumbs. "But not you. Oh, Rachel. You just want to fix and help everyone. Who could possibly blame you?"

God, she broke his heart. It hurt just to look at her and see all that hope in her eyes. She wanted to believe him. She really did. Just like he wanted to believe that she could fix him, too.

Her hands came up to grasp his lapels, and when she pushed her head against the prison of his hands, he let her go, surprised when she lowered her forehead to his.

A tear fell on his nose, followed by another. Wrapping his arms around her waist, Brave pulled her from the chair, so that she dropped to his lap, the skirts of her berry-hued gown frothing around her like a meringue.

She clung to him as though he was the only thing in the world she had left, and he held her as tightly as he dared, frightened by how deeply she touched him.

Another tear slid down his cheek, and as he tasted its salty coolness against his lips, Brave realized that he didn't know if the tear was hers.

Or his.

How much longer was it going to take?

Sighing in frustration, Rachel hugged herself and stared at the door to her mother's room.

As if he hadn't kept them waiting long enough downstairs, Dr. Phelps was now keeping them waiting in the corridor outside her room. Reynolds had knocked on the study door almost twenty minutes ago to tell them that the doctor was almost ready for them.

If this was his idea of "almost," she would hate to experience what the good doctor would consider a long time.

By the time they'd answered the summons, Rachel had regained control of herself. She'd been horrified to see the mess her tears had made not only of her own appearance, but of Brave's as well. But if Brave's mother or any of the servants had noticed the damp patches on her gown or Brave's jacket, or the streaks on their cheeks, they didn't let on. And for that, Rachel was grateful.

She was even more grateful for Brave himself. She wasn't completely certain she believed everything he'd said to her in the study—she couldn't even remember much of it. But she remembered that smile he'd given her—one that had actually reached his eyes. And she remembered how passionate he'd been as he tried to convince her that she was without blame for her mother marrying Sir Henry. And she remembered the way he'd held her as she cried.

Maybe he was right. Maybe she hadn't been completely to blame for her mother's ill-fated marriage. Maybe at the time she had been too young to change things, and maybe her mother had made the decision on her own, but that all changed when Rachel grew into adulthood. And she still couldn't help feeling that there must have been something— anything—she could have done to keep this from happening. Because if there wasn't, then it meant that she might not be able to prevent it from ever happening again.

Brave placed his arm around her shoulders and pulled her against his chest. It was a comforting gesture, and she was more grateful for him than he would ever know. He hadn't tried to force her into conversation. In fact, he'd hardly spoken at all. He'd let her know he was there for her with little more than a concerned glance or a warm touch. It was nice, knowing that she had someone to lean on.

Finally, the door opened, and two maids scurried out. Slowly, Rachel rose to her feet. The shock of the morning had left her knees like jelly, and she had no desire to make even more of a spectacle of herself by collapsing. Casting up her accounts in the foyer had been humiliation enough.

Phelps stepped into the hall and fixed her with a gentle smile.

"How is she?" Brave asked before Rachel could find her voice.

"She's as well as can be expected," the physician replied bluntly. "However, I've determined that none of her injuries should result in permanent damage. I expect her to make a full recovery."

Clutching at Brave's hand, Rachel smiled in relief. He gave her fingers a reassuring squeeze.

"However," Phelps continued, "it could take several weeks before she's up and around. She suffers from bruised ribs and a dislocated shoulder, neither of which is going to be very comfortable for a while. The cuts and bruises will begin to heal and fade in a few days, and you should notice a reduction in the swelling by then as well."

"Can I see her now?" Rachel asked.

Phelps stepped away from the door. "Of course you may. She's been asking for you. She'll be a little groggy. I've given her laudanum for the pain."

Rachel thanked the doctor and made to enter her mother's room, but before she did, she turned back to her husband. Wrapping her arms around his ribs, she hugged him as hard as she was able, absorbing as much of his essence and strength as she could. He tensed in surprise, but didn't try to pull free, even though the doctor and the maids were watching.

"Thank you," she whispered, and before he could reply, released him and darted through the open door.

The sight of her mother's face was less grisly, but no less horrifying than it had been an hour ago. Dr. Phelps and the maids had cleaned away all the blood and dirt, but Rachel could see clearly how much damage had been done.

"Rachel, is that you?" Marion's voice was thin and hoarse.

She closed the door. "Yes, Mama. It's me."

"I can't see you. Come sit beside me."

Her mother couldn't see her because both of her eyes were swollen almost completely shut. It occurred to Rachel that Sir Henry often blackened her mother's eyes so that they swelled in such a manner, as though he didn't want to look her in the eye while he beat her—or after.

Rachel eased herself onto the bed, taking care not to jostle the mattress too much. She couldn't tear her gaze away from her mother's face. The sight would break the hardest of hearts, and Rachel had no doubt that the next time she looked upon those hideous shades of red and purple she would sob like an infant. She was much too angry, too cold inside to do anything but study them dispassionately. She wanted to memorize every swollen inch so she could paint the picture perfectly for those men who would decide whether or not her mother deserved to be free of her husband.

In fact, drawing a picture might be the best course of action. If she sketched her mother as she looked right now, certainly there would be no way anyone could side against her.

Her mother reached out a hand. Rachel took it. There was blood beneath her fingernails. Her other hand was clean, save for a little dirt around the pads of her fingers.

"Are you in much pain?"

"Dr. Phelps gave me a tonic for it. He wouldn't leave until I'd taken some of it."

"Good."

Her mother squeezed her fingers. "Don't worry yourself. Giving birth to you hurt more than this."

Rachel's heart swelled at her mother's attempt at lightness. "Well, that makes me feel much better, Mama. Thank you." Tears threatened again. She couldn't be as cavalier about this as her mother was. She just couldn't.

Marion's lips twitched in a faint and twisted semblance of a smile. How could she possibly find anything to smile about?

"I meant that it's not so bad. The tonic seems to be helping. Besides, physical pain eventually fades."

But what about the deeper scars? Would her mother ever recover from Sir Henry's brutality emotionally? Would she ever regain her strength and independence?

"Tell me what happened." Her voice was hollow in her

own ears, as though she was listening to herself through the end of a long tunnel.

"Why?"

"Because I want to be able to write it down for when we petition for a divorce."

Even such a simple gesture as moistening her lips looked painful when her mother did it. "Do you really think he can protect me from Henry?"

Rachel didn't know what Brave would or wouldn't be able to do, but there was no way in hell that Sir Henry was ever going to touch her mother again.

"You'll be safe," she promised.

Sighing, Marion winced and laid her other hand across her ribs. "I'm so sorry, dearest."

"Sorry? For what?"

"For not listening to you in the first place. You knew his character better than I did, and I should have known, but I so foolishly wanted to believe . . ."

"Of course you did," Rachel replied without censure. She reached out to stroke her mother's hair. Dried blood was caked between the fine strands. She withdrew her hand.

"Tell me what happened, Mama. Don't leave anything out."

Marion drew a shallow breath. "Everything was perfect until this morning when I received your invitation to tea. When I told Henry that I planned on visiting you he forbade me to leave the house. When I protested he hit me, and—" her voice broke.

Rachel remained frozen in furious silence as she waited for her mother to continue.

"And when I tried to fight back he went insane. I lost consciousness, and I assume that's when he stopped."

"Then what did you do," Rachel prodded gently, carefully keeping her anger from her voice. She felt sick.

"I left the house and started walking for here. I fell in one of the fields and couldn't get back up. I dragged myself for what felt like forever until one of Braven's tenants found me and brought me to you."

A huge, hard lump gathered in Rachel's throat. How could she have ever thought this woman weak? Naive perhaps, but no one who could stand up to someone more than twice her size and drag herself across the ground on injured ribs could ever be mistaken for weak.

She blinked back tears. "You did the right thing, Mama."

A few seconds passed before her mother spoke again. "Rachel, I think Dr. Phelps's tonic is starting to take effect. Would you mind if I rested for a bit?"

"Of course not." She leaned down and kissed her mother lightly on the forehead. "I'll check in on you later."

"All right. Don't let Henry take me home."

"Never," Rachel vowed, her jaw clenched so hard her shoulders trembled with tension.

Silence. She was already asleep.

Rising to her feet, Rachel thought about her mother's last words. Sir Henry would come looking for her, of that there was no doubt, and while she had little doubt that Brave could deal with him, what happened when he returned with the law? Would they allow him to take her mother back to Tullywood?

Surely no one could be so cruel and heartless.

Her gaze went to her mother's face. There was firsthand evidence of just how heartless and cruel some people could be.

She knew what she had to do.

Leaving her mother's room, Rachel was relieved to find the corridor empty. She didn't want to have to deal with Brave just then. The less he knew the better.

She hurried down the stairs, holding her skirts up with one hand while the other held the banister for support. The trembling in her legs still hadn't completely ceased.

Reynolds was at the bottom, watching her with a worried gaze. "Might I inquire after your mother, Lady Braven?"

"She's resting now, Reynolds. Thank you for your concern."

The diminutive butler looked so relieved that Rachel was touched by it.

"Where is my husband?"

"He's in his study with Dr. Phelps and the dowager countess, my lady. He asks for you to join him there."

Rachel thanked him and turned down the hall toward the study, but instead of continuing all the way down, she went into the library instead. Once inside, she went to the desk and opened the bottom drawer on the right side and withdrew a polished mahogany box.

The pistols were a few years old, but she'd seen Reynolds cleaning them just the other day and knew they were in fine working order. Balls and powder were also in the box, and she loaded one of the pistols before putting the other and the box back in its drawer.

With her weapon hidden in her skirts, she stuck her head out of the library door. The coast was clear.

All she had to do was get to the stables and ride to Tullywood.

And then she was going to kill her stepfather.

"Hello, Potts. Is Sir Henry here?" Keeping her tone deceptively light, Rachel slipped past the portly butler to enter Tullywood's front hall.

"I don't know," was his only reply.

"You don't know?" Scowling, she whirled around to face the man who had always been more friend than servant. "Did he go out? Is he in the house?"

"I have no idea where he is, Lady Braven," the elderly man replied as he slipped into a brown-wool overcoat. "And you may rest assured that I don't care if I ever see the blackguard again."

Rachel was taken aback. Potts, for all his loyalty to her and her mother, had never spoken disrespectfully of Sir

Henry. It was then, as her anger toward her stepfather eased somewhat that she noticed the satchels at his feet.

"Potts, whose bags are those?"

Plunking a worn hat on his head, Potts peered down at the luggage. "They're mine, my lady. I'm leaving."

Rachel couldn't believe her ears. "Leaving?"

Potts nodded, a sharp jerk of his snowy head. "When I heard what he did to dear Lady Marion, I realized I could not countenance another moment under this roof. I'm staying with my daughter until I can find another position." He picked up both valises. "I should like to call upon your mother in a day or two if that is agreeable to you."

"Of course it is. I shall speak to Lord Braven about a position for you—if you would like." She'd have to make sure Potts wouldn't be a painful reminder of Sir Henry's cruelty to her mother first, however.

"You're too kind, my lady." He bowed and turned to leave.

"You're not even going to ask what I'm doing here, are you, Potts?" Rachel called.

The aging servant looked over his shoulder. "Lady Braven, you can burn this place and its master to the ground for all I care." And with that, he was gone.

Rachel searched the upper floors first, pistol clutched at her side. Nothing.

The downstairs rooms were next. Her frustration mounted as she went through them one by one. Her stepfather was nowhere to be found.

She paused outside the library. If Sir Henry was anywhere in the house, this was going to be it. It was his favorite room, even though he had the literary appreciation of a goat.

The door swung open silently, hitting the wall with a gentle thud.

She peered inside to find Sir Henry staring at her.

"Damn." She was disappointed, even if a part of her was

secretly glad that it was only a portrait watching her and not the man himself.

Where was he? She couldn't kill him if he wasn't there.

Who was she trying to fool? She couldn't kill him anyway. She'd known when she left Wyck's End that she wouldn't be able to pull the trigger, just as she'd known that her stepfather was unlikely to be at home. He was no doubt out hunting with Charlton or one of his other cronies.

In fact, she would have been more alarmed to find him at home. What would she have done then? She very well could have ended up with blood on her hands if they'd argued, or if he'd attacked her like he had her mother. Or worse yet, Sir Henry could have turned her own weapon against her and killed her. No one at Wyck's End knew where she was. Only Potts had seen her—one or two of the other servants might have, but she doubted any of them would turn against their master.

She'd just wanted to feel in control of the situation. And maybe a small part of her had hoped to frighten Sir Henry into staying away from her mother. She hadn't thought of how easily the tables could turn against her. And she certainly hadn't thought of what the consequences might be if she actually killed him.

Aghast at her own foolishness, Rachel shoved the pistol into her cloak and left the house. She rode fast back to Wyck's End, a mixture of fear and relief making her reckless. She had scared herself by acting as she had. She'd let her anger get the better of her, and by doing so she could have made herself a murderer. Not that anyone in a twenty-mile radius would miss Sir Henry if she had killed him, but she would have lowered herself to a level beneath even Sir Henry himself, and she could have done it easily. That's what was so frightening.

Thank God she hadn't been at Tullywood when Sir Henry had hurt her mother. No doubt one of them—either she or her stepfather—would be dead.

"Idiot!" she cried, unable to keep it inside.

Stone-faced and stiff with anger, Rachel left her horse with a bewildered groom and stomped to the house, cursing herself every step of the way.

She was contemplating her stupidity for what felt like the thirteenth time when she entered the library to replace the pistol. What she saw as she opened the door, pistol in hand, made her halt in mid-stride and begin on contemplation number fourteen.

Brave stood at the desk, the pistol box in his hands and a thunderous expression on his face. Rachel had never seen a more intimidating sight. His gaze went to the gun in her hand. Rachel watched in frozen awe as his face darkened even more.

"Just where the hell have you been?"

Chapter 13

Brave had known who had stolen the pistol the minute he discovered it missing. His heart still froze when he saw the weapon in Rachel's hand. He prayed she hadn't done anything stupid.

"Well?" He sounded so calm, not like he felt at all. "Where have you been?"

Closing the door behind her, Rachel came into the room and toward him. She laid the pistol on the gleaming surface of his desk and stared at it a moment before raising her gaze to his. "I went to Tullywood to kill Sir Henry, but he wasn't there."

Thank God. What the hell had she been thinking? "So the pistol is still loaded then?"

"Unfortunately, yes."

Whether she was disappointed or disgusted, Brave couldn't tell. He wasn't certain of his own feelings either. He'd been so scared and angry when he found the pistol missing and realized who had taken it. Scared that she might

actually use it, and mad as hell that she hadn't trusted him
enough to come to him.

And furious that she'd put herself in that kind of danger—
angry that she would have tossed their marriage aside so easily
for the sake of putting a lead ball through her stepfather's skull.

"Just what had you planned to do if he had been home,
Rachel?" He couldn't keep the anger from his voice. "Did
you plan to frighten him a bit? Intimidate him? Or could you
have actually pulled the trigger? Could you have killed him
in cold blood?"

She shook her head as though she didn't understand his
questions or his rage. "I don't know. I had to do something—"

"Had to? Or wanted to?"

Scowling, she stared at him. She obviously hadn't expected him to question her motives. "*Had* to."

"What do you suppose will happen when Sir Henry learns
you were there?"

Rachel's delicate features hardened. "If he comes near me
or my mother again, I'll kill him."

He didn't know whether to strangle her for being so foolish or kiss her for being so brave. "And then what will happen to your mother?"

Her scowl deepened. "She'll be free of that bastard."

"Yes, she will. And she'll watch you hang for it. Is that
what you want?"

She didn't reply. She didn't need to.

"Didn't think that far ahead, did you?" Folding his arms
across his chest, he moved toward her. "I'm starting to realize, Rachel, that you tend to act before you think." He kept his
tone light to soften his words. "Someday you're going to do
something rash that you won't be able to walk away from."

Like their marriage perhaps? If either of them managed to
survive it unscathed, Brave would be amazed. He knew himself well enough to realize half his anger was because he
cared what happened to her. He cared about her.

"I'm sorry," she said softly.

Leaning his hip against the edge of the desk, Brave regarded the top of her bowed head with a slight smile. "You don't have anything to apologize to me for."

Their gazes locked. "Yes I do. I should have come to you, but I didn't. I let my emotions rule me, and I could have made an awful, awful mistake." She looked away. "It's hard for me to depend on someone else."

How much had it cost her to make such a confession? She was a very proud woman, and he didn't doubt that pride was pretty bruised at that moment.

"I understand."

"He did it because I'd invited her for tea. He didn't want her to come."

A sharp pain pierced Brave's chest at the tortured expression on her face. He knew what it was like to blame oneself for another's actions.

"It's not your fault."

She glanced at the floor. "If Sir Henry brings the law after me—"

"For going to his house? I doubt he will. He'd risk exposing what he did to your mother. Unless he's feeling fairly cocky, he's more likely to retaliate on his own—if anyone even tells him you were there."

Rachel lifted her chin. It quivered. "I'll deal with him."

Brave didn't know whether to yell at her or laugh, so he did both. "Oh no you won't! *I'll* deal with your stepfather if he comes to call. That way he might actually survive the visit. Meanwhile, I'll send a letter off to my solicitor. Your mother's unfortunate condition has given us the evidence we need against Sir Henry."

She stared at him. Something in her eyes stirred his blood and other body parts.

Rising to her feet, she stepped toward him. Brave's heart accelerated.

"You've done so much for us. Why?"

"Because I couldn't live with myself knowing I could have helped you and didn't," he replied honestly.

"Most people wouldn't have cared."

Held by the darkness of her gaze, Brave was powerless to resist. "I care."

"Yes," she replied, searching his face for God only knew what. "I believe that you do."

"What are you doing?" he asked when her close scrutiny continued.

She smiled. "I'm looking for a clue as to why you, of all people, should care what happens to me or my mother. Why should you care about two people you hardly know?"

He should tell her about Miranda. He should confess to wanting to allay his guilty conscience, but those weren't the words that leapt to his lips.

"I care," he told her, his voice hoarse, "because one of them is you."

Her eyes widened. He watched as surprise blossomed in the lavender-blue depths. Before she could speak, he reached out and seized her by the hips, hauling her against him. She stumbled, knocking him back so that he was pinned between her and the desk.

He kissed her, pouring all of his fear and leftover anger into his desire for her. The kiss was hard, his lips and tongue insistent as they forced her mouth open under his. Her fingers clutched the lapels of his coat as she yielded to his embrace. A burst of longing exploded low in Brave's stomach as she pressed herself against him, her sweet, moist tongue tentatively stroking his.

It was terrifying, this excitement he felt when they touched. His need for her was almost unbearable, yet he cherished the ache. There was something precious that he couldn't identify in the way he wanted her, as though it wasn't just the union of their bodies he longed for, but their souls as well. He wanted to be a part of her as she was becoming a part of him.

He slid one hand up the generous curve of her hip, to the gentle indent of her waist, spreading his fingers wide as they met the swell of her ribs. He could feel her heart pounding beneath her ribs, its rhythm increasing as his palm came up to cup her breast. Warm and heavy in his hand, he thrilled at the feel of it, his erection throbbing in response as her nipple hardened with his touch.

Rachel made a low, moaning sound deep in her throat as he traced the outline of her nipple with the tip of his thumb. Her hips shifted against his with an uncertainty that was more arousing than anything Brave had ever experienced before that moment. His other hand flattened against the small of her back, pressing her deep into the V of his legs.

He couldn't take away what Sir Henry had done to her mother. He couldn't snap his fingers and make everything better, no matter how badly he might wish it. And he certainly wasn't about to take advantage of her emotional state by seducing her when she was in such turmoil, no matter how much his throbbing flesh insisted he do so. He wanted her to give herself to him because she wanted and needed *him*, not because she needed something—anything—to quell the storm brewing within her.

But he could help alleviate the tempest.

Still holding her, he pushed away from the desk and walked them both to one of the chairs. Without breaking their kiss, Brave lifted her in his arms as he sat, settling her in his lap so that their torsos were touching and her legs dangled over one armrest.

His hand went back to her breast. Tugging on the neck of her gown, he pulled until one pale globe was free. Then, tearing his mouth free of hers, he lowered his lips to the hard, pink bud that tightened even further with just the touch of his breath. Drawing it into his mouth, he laved it with his tongue, and then with deliberate pressure, he closed his lips around it and sucked. Rachel gasped above him, her hands coming up to press his head against her chest.

Body humming with the force of his lust, Brave shoved his hand under her skirts as he tongued her nipple. Shoving the layers of fabric aside, he slid his fingers up the silky stocking covering her calf, past a garter, along the drawers that covered her thighs, to the slit between. The thin lawn was warm and damp with her juices. His body tightened with the evidence of her desire, and he groaned as she lifted her hips to his touch.

Nipping her lightly with his teeth, he slipped his hand inside the delicate underclothing, brushing his fingers along the springy curls beneath. Rachel gasped, her pelvis jerking against the contact. So hot, so sensitive, the barest touch made her body flush with heat and increased the moisture that greeted his questing fingers.

God, but he wanted to be inside her! Wanted to drive himself into her until the world became nothing but a maelstrom of color and sensation. No woman had ever driven him so close to losing control. No woman had ever made him want to lose it.

He slid his fingers along those curls, easing them into the warm, wet cleft. A more patient man would have slipped a finger inside her and stoked the fire within her. A more patient man would cherish taking his time, but Brave was far from patient, and he wanted to make Rachel scream. Now.

He found the source of her torment with the pad of his thumb. Stroking the hooded nub, his cock pulsated his response when Rachel cried out, shoving herself against his hand. Relentlessly, he worked her sensitive flesh with a rhythm that was neither fast nor slow, hard nor soft, but demanding and insistent. Feeling her thighs tremble as they clamped around his wrist, he pulled his mouth free of her breast and leaned back against the chair so he could watch her face.

She gripped the top of the chair with one hand, the other arm was bent behind her, her palm braced against his knee, lifting her weight as she rode his hand. Her head was tossed back, her face contorting in mounting pleasure. Her chest was thrust forward, her bare breast just inches from his face. Increasing the movement of his hand, he flicked her nipple with his tongue just so he could watch the sensation furrow her brow.

"That's it," he urged as the jerking of her hips became more frantic. "Let it go."

Sweat beaded on Brave's upper lip. The need for her release was almost as sharp as the need for his own. He matched the tempo of her hips with his thumb, and when her cries became more and more urgent, he increased the pressure.

Her body went as taut as a bow as the first spasms hit. A high, keening cry broke forth from her parted lips as her hips gave one final thrust against his hand. And Brave pressed his face against her breast and concentrated on not humiliating himself by coming with her.

She collapsed on his lap in a limp heap. The swell of one buttock pressed hard against his groin. Gritting his teeth, he shifted in the chair to ease the pressure. She was his for the asking. He could take her right there and she wouldn't offer any discouragement, but that wasn't the way he wanted it. If anything, this experience had taught him just how much he wanted her to come to him. He wanted her desire to match his, wanted her to give herself to him because she couldn't stand to be without him another minute.

He didn't care what it meant, didn't want to consider a deeper meaning. It was just the way it had to be. And if he had to put her pleasure before his, had to make her explode with his fingers and tongue every day for the next six months before her surrender was complete, then so be it.

Although he prayed to God it wouldn't take six months to seduce her. He didn't know how many more episodes like this he could endure.

He straightened her skirts and her bodice. "Are you all right?" he asked, rolling her body toward his so he could see her face. She was quiet. Too quiet.

Tears trickled down her cheeks as she nodded. "I . . . it . . ." She pressed a hand to her mouth as the tears increased. "I'm not sure what's wrong with me."

Brave was. The physical release of her climax had brought forth a need for emotional release as well. One of her worst nightmares had come true that day, and it was too much for her to bear. It would be too much for anyone to bear alone.

"It's going to be all right," he whispered, guiding her head to his shoulder. He pressed his lips against her forehead as she began to sob. "I promise he'll never touch you or your mother again."

He held her like that until the sobs stopped and the tears had soaked through to his skin. He held her until her sniffles disappeared and her breathing fell into the shallow rhythm of the exhausted.

And then he carried her up to her room and put her to bed, sitting with her until he was certain she wasn't going to wake anytime soon.

Planting a brief, firm kiss on her brow, Brave rose from his seat on the mattress and crept to the door. There was a strange lightness inside him even though he felt the weight of responsibility lying heavily upon his shoulders. Suddenly, Rachel's problems were much more important than his own. Her fight was now his fight. He'd do anything to make her feel safe and happy again.

And God help anyone who got in his way.

Rachel didn't wake until early the next morning, feeling more rested and relaxed than she had in a long time. She didn't have to wonder why. The answer was there in the stretched neck of her gown and the slight tenderness around the nipple on her left breast. Brave had done this. He had taken the weight of the world off her shoulders and replaced it with a sensual awareness she'd never known existed. He'd taken her fear and anxiety and replaced it with strength and a burgeoning sense of trust.

As she stared out the window at the rising sun, things seemed much clearer to her. She'd been an idiot to go off after Sir Henry as she had. She knew that. She also knew that despite her stupidity, Brave still wanted to help her. He cared about her, and that was more than she ever dared to expect.

It was probably too much to ask then, that none of the servants would mention her visit to her stepfather. No doubt there were some who would be all too happy to tell him she'd searched the house for him like a madwoman, either in hopes of intimidating him or earning his gratitude. She could only hope that Brave was right when he said he didn't think Sir Henry would risk exposing himself by bringing the law after her, but if he did, then Rachel would face it just like she faced everything else. She'd do whatever she could to get out of it, but if she had to pay for her actions, then she'd make certain Sir Henry paid for his as well.

Yawning, she stretched her legs out in front of her and sat up. The fire in the hearth was low and she shivered as the chilly morning air seeped through her clothes. Pulling a coverlet around her shoulders to ward off the cold, she leapt out of bed and ran across the carpet to pull the bell for Meg, the abigail Brave had hired for her.

She needed a bath. After she dressed, she'd go down to breakfast and ask Brave—how she was going to face him, she wasn't sure—if Dr. Phelps would be coming by to check on her mother that morning. Rachel had a few questions she wanted to ask him.

A few minutes later Meg arrived, looking far more chipper than anyone had a right to first thing in the morning. And shortly after that, there was a steaming tub waiting for Rachel in front of a blazing fire in the dressing room adjoining her chamber.

Rachel's stomach growled as Meg brushed her hair. She'd missed dinner the night before and was surprisingly hungry. She wondered if she had Brave to thank for that as well. He'd certainly awakened a hunger within her, but she wasn't sure it was for food.

Blushing, she met the maid's questioning gaze as she rose to her feet and allowed her to unfasten the back of her gown.

"Meg, would you be so good as to bring me a cup of chocolate when you have a moment? I should like to drink it in the bath."

"Certainly, my lady," the young woman replied with a curtsy as she left the room.

Alone in the quiet warmth of the dressing room, Rachel stepped naked into the tub, sighing as the hot, fragrant water closed around her.

Stretching her legs out as far as they would go, she leaned back against the warmed copper and closed her eyes in relaxed bliss. She was up to her neck in hot, soapy water and dangerously close to falling asleep again when a knock sounded on the dressing-room door.

"Come in," she called. Then when the door opened, "Just put it on the table beside the tub, Meg, thank you."

"Put what on the table?"

Rachel jumped at the sound of Brave's voice, sloshing water over the sides of the tub. Instinctively, her arms crossed her chest.

"Brave, what are you doing here?"

His footsteps were heavy behind her, each slow, deliberate stride bringing him closer and closer. Her nipples tightened. Traitors.

"I came up to tell you that Phelps sent word that he will be coming to look in on your mother later this morning, but now that I'm here—" The footsteps stopped. She felt his breath hot against her neck. "I would be remiss in my husbandly duties if I didn't wash your back."

Rachel shivered. The tremors raised gooseflesh on her arms and shoulders and spiraled down to her breasts and between her legs. How did he do this to her without so much as a touch?

He moved around to the front of the tub like a tomcat stalking a mouse. When he turned to look at her, Rachel knew she was that mouse.

She kept her gaze glued to him as he removed his coat. He tossed the dark green superfine onto a nearby chaise. His amber waistcoat followed. The linen of his shirt pulled across his incredibly wide shoulders as he rolled up his sleeves. His forearms were long and well-defined, the muscles clear beneath the dusting of golden hair.

He came toward her, dropping to one knee beside the tub. Not seeming to be able to find her voice, Rachel stared at him, her heart pounding wildly against her ribs.

Brave took the washcloth from the side of the tub. "Where's the soap?"

In her left hand. In order to give it to him, she was going to have to take her arm away from her breasts, revealing more of herself to him.

What difference did it make? He'd already seen her breasts. He'd kissed them, for heaven's sake! Yet, the fact that she was naked while he was fully clothed made her feel infinitely more vulnerable than she had on any other occasion.

She handed him the soap. As if sensing her hesitancy, Brave kept his gaze locked with hers, never once glancing at her breasts. How did he always know just what to do?

"Lean forward."

She did, hugging her knees to her chest. "You don't have to do this."

"But I want to," he replied, a mischievous twinkle in his eyes as he soaped the cloth until it foamed with lather. "Besides, when was the last time you had someone scrub your back?"

Longer than she cared to admit. Her mother had done it for her a few months ago when she was sick, but other than that, she always had to stretch and strain to do it herself.

And, of course, it had a completely different effect on her when her husband did it.

The cloth was cool as Brave slapped it against her skin, but it felt so good as he rubbed it along her back that Rachel didn't care.

"Mmm." Every stroke just served to relax her even more. If he didn't stop soon, she really was going to fall asleep.

He rinsed the soap away with handfuls of hot water. "All done." His lips brushed her shoulder, nipped at her neck. "Want me to do your front as well?"

"Meg will be back soon . . ." The protest died on her lips as he slid one hand beneath the water to cup her breast. He gave her nipple a light pinch. She gasped.

"I spent the entire night thinking about you." His voice was low against her ear as his fingers toyed with her tightened flesh. "I couldn't stop thinking about touching you, feeling you respond to me."

Like she was responding to him now. One touch and some seductive words and a familiar throbbing started between her legs. This was madness. It had to be wrong. Nothing that felt so good could possibly be right.

"I keep picturing you with your head thrown back, moaning as you came." He moved his hand to her other breast, teasing the nipple until it puckered almost painfully. "I've never seen anything so beautiful."

"You shouldn't say such things." Even as she spoke, shivers of desire shook her. His words excited her, aroused her, and she wanted him to make her feel like he had the day before. She craved that head-spinning pleasure. It would be so easy just to lean back and let him do whatever he wanted to her.

"I want to touch you all over," he continued, as if he hadn't heard her pathetic admonishment. "I want to explore every part of you." His lips brushed her jaw. "And then I want to put my mouth everywhere my hands have been."

Rachel's eyes flew open. "Everywhere?" Surely not . . .

"Everywhere." She could feel his smile against her cheek. "What I can do with my fingers I can do even better with my tongue."

It was on the tip of *her* tongue to invite him into the tub to test that theory her when another knock came, this time from her bedroom.

"It's Meg!" she whispered. "You have to get out!"

He jumped to his feet and snatched up his discarded clothing. "We'll finish this later," he promised with a hard kiss on the lips and a saucy grin. "Too bad Phelps is coming by, or I'd just wait for you in my chamber."

He was going to leave her there, frustrated and wanting. Unless she told him otherwise, he wasn't going to do anything to relieve the ache between her legs or the straining bulge in the front of his trousers. He was keeping his word that the actual consummation of their marriage would be up to her. His last remark was just a reminder that she would have to go to him.

He'd torture her, tease her, but he wasn't going to give her what they both wanted. It would be very easy for her to hate him at that moment if she didn't want him so badly.

"Get out," she muttered, completely petulant and not caring if he noticed.

He chuckled—a joyous sound that both thrilled and angered her. He was absolutely breathtaking when he laughed. She just wished it wasn't at her blasted expense!

"Don't keep me waiting too long, Rachel. I'm anxious to hear you scream again."

She flushed right to the roots of her hair.

Chuckling, Brave slipped back through the connecting door to his room just as Rachel called for Meg to enter. If the maid wondered why her mistress had such a scowl on her face sitting alone in her bath, she had the good sense not to ask.

"Your mother is an incredible woman."

Rachel smiled at Dr. Phelps as they descended the stairs side by side. "I know. Thank you so much for taking care of her, Dr. Phelps. I should never have been able to do it on my own."

"You don't need to thank me, Lady Braven. I'm glad to be of service. It's been a long time since I've had to deal with physical injuries like your mother's. I hope never to have to see the like again." The doctor's tone was somber.

"I hope you never have to again either, Dr. Phelps," Rachel replied, as they stepped off of the stairs and rounded the corner toward Brave's study. "Nevertheless, I do appreciate your taking time away from your busy practice to come here."

Dr. Phelps stopped. "You know about my practice?"

"Er, yes." Rachel was a little confused. Why would he sound so surprised. Weren't all physicians kept fairly busy? "Lady Braven told me you tended to the earl." The late earl, she meant to say, but of course Dr. Phelps would know that.

"She did?" The doctor began walking again.

"Yes." Again, she didn't understand why he seemed so surprised. "Do the majority of your patients come to you or do you spend your days visiting patients at their homes?"

Dr. Phelps still seemed quite nonplussed. "Both actually. And of course, there are my extended-care patients, who often stay at the house with me."

What an inventive idea! Patients would be able to receive round-the-clock medical care. Dr. Phelps must love his work very much to devote so much time to it.

"You're a good man, Dr. Phelps," Rachel said, as they entered the study.

"Thank you, Lady Braven. I must confess I'm a little surprised. Ladies of your station don't normally express much of an interest in medicine of the mind, but I suppose given your circumstances . . ."

Circumstances? What the devil was he talking about? "Medicine of the mind?"

Phelps's pale cheeks flushed. "I beg your pardon. I should explain. I use the term to describe anyone with some kind of sickness of the mind, be it delusions or an irrational fear, or simple brain fever. Of course, as you know, Lord Braven's condition is neither."

"Of course not," Rachel replied, her voice hollow. Brave's condition? This was why he was seeing Phelps, because he was mad?

No, not mad. Sad, solemn and perhaps a little antisocial, but Brave was not mad. There was nothing in this world short of him foaming at the mouth and speaking in tongues that could convince Rachel that her husband was a lunatic.

She should stop him before he told her anything else. She'd wanted to know what was wrong with Brave, but she was certain this was the kind of thing he wouldn't want her knowing—no wonder he'd gotten so upset before. But what if there was something she could do?

"How would you describe Brave's condition, Dr. Phelps?" Keeping her voice even, Rachel closed the door behind them so servants walking past—or Brave himself when he arrived—wouldn't hear.

"Extreme guilt, Lady Braven. His inability to keep Miranda Rexley from committing suicide, despite it being completely out of his control, resulted in a pattern of destructive behavior that eventually gave way to a feeling of responsibility." He smiled. "But I think his marriage to you is putting an end to all that."

"Oh?" Rachel was too stunned to speak. So Miranda Rexley's death did have something to do with his perpetual sadness! She should be pleased that she'd ferreted out the root of Brave's withdrawal, but instead all she could think of was how much he must have loved Julian's sister to cling to her memory like he did.

Before Dr. Phelps could elaborate further, the door opened. Brave stood there with a sly smile on his face.

"Good morning, Phelps. Ah, Lady Braven. I hadn't expected to see you again so soon."

Rachel blushed at the memories and sensations his words conjured. Averting her eyes so he couldn't see the guilt and the desire there, she mumbled something vaguely coherent in reply.

"I'll leave you two gentlemen to your business." Head bowed, she bolted for the door.

"You know where to find me if you need me," Brave called after her.

The sensual promise in his voice sent a shiver down Rachel's spine at the same time her heart lurched in apprehension. She nodded in his direction, and his answering chuckle echoed in her ears.

She closed the door behind her and collapsed against the wall, one hand pressed against her pounding heart. What was she going to do? She had to tell him that she knew. He wouldn't be pleased, but he would be even angrier if she didn't confess, and he found out some other way. Phelps might even mention it to him during their conversation.

Phelps had said he hoped that she might help Brave recover from his guilt. After all Brave had done for her, she was honor-bound, not to mention bound by her feelings, to do the same for him. But first, she had to know the whole story.

She turned down the hall toward her mother-in-law's favorite drawing room, the one in which Brave had offered her his name and protection. She had jumped at his offer, as usual acting without consider the consequences. Still, she didn't regret it. The only regret she had was that Brave hadn't trusted her as wholly as she had trusted him. Perhaps there was still time to fix all that.

Or she could just walk away, mind her own business, and deal with his anger with feigned disinterestedness. Sir Henry would no doubt be coming for her mother soon, and she had to be prepared to face him. She couldn't afford to invest more of herself into this sham of a marriage. If she did, she was in danger of forgetting just how much of a sham it was. If Brave opened his soul to her, there would be no way she could just walk away in the end.

She entered the drawing room. Annabelle looked up from her needlework with a smile that faded when she saw the expression on Rachel's face.

"My dear, Rachel, whatever is the matter?"

Shutting the door, Rachel faced her mother-in-law with an uneasy determination. "I want to know everything about Miranda Rexley. Now."

Chapter 14

❝I have something I'd like for you to take a look at, Lord Braven.❞

Swirling the brandy in his glass, Brave fought the urge to smile. Of course Phelps had something for him to look at! The man never called at Wyck's End without putting him through some new kind of test or procedure. Usually the physician's tenacity annoyed him, but today, Brave was too pleased with how things were going with Rachel to let Phelps get to him.

"What is it?" He asked, reaching out for the papers Phelps offered him.

"Take a look."

I don't believe it." Brave remarked a few moments later as he sifted through the sheets. "What does it mean?"

He was looking at the notes Phelps had taken during their last visit, when they'd discussed Miranda, compared to those he'd taken almost a year earlier.

"It means that Miranda is no longer the problem," Phelps replied. "You are."

Again, Brave read the paper, his gaze freezing on those answers that seemed to jump off the page at him.

"When you think of Miranda now, how do you see her?"

A year ago he'd described her as *"The most beautiful, selfless girl in the world."* A few days ago his response had been, *"Willful, a little spoiled. Pretty."*

"Describe your feelings for her."

"She's the only woman I've ever loved." followed by, *"I suppose I fancied myself in love with her."*

"And how do you feel about the fact that she didn't accept your help, that she didn't love you as you wanted?"

"How do you think I feel?" Brave almost smiled at his own melodramatic response until he read what he'd said during that last session. *"I feel guilt."*

That was it? He'd wanted to die when Miranda killed herself, and now all he could say was that he felt guilty? Had his feelings for her really been so shallow? Or was he just finally seeing things as they really were? Miranda hadn't loved him, and he hadn't truly loved her.

He held up the papers. "It doesn't change the fact that I'm responsible for her death." Nothing could change that.

Phelps gave a decided Gallic shrug. "Doesn't it? I think it does. For reasons only you can know you've clung to the belief that her death was all your fault. You've continued to punish yourself."

Eyeing him suspiciously, Brave frowned. "Because it's my fault."

Phelps stuffed the papers into his satchel and closed it with a decided *click.* "That, my dear boy, is something only you know for certain. I believe if you take a good long, honest look at the situation, you'll eventually see the truth."

"I know what happened, Phelps. I know the truth." Brave sipped his brandy, silently daring the doctor to disagree.

But Phelps only smiled that infuriating smile of his. "I'm sure you do, my lord, but sometimes a new perspective offers up a whole new truth." He hoisted the satchel off the table. "I must tell you that I think confiding in your wife was one of the best courses of action you could have taken."

Brave stilled. His fingers tightened on the snifter until his knuckles were white and his arm shook. Everything around him stopped except for the incessant, thunderous pounding of his heart.

"What do you mean, confiding in my wife? My wife doesn't know anything about this."

Phelps's already pale face whitened even more. "B-but she does. She and I were talking about it when you came in."

Blood roared in Brave's ears. Rachel knew? How the hell had she found out? He'd told her it didn't concern her. He should have known better than to say such a thing to a woman. It was like waving a red flag in front of a bull.

Where was she now? She'd had almost a full hour to digest the information. Was she plotting to leave and take her poor battered mother somewhere safe—somewhere away from her murderer husband? Or perhaps she was waiting just outside the door with a dueling pistol planning to put a bullet through him as she had Sir Henry? Or maybe she was waiting for him to explain things to her before she left him or tried to kill him.

Well, he thought, anger churning inside him, he wasn't about to disappoint her. Not that he probably hadn't already.

"We're done here, Phelps. In fact, I think this might very well be our last appointment. You will of course continue to treat Lady Marion." Regardless of whether or not Rachel wanted to leave him, he wasn't about to allow her to take her poor mother anywhere. Not until she recovered.

Phelps nodded absently, as though he realized it had been an order rather than a question.

"Good." Turning on his heel, Brave stomped to the door. "Pray excuse me, I have business to attend to."

And he had a fairly good idea just where that business would be waiting for him. Rachel wasn't the type to wait on safe ground. She'd march right into the enemy camp and start shooting. She was either incredibly brave or incredibly foolish.

He took the stairs two at a time and ran down the corridor to his chamber. Emotions raged deep within him—fear, anger, relief. Fear of how Rachel would react to the truth. Anger that she hadn't left well enough alone. And relief. Relief that he didn't have to worry about her finding out anymore.

The door to his rooms swung open, hitting the wall with a loud thud.

She was standing by his bed.

The door swung shut behind him. "How long have you known?" There was little point in beating around the bush.

To her credit, she didn't even pretend to misunderstand. "Since I spoke to Dr. Phelps earlier."

That was it? "Phelps was under the impression that you already knew."

Clasping her hands in front of her, Rachel nodded. "Yes. I'm not certain how he made that assumption, but he did seem to think you had already told me."

"And, of course, you didn't bother to correct him." He kept his expression carefully blank. He had to keep his emotions under tight control; otherwise, he was going to unleash a year's worth of repression on her, and that would not be pretty.

Her chin came up a notch. "No. I wanted to know what was wrong with you."

As he moved toward her, Brave held his arms out at his sides. "And what do you think now that you know?" He wanted to hear her tell him she pitied him. It would make his humiliation complete.

"I think I would like to kick you in the buttocks, Lord Braven."

Which was more of a shock, that she wanted to kick him, or her use of his title?

"You want to kick me?"

"Somebody needs to. In fact, someone should have done it a long time ago."

Forget humiliation, Brave was just plain mad. How dare she talk to him like that! He'd gone out of his way to offer his assistance to her and her mother—

"And since everyone seems to think that I can 'cure' you," she said, stepping forward, "I think the pleasure might as well fall to me."

Brave stopped in the middle of the room, his blood cold. How did she know about that? He hadn't told anyone but Gabriel and Julian about his reasons for marrying Rachel.

"How are you supposed to cure me?"

This time she advanced on him. "I'm not quite clear on that myself. I think they believe we're a love match, Brave, or that we will be." There was sadness in her eyes as she gazed at him. "And you know what they say about love. It conquers all."

He didn't know what surprised him more—that she could paraphrase Virgil, or that she she didn't sound like she believed it.

"Maybe it does," he heard himself reply.

She met his gaze squarely. There was nothing but darkness in her eyes. "It didn't help you much where Miranda was concerned, did it?"

The blood rushed from his face as her point hit home. So she didn't just know that he'd been under Phelps's care, she also knew why.

"No." He looked away, unwilling to face whatever condemnation waited in her countenance. "It didn't."

Standing directly before him, only inches of space between their bodies, Rachel reached toward him. Brave braced himself for a slap or a punch—something that would prove just how much he had let her down.

"Belinda told me about her first. I forced your mother to tell me about her this morning." The lightest of caresses brushed his cheek. "Do you want to talk about her?"

Brave jumped at the touch as well as the question. Slowly, he turned his head toward her. "I would have thought you'd know everything, given how many people you've spoken to." He sounded defensive, childish.

"I know that you proposed and were refused. I know she took her own life and I know . . . that you still grieve her."

Grieving. Was that what he was doing? Weren't you supposed to miss the person for that?

Something shriveled inside him. His conscience maybe. He was completely numb except for the burning need to tell her anything she wanted to know. He'd risk her anger and her disappointment if only she wouldn't look at him as though she understood. There was no way in hell she could possibly understand. She didn't have blood on her hands.

"What would you like to know?"

He watched as she walked away from him, toward the bed. His gut tightened with remorse. He couldn't help but feel their relationship was about to change, and he had liked the way it had been going before she found out about Miranda.

"Whatever you'd like to tell me," she replied, seating herself on the bottom corner of the mattress. Her expression was blank. "I confess to having an unnatural curiosity about the woman you would have chosen for your bride."

Meaning he hadn't chosen Rachel herself. Was it possible she was a little jealous? God, she had no reason to be. There was no comparison between her and Miranda.

"She must have been a fascinating woman."

She *was* jealous.

"Not really," he replied, folding his arms across his chest.

"Not really a woman, that is. Miranda always seemed like more of a girl." A very young girl, now that he thought of it, although she and Rachel would have been of an age had Miranda lived.

"But . . . you loved her."

Brave smiled at the confusion in her tone. "Yes, I suppose I did." He crossed the room to the window, his boots silent on the carpet. Staring out at the countryside, Brave watched the rain stream down from the heavens, felt the cold and the damp through the thin layer of glass. It was a fitting day to dredge up the past.

"I've always been a bit of a brooding character," he admitted. It was easy to do so when he didn't have to look at her face. "I suppose I thought it made me more romantic, more appealing to the ladies." He laughed self-consciously.

"I don't remember you like that," came Rachel's voice from far behind him.

He didn't turn. "I never tried to seduce you."

Silence.

"I'd known Miranda for years. I watched her grow into a beautiful young woman, and I wanted her." If he closed his eyes, he could picture her elegant beauty in his head. He kept his eyes open.

"As Julian's sister, she was the perfect candidate for the future Countess Braven. It never occurred to me that she might have different plans." No, the idea of being refused had never crossed his mind. He'd rarely been refused anything in his life; why should the wife he wanted be any different?

"And those were?" Rachel prompted.

Brave started. He hadn't realized he'd fallen silent. "Not to marry me, I can assure you. She refused my proposal without hesitation."

"She was in love with someone else. Belinda said he worked for her father."

He chuckled mockingly. "I should have known that would be one aspect of the story you would be certain to be told." He glanced over his shoulder at the woman on his bed. She waited expectantly for him to continue.

With a bitter smile, Brave turned back to the window. "Miranda had fallen in love with one of the grooms in her father's stables. The blackguard claimed to love her as well. He bedded her and got her with child." He waited for his wife's outraged gasp. There wasn't one.

"When Miranda told him of her condition, he refused to marry her. I think he must have been rather cruel about it because she was in a state of shock when she came running back to me."

"She came back to you?"

Ah, here it was. Closing his eyes, Brave nodded, filled with a perverse sense of satisfaction. No one had told her this part. How could they? No one but Gabriel and Julian knew.

If this little tidbit of information didn't ruin any illusions his wife might have about him, nothing would. And although disillusioning her was the last thing he wanted to do, he couldn't help but want to see her face when he did it. Her reaction would be his validation.

Turning, he rested his shoulder against the window frame. Their gazes locked. "Yes. She came back. She came back and begged me to help her. To marry her. I refused."

Rachel stared at him, her expression still carefully guarded. "And then she killed herself."

Why wasn't she revolted? "Yes. She drowned herself when I refused to marry her. I was angry and hurt, and I wanted to punish her."

Rising from the bed, Rachel skirted around the footboard to move toward him. "And you were so overwhelmed by grief that you almost destroyed yourself until your friends and family urged you to enter into Dr. Phelps's care."

He nodded.

"And you've been burdened by guilt ever since."

What the devil was wrong with her? Hadn't she heard a word he'd said? "Of course I have been. She killed herself because of me."

Shaking her head, Rachel looked away with a rueful smile. "I would have thought you'd be smarter than that."

What the—? Before Brave could open his mouth, she turned her gaze back to him, pinning him with the multitude of emotions there. Anger, sadness, even a glimmer of amusement, but there was no disappointment.

"Does she have anything to do with why you married me?"

Brave froze. He should have known this would follow. Rachel wasn't stupid. "What do you mean?"

Vulnerability, naked and raw shone in her eyes. "You saved me from dying the same way Miranda did. You married me as you wanted to marry her. Am I . . . am I merely a replacement for a woman you couldn't have?"

How could he tell her? How could he tell her that yes, in a way she had been a replacement, but not in the way she thought? He'd married her to right a wrong, not as a substitute for another woman. He couldn't tell her, not and make her understand. Because then he'd have to tell her how she made him feel, how he wanted her, why he wanted her, and these were things he didn't quite understand himself.

"When I offered to marry you, I was sincere in my wish to help you. I wasn't trying to make you into someone else." It wasn't a complete lie. He'd only thought to use her to atone for someone else. And now . . . now, he realized that atoning for Miranda's death paled next to the need to keep Rachel in his life. Yes, he wanted to make amends for the past, but he also wanted to protect Rachel and her mother.

And Rachel made him think of the future. For the first time in a long time, he wanted to go forward. He wanted children, and he wanted Rachel to give them to him.

He opened his mouth, searching for the words to tell her just that. They wouldn't come, and he was left standing there, gaping like an idiot. He closed his mouth.

Rachel looked away, but not before he saw the shimmer of tears in her eyes. She shrugged. "I had to ask. I suppose it's one less thing to kick you for now."

If she'd meant the remark to be funny, Brave didn't take it as such. He was still reeling from her question and his answers to it.

"How can I help you?"

His attention snapped back to her. She was staring at him with an intensity that made him uneasy. "What do you mean?" Help him? She wanted to help him? Didn't she realize how much she'd already done for him?

Of course not, because he couldn't find the words to tell her. He didn't know how to tell her.

Her gaze was guileless as it locked with his. Prying his arms away from his chest, she took one of his hands and placed it on her breast. "You can take your pain out on me if you want. Let me take it away."

Brave could only stare at her. Had he heard her correctly? Was she truly offering to let him pour all the rage and self-pity of the last two years into her virginal body?

It made sense to him when he thought about it. Looking into her eyes only confirmed it. For whatever reasons, Rachel needed to save him just as he had needed to save her. She felt responsible for her mother's marriage to Sir Henry, and for the physical condition her mother was now in. If Brave made love to her now, she would regain some of her control over her life.

Two weeks ago, perhaps even two days ago, he might have taken her up on it, but not now. No, when he and Rachel finally shared a bed there wasn't going to be anyone else in it with them.

Peeling his hand away from the warm temptation of her

breast, Brave cupped both his hands around her shoulders. He wanted to shake her but he didn't.

"There are many emotions I want to 'take out' on you, Rachel. Desire and passion are two that come immediately to mind, but grief and pain are not on the list." He searched her face for any evidence that his words made sense to her.

"When I make love to you—when you give yourself to me—I want it to be because you want me inside you, not because you have some need to martyr your maidenhead. You've draped yourself across enough altars. I don't want to be part of just another sacrifice."

Rachel jerked out of his hold. Angry red splotches stood out on her pale cheeks. Her eyes snapped with indignation. "Is that what you think I'm doing? Sacrificing myself?"

"I know that's what you're doing." And oddly enough the knowledge touched him, because Rachel only made such sacrifices for people she cared about.

She stood before him like a chastised child—a child more sorry for being caught than for the offending action.

"Go see your mother," he commanded softly. "Listen to her when she says that you are not to blame. Come back to me when you're ready to face the fact that you want me for yourself—not to save someone else."

Rachel's jaw tightened. Turning on her heel, she walked stiffly toward the door. Hand on the knob, she turned. "Would you believe Miranda if she told you that you weren't to blame?"

She was gone before Brave could find his voice. It was just as well. He didn't know the answer himself.

"Then what happened?"

Rachel turned away from the window and the relentless rain to stare at her mother's swollen eyelids. Beneath one fringe of lashes, the barest hint of white was visible. Rachel wondered how much her mother could see through that little slit.

"I left and went to my room to think, and then I came here." She didn't tell her mother that once she got to her room she had flung herself on the bed and sobbed for nearly an hour, or that she probably could have gone on for at least one or two more.

And there were certainly some details she left out of her story—like her idiotic offer to take away Brave's pain, and his remark about coming back when she was clear on her reasons for wanting him.

She felt ten times a fool. A fool for the way she'd behaved, awful for the way she pouted when he refused to make love to her. And she felt awful because almost everything he'd said to her was true. She had been thinking only of her own plans, and she was vexed because Brave's attention hadn't been focused solely on her.

She'd been sharing him with a girl who had been dead for almost two years. She couldn't compete with Miranda any more than Sir Henry could ever compare to her father. Oh, she knew Brave said he didn't compare her to Miranda, but how could he not? She was the one he'd wanted, and Rachel was the one he got instead.

At least Rachel had been smart enough to appreciate him. Miranda Rexley didn't know what she'd turned her back on. Stupid twit.

"He trusted you enough to tell you the truth," her mother replied, her voice soft and hoarse. "You should be happy."

"Should I?" She wrapped her arms around herself and shrugged. "Perhaps I will be later. Right now I'm just too tired."

"And your pride's too bruised to think of much of anything other than licking your wounds."

"That too," Rachel admitted with a sigh. She was feeling pretty sorry for herself, but it would pass. It usually did.

Marion's lips curved slightly. "And you're in love with him."

There was no point in denying it. Her mother had a way of knowing these things—just like she knew about Rachel and Belinda giving Mrs. Dane's sheep dog a haircut when they were twelve.

She chuckled self-consciously. "When you're right, you really like to be right, don't you?"

"It happens so rarely that I like to do it properly." Marion patted the bed beside her. "Come sit."

Rachel looked at that empty spot on the smooth coverlet. She wanted nothing more than to sit there and pour her heart out to her mother. She was in dire need of some hair stroking and shoulder patting. "The last thing you need to hear right now are my paltry problems."

"You're my daughter. If you had a hangnail, I'd consider it a matter of grave importance. Now sit."

Smiling, Rachel obeyed, taking care not to cause her mother any discomfort as she sat.

She didn't know where to begin. "It seems so foolish to be in love with someone I hardly know."

Her mother's eyelashes fluttered, the only indication that she was even looking in Rachel's direction. "Your heart obviously thinks you know him well enough."

"I don't even know how it happened," Rachel said, toying with the lace on the sleeve of her mother's nightgown. "Is it possible to just wake up one morning in love?"

"I daresay it probably is." There was no ridicule in her mother's voice. No doubt she could tell her mother she wanted to fly, and her mother would give her full support. Then again, her mother also seemed to think that Rachel could have the man of her dreams.

Staring out the window at the wet grayness beyond,

Rachel played back every major detail of her relationship with Brave in her mind. "I suppose it could have happened the night he saved me."

"It could have."

She thought some more. "Or the night he kissed me at Lady Westwood's."

A moment of silence, and then, "He kissed you at Lady Westwood's?"

Rachel was glad her mother couldn't see her flaming cheeks, else she'd know that wasn't all Brave had done. As a married woman, it was expected, but there were some things a woman didn't want to share with her mother.

"It hardly matters how I feel about him," she remarked, hoping she sounded more convinced than she felt. "I've more important things to think about—like getting you a divorce from Sir Henry and keeping you safe until then."

"I sincerely doubt Henry would put up that much of a fight to get me back right now, Rachel," Marion drawled, shifting her position ever so slightly. Her swift intake of breath betrayed just how much pain she was in.

Rachel didn't say anything. Sir Henry wanting her mother back wasn't what scared her. It was Sir Henry deciding that if he couldn't have her, then no one would.

"You don't think Braven could protect me?" her mother asked once she was comfortable again.

"I have no doubt that Brave could do anything he set his mind to," was Rachel's honest reply. "He promised to protect you, and that's what he'll do."

"Perhaps," her mother said, watching her through that tiny crack in her eye, "his feelings for you are why he made that promise."

Rachel tugged on her sleeve. "Perhaps you should stop grasping at straws. I appreciate your confidence in me, but I have no idea how Brave feels about me, and after this afternoon I'm not sure I want to know."

"Coward."

Rachel laughed at that. "Admittedly so. We shall just have to content ourselves with the knowledge that at least one of us experienced perfect love in her lifetime."

"You think your father and I had the perfect relationship?" Coming out as hoarse as it did, the question sounded positively ludicrous.

"Didn't you?" Rachel's own voice sounded just as questioning. Everything she remembered about her mother and father, everything she'd been told proved her theory correct.

"Rachel, when your father and I met, he neglected to tell me he was already betrothed to someone else."

"What? No!" She couldn't believe it. Her father? Betrothed to someone else? "The cad!"

Her mother nodded. "It's true. He was engaged to be married to one Lydia Bunst, a buxom blonde with a fortune as large as her other attributes."

Rachel leaned forward, resting her forearms on her thighs. This was a story she'd never heard before. "What happened?"

"He courted me for close to a month before I found out. I unexpectedly encountered the two of them at an assembly."

Rachel almost squealed. "You saw them together? What did you do?"

"I introduced myself to her and told her what he'd been up to. She jilted him right there on the spot."

In her mind, Rachel pictured her mother as a young woman confronting her father and his blond goddess. It was difficult to imagine her mother being so brazen. "He must have been mortified."

"Mortified?" Marion laughed out loud, and then placed a hand against her ribs. "He was ecstatic! He thought I'd done it just so she'd cut him loose and we could be together."

"And had you?"

A hint of a sly smile curved her mother's lips. "Perhaps. I

didn't make it easy for him, however. I put him through agony before I finally agreed to marry him."

Rachel's good mood soured somewhat. "At least you knew how he felt about you."

"I knew no such thing! After I found out about Miss Bunst I thought he'd just been toying with me. I was crushed."

"Then why did you go to such lengths to have him?" Rachel asked with a frown. She didn't understand how her mother could take such a chance and risk public humiliation when she didn't know what the outcome would be.

"Because I knew how *I* felt about him." Marion's voice rang with confidence. "And I knew that a truly honorable man wouldn't jilt one girl just so he could have another, even if he had been thoughtless in his behavior."

Rachel was still confused. "But Brave has no such reason to hide his feeling for me—if indeed he has any."

"Does he not? You've hidden yours from him, and he isn't the one who entered into this marriage for his mother's sake." She paused. "Can you honestly tell me that if it weren't for me you wouldn't have made your feelings more obvious?"

"If it weren't for you," Rachel said, keeping her tone light, "he never would have offered to marry me and we wouldn't be having this conversation."

"But we are, so answer me."

Sighing, Rachel knotted her hands in her lap. "No, I can't tell you that. If circumstances weren't what they are, I would probably be more honest about my feelings."

"But you won't, will you?"

Rachel shook her head. "Not now. No."

Marion sighed. "You've got your father's foolish pride."

"And his honor," Rachel added with a smile. "I won't jilt you just so I can be with Brave."

"So you're going to risk having a happy life with him because you're afraid."

Rachel's smile faded. How could she make her mother understand? She couldn't admit her feelings to Brave until she was certain of his. She wouldn't give her heart until she was certain of one in return, and even then she'd be cautious. She'd seen what losing her husband had done to her mother. It wasn't something she wanted to experience.

"Yes," she replied with false conviction. "I'm going to risk it all."

"Then why did we just have this conversation if you already had your mind made up?"

Rachel's tired eyes filled with tears. Embarrassed, she swept them aside. "I needed to talk."

Her mother gave her hand a light squeeze. "You can always talk to me. You know that."

Her throat tight, Rachel nodded. "I know." She paused. "I should go. It's time for you to take your medicine." She reached for the bottle on the bedside table.

"What are you going to do?"

She removed the stopper and held the bottle against her mother's lips, slipping a hand under her head to help her drink. "I think I'll go for a walk. That always helps me clear my head."

Swallowing, her mother leaned back against the pillows. "Don't run away from him for too long, Rachel. Admit your feelings. Give him a chance to tell you his."

Did she want to hear Brave's feelings? Not if it included all the virtues and aspects of Miranda Rexley, no she didn't.

She kissed her mother on the forehead. "Sleep well, Mama. I'll come back this evening."

"Take care, dearest," Marion advised, as Rachel rose to her feet and strode across the carpet. "Don't do anything rash."

A dull ache twisted Rachel's chest as she opened the door. "I won't, Mama," she replied over her shoulder. "The consequences are becoming far too painful."

Chapter 15

~~~OO~~~

Bundled up against the late-afternoon chill, Rachel went for that walk she so desperately needed. The rain had stopped, leaving nothing but bitter dampness and grass that soaked her boots and darkened the hem of her skirts as she strolled down the smooth path that led from Wyck's End to the river. It seemed the perfect place to think about Brave and their relationship.

Standing on the bank beneath the oak tree, Rachel watched the dark water as it navigated its course. How nice to have a path laid out for you and all you had to do was follow it. The river of human existence had far too many little brooks and tributaries—too many places for a young woman to get caught up in and lose her way.

So Rachel had set her own path. It had all seemed so perfect, so definite until Brave hung upside down from this old tree and pulled her to safety and into his arms. He had saved her and damned her, it seemed, all with one heroic act.

Miranda Rexley had committed suicide by drowning. The

267

irony of it was not lost on Rachel. How had it affected Brave? What had gone through his mind when he came through the trees and saw his chance to save a young woman from drowning? Had he thought of his lost love, or had he simply acted?

And when he pulled her from the water, had he been saving her or Miranda?

Oh she knew what he'd told her, and for the most part, she believed him. But at that moment certainly his lost love must have crossed his mind.

Her mother had been right about her pride. It was wounded. Battered in fact. She'd never gotten much attention from young men because of her circumstances. No one in their right mind wanted to align themselves with Sir Henry, and so Rachel had never really been courted, except by David, and even he hadn't wanted to get under her skirts badly enough to fight Sir Henry. His desertion had hurt, and it made her all the more leery of depending on a man after that, but her heart hadn't been broken. Rachel had never truly known what it was like to lose her heart to someone.

And now she didn't know what to do. Could she take a chance on a real marriage with Brave? What if he left her like her father had? What if, like almost every other young man who'd ever courted her, he was only interested in her virginity? There was no denying he wanted her. He'd told her. But what if he lost interest after that? It certainly wasn't unheard of—young women spent their entire lives being warned about the fickleness of young men's attentions.

Marrying Brave wasn't supposed to have been so complicated. It had simply been a way to get out of a bad situation. She'd done what she had to do to get her mother away from Sir Henry, just as her mother had done what she had to do when she married the baronet. Perhaps that was where Rachel got her penchant for rash decisions.

Her mother hadn't even thought about the consequences

of marrying Henry Westhaver. And even if she had, Rachel had no doubt her mother would have married the ogre anyway. She'd thought only about Rachel's welfare. Something mother and daughter had in common, because every time Rachel acted impulsively it was with her mother in mind.

Both Brave and her mother thought she didn't think before she acted. Of course she thought. She thought about what might happen if she didn't act. Rachel always found the unknown less frightening than her immediate circumstances. How could it possibly be worse? Another thing to blame Sir Henry for.

She'd blame her stepfather for this mess between her and Brave if she could, but she couldn't. True, she'd seen Brave's proposal as a way to get her mother away from Sir Henry, but she'd also been thinking of herself. She'd been thinking with the part of her that always dreamed of having a handsome, rich husband who adored her.

Well, two out of three wasn't bad.

"Well, well. Will you look at what we have here."

Rachel froze, legs rooted to the ground by pure and icy fear. Somehow, she managed to will her head to turn, to face her stepfather. He sat atop one of his prized horses, not ten feet away. Caught up in her own thoughts and the rushing of the river, she hadn't heard his approach.

"A little housebreaker." Sir Henry smiled bitterly as he dismounted. "And without her protector."

She remained silent. Not because she didn't have anything to say but because she didn't want him to hear her voice tremble when she said it. She didn't even remind him that she'd been let into his house by Potts. It hardly made a difference.

"I was just on my way to Wyck's End to pay a visit." He stepped toward her, so close that she could smell the liquor on his breath, see the unfocused gleam in his eyes. "And now I'll have the countess with me."

His arm flashed out with surprising speed for a man so deep in his cups. He seized Rachel by the wrist and pulled, hauling her off-balance.

It hurt, but she would rather die than let him know that. Bent at an odd angle because of how he pulled on her arm, Rachel lifted her gaze to his, wondering if he could see how much she hated him.

"Imagine my surprise when I returned home from a hunting trip to find not only my wife gone but my butler gone as well." He smiled, a twisted, humorless expression that made Rachel's heart heavy with fear. "Even more of a surprise was news that you had apparently paid me a social call earlier in the day—with a pistol."

Rachel clenched her jaw to keep her chin from trembling. "What do you want, Sir Henry?" As if she didn't know.

He gave her arm a quick jerk, almost sending her falling to her knees as he began to walk. He hauled her along behind him, his thick fingers cutting off the flow of blood to her hand.

"I want my wife, Lady Braven. And you're going to give her to me."

For the first time in easily a dozen months, Brave wanted to hit something. He wanted to bruise his knuckles until sweat dripped off his brow and he was too tired to think. Maybe then, Rachel would get the hell out of his head for a while.

He raced upstairs, to the old nursery he'd converted to a sporting room. It was where he and Julian and Gabe would box or fence when his friends came to visit. For the last two years it had been draped in holland covers, but all of the equipment was still there.

It was the large, sand-filled leather bag hanging from the ceiling that he wanted. He didn't even bother to brush the dust off it before starting to pummel it with his fists.

He'd lost such control of himself after Miranda's death that he'd spent much of the last dozen or so months making up for it by keeping himself in complete control. He had so much bottled up inside him it was a wonder he hadn't lost his mind.

Although he couldn't say he wasn't losing something infinitely more valuable to his wife. She awakened feelings in him, tender feelings, and urges that weren't always sexual, but protective and possessive. For all her impulsiveness, her stubbornness, he wouldn't have her any other way. And when she wept, all he wanted to do was fix the world to her liking so he wouldn't have to see those tears anymore.

He struck the hard leather, feeling the blow all the way up to his shoulder. That was for making such a cake of himself over Miranda.

Another blow. That was for being such an idiot after she killed herself.

He struck again, and again, until his fists were a blur of motion and his shoulders burned. Finally, he collapsed to his hands and knees. His arms shook under his weight. *That* was for thinking he could fix the past by marrying Rachel and not have to face the consequences in the present and the future.

Brave rolled onto his back. The wood was hard and unyielding against his shoulder blades. He was hot and sweaty, his muscles tired. All those years of his youth spent trying to be a true Corinthian, and he'd never realized just what kind of healing properties a good sweat offered.

Things seemed so much clearer now. He knew what he had to do. He had to tell Rachel how much he cared about her, that he wanted to make love to her, not to Miranda or anyone else for that matter. He would have to be completely honest with her. She wouldn't like it, but hopefully she would forgive him for having been such a stupid, misguided ass.

He'd certainly spend the rest of his days begging for her

forgiveness if that was what she required. And he could think of several other things he could do while on his knees.

"Balthazar, what are you doing on the floor?"

Smiling, Brave didn't bother to open his eyes. "I'm thinking, Mama. Would you like to join me?" He knew she had told Rachel about Miranda, but somehow he couldn't bring himself to be angry with her. No doubt Rachel had given her little choice.

Brave had been the only child his mother and father had that lived. Three infant brothers and one sister were buried in the small family crypt behind the village chapel. As a result, Annabelle Wycherley had taken more interest in her son than other mothers of her rank and generation did. She would often sneak up to this very room and play games with Brave. One of those games had been lying on their backs in the middle of the floor and "thinking" out loud about anything that came to mind. Sometimes it was something as foolish as whether or not butterflies had feelings. Once it had been where babies came from.

Brave still wasn't sure he'd made sense of his mother's cryptic answers on that one.

He listened to the soft *click* of her heels as she crossed the polished floor toward him. Her skirts rustled, and then he felt the weight of her settle beside him as she sat down. She reached out and placed her hand in his. Brave smiled. He could remember a time when his mother's hand dwarfed his; now he was amazed by how dainty she was.

"What are you thinking about?"

He opened his eyes. "About what an idiot I've been."

Annabelle smiled. "How wonderful. Most men don't realize it until it's too late to change."

Brave's lips twitched at that. Pushing himself up into a sitting position, he released her hand and wrapped both arms around his bent knees.

"Did my father realize before it was too late?"

His mother's eyes twinkled. "With a little help."

Brave's smiled faded. "Then it seems I'm a little like him after all."

"A little!" Annabelle's tinkling laughter echoed throughout the room. "Darling, you're *exactly* like him!"

That wasn't what he expected to hear. "Really?"

Annabelle nodded, her expression hard to read in the fading light. "He had a tendency to take everything personally as well. I used to say he wasn't happy unless he had something to brood about at least once a week."

Brave had never known that about his father. He'd known him to be a serious man, but he hadn't seemed the type to waste time blaming himself or worrying over what couldn't be changed. Would he have been disappointed to have his son turn out the same way?

"Was he proud of me?" He cringed at how needy that sounded.

Now it was his mother's turn to look surprised. "Every day. And he would be even prouder if he was alive today."

Brave arched a dubious brow and his mother laughed. "He'd be especially proud of you for what you've done for Rachel and her mother."

But not for the motivation behind it, Brave would wager.

"And what do *you* think of what I've done for Rachel and her mother, Mama?" Rising to his feet, he held out his hand to her.

Annabelle took it and also stood. "I'm more interested in what Rachel's done for you, Balthazar. I think she's just the kind of woman you need."

Now this was interesting. "Oh?" He could barely suppress a grin. "Why, because she's as stubborn, willful, and meddling as you were with my father?"

Shaking out her skirts, Annabelle smiled. "There's that.

And the fact that between the two of you there's enough guilt to keep the Church of England in business until the end of the world."

He laughed at that. His mother always did have a sharp sense of humor.

She stared at him, her eyes filling with tears, and Brave's laughter faded. "What is it?"

"My boy," she whispered, her hands coming up to cup his cheeks, "I never thought I'd see you again, but there you are."

The lump in Brave's throat swelled until it threatened to choke him. He didn't want to know how his behavior over the past two years had affected his mother. That was more responsibility than even he could bear. "Let's go downstairs and have some tea."

They strolled arm and arm from the darkening room. The sconces in the corridor were already lit as the days were becoming shorter and shorter, and Brave found he preferred their warm glow to the murky daylight that had lit the house up until that point.

Talking to his mother had lightened his heart more than the lamps' golden glow ever could, however. It gave him hope. Hope that someday the fog that had settled over his life would lift. Already he thought he could see a clearing on the horizon. And that distant sunrise could only be attributed to one person.

Rachel. How she had done it he didn't know and didn't care to. All he knew was that his life had been forever altered the day she entered it, and while the future was all the more intimidating for her presence in it, Brave had never looked forward to something quite so much.

It was because of this newfound lightness of being that he was quite unprepared for what was waiting for him at the bottom of the stairs.

Sir Henry Westhaver stood just inside the door, the cold autumn air whistling in past him. He held Rachel by the wrist in front of him, her arm bent so far behind her back her torso arched. Reynolds and two footmen surrounded them, but no one moved.

"What the hell are you doing here?" Pulling free of his mother's grasp, Brave hurried down the last few steps.

A sharp gasp from Rachel brought him up short as his feet hit the marble floor.

"Not too close, Braven," Sir Henry warned. "Or I'll snap the countess's arm like a twig."

One look at Rachel's mutinous expression and Brave knew she didn't care if he broke her arm or not, so long as Brave kept her stepfather from reaching her mother.

But he cared.

"What do you want, Westhaver?"

"I want my wife!" Holding Rachel like a shield in front of him, he stepped farther inside. "Tell her to come down."

Brave clasped his hands behind his back, willing his expression into one of outward calm. He even smiled a bit. "It doesn't make one bit of difference what I tell her, Sir Henry. She can't come down."

"Why the bloody hell not?"

Rachel struggled against his hold. "Because you beat her so badly she can't walk, you bastard!"

She cried out as her arm was brutally wrenched upward.

"All right!" Brave shouted. He couldn't stand to hear her pain.

Sir Henry stilled. His flushed and fleshy face was bright with the prospect of victory. "What was that?"

Fighting to keep his expression neutral, Brave nodded. "I said all right. You can have Lady Marion."

Rachel stared at him in horror. "Brave, no!" He met her gaze evenly, hoping she knew she could trust him.

Sir Henry smiled. "I knew you'd come to your senses."

"But you have to go up and get her yourself." God, let him be doing the right thing.

Disappointment shadowed Rachel's stricken features. Brave couldn't bear to look at her. He looked at Sir Henry instead.

Rachel's stepfather cast her aside, flinging her to the floor like a discarded doll. "With pleasure," he announced, moving toward the steps.

Brave nodded at Reynolds. The butler shut the door. Then Brave held his ground at the foot of the stairs.

"You can have Marion, Westhaver. But you have to go through me first."

Sir Henry actually looked surprised by this turn of events.

"Did you really think I'd just hand her over?" Brave asked, his voice silky. "I'd let you break Rachel's arm before I'd let you walk out of here with her mother."

Rachel actually brightened at his words as she picked herself up off the floor. If he lived to be a hundred, he didn't think he'd ever figure her out.

"I want my wife," the baronet snarled.

Brave flashed a condescending smile. "And I always wanted an elephant, but some wishes just aren't meant to come true. Now, why don't you leave before I throw you out?"

"You can't keep me from my wife! The law's on my side!"

Smile fading, Brave cocked his head to one side. "Well, my title is bigger than yours, so I say I can do whatever I want. But why don't you come back later, and bring the law with you, and then we'll see whether or not they'll let you take Marion back to Tullywood? Make no mistake, Westhaver, there's only two ways you're going to take her. Through me, or through the courts."

Obviously Sir Henry was in a bit of a hurry, because he took the first option.

The first blow made Brave stumble. The second knocked him on his back on the stairs. Sir Henry reached down to grab him, and Brave retaliated with a boot to the face, knocking the baronet to the floor.

"Get him out of here," he instructed the footmen, and the three of them dragged the struggling and swearing Sir Henry across the floor to the door. Brave followed, half-hoping for another chance to pummel the bastard.

"You've not seen the last of me, Braven!" The baronet shouted from the steps. He raised one meaty fist and shook it. He looked ominous in the deepening darkness. "I'll be back."

"I'll be here," Brave replied, pressing a finger to the tiny cut inside his lip. "And so will Marion."

And then he slammed the door.

"I notice Lord Braven has retired early this evening as well." Meg grinned as she began unfastening the hooks on the back of Rachel's gown

"Really?" Rachel tried to keep her tone devoid of interest.

Meg only smiled and nodded, her assumption clear. She obviously believed that Brave and Rachel had an assignation planned. If she only knew the truth! That their marriage had yet to be consummated—something Rachel planned to remedy that night.

Meg folded the discarded gown over her arm. "I'll have this pressed for you, Lady Braven."

"Thank you, Meg. You can go now. I'll manage by myself."

Meg flashed her a grin that said she doubted Rachel would be by herself and left the chamber with a cheerful good night.

It had taken three glasses of wine to gather the courage to seduce her husband. After that scene with Sir Henry, Rachel could think of nothing she wanted more than to make love to Brave. He'd stood up for them. He'd refused to allow her stepfather to take her mother—even as Sir Henry threatened her own safety.

Did he have any idea how much that meant to her? Of course she had a sneaking suspicion that Brave would have cheerfully killed Sir Henry if he actually had broken her arm. She'd never felt so safe and protected in all her life.

She trusted him. Not just with her own life, but with her mother's as well. She loved him. Loved him so much that when he'd first told Sir Henry he could have her mother it had felt as though her heart had been ripped right out of her chest.

She wanted to be a wife to him—a proper wife. Giving him her body was just the first step. He'd willingly offered his. She only hoped that when she offered him her heart he'd be equally as generous.

Rachel was glad for the wine-induced fog in her brain as she turned down the bedclothes. Had he found her note yet? Did he know what she had planned?

Smiling, she didn't even look up at the knock upon her door. "Come in! Did you forget something, Meg?" she asked as the door opened.

"I'm not Meg."

The sheets dropped. She didn't look up. He was early.

"I got your note. You mentioned something about a drink before retiring?"

Rachel raised her head, trying to retain a measure of calm—or at least give the appearance of it.

Brave stood by the door that separated their rooms. She hadn't even noticed which direction the knock had come from. He was wearing a gold-velvet robe. And judging from the way it hugged his shoulders and revealed a shocking amount of muscular chest, Rachel guessed he wasn't wearing much—if anything—beneath it.

Oh yes. A drink would be good.

"Shut the door." Oh, that was subtle! Why didn't she just tell him to drop his robe while she was at it?

He did as she bid, turning to face her with a curious expression.

"I thought we could sit by the fire," she blurted, gesturing to the rug. It had seemed like such a good idea earlier, but now she thought it was entirely too transparent. He had to know why she invited him to her room.

But blast him, he wasn't giving it away if he did know. His bare feet were silent on the carpet as he walked toward the fireplace and the thick, plush rug where a bottle of wine and two glasses waited. His robe flared around his legs as he walked. Rachel caught a glimpse of a strong, hairy calf. No, he wasn't wearing anything underneath that soft velvet.

Her mouth dry, Rachel trailed after him, clutching the neckline of her wrapper closed with one hand. The velvet didn't just cling to his shoulders, it hugged his hips and buttocks as well. Would he feel as firm as he looked?

He knelt on the rug before the fire and set both glasses in front of him. Rachel stood to the side, not sure if she should join him or not.

Brave didn't even look at her as he liberally filled both glasses. Recorking the bottle, he set it aside and picked up both glasses. He held them both at chest level and gazed up at her.

Subtle. With a sigh, Rachel sank to the floor as gracefully as her gown would allow. Despite all her efforts at modesty, she still ended up showing a shocking amount of ankle. She'd set out to look seductive but ended up—literally—with cold feet. But what did it matter when the man across from her displayed both his legs from the mid-thigh down? Why, he was just inviting her to stare at the dark V between his legs! If that robe fell open any farther . . .

Yanking her gaze away from his legs, Rachel took the glass he offered her and downed half of it.

"Your mother shows much improvement," he remarked.

Her mother? This wasn't the kind of conversation Rachel expected. She expected him to ask her what she was up to, or even play upon their attraction. This talk of her mother was . . . was . . . *disappointing*.

"I believe she's recovering quite well, yes. Dr. Phelps believes it will still be several weeks before she's able to move around very much." She took another drink of wine and tried again to tug her gown over her chilled toes.

"What's wrong?" He gestured toward her feet.

Her smile was sheepish. "They're cold."

"Stretch them out so they're closer to the fire."

Doing so would reveal even more of her legs to him, but the idea of warming the frigid appendages won out over modesty. Tentatively, she uncurled her legs. Brave didn't even seem to notice. He drained his glass.

He poured himself more wine and topped up her glass as well. She shouldn't drink it, but it tasted so good and warmed her insides. Was it more than one drink if she never finished a whole glass?

"Are your feet still cold?"

They were. She nodded.

Setting aside his glass, Brave patted his lap. "Put one up here."

There? Rachel stared at his hand and at the bulging velvet just behind it. Why did he want her to put her foot there? And why did it suddenly feel as though she was the one being seduced and not the other way around?

"I'll rub it," he explained when she didn't move. "It will warm it."

"There's no need—"

He scoffed at her hesitation. "I did it the night I pulled you from the Wyck, remember? It worked then, and you're not nearly as cold now."

He had a point, and her feet were awfully cold . . . well, what harm could a little rub do? Eager to be warm, Rachel plopped her right foot into his lap. It nestled comfortably in the hollow between his legs—just scant inches from his groin.

"Oh!" she cried when his hands touched her chilled flesh. Oh dear, but he was warm!

There was a chair behind her and Rachel propped one arm up on the cushion so she could lean against it. Sipping her wine, she sighed in pleasure as Brave massaged warmth back into her toes. This was becoming a habit, him rubbing her feet.

As he rubbed, he talked and Rachel began to relax. The sound of his voice, the heat of his hands and the mellow flavor of the wine all served to make her muscles as languid as a kitten's.

Brave told her stories—humorous, personal stories about his days at school with Gabriel and Julian. Some of the stories were hilarious. Some were touching, and others were so scandalous Rachel couldn't possibly believe they were true.

"You did not!" she protested when he told her about the time they paid a prostitute to dress up like a nun and proposition one of their classmates.

He held up one hand and reached for the bottle with the other. "I swear it is the absolute truth. Brentwood thought he was quite the rake after that. Poor fellow didn't even know enough to realize that the nun wasn't a virgin."

Rachel took a long swallow from her glass, and then held it out for Brave to fill again. "Can you tell?" At his puzzled glance, she added, "If someone's a virgin?" She'd always wondered about it, ever since Belinda told her about a girl in London pretending to be a virgin on her wedding night so her husband wouldn't know she'd been ruined.

He choked on his wine. Rachel laughed at the coughing that ensued. She'd shocked him!

"For the most part," he responded, wiping his eyes with the back of one hand. "The maidenhead is the easiest way to prove virginity, but all women are different and some have thick barriers and others have little or nothing at all."

"And how does it feel?" She took another sip.

Brave actually blushed. "That's different for every woman as well."

She shook her head. *Whoa!* Spots danced before her eyes. "No, I meant what does it feel like for *you*, for the man?"

His flush deepened. "I don't know. I've never made love to a virgin."

"I'm a virgin," Rachel announced, leaning heavily on her chair. It felt naughty and deliciously scandalous to discuss such things with him. It was also dangerous and she liked it.

Something brightened in Brave's gaze, like the flare of a lamp in a dark room. "I know."

"So I'm afraid I can't tell you how it feels either. Mmm." She moaned as Brave's hand slid up her foot to her calf and massaged the muscle there.

Closing her eyes, she lost herself in the gentle motion of his caress. Lord, but it felt good! His hands slid higher. He was rubbing both legs, and his fingers brushed the sensitive skin behind her knees. She gasped.

"Do you like that?" His voice was barely a whisper.

Rachel squirmed. "It tickles."

Something soft rubbed the inside of her legs. It was Brave's robe. Opening her eyes, Rachel raised her somewhat fuzzy gaze to see him kneeling between her splayed thighs. When had that happened? And how had her nightgown ended up around her hips? It was indecent. He could see her privates.

Curious, but she had no desire to cover herself. Let him look. And the thought of him looking led to the thought of him touching and that led to a flood of warmth rushing to the very spot revealed to him.

Licking her lips, Rachel watched as his fingers spread across her thighs, inching closer and closer to the bunched hem of her gown. His fingers were dark golden brown against her pale flesh, and just as hard as she was soft.

His hands slipped back down behind her knees and Rachel gazed at him questioningly.

Suddenly, he yanked her closer. Her elbow slipped off the chair. Wine spilled down her arm, and the glass fell to the rug as he jerked her body to his.

Heart hammering, Rachel stared up at him. The firelight illuminated one side of his face, the flames reflected in the golden darkness of his gaze. His lips parted as his fingers brushed her upper thighs.

Her nightgown was now up around her waist, and his knees were flush against her backside. The soft velvet against her naked skin was one of the most erotic sensations Rachel had ever experienced.

He knelt above her, an expression on his face that she had never seen before. He looked intense, dangerous, and utterly determined. She shivered.

His palm drifted from her thigh to her hip and up to her belly. A trail of fire seemed to blaze in the wake of his fingers. "Would you like me to stop?"

"No," Rachel whispered. "I don't want you to stop."

Closing her eyes, Rachel lost herself in the touch of his hands on her bare skin. Her knees straddled his hips and the velvet of his dressing gown caressed the sensitive flesh inside her knees. The hair on his legs tickled the back of her thighs, and all the while, his fingers stroked her hips and thighs, coming close to that eager place between her thighs, but never quite touching it.

Slowly, his hands slid up, following the curve of her hip to the indent of her waist and out again to the swell of her ribs. Underneath the fine lawn of her nightgown, Brave's thumbs brushed the underside of her breasts. Her nipples tingled and tightened in response. Her breathing quickened.

He knew exactly how to touch her. It was as though her

body and his hands had been made for each other. Every touch only served to heighten her awareness of him, to make her want him more.

His hands cupped her breasts. Rachel drew a shaky breath as his thumbs grazed the hardened peaks with a touch as gentle as the brush of a butterfly's wings. It was just enough to tease her, to sharpen the ache, but not nearly enough to content her.

"Untie your robe." His voice was low and deliciously hoarse. The command sent a thrill of desire through Rachel's heavy limbs. How she managed to lift her hands, she didn't know, but suddenly they were there, her fingers fumbling with the bows that held her wrapper closed as Brave's fingers expertly coaxed her nipples into exquisitely painful arousal.

The wrapper fell open and Rachel knew the thin material of her nightgown hid very little from his hungry gaze. His hands came out from underneath the froth of linen and went to the gown's neckline. With one tug he pulled it down enough to expose both breasts. He pushed them up so that the stretched neck cupped them, offering them up like some kind of exotic delicacy for him alone.

Rachel couldn't help but watch as he lowered his head to first one then the other. The tip of his tongue flicked one swollen nipple, sending a jolt of pleasure from her breast straight to the juncture of her thighs. Her body throbbed in response.

Her fingers tangled in his hair, pressing his head against her as he licked and suckled her breasts. His tongue swirled and flicked around her sensitive flesh until her hips arched and she moaned aloud.

Suddenly, she was yanked upright so that she sat straddling his lap. Her wrapper slid off her arms as Rachel's head swam with dizziness. "What are you doing?" she demanded when he pulled the nightgown up over her head and tossed it to the side. She was the one who was supposed to be in charge!

He only smiled and smoothed the hair back from her face.

She was naked. Completely bare, and something hard and velvety was pressed very intimately between her legs. Instinctively, Rachel spread her thighs wide, lowering her weight onto that delicious pressure.

Brave gasped and grabbed her by the arms. His hips lifted against hers, pressing his hardness flush against her. Heat and longing coursed through her and she reached out blindly for something to hold on to, seizing the soft lapels of his robe.

He kissed her, his lips demanding as they moved on hers. Willingly, wantonly, Rachel opened her mouth to his, sighing when he slid his tongue against hers. Nothing else existed outside of this moment. The touch and taste of their bodies was the only thing that mattered. Nothing had ever felt so right to her in her life. She'd never wanted anything so badly.

Her tongue swept against his. He tasted of wine and something that was inherently Brave, something hot and sweet. Her hands traced the line of his lapels, down to the ties that held his robe closed. With surprising deftness, she released the knot and lifted her hands to push the heavy fabric off his shoulders so that he was left as gloriously bare as she.

His flesh was warm and taut beneath her hands. The knobby bones of his shoulders were hard against her palms, and the smooth planes of his back flexed as he slid his hands to cup her buttocks. Rachel gasped against his lips as his fingers kneaded her sensitive flesh.

The hair on his chest rubbed along her torso, teasing her nipples and abrading the delicate skin of her breasts. She pressed against it, reveling in every sensation. The head of his sex pushed against her, hot and insistent.

Reality stepped in.

For one brief moment Rachel panicked. "Brave—"

"Ssh." He silenced her with a kiss. "It's all right. I'll take care of you."

And she knew he would.

He slid a hand between their bodies, easing a finger into the damp cleft between her legs. His thumb brushed her most sensitive spot. A shudder wracked her and she clung to him, biting her lip to keep from crying out.

"You like that, don't you?" His breath was hot against her lips as he teased her most sensitive spot with his thumb. She pressed down with her hips, increasing the pressure, spreading herself farther for his hand.

Groaning, he slid a finger inside her. "Trust me," he murmured, his finger sliding in and out of her while his thumb caressed that sweetly tight bud with maddeningly controlled strokes. "I would never do anything to hurt you, Rachel. I promise."

And she believed him, believed him as wholly and as powerfully as she needed him inside her. The rhythm of his thumb increased, stoking the fire within her until she thought it might consume her.

And then his hand was gone, and she was left wanting with dampness on her thighs and her body humming with tension. Crying out at the injustice of being brought so close, Rachel opened her eyes and met his black gaze.

"I want to be inside you," he told her, and her entire body clenched as if he already were plunging within her.

"I want you inside me." Something wild and primitive within her didn't care what happened after this night, didn't care what the consequences were, just wanted release. Now.

The head of his sex probed the entrance to her body. It was big and blunt, but she was too far gone to be afraid of it. In fact, it took every ounce of her control not to just impale herself on it.

"Go slowly," he cautioned. "I don't want to hurt you."

Rachel could scarce believe this was happening as she began lowering her body by agonizingly slow degrees. The head penetrated her. There was a twinge of sharp discomfort and Rachel stilled, waiting for it to pass, fearful that it wouldn't.

As if sensing her discomfort, Brave cupped one of her breasts, raising it to his mouth. Gently, he grazed the nipple with his teeth, sucking it until the incredible sensations caused by his mouth began to overpower everything else.

His hand was between them again, his thumb finding the center of her pleasure effortlessly, teasing the nub into full arousal with one stroke.

With such promise driving her toward fulfillment, Rachel lowered herself farther onto Brave's shaft, feeling herself stretch to accommodate him. It burned a bit, but the burning mingled with the insatiable ache, creating the most intense sensation of pleasure/pain she'd ever experienced. She threw herself against it, opened her body to it, until sweat beaded on her brow and blackness swamped the edges of her mind.

Brave's hips rose to meet hers. His mouth had left her breast and his head rested back against his shoulders, his expression one of such intent concentration that Rachel quickened her movements, wanting to break it, wanting to watch as he lost himself as completely as she was about to.

The tension mounted, shaking her as a storm flails against a tree. Rachel gave in to the tempest, thrusting her body against Brave's hand, shoving herself down onto him until the burning became a fire and her body exploded into a cascade of sparks.

It raged through her, tightening her muscles as she wrapped her arms around Brave's neck and screamed against his flesh, half pleading for it to stop and half begging for it to go on forever.

A ragged cry tore from Brave's lips as his hips lifted in a powerful thrust. Holding her tightly by the waist, he plunged deep within her, filling her with warmth as his own release shook his body.

Weak and exhausted, Rachel clung to him. The room was quiet save for the heavy sound of their breathing and the crackling of the fire. Rachel didn't mind the silence. She was his now. And he was hers. What more could there possibly be to say?

Chapter 16

He'd just taken his wife's virginity on her bedroom floor.

And instead of being upset about it as he assumed most virgins would be, Rachel was draped bonelessly against him, her arms hanging limply over his shoulders, her head nestled in the hollow of his neck.

"You all right?"

Her hair brushed his jaw as she nodded. He felt her hum "Mmm" against his flesh.

Brave couldn't help but chuckle. His little seductress was exhausted—not to mention well on her way to becoming thoroughly foxed.

Gingerly, he withdrew his body from hers. She mumbled in protest as he did so and wrapped her arms even tighter about his shoulders, as though she was afraid he would leave her completely.

The gesture touched Brave. She could cling to him all she

wanted. He wasn't going anywhere. There was no place he'd rather be.

He maneuvered her so that he could scoop her up into his arms as he rose to his feet. His knees screamed in protest as they unbent, stiff from having been locked in one position for so long.

"Where are we going?" Rachel asked in a sleepy voice.

"You'll see."

He carried her into the dressing room, where the bath he'd taken before coming to her awaited by the dying fire. The water was still warm as he stepped in. Kneeling, he lowered both of them into the water, positioning them so that Rachel reclined lengthwise in the bath while he knelt between her legs.

"This feels very familiar," she purred, flipping her hair over the side. A spray of water flew up into Brave's face from the wet strands as she did so.

Chuckling, Brave wiped the water from his cheek and reached for the bar of soap on the side of the tub.

"I like it when you smile," Rachel remarked, her gaze lazy.

Brave's heart swelled painfully. "You make me want to smile." Lathering a cloth with the soap, he leaned toward her.

"What are you doing?"

He set the soap aside and ran the cloth along the top of her breasts. God, she had incredible breasts!

"Washing you." He brushed the cloth across one pale pink—not rose but a soft petal-pink—nipple.

"Why? I'm not dirty."

Staring at the delicate bud that puckered and hardened at his attentions, Brave smiled. "I want to."

Transferring the washcloth to his other hand, he ran the pad of his thumb across the tip of her breast, feeling his own flesh tighten in response when Rachel moaned.

She was so responsive, as though her body had been specifically designed for his touch. Reaching below the surface of the water, he pressed the cloth against the juncture of her thighs.

"Are you sore?" The last thing he wanted was to hurt her, but he knew that was often inevitable the first time.

Her gaze met his, heavy and bold from the wine she'd drunk. "Some spots are tender," she replied. "Others aren't."

Brave jumped as her fingers closed around the hardening length of his erection. "You're very bold, Lady Braven," he teased, pushing his hips against her hand.

She stroked him, instinctively knowing just how to drive him mad with desire. "I know. Do you not like it?"

Washcloth forgotten, Brave used his fingers to part the delicate flesh between her legs. Bracing the other arm against the rim of the tub, he angled himself over her, finding the hardness he sought within her.

"I love it." Gritting his teeth against the heavy pressure building between his legs, he flicked his fingers against her, rapidly bringing her to a keening climax.

The sound of her cries were almost his undoing. Jerking free of her hand, he jumped to his feet, sloshing water over the side of the tub and almost losing his balance. He climbed out of the tub, grateful for the chill that hit his wet skin.

"Where are you going?" Rachel demanded, resting her chin on her forearms on the rim of the tub. Obviously, her second orgasm had revived her somewhat.

Brave hauled her to her feet. More water sloshed onto the floor as he swept her, squealing, up into his arms.

"We're going to bed," He informed her as he carried her, dripping bathwater, into his bedroom. "This time I'm going to make love to you properly."

And he did. Slowly, tenderly, Brave entered her, bracing his palms on either side of her head so that he could watch her face as he filled her. He swore he would stop at the first sign of discomfort, but he saw none. Nothing but sensation and pleasure flickered across her delicate features.

He made it last as long as he could, until his arms trembled with the strain and Rachel begged him to give her the release she wanted—until he couldn't hold out any longer. And then he quickened the pace, bringing them both to a shattering climax that rendered him incapable of thought and made colors dance before his eyes.

Afterward, he held her against him, breathing in the scent of her hair as sleep started its mellow assault on his senses.

"Why did you come to me tonight?" he asked, brushing his lips across the velvety softness of her cheek. "What made you do it?"

It shouldn't matter, he knew, but he wanted to hear. He wanted her to tell him that she wanted him as badly as he wanted her, that she was as powerless against him as he was against her.

"Wanted to," was her sleepy reply as she snuggled against his chest.

Smiling, Brave wrapped his arms around her. *Wanted to.* That was probably the best answer he was going to get out of her that night.

Darkness closed in on him. Yawning, he tucked her bottom into his groin and pressed his chest against her back.

"Wanted to . . . thank you."

His eyes opened, his whole body became very still. She'd wanted to thank him? Is that why she'd let him make love to her?

"For what?" It was hard to speak with the icy band that tightened around his chest.

Rachel sighed, burrowing further under the blankets. "For today . . . for Sir Henry."

He'd been trying to get drunk for two days.

Sitting in his study, with the door locked against the outside world, Brave nursed a bottle of brandy. He'd given up on using a glass the day before. Getting foxed wasn't as easy as he remembered. No matter how much he drank he couldn't seem to reach that mind-numbing blankness that made thought impossible.

On the contrary, the more he drank the more he seemed to think about things, specifically Rachel. He thought about her face, her voice . . .

The fact that she thanked him for kicking Sir Henry out of his house by giving him her sweet, tight body. He thought about that a lot. It had a decidedly sobering effect that made him wish he could stop thinking about it, especially since her "thank-you fuck" was the one thing he was drinking to forget.

Raising the bottle to his lips, Brave drained the last few swallows of brandy from it.

Now what? All his liquor was gone, and short of ringing for Reynolds to bring more, there was nothing he could do but face sobriety like a man.

Damn it.

Something tapped against the window closest him. Closing his eyes, Brave sighed in frustration. They'd given up knocking on the study door the previous evening. His mother, Rachel, Reynolds . . . all of them had professed to be terribly worried about him. Bollocks. They just couldn't stand not knowing what he was doing.

When they realized he wasn't going to answer the door, they tried other inventive ways to get his attention. It was a sad state of affairs when a man couldn't get drunk in his own house without his butler trying to sneak in through the secret passage in the wall.

Brave had to put all his weight against the panel to keep the little bugger from getting in, too.

Now, turning his head toward the window and the overcast morning outside, he saw his wife's face pressed up against the glass.

He should just shut the drapes, he thought as he reluctantly rose to his feet. The world tilted and swayed a bit before falling back into place. He was a little drunker than he thought. Excellent. He staggered toward her.

Rachel's expression was one of disappointment and concern. The concern didn't bother him; he rather liked it. It was the disappointment that rubbed. He didn't like knowing he'd disappointed her. But she had disappointed him too, damn it!

He was tempted to run up to the glass and press his mouth wide against it and blow—puffing his face up like something out of a traveling sideshow. That would teach her to come knocking on windows.

Flicking the latch, he pushed the window open. She had to jump back to avoid being hit by it.

"What?"

Her pert little nose wrinkled as she took in his appearance. "I wanted to make sure you were all right."

Spreading his arms wide, he revealed the full glory of his sweat- and brandy-stained shirt. "As you can see, I'm fine."

She pressed a gloved hand over her mouth and nose. "You stink."

Perversely, Brave leaned out the window, letting the chilly breeze carry the full extent of his aroma to her offended sensibilities. "When one doesn't bathe and wears the same clothing for two days, one tends to become somewhat fragrant. Does it disgust you?"

She lowered her hand, and, closing her eyes as though for strength, Rachel drew a deep breath. Brave smiled when she shuddered.

"Nothing you could do would disgust me, Brave."

"What if I pulled you over the sill and took you right here where anyone could see?"

Her eyes flew open, and he laughed out loud at the shock on her face. She scowled at him.

"You're drunk."

Sadly, he shook his head. "Not as much as I'd like to be, I assure you."

Another breath. Another shudder. "I can't help but feel responsible—"

"Of course you can't." he cut in.

Rachel scowled again, this time so deeply her eyebrows merged into one blond "M." "Can you deny that *this*"—she gestured up and down the length of him with an expression of dismay—"has nothing to do with the fact that you haven't spoken to me since we made love?"

"Purely a coincidence," he lied.

Her expression softened. Oh, he hated it when she looked at him like that. It usually meant she was going to say something that would make him want to hold her and tell her everything was all right.

"Then you're not feeling guilty?"

Guilty? He wasn't the one who had anything to feel guilty about!

"No. I'm not." He leaned closer. "How 'bout you?"

She pulled back as his breath hit her. "Well, I do have to wonder if I've done something wrong."

There it was. He knew she'd say something to tug at his heartstrings. How could he tell her she'd done everything right? Too right. That was why her thanking him had hit so hard. He hadn't expected it. He'd foolishly believed she'd just wanted to be with him.

"You mean you don't know?"

She paled. And Brave silently cursed himself. He hadn't meant for it to come out like that.

"I see," she replied, her tone as cold as the breeze that raised gooseflesh on Brave's arms. "Obviously, I've intruded where I'm not wanted."

He met her gaze as evenly as his swimming vision would allow. "Obviously. Now, if you will excuse me, I'd like to get back to my drinking and stinking." He reached past her for the handle. The movement shoved his armpit practically into her face. If possible, she turned even whiter.

Backing away, her eyes watering, Rachel looked at him. "What is *wrong* with you?"

Brave shook his head. If she didn't know, he was in no shape to try to tell her. Let her figure it out on her own, the heartless wench. How could she not know? Unless she didn't remember, in which case he wasn't so certain now was the time to remind her.

He closed the window before she could say anything else. It was rude he knew, but if he talked to her any longer he was liable to make a fool—an even bigger fool—of himself again, and that was something he just didn't care to do.

She watched him through the glass, and when he could bear the sad expression on her face no longer, he closed the curtains, blocking out the daylight and the sunshine that was Rachel.

Unsteadily, he made his way to the commode in the corner and removed the chamber pot from inside it. To his surprise, there was another bottle of brandy in there as well. The dust on it implied that it had been in there for some time. Why hadn't he noticed it before?

After relieving himself, Brave and the bottle sauntered over to the chaise lounge underneath the Ingres on the far wall. Gabriel and Julian had written, announcing they would be arriving sometime that day, and so Brave reclined like a pasha awaiting his harem and drank, waiting for his friends to arrive and see how married life agreed with him.

Don't you know?

She knew it was dangerous for her to leave the house alone, but she needed to talk to someone. As the carriage bumped and rolled up the lane to Belinda's house, Rachel pondered Brave's cryptic remark for what must have been the tenth time since he uttered it not even half an hour earlier.

What did he mean, didn't she know? Surely she would know if she'd done something to offend him. And since she didn't know, why didn't he just tell her? He was hardly in the right frame of mind to discuss anything just then, but why hadn't he told her when she committed whatever offense he found her guilty of?

Had she done something wrong when they were making love? She was no expert on these things, but everything *felt* as she thought it should—better even. Good enough to make her blush with the memory of it.

Was that it? Had things gone too well? Had she not acted as a virgin should? Brave had said he never made love to a virgin before. Had her wantonness led him to believe that she wasn't actually pure? Did he now lump her into the same category as Miranda?

No, that was unlikely, she thought bitterly. He'd loved Miranda.

It was unfair, she knew, to compare herself to the woman Brave had once loved and lost. Unfair, because Brave had never offered her love. In fact, he'd made it very clear that he wasn't interested in the emotion at all. And it was unfair in more ways than one because Rachel actually loved Brave— something Miranda hadn't had the good sense to do as well.

And Rachel thanked her for it. If Miranda had returned Brave's feelings, he would have married her instead of Rachel, and, quite frankly, Rachel didn't know what she would have done had Brave not walked into her life.

But the nature of her supposed trespass was still a mystery to her. It had to have happened sometime during or shortly after their lovemaking, because Brave certainly hadn't acted displeased with her before then. In fact, he'd seemed happier than she had ever seen him, right up until she fell asleep.

Vaguely, she remembered talking to him just before falling asleep. He'd asked her why she'd decided to make love to him, and she'd told him that she wanted to. She'd been too tired to give a more detailed response.

Good Lord, she hadn't told him she loved him, had she? Surely she would remember if she had. She remembered thinking it, along with the fact that she hadn't thanked him for disposing of Sir Henry earlier.

Pressing a hand against her stomach to quell the nausea there, Rachel rocked back and forth against the padded squabs. What if she *had* told him she loved him? Was that what had driven him to hide away in his study and reek of brandy and stale sweat? Was having her love him that awful?

Oh Lord, she hoped not! That would be just too painful.

But she couldn't remember saying anything of the sort, which led her right back to wondering just what she had done to warrant such treatment.

But before she could give the subject any more thought, the carriage rolled to a halt and the door swung open. A gloved hand appeared to help her to the ground.

How quickly she'd become accustomed to the footmen and the grand carriage and the new clothes, but none of them meant anything if her husband didn't want her anymore. She had to find out what had Brave so upset. Otherwise, she wouldn't be able to fix it, and she *would* fix it. She was not prepared to spend the next forty or so years of her life in a miserable marriage. And she was certainly not going to have children with a man who punished her for something she didn't even know she'd done.

With that vow strong in her heart, Rachel finally put all thoughts of her husband aside and climbed the steps to Belinda's door. The butler opened it immediately, and, once her outerwear had been taken away, Rachel was shown to the parlor, where her friend waited.

Belinda greeted her with the scent of roses and a quick squeeze of her hands, and steered her toward the low table laden with an assortment of sandwiches and cakes.

"I'm so glad you decided to join me," the darker woman gushed, pouring tea into two delicate china cups. "Mama has been an absolute bore all morning. For some reason she's got it into her head that I must decide on the flowers for the wedding *now*. Not next week, not in a few days, but today. Two lumps?"

Rachel nodded, thankful not only for her friend but for her chatter. Getting out of the house—and away from Brave and his moods was the best impulsive decision she had made in a long time.

She took the plate of cakes Belinda arranged for her, balancing it on her lap as she sipped the hot, soothing tea. She was starving. She hadn't eaten much in the last two days— since concern for Brave had diminished all other normal behavior. Now, away from the gloomy atmosphere of Wyck's End, her appetite returned with a vengeance.

"But enough of my prewedding babblings," Belinda remarked some ten minutes and three cakes later. She took a sip of tea. "Tell me how you managed to persuade that magnificent husband of yours to let you out of his sight long enough to come visit me."

Rachel swallowed what was left of cake number four. The mere mention of Brave had turned the sweet, moist treat to dirt in her mouth.

"I doubt very much he even misses me," she replied with false lightness, licking a crumb from the corner of her lips.

Belinda's cup froze halfway to her mouth, her eyes widening in surprise. "I'd almost believe you were jesting if not for the fact you were looking everywhere but at me when you spoke."

Rachel forced herself to meet her friend's gaze. It was

nearly torture to do so. "I don't know what you're talking about." As if to prove her point, she crammed another cake into her mouth.

She must have looked truly ridiculous because Belinda burst out laughing. "Rachel, my dearest friend, you cannot hide these things from me!" Her expression changed to one of hurt bewilderment. "And even if you could, why would you wish to?"

Forcing the cake down with another gulp of tea, Rachel sighed inwardly. Not only had she managed to offend Brave in some unknown way, but now she'd hurt Belinda's feelings as well. Splendid.

Belinda set her cup aside. "Have you and Braven had a fight?"

Rachel dabbed her mouth with one corner of her pale pink napkin. "Fighting generally requires speech, Belinda. This morning was the first time in two days that my husband has condescended to even face me, let alone speak." She didn't even want to think about the cool words that had come out of his mouth once he'd opened it.

Now her friend looked truly shocked. "Why?"

Shrugging, Rachel drained her cup. "I haven't the foggiest notion."

Belinda shook her head. "But that makes no sense. No one in his right wits just stops speaking to someone. What happened the last time you saw him?"

Rachel blushed clean to the roots of her hair as she thought about the things she and Brave had done to each other that night.

Belinda's eyes widened even further. "Oh." Clearing her throat, she leaned forward, glancing about as though she feared someone might be listening. "Did Braven—" she lowered her voice, "Did Braven have trouble . . ." She lifted her hand in a rising motion.

Rachel's blushed deepened. "Certainly not!"

Her friend visibly sagged in relief. "Oh, I must confess I would have been disappointed if you'd said yes." Then, as though the thought just occurred to her, "Dearest, he didn't hurt you, did he?"

Were it not for her acute embarrassment, Rachel would have been warmed by the concern in Belinda's gaze. "No. He was very . . . considerate."

Belinda wrinkled her nose. "Just considerate?"

"Oh for heaven's sake, Belinda!" Rachel cried, tossing her hands into the air, almost spilling her last cake to the floor. "It was marvelous! Are you satisfied?"

At that point, Belinda was sitting as far back in her chair as she could, her eyes as wide as saucers. Rachel was instantly contrite.

"Forgive me." She reached around to massage the back of her neck with one hand. She was as hard as rock. "I'm afraid I'm not quite myself today."

"Obviously," Belinda agreed, straightening. "So . . . you liked it?"

Rachel couldn't help it. She started to laugh. "Yes, I liked it. And I've no doubt you will as well. That's what you've been wanting hear, isn't it?"

Now it was Belinda's turn to blush. Her eyes bright, she ran a hand over her sable curls. "Yes. I've thought often about my wedding night. I've thought about it a lot." Again she leaned forward, and this time Rachel glanced about for imaginary eavesdroppers.

"Winchelsea and I, we've never . . . well, we've . . ." She waved her hand. "We have a bit, but he wants to wait until we're married."

Rachel raised a brow, smiling at her friend's disappointed tone. "And you're impatient?"

Belinda looked surprised. "Well, yes. But then Mama decided we needed to have 'the talk' and what she told me makes absolutely no sense when I think of how Win makes me feel."

Rachel could just imagine the kinds of things Belinda's mother had told her. Twenty-some years of sharing a bed with Mr. Mayhew would be enough to sour any woman.

"You'll be fine," she assured her friend with a gentle pat on the hand. "Although, I'm not sure I'm a good one to ask. After all, my husband stopped talking to me after we made love the second time."

"The second time?" Belinda suddenly looked very interested. "I thought you said it was the first time."

Rachel had blushed more in the last ten minutes than she had in the last three years, she was certain of it.

Belinda's face was positively glowing with curiosity. "You mean they can do it more than once?"

"It would appear so, yes."

"And did you . . . could you . . . ?" Crimson blossoms appeared on Belinda's pale cheeks.

"Yes," Rachel replied between clenched teeth, well past humiliation and slowly sinking into mortification. "And judging from the way my husband is treating me, I won't again for some time. Now can we talk about something else, please?"

"Yes," Belinda conceded. Her contrite expression did not last for long. "What are you going to do about Braven?"

Taking a bite out of her last cake, Rachel shrugged. "There's not a lot I can do until he's sobered up. Then I'll demand that he tell me what the devil has him in such a wicked temper?"

"Demand?"

"Forcefully request."

Belinda smiled slyly. "And if that doesn't work?"

Rachel swallowed and set her plate aside. "I won't leave him alone until it does. I agreed to a real marriage, not a lifetime of making the best of a bad situation as my mother has tried to do." Holding out her cup, she smiled as her friend poured more tea into it. She felt better than she had in days.

"The Earl of Braven has a wife now, and he's going to have to deal with her."

"You're a complete idiot."

Angrily, Brave turned to face his friends. Julian was angry. Gabe was . . . well, Gabe looked like he always did when Julian got his temper up. Gabe looked amused.

"You think I don't already know that?" Without any aid from the groom, Brave swung himself up onto his horse's back and started off.

His friends had arrived earlier that day—while Brave was still languishing on the sofa in his study. A cold bath and some black coffee had followed. And once he'd shaved and dressed, Brave felt almost sober. It had been Gabriel who suggested the fresh air. And when Julian had asked if perhaps Rachel would like to join them, Brave had to confess that he didn't know where his wife was. And for some foolish reason he hadn't yet deciphered, he'd also decided to tell them *why* he didn't know where his wife was. The confession was supposed to incite his friends' compassion. It seemed to have achieved just the opposite—from Julian, anyway.

"Don't you think," Julian had said with more emotion than even Brave was used to seeing him display, "that if Rachel had wanted to 'thank you' in such a way, she would have done it when you actually agreed to help her and not have waited until now?"

He'd had a point, but Brave wasn't entirely convinced.

"And," Julian continued, "did it not occur to you to simply ask her what she'd meant? Of course not! That would have been too easy, wouldn't it?"

Brave would have taken offense to that, had he not agreed. He should have asked Rachel. Instead, he jumped to conclusions, basing his assumptions on his own battered self-esteem. At the time, he'd simply assumed the worst. And then his pride had prevented him from acting like a mature adult. Instead, he'd gone off to lick his wounds, not even considering that they might be of his own making.

As they cantered away from the stables, Julian's horse came up beside Brave's.

"So what are you going to do?"

Brave shot him a weary glance. "When she comes home I'll talk to her." He didn't add that he was going to talk to her because it was the right thing to do and not because Julian wanted him to. Let his friend claim responsibility. It would be something to needle him over if Brave ended up being right in the first place.

For the first time in his life he *wanted* to be wrong.

And not knowing where Rachel went, there could be no knowing when she would return home. Brave wouldn't blame her if she stayed away for a few days and let him stew for a bit, but if he knew Rachel, she wouldn't stay away from her mother for very long. Perhaps someday he would inspire such loyalty.

He refused to think of what might happen if she ran into her stepfather. At least he could be certain that Rachel hadn't left him for good. First of all, she wasn't that flighty a female. Secondly, she wouldn't go anywhere without her mother, and Marion Westhaver was in no condition to travel. And thirdly, Rachel wanted her mother free of Sir Henry's clutches, and the only person that could help her achieve that was Brave himself. That alone would buy him enough time to set things right between them.

It was also going to give Westhaver enough time to retaliate.

The perfect solution would be if Henry Westhaver simply fell off the face of the earth, but that wasn't very likely to happen, was it?

Not a bloody chance.

Once in the field, Brave let the gelding go, bending over its back until his face was almost level with its neck. Gabriel and Julian followed, their mounts easily picking up the pace until the three of them were nothing more than blurs racing across the countryside. They sailed over the hedgerows and stone fences, past tenant farmers laboring in the fields, and still the horses showed no sign of tiring. Brave's eyes stung from the cold, and he almost lost his hat twice, but on they went, until his bleary vision caught sight of something unusual up ahead, near one of the low stone walls.

He tugged on the reins, slowing his horse to a walk. Gabriel and Julian did the same, each coming up to flank him. As the three of them drew closer to the wall, Brave noticed it was a horse lying on the grass. A fine-looking bay— or least it had been. The poor thing was on its side and from the position of the carcass, obviously dead. How had it gotten there? It wasn't one of his mounts, so where was its rider? And there had been a rider because the saddle was still cinched around its belly.

"Do you recognize it?" Gabriel asked, his brow furrowed.

"No," Brave replied. Easing out of the saddle, he dismounted and walked closer to the corpse. A shiver of dread raced down his spine. He didn't want to look . . .

Oh dear God.

The body of a man lay beneath the horse, pinned to the ground by its weight. But it wasn't that the man was still alive that shocked Brave, nor was it the fear or the pain in his eyes as he stared at him. No, Brave was shocked because the man on the ground was desperately trying to reach his rifle. And because he was Sir Henry Westhaver.

Chapter 17

It took several men and a great deal of strength, but with the aid of his friends and some of his tenants, Brave finally managed to pull the dead horse off Henry Westhaver. Then Phelps supervised as Brave and two others lifted the baronet onto a crude stretcher and loaded him into the back of Phelps's wagon.

"Wrap him in the blankets," Phelps instructed as they set him down. "And place those heated bricks I brought around him. That should keep him warm until we get him back to the farm."

It was a miracle—depending on how one looked at it—that Sir Henry wasn't already dead. He'd been trapped beneath that horse for two nights. Phelps believed the only thing that kept him from succumbing to the elements was the warmth of the horse's carcass.

From what little Sir Henry had told them, Brave managed to deduce the baronet's plan.

After their scuffle at Wyck's End, Sir Henry had gone

home, only to feel his anger grow. Finally, he'd decided that if Brave didn't want to hand over his wife, then he'd take her by force. Brave had no illusions about Westhaver's intentions. The rifle proved he had planned to kill anyone who got in his way—specifically Rachel and Brave himself. Given the baronet's tenuous hold on his temper, he no doubt would have shot Marion as well if she'd dare refuse him.

But Sir Henry had come after them drunk, riding hell-bent for leather across fields neither he nor his mount was used to navigating, especially in the dark. Westhaver tried to force the unfortunate horse into a jump and had botched it. The horse went down, breaking its neck and pinning Sir Henry beneath its carcass.

"Sometimes," Brave remarked to one of his tenants as Phelps's wagon departed with its injured cargo, "there's no such thing as justice."

The farmer nodded. "I know what you mean, m'lord. 'Tis a pity to see such a fine animal dead whilst that fat arse lives."

"Well said, Jones." Turning, Brave walked through the short grass toward where Gabriel and Julian waited with the horses. "Now, I must return to Wyck's End. No doubt the magistrate will want to know what's happened, just in case Westhaver doesn't survive."

The magistrate wasn't the only one wanting answers. Rachel was waiting for him in the entrance hall when he came through the door.

"The servants say there was an accident. Is it true?" she demanded without so much as a hello. "Is Sir Henry dead?"

He supposed he couldn't expect her to greet him with a kiss after his behavior these last two days. He wanted to explain to her, but he was in desperate need of clean clothes, especially since the magistrate would no doubt be paying a call as soon as he heard the news.

"No, he is not." Handing his hat and greatcoat to

Reynolds, he made for the stairs, taking them two at a time. "Now if you will excuse me, I need to change before the magistrate gets here."

"Magistrate?" Skirts hiked up above her ankles, Rachel gave chase. "The magistrate is coming here. Why?"

"Because your stepfather might very well die," Brave replied, picking up speed. "And if that happens, I want everyone to know that his death was an accident and not murder."

She struggled to keep up. "Why would anyone think it was murder?"

At the top of the stairs, Brave turned down the corridor toward his rooms. He slowed his pace. "Because he almost killed your mother and because he and I came to blows over it. And because you were seen by several of his servants in his house with a pistol. Anyone with any inkling of how Sir Henry treated your mother will wonder if either you or I finally decided to kill the bastard."

He found little satisfaction in the way the blood ran from her face. Rachel had already paid more than amply for her rash attempt at confronting her stepfather, she didn't need to know there might be more consequences.

"But it was an accident," she insisted, her breath shallow as she hurried. "Meg said it was an accident."

"So it was." He stopped outside his bedroom door. "And I want the magistrate to know it. Now, if you'll excuse me, I wish to be in a more presentable state when he arrives."

Rachel clasped her hands in front of her. "What are you going to tell him?"

"I've always found the truth to be most useful." He opened the door.

"Even about our marriage?"

Pausing in the doorway, Brave turned to her. So that's what this was all about. "That I plan to discuss as little as possible—with the magistrate. You and I have much to talk about, however."

She flushed, and a stab of guilt pierced Brave's gut, but not for long.

"Of course," she agreed. "You'll find me after the magistrate leaves?"

Brave nodded. "I don't think you could avoid it if you tried."

And then, before he could do anything foolish, like fall to his knees and beg her forgiveness, he turned and entered his room, shutting the door firmly behind him.

Brave didn't have to worry about Rachel avoiding him. As soon as the magistrate left, she sent Reynolds with a message that she was waiting for him in her chamber. Would he please join her there at his earliest convenience?

Earliest convenience? With a snort, Brave crumpled her note in his hand and ran a hand through his hair. There was nothing convenient about their situation. Nothing at all.

And did he mind? Not really. Having a wife was new to him, but he couldn't exactly say it was a bad thing, even given the circumstances. In fact, if it wasn't for the fact that he was terrified that Rachel was going to confirm his suspicions about her motives for making love to him, he'd feel rather content being a husband.

He didn't want his wife to make love with him out of gratitude. He wanted passion and desire and affection. And while he couldn't deny that Rachel had wanted him, and had enjoyed it, he couldn't help but question why.

He took the stairs in his usual two-at-a-time manner. There was no sense in putting this off any longer. Regardless of her answer, he would deal with it. Even if she had slept with him as a means of thanking him, it didn't mean that she wouldn't want to be with him again, and this time for the right reasons.

He'd barely knocked when the door to her chamber flew open.

"What did the magistrate say?"

Always right to the point was his Rachel, especially when the situation directly involved herself or her mother. She couldn't stand not knowing exactly what was going on.

"And good day to you as well," he replied smoothly, slipping past her into the room.

The door shut behind him. "I'm not sure you deserve such courtesy after the last few days."

That stung, but it was true. How could he expect her to be cordial after he'd behaved so badly?

He turned to face her. With her arms folded across her magnificent bosom and a cool expression on her lovely face, she looked just like an Amazon warrior daring him to make the first strike.

"The magistrate is convinced Sir Henry's accident was just that, an accident. He did say that your stepfather has some explaining to do as to why he was coming here with a rifle."

She paled. "What if he decides to let Sir Henry take my mother back to Tullywood?"

Brave shook his head. "He won't. Sir Henry was coming here to take her home, and he didn't mind if he had to kill someone in the process. The magistrate is not likely to forget that."

He shouldn't have mentioned Sir Henry's intent. If it was possible, Rachel's face whitened even further, and Brave feared she might faint.

"He was going to kill her," she whispered, pressing a hand to her mouth.

In an instant, Brave crossed the pale green and gold carpet to where she stood. He curled his fingers around her shoulders. "We don't know that for certain. It could have just as easily been me he was after."

She didn't seem relieved by his words.

"I should think you'd be glad to be rid of me," he joked.

Some of the blood rushed back to her cheeks. "That's odd. I was thinking you wanted to be rid of me."

There was a deep hurt in her gaze, and Brave could kick himself for having treated her so poorly. Julian was right. She deserved better. She deserved honesty and trust.

"Why did you let me make love to you?" So much for being subtle.

He'd shocked her. She hadn't been expecting that.

"I told you," she replied, her tone confused. "Because I wanted to."

"You told me you did it because you wanted to thank me for handling Sir Henry."

There was no way she could have pretended the anger and surprise on her face. "I most certainly did not!"

"Rachel," he said with conviction. "I heard you say it."

"Then you heard wrong!" she cried, pulling free of his hold. "I would never had said such a thing because it's not true!"

He wasn't convinced. Miranda had said things she claimed not to have meant either, especially when she tried to convince him to propose again.

"Then you didn't want to thank me?"

"Of course I did!" she cried, throwing her hands into the air. "But I can do that with words, Brave. I certainly wouldn't do it by offering my virginity. It's not that much of a prize."

"I beg to differ."

The words were spoken softly, not suggestively at all, but she still blushed.

"Besides," she continued, "I didn't just give you my virginity, I gave myself to you, and I certainly wouldn't do that where a simple 'thank you' would have sufficed."

Staring into her eyes, deep indigo with conviction, Brave believed her. She might not think much of her maidenhead, but she thought something of herself, of her control and her freedom.

And then it hit him just how much of a gift she'd given him, and he was humbled by it.

And shamed. Ashamed of how he had reacted because his pride had been pricked, ashamed because he'd been too caught up in himself to see her true motives.

"Forgive me?" he asked, reaching out for her once again.

She came willingly into his embrace, pressing her cheek against his shoulder. "Yes."

He smiled against her hair. Every man should be this blessed. "Show me."

She laughed and lifted her head to meet his gaze. "You don't want me to thank you with my body, but you're willing to let me forgive you with it?"

"It's not the same thing," he teased.

"Isn't it?"

"No." He pulled her closer, so that her hips pressed against his. "Thanking someone is an act of kindness. Making love shouldn't be done out of kindness, but it can be done out of forgiveness. And you know what forgiveness is."

She raised a brow. "What?"

He grinned. "Divine."

She laughed. Not a demure giggle or a throaty chuckle, but a deep, full-blown laugh that filled the room and his heart.

Leaving his embrace, she moved toward the bed. Climbing onto the mattress, she turned to face him with an expression that made his blood run hot and his groin tighten in anticipation.

"Come get your forgiveness."

She was his, finally his, and all the anger and anxiety of the past few days slid to the farthest recesses of his mind. Right now all that mattered was that she was there, offering herself to him, and he meant to take her.

And to give himself in return.

Toeing off his boots, he kicked them across the room and climbed onto the bed to face her.

He reached out, his fingers brushing the soft indent of her temple and trailing down the curve of her cheekbone to her stubborn jaw.

"You're the most beautiful thing I've ever seen."

Her chin quivered, and her eyes were suddenly bright with tears. "Really?" Her voice was little more than a tiny whisper.

He answered her by grabbing her by the waist and hauling her against him. Lowering his head to hers, he kissed her with all the emotion he had to give her. Every overwhelming ounce of emotion and passion poured out of him as he slid his tongue between her teeth, tasting her, drinking her.

His fingers deftly unfastened the handful of buttons on the back of her gown. Drawing it up over her head, he tossed it across the room. Her shift followed, until finally she knelt before him in nothing but her stockings and garters.

"Beautiful," he whispered, his eyes never leaving hers, even though he longed to look at her nakedness.

Her arms wound around his neck as he lowered them both to the mattress. She was soft and warm beneath him, and he wanted to melt into her so he could truly feel every inch of her at once.

He kissed her until he thought his lungs would burst. His tongue licked the hollows of her mouth, tasted the salty sweetness of her lips. Everything about her was a delicious shock to his senses and his body trembled with the force of his emotions.

Gasping for air, Brave stared down at her, into wide blue eyes that were dark with desire.

"Are you sure this is what you want?"

She lifted her hips against his. Just the feel of her feminine heat caused his shaft to throb and thicken.

"Yes," she replied. "This is what I want. I want you."

He kissed her again, sliding his mouth down her jaw to the slender column of her throat. His teeth nipped at the delicate skin there, and he pressed his lips against the rapidly beating pulse in the hollow at the base of her neck, feeling the frantic throbbing of her excitement.

Lifting himself on one arm, Brave lifted the other hand to her breast, watching her skin flush softly as he brushed his thumb across one taut nipple.

"Do you like that?" he asked, stroking the puckered pink bud until her breathing quickened and her hips began to move beneath his.

"Yes," she answered, pushing against his hand. "I like it very much."

Her reply sent him into full arousal, both physically and emotionally. Nothing else mattered but her and joining himself with her.

His erection strained painfully against the confines of his trousers as he lowered his mouth to her nipple. Greedily, he sucked at her, drawing her deep into his mouth until her soft moans became sharp cries and her fingernails dug into his shoulders through his shirt. He moved to the other breast.

Rachel's hands slid down his back to his waist, her fingers clawing at his shirt until she succeeded in pulling it free of his trousers. "Off," she demanded, groaning as he tongued her nipple with ruthless abandon. "Take it off."

Releasing her breast, Brave rose up on his knees. As his fingers fumbled with the buttons on his waistcoat, his gaze feasted on the sight of her beneath him. Her eyes were dark, her skin flushed a pale petal pink—the color of arousal, and one he knew perfectly. Her lips and nipples were a darker shade of rose, one he found as entrancing as the shade of her flesh. And farther down her body was an even softer pink, peeking out from between the downy lips of her sex. And that pink, Brave could tell anyone, was the exact color of heaven.

His waistcoat flew across the room. Grabbing the hem of

his shirt, he hauled it upward, almost getting tangled in the fabric when Rachel's curious fingers caressed the length of him through his falls. He pulsated against her hand.

"Shall I remove those as well?" he asked, as his shirt flew off to join his waistcoat.

Rachel nodded, smiling coyly. "Yes. Take them off."

He did, watching her as she watched as he slid the buckskin and linen drawers down over his hips and down to his thighs. His arousal sprang free, hard and anxious, the head dewy with anticipation. Rachel's eyes glittered at the sight of it.

"It will feel different this time, won't it?"

Kicking the trousers and his stockings onto the floor, Brave leaned over her. "It will. There won't be any discomfort this time. Only pleasure." To emphasize his point, he slid a finger down her abdomen, to the golden curls between her thighs. Her legs parted, and he slid a finger inside her, gasping as her wet heat closed around him. She gasped too.

"Like this." He began moving his finger in and out of her. "Only better."

Bending down, he planted soft kisses along her throat and breast before moving down. He kissed her ribs, and the soft flesh of her belly, gently rolling the tip of his tongue along the hollow of her navel. He nuzzled the soft honey-colored curls between her thighs.

He withdrew his finger from her and, lifting his head, made certain she was watching when he raised it to his mouth. The scent of her heated his blood to a hot rush of sensation. She tasted delicate and musky, all salty sweetness.

Rachel's eyes widened. "What are you doing?"

"Tasting you," he replied, sliding down between her legs. "And now I'm going to taste you some more."

She tensed when his fingers parted her flesh. Placing his mouth against her warm wetness, Brave teased the sensitive bud hidden there with the tip of his tongue, drawing a sharp gasp from her and making her arch her hips against him.

Slowly, he stroked her with his tongue, tasting her, teasing her. Rachel's heels dug into the mattress, lifting her hips even higher, moving them in rhythm with his attentions. She made a low, keening sound deep in her throat, and the hands that she tangled in his hair pressed him deeper into her.

Brave was merciless. His hands slid under her buttocks, holding her in position as he plunged his face between her legs. His senses were filled with her and the urge to feel her shudder around him. To taste her as she shivered in completion was the only thing that existed for him. Faster and harder he stroked her, until her thighs clamped down hard on his shoulders, and her cries rang out above him.

Breathing heavily, he raised himself above her, teasing her wetness with the head of his shaft. She gasped, pressing her head back against the cushions. She tried to arch her hips, urging him to enter her, but he held still, watching as the last shiver shook her.

Slowly, he pushed against the entrance to her body. Inch by inch, he ground his teeth and slid into her, teasing them both with ever-languid pushes. He wanted to thrust his hips hard, drive himself into her and find release from the torrent of emotions spiraling through him. The moans escaping her throat were sharp, keening sounds, almost as if she were in pain.

"Do you want this?" He pushed deeper, watching pleasure play across her features.

"Yes." She squirmed against him, pushing up even as he held back. "Do it, Brave. Do it now!"

He needed no further encouragement. Colors spun behind his eyes as he drove himself into her, and he had to stop and gather his control. She was so tight around him, so hot and wet and like nothing he'd ever felt before.

Slowly, he moved within her. He wanted to take his time, wanted to make her come again. Every muscle in his body was rigid as he fought to maintain control. God, he wanted this to last forever.

She raised her hips against him, flexing her internal muscles so that they clenched hard around him. Brave gasped, tearing his mouth away from her breast and arching his spine as spasms of pleasure pooled in his groin. He wasn't going to last, not like this.

He rolled over onto his back, taking her with him so that their positions were reversed. She sat astride him, her body firmly wrapped around his. He gripped her hips and held her there. The sensation was maddening, intoxicating, and threatened to send him over the edge at any second. As the urgency subsided, he released his grip and allowed her to set the rhythm.

Brave's fingers fisted in the sheets, pulling so tightly he could feel the tendons in his arms tremble as he raised his hips clean off the bed to bury himself deeper within her. Her movements quickened, became more and more urgent as she rode him. Her breathing was harsh, her face intent as she drove her body down on his.

She shuddered, crying out as she fell forward. The pressure in Brave's abdomen reached its peak and maintained it for only seconds before pitching him over the edge. He could not silence the shout of gratification that pushed its way past his lips any more than he could stop the incredible spasms that shook his entire body.

Rachel slid down to his side. He closed his arms around her with what little energy he had left, and holding her against him, pressed his lips against her forehead.

"Feel free to ask for my forgiveness anytime," she whispered, her breath hot and shallow against his neck.

Laughing, Brave met her heavy-lidded gaze. "Give me a few minutes."

"Is it true?"

Closing the door behind her, Rachel crossed the room to her mother's bed, perching herself in her usual spot. Her mother was sitting up, supported by her ever-present mountain of pillows. Her ribs still gave her discomfort, but her bruises had begun to yellow, and the swelling was almost completely gone. Her anxious expression was all too familiar.

"He's not dead," Rachel replied. "But from what Brave told me, it doesn't sound good."

Her mother drew a shaky breath. "Is it wrong of me to be so hopeful?"

"Hopeful that he'll die, you mean?" At her mother's hesitant nod, she continued, "I don't think so. I'd say it's to be expected given all he put you through. I hope he dies, too."

"You shouldn't say such things out loud," Marion admonished, her gaze darting toward the ceiling.

Rachel chuckled. "Mama, God can hear me think it just as well as he can hear me say it. I don't think he'll blame either one of us for wishing for it."

Dragging her gaze downward, her mother smiled sheepishly. "I suppose not." Her smile faded into an expression of concern. "How did your discussion with Braven go?"

She plucked at a nub on the quilt, trying to hide the blush that flooded her cheeks. "It went well."

"You never did tell me what happened to make you both so upset."

This time Rachel couldn't hide the hot flush that crept up her neck. Sometimes she believed her mother could read her thoughts just as easily as God could.

"Let's just say Brave questioned my motives for doing something. He now knows he was mistaken." Lord, even saying it so cryptically, the meaning sounded perfectly clear to Rachel!

"Remind me to thank Lord Braven for all the kindness he's shown us."

The irony of her mother's words brought a smile to

Rachel's lips. "I'm sure he knows how thankful we are." But did he know how loved he was?

Marion reached up and tentatively placed her fingers against her bruised cheek. "No, I'm not sure that he can."

Rachel's heart rolled over in her chest. She reached out and seized her mother's other hand in both of hers. "I'm so sorry this happened, Mama. I'm so sorry I wasn't there to stop it, to help you. It will be all over soon, I promise. Soon you won't ever have to fear for your safety again. You won't ever have to fear Sir Henry again. I'll make sure of it."

"You have nothing to feel sorry for, darling."

The old guilt surfaced with a vengeance. "Yes, I do."

Her mother smiled sympathetically. "You don't think I blame anyone but myself for my marriage to Sir Henry, do you?"

Rachel's head snapped up. She opened her mouth, but nothing came out.

"I'd heard stories about him, but I foolishly believed that he'd changed. I was tired of going hungry and relying on charity, and when he proposed, I saw it as a chance for a better life for both of us. I could have gone into service somewhere, but I wanted a better life than that for you." Marion laughed humorlessly. "And what a life it was, hmm?"

"It wasn't your fault, Mama."

"No? Whose was it then? Yours?"

Rachel averted her gaze.

"Rachel, I did not marry Sir Henry because of you. I married him because of me, because I didn't want to get calluses on my hands, because I didn't want you to get calluses on yours. I was afraid to be alone and scared, and so I jumped at Sir Henry's proposal because he offered to take care of us and flattered me. If I hadn't been so scared and still grieving for your father, I would have had more sense, but I didn't."

Looking up, Rachel couldn't believe her ears. "You didn't marry him just to put a roof over my head?"

Her mother chuckled. "That was certainly part of it, but it wasn't all for you, no."

Rachel couldn't believe how much of an idiot she'd been. How self-absorbed. She automatically assumed everything was about her, either for her or against her.

Marion squeezed her hand. "Dearest, I know you married Braven to help me, but he's a good man, a good man who will treat you as you deserve. I hope you find the happiness you deserve with him."

Rachel didn't tell her mother that Brave already made her happy. She wasn't sure how, but he did. He made her feel safe and secure, something she hadn't felt since she was a child. He made her want to make him smile again. And when he did laugh or smile, it was as though the full radiance of the sun was released upon her. All she could do was bask in his joy.

He was everything she'd ever wanted—someone who'd look after her and protect her. She'd been the one doing the protecting since she was a young girl. It would be nice to have someone to run to when she got scared instead of trying to find a way out herself. Not that she wanted someone to hide behind, but someone to lean on would be nice.

Could she take the chance and offer him not only her body but her heart as well? Brave could give her the kind of life she'd only read about in romances and fairy tales. He could give her a happily ever after. He could give her those fat babies. She already knew he gave wonderful foot rubs.

But could he give her love? Was there room in his heart for another when Miranda Rexley still lived there?

And what of her? Could she give her heart to him while so much of her attention was focused on getting her mother a divorce? It had been her mission for so long she wasn't sure she knew how to pursue anything else, let alone the husband she never thought to love.

She couldn't give their relationship the attention it needed until she knew what condition Sir Henry was in. If he was going to recover, they would need to take extra precautions where protecting her mother was concerned, and that might mean leaving Wyck's End—and Brave—for a while.

The fact that Rachel couldn't imagine being safe anywhere else spoke volumes.

She slipped off the bed, careful not to jostle her mother in the process. "Mama, I have to go."

Her mother eyed her warily. After twenty-four years, Marion Westhaver knew when her daughter was up to something. "You're not going to do anything foolish, are you?"

Rachel frowned. "Like what?"

"Like burn down Tullywood or something."

Laughing, Rachel shook her head. "Nothing that extreme, Mama. I promise." She kept her smile bright. "I just have someone to go see."

Sir Henry didn't look so intimidating when he was unconscious. In fact, he looked almost harmless. Perhaps that was how her mother had first seen him as well—harmless.

"Will he live?" she asked, glancing over her shoulder to where Dr. Phelps stood.

The doctor came up beside her. "I honestly don't know. I suspect he sustained internal injuries during the fall. Whether or not he recovers depends on the extent of those injuries."

Rachel stared at the man in the bed, surprised at just how little she felt. She always thought she'd be happy or relieved to hear that her stepfather might die, but she felt nothing except the slightest bit of irony. How convenient would Sir Henry's death be? She and her mother would be free to do whatever they wanted.

And if he lived, there was still the matter of his coming to Wyck's End with a rifle. Given his earlier altercation with Brave, there was every chance he had been on his way to kill them all. Surely the law would have to take that into consideration and grant her mother a divorce. Perhaps Sir Henry would be jailed for making such a threat against a peer of the realm.

The worst thing that could happen was that Sir Henry would win. And if that happened, Rachel was prepared to take her mother someplace Sir Henry would never find her.

But that would involve leaving Brave, and Rachel didn't even want to think about that. She couldn't imagine never feeling the touch of his hands or lips again. Couldn't bear to think a time might come when she would never have him inside her.

Could she leave him if it came to that?

She knew exactly what her first instinct would be, but thankfully if it ever came to that, she would have time to think things through. No more rash decisions; they'd gotten her into enough trouble already.

"Do you think I could have a moment alone with him?" she asked, not taking her gaze from the corpulent form.

"I'm not certain that would be wise, Lady Braven."

Rachel smiled. She wasn't certain whether to be insulted or flattered that the doctor considered her a threat to his patient.

"You could sit by the door and keep an eye on me," she suggested, turning that smile on him. "Make sure I don't suffocate him or anything."

Dr. Phelps flushed bright crimson right up to the roots of his hair. "My lady, I didn't mean to insinuate—"

"Of course you did. And it's quite all right. I don't blame you. I wouldn't leave me alone with him either."

Eyes downcast, Dr. Phelps nodded. She'd obviously embarrassed him, for which she was sorry.

"It really is quite all right, Dr. Phelps."

He looked relieved. "Thank you, Lady Braven. I'll sit by the door so you can have some privacy."

Rachel was cautious as she moved toward the bed. Unconscious or not, her stepfather was still intimidating. She remembered the strength with which he struck her after she refused Charlton. With any luck, he'd never strike anyone again.

She sat down on a chair beside the bed, dragging it forward so that it touched the mattress. She wanted whatever she said to be for his ears and his ears only.

"Hello, Sir Henry," she whispered. "Can you hear me?"

No response.

"I hope you can." Her gaze swept over the slackness of his features. "My mother has begun to recover from what you did to her. In fact, I believe she's almost recovered from *you*. I know you wanted to break her. To be honest, I thought you had, but I was wrong. She's stronger than either of us ever gave her credit for."

Still nothing. Rachel was both relieved and irritated. She wanted him to hear her.

"You couldn't break her and you couldn't take the place of my father. She still loves him, you know. The only thing she feels for you is disgust."

One eyelid twitched and Rachel thrilled at the sight of it. He understood her! She leaned closer.

"You'll not defeat us, Sir Henry, do you know that now? No matter what happens, we will be free of you, even if you live. And if you die, I want you to know that no one will mourn you. Eventually, you'll be nothing but an unfortunate memory to my mother. You couldn't compare to my father in life; you certainly won't compare to him in death."

Another little twitch, this time around the doughy flesh of his mouth.

She looked down at her stepfather, drunk with the power his responses gave her. "I came here to tell you how completely insignificant you've become. It gives me a great deal of satisfaction to tell you these things. Rest well, Sir Henry.

You're not likely to find such peace again for a long, long time."

Rachel jumped when his arm twitched against her. For one split second, she envisioned him bolting upright in the bed and attacking her. He didn't. Except for that one spasm, he remained motionless.

"Is everything all right, Lady Braven?" Dr. Phelps called from behind her.

Staring at the headboard, Rachel inhaled deeply, trying to slow the pounding of her heart. "I'm not sure. His arm just moved."

Dr. Phelps left his chair and came up on the other side of Sir Henry's bed. Leaning down, he placed his fingers on the side of the baronet's neck. Then he checked his wrist.

Rachel watched as the physician paled.

"What is it?" she asked, both terrified and hopeful of his answer.

Phelps met her gaze with an expression Rachel couldn't quite read. "He's dead."

Chapter 18

Lady Marion wept a little when they told her the news. Whether they were tears of sorrow or relief, Brave couldn't tell. Perhaps they were both.

But despite Sir Henry's passing, Wyck's End was not a house in mourning. That evening at dinner, everyone wore their finest, most splendid attire. Even Marion, who hadn't been able to leave her room since her arrival, managed to make it downstairs for after-dinner refreshment in the music room. Brave carried her down himself and placed her on a comfortable chaise.

If it seemed odd to celebrate death, no one commented upon it. In fact, it seemed perfectly natural to say good-bye to Sir Henry by embracing life and the future. A future without the baronet's tyranny.

Only Rachel seemed a little out of sorts. Brave thought that decidedly strange, considering no one had wanted Sir Henry out of the way more than her.

He offered her a glass of sherry. "You're subdued."

She looked up. "I suppose I am. Thank you." She took a sip.

Flipping out the tails of his coat, Brave seated himself on the green-velvet sofa beside her. What he really wanted to do was sling her over his shoulder and carry her upstairs. In fact, he wanted to make love to her until there were no thoughts in that thick head of hers but thoughts of him and how good he felt inside her.

He wanted to be with her, wanted her to trust him completely. It scared him.

"So what's got you worried now?"

Rachel chuckled, her eyes brightening at his teasing. "Am I that transparent?"

"Only to someone whose powers of deduction are as keen as my own," he replied with mock arrogance. "What's the matter? I thought you'd be happy finally to be free of your stepfather."

"I am happy." She smiled ruefully. "That is the problem. It's one of the few times my impulsiveness resulted in something good."

Brave nodded, wondering if their marriage was another one of those good decisions. "Feeling a little guilty for being so happy, are you?"

Another smile. "I'm feeling guilty because I *don't* feel guilty. Does that make any sense?"

"Perfectly." He turned his body toward hers. "No one blames you for feeling relief, Rachel. No one condemns you for feeling happiness. Other than his tailor, I seriously doubt there's anyone in the county who's going to miss Henry Westhaver."

She placed a hand on his thigh and squeezed. Every nerve in his body jumped at the contact. This was ridiculous! He was as randy as a boy whenever she was within two yards of him.

"Thank you. You must get so very tired of easing my foolish worries all the time."

Brave grinned. "Not at all. It gives me something to do with my day."

Rachel laughed, and he could feel her blue mood lift.

"You've been smiling an awful lot lately," she remarked. "A few weeks ago I wondered if you even could smile."

A few weeks. Was that all it had taken him to fall in love with her? It seemed longer somehow.

Love. Is that what this feeling was? It was different than he expected. He'd pined for Miranda, ached for her—even when he was with her. But with Rachel, he felt whole, like a part of him had been missing and she was it.

He placed his hand over hers. Her fingers were cold. "You make me want to smile." That was it? Hadn't he just been thinking about how much he loved her? Why couldn't he just tell her?

Something flickered across her face, and he thought for a moment, he wondered, if she'd been hoping for something more, but then it was gone and she smiled. Did she love him as well? Was that what she'd wanted to hear, a declaration? He didn't know if he could.

Coward.

Her gaze drifted across the room and Brave's followed, to where their mothers sat, chatting. Marion still looked awful, but her spirits were high. Brave admired her for that.

"What do you think is in the will?" Rachel asked, staring at her mother as Annabelle patted her hand.

"I'm not sure. I suppose we'll find out tomorrow." At exactly three o'clock the next afternoon, Sir Henry's solicitor would descend upon them to read the will. They probably could have read it that evening were it not for the fact that Sir Henry's heir had to be notified of his inheritance. Since the young man lived just over in Sherif Hutton, he would arrive the next morning.

"Let's go to bed," he suggested after several moments of silence.

Turning, Rachel flashed a coy smile. "What did you have in mind?"

With feigned innocence, Brave shrugged. "I don't know. I thought we could play a few hands of piquet, or mess up the sheets some more so the servants really have something to talk about."

She blushed. She blushed so easily and so brightly, Brave was enthralled by it.

They said good nights to their mothers, who barely seemed to notice their departure, they were so engrossed in their own conversation.

Once inside his chamber, Brave stoked the fire, blew out all the candles save for one by the bed, and then undressed his wife by its soft light. His own clothes followed and he joined her on the bed, kissing every silky pink inch of her until he was ready to burst with wanting her. And then she kissed every inch of him, and he almost did burst. Finally, he sank into her with a sigh of contentment. If ever it was possible for a body to be at peace, Brave found his in Rachel's arms.

And afterward, as he held her in the dark, he tried to find the words to tell her how he felt about her, but he was afraid to say them. The last time he'd told someone he loved her she'd rejected him. It didn't matter that he now realized he hadn't loved Miranda, what mattered was that he didn't want to say the words and then put Rachel in the awkward position of having to respond. He was afraid the fragile bond between them wouldn't be able to survive such an uncomfortable situation if she had to tell him she didn't feel the same way.

And if she didn't feel the same way, he didn't want to know.

The funeral was small, as was expected.

The day was cold, but strangely bright and sunny, as though nature itself celebrated the baronet's passing. Very few of the townspeople were in attendance, and those who were only came to make certain Sir Henry was indeed dead.

Marion was still too sore and physically fragile to attend, and Brave thought it for the best. The last thing that poor woman needed were her neighbors staring at the bruises on her face. There were enough rumors circulating about the true nature of Sir Henry's death. It seemed most of the town still wanted to believe it was murder, despite the magistrate's findings. One look at Marion and the rumors would worsen. It was as though the townsfolk *wanted* Rachel or Brave to have killed Sir Henry. It suited their sense of justice.

After the service, Brave, Rachel, Sir Henry's solicitor, and the new baronet journeyed back to Wyck's End for the reading of the will.

Sir Henry's nephew turned out to be as different from his uncle as anyone from the same family could be, which was a great relief to everyone involved in the reading of the will. Marcus Westhaver was young, handsome, and possessed a charming disposition. He was also well educated and, unlike his predecessor, had a fine head for business.

He hadn't dressed in mourning either.

"I knew my uncle well enough not to miss him," Marcus informed them in a carefully neutral tone when Marion asked him to excuse the lack of black in the room.

When everyone was seated and had a cup of tea or something stronger, Sir Henry's solicitor, Mr. Smith began the reading. Apparently Sir Henry had a new will drafted after Brave had been so kind as to take Rachel off his hands, and Sir Henry's prosaic style certainly reflected the strange light-heartedness the baronet had felt at finally being rid of his stepdaughter.

It took poor Mr. Smith almost a full quarter hour to get through all that Sir Henry had to say about himself, the strength of his character, the soundness of his mind and the goodness of his heart. All of which had those listening exchanging puzzled, if not appalled glances.

Finally, Smith got to the point. "To my nephew Marcus

Westhaver of York, I bequeath my baronetcy as is his birthright. I leave him nothing more than what the title dictates as he deserves no more." Mr. Smith flushed as he read on. "If he is anything like his father he has no doubt pinched every penny he's ever had until it bled, and has no need for my funds as well."

Marcus smiled at that. "Why, thank you, Uncle. You're quite right."

Brave glanced over at Rachel. She winked.

"To my stepdaughter Rachel Ashton Wycherley, Countess Braven, I leave nothing more than the hope that she learns her place." Mr. Smith flushed deeper as Rachel snorted. "And to her husband Lord Braven, I leave the hope that he will be the man to put her in it."

The laughter bubbled over before Brave could stop it. The nerve of the old bastard! He was as miserable and mean in death as he had been in life. Only now he was no longer a threat to any of them and little more than a bad joke.

"To my dear wife, Marion—"

Obviously the will had been written before Marion left him. Brave was surprised Westhaver hadn't changed it out of spite. He supposed the baronet hadn't thought of that. He'd only thought of getting her back.

"I leave all my worldly possessions, including my horses, in the hopes that they will serve as a loving reminder of our marriage."

Rachel's gaze flew to her mother, and Brave's followed. *Loving reminder?* How would Marion react to that? Mr. Smith, poor man, looked about ready to crawl under the desk, he looked so pained. And why wouldn't he? Three of them had laughed out loud at their various sections of the will. And Marion, whom Sir Henry referred to lovingly, was reclining on a chaise with all the "loving reminders" she needed fading on her face.

But Marion didn't even blink. She smiled and nodded,

even faced with Brave and Rachel's amazement. She didn't even speak, not until all the will business had been concluded.

"Mr. Smith," she said softly, garnering the attention of the entire room.

"Yes, Lady Marion."

"I would like for you to arrange for the sale of my late husband's possessions, please. I'm not going to need them where I'm going."

"Going?" Rachel demanded, looking shocked. "Where are you going?"

Brave was shocked, too. He'd expected Marion to leave eventually. She'd told him she wanted to, and his mother had told him that she'd invited Marion to take a trip with her, but he hadn't expected her to announce it so soon. Neither had Rachel apparently.

Marion glanced over her shoulder toward her daughter. "Annabelle's invited me to tour the Continent with her. I'll tell you all about it after Mr. Smith and I finish our business."

Brave wondered if Rachel found Marion's light tone as forced as he did. He had no doubt that Marion wanted to make as little fuss over leaving as possible. He also knew that if she could, his wife would blow it completely out of proportion.

He watched as she fidgeted with the lace on her cuff, her head bowed. Even if he could read her mind, he wasn't certain he wanted to.

Was she worried about letting her mother go off on her own? Surely she didn't think there was anything to fear now that Sir Henry was gone?

Or was it being left alone with him that bothered her? No, that didn't make sense either. Then again, very little about Rachel did.

He smiled when she glanced in his direction. She smiled back. That was a good sign.

Marcus Westhaver was the first to depart, followed by Mr.

Smith. Once the old solicitor had taken his leave, Brave rose to his feet.

"I'll leave the two of you alone," he said. "Unless, you'd like me to take you back upstairs, Marion?"

His mother-in-law waved her hand. "That's quite all right, Balthazar." She'd refused to call him Brave, and he wouldn't have her call him by his title, so he had to get used to hearing his Christian name on her lips. His father had named him, said all the men in his family had strong names. His own father, Brave's grandfather, had been named Ulysses.

If he and Rachel ever had a son, he was going to name him George.

"As you wish. Ring for a footman or have someone come fetch me when you're ready." Over her head, his gaze locked with Rachel's. He blew her a kiss. "I'll be in my study."

He left them sitting there in silence. Whatever it was Rachel wanted to say to her mother, she didn't want him to hear any of it.

His own mother was waiting for him when he closed the door.

"Well?"

He started down the hall. "Well what?"

"Well, what happened?" She fell into step beside him.

"The nephew inherited the title and not a penny more," Brave informed her in a fair imitation of poor Mr. Smith. "Rachel was left the fond hope that she be put in her place, and Sir Henry charged me with the task of putting her there."

Annabelle laughed. "You're joking!"

Clasping his hands behind his back, Brave shook his head with a grin. "I'm afraid not. He left everything else to Marion."

"Wonderful!" His mother clapped her hands. "Is it enough to afford her a little independence?"

Brave tilted his head. "Sir Henry had quite a fine stable. The horses alone should fetch a fair penny. Not to mention his jewelry and personal items. Yes. I think she'll be able to live quite comfortably for a number of years, especially if she's frugal."

"Oh, she must be so pleased! Now I know she'll come abroad with me."

Brave stopped and turned to face her. "Why didn't she tell Rachel her plans? Do you know?"

Her smile faded to an expression of discomfort. "I shouldn't tell you this."

"The fact that you feel that way is all the more reason to tell me." He looked around for eavesdropping servants. "Now."

His mother sighed. "Marion was concerned that despite Rachel's feelings for you she might decide to accompany her."

Brave frowned. "But I'm quite certain Rachel never expected Marion to live with us forever."

"Yes, but I doubt she expected it to happen this soon. Marion thought Rachel's sense of loyalty might make her feel as though she had to choose between the two of you. Marion didn't want to give her time to think about it. I told her I thought that was ridiculous, but Marion said the girl has an incredible sense of loyalty. Foolishness is what I call it."

Brave was tempted to agree, especially given Rachel's penchant for impulsive decisions. "So Marion thought that if she didn't give Rachel time to think about it, then she couldn't do anything foolish."

Annabelle nodded. "Exactly."

"That's the worst thing to do where Rachel is concerned!" Sighing in frustration, he raked his fingers through his hair. "Rachel makes some of her best mistakes with no thought whatsoever."

His mother's eyes widened. "Balthazar, this girl sounds quite unstable."

He burst out laughing. "She just thinks she can fix things

better than anyone else, Mama. It's actually very charming once you get used to it."

She didn't look very convinced. "If you say so. Do you think she'll try to interfere with Marion's plans?"

"I don't know." And he was ashamed because he honestly didn't. In his gut he felt certain that Rachel wanted to stay with him, but he knew how she often acted without thinking.

"But I'll tell you something I do know."

"What's that?" his mother asked, frowning at the determination in his voice.

Brave met her gaze evenly. "There's no way in hell I'll let her go that easily."

"You could have at least told me you were planning to leave."

Sighing, Marion leaned back against the cushions. "And would you just let me leave?"

Rachel scowled so deeply she could see her own eyebrows. "I'm not Sir Henry, you know. Is that why you didn't tell me? You thought I'd try to stop you?"

"I thought you'd try to come with me."

Good lord, had she truly been that bullheaded that her own mother had to resort to trickery to keep her from interfering? She thought she'd been doing the right thing.

"Mama, I'm married to Brave. Even if it were possible, I can't believe you'd think I'd turn away from him that easily."

"It's not that I thought you'd turn away from Balthazar, dearest. It's that I thought you wouldn't be able to turn away from me."

"What?"

Marion flushed. "You've spent so many years trying to protect and look after me that I was worried you wouldn't be able to let go so easily."

"It was a lot easier than I thought. I'm not certain I ever had a choice." Scowling again, she added, "I might not always make the right decision, but once it's made, I stay with it."

Her mother had the audacity to chuckle at that. "Yes, dear. I know."

Perhaps Rachel hadn't always made the best decisions, and perhaps the consequences weren't always clear in her head when she made them, but her intentions were generally good. And for the past few years she'd thought of nothing but her mother and giving her a better life. And now she'd achieved it—or at least played a part in it. So why did she feel as though she was being abandoned?

Tears stung her eyes. "For years, I've thought of nothing but getting you away from Sir Henry, and now that it's done you're leaving, and I . . ." She swallowed hard against the lump in her throat. "I'm not sure I know how to do anything else but try to protect you."

Her mother stared at her, her own eyes filling. "And I've spent the last twenty-four years trying to protect you."

Startled, Rachel stared at her mother, wiping her eyes with the backs of her hands until her vision cleared.

"Now it's time for you to look after someone else, and let him look after you. It's what husbands and wives do. I think Balthazar will be good at it. He reminds me a bit of your father, you know."

Rachel couldn't help it. The dam burst, and all the tears she'd held at bay came pouring forth. She'd become such a watering pot lately! Lord, it felt good to let it all out.

Somehow, her mother had struggled to her feet, because she came to her and wrapped her thin arms around her.

"I'm so sorry, dearest," she murmured against Rachel's hair. "I never knew how much all of this affected you."

"You laughed at me." Rachel sniffed. How petulant she sounded.

"But not cruelly, dearest. Not cruelly. I only meant that I knew how stubborn you could be once you've made up your mind. And I'm thankful for that stubborness. Truly, I am.

Were it not for that I might very well be dead now." Her hands stroked Rachel's hair and lifted her head. "You've always been my little warrior queen."

Rachel couldn't help but laugh. Drying her eyes with the backs of her hands, she pulled away. "You shouldn't be standing," she said, once she'd found her voice. Sniffing, she accepted the handkerchief her mother pulled from her sleeve and soundly blew her nose.

"I'll be all right for a few moments," her mother replied blithely. "What about you? Are you all right?"

Rachel nodded. "Yes."

Her mother smiled. "You'll see, everything will work out for the best, as it usually does—thank heaven." Her smiled faded. "I'm very sorry I didn't tell you about my plans earlier."

"I understand why you didn't. I probably wouldn't have told me either." She sniffed. "I have no intention of trying to follow you, Mama. I don't think I could leave him if I tried."

Gingerly, her mother drew her into a soft, perfumed embrace. "I hope he knows what a lucky man he is, dearest. If he's smart, he won't ever let you go."

Gabriel and Julian were waiting for Brave in his study. His friends hadn't planned to stay for long. They'd only returned to finish the hunting trip they'd first embarked upon weeks before at Julian's, and to see how Brave's marriage was faring, but Sir Henry's accident had persuaded them to postpone indefinitely their ill-fated hunting trip at least until this mess was resolved.

And it didn't get any more resolved than death, so why were the two of them still there?

They were like two nosy old women, those two. It was a trait Brave despised in most people, but easily forgave in those closest to him. He couldn't blame them for wanting to know what was going on, for checking up on him. He'd certainly given them enough reason for concern over the last couple of years.

"How did the will reading go?" Gabriel asked as he sipped brandy in a chair by the fire.

Brave strolled across the room to the liquor cabinet and poured himself a drink. He opted for scotch, not brandy.

"It went well all things considered. The heir got the house and the title, Lady Marion got the horses and the personal effects."

Julian let out a low whistle from his chair opposite Gabriel. "That should bring her a fair price."

Brave drained his glass in one gulp. "She plans to take an extended trip with my mother. They hope to leave within the week if Lady Marion's well enough to travel." He poured another measure of scotch into his glass and moved to the sofa closest to his friends.

"That must give both you and Rachel some comfort," Julian remarked, "knowing that Lady Marion will be well looked after."

With a sigh, Brave leaned back against the padded brocade. "Speaking solely for myself, I do like the idea of Mama having someone with her when she traipses across the Continent. I'm not sure how Rachel is taking the news. Today is the first she's heard of it."

Something in his voice must have given away his concern, for both Gabe and Jules turned to stare at him.

"You don't think she'll want to go with them, do you?" Julian asked, his tone incredulous.

Julian always did have a knack for seeing deeper than Brave was comfortable with. "I don't know," he replied.

"What do you plan to do?"

Gabriel scowled. "What do you mean, what does he plan to do? He's her husband. If he wants her to stay, she stays."

Brave smiled at his friend. "I'm not that much of a tyrant,

and you know it, Gabe. I'd never force Rachel to stay with me against her will." He gazed into his glass. "I tried to control a woman once before, and we all know how that ended up. I'll not do it again."

"So you'll just toss her aside?"

"I'm not tossing her aside," Brave chided. "I'm not doing anything yet. Rachel hasn't even told me what she wants to do. I don't plan to let her go without a fight, but neither do I plan to dragoon her into doing something she doesn't want to do."

Gabe was like a dog with a bone. "But she's your *wife*. You made vows—"

"What I vowed was to protect her and her mother from Sir Henry. I promised to help her mother obtain a divorce. There's no need of that now." Brave swallowed another mouthful of scotch. It was true. He'd made a promise to Rachel, and fate had made it impossible for him to keep it. How did Sir Henry's death affect his own hope to make amends for Miranda? Was her death still on his soul? And why didn't the thought of her fill him with that familiar guilt? All he felt when he thought of Miranda was sadness.

"And so your vows mean nothing?" Gabe looked angrier than Brave had seen him in some time. "What of the promises she made you?"

Brave couldn't help but wonder if Gabe was talking about him and Rachel, or something else.

Rachel had promised him an heir, but he didn't want an heir. He wanted a child. His and Rachel's child.

"I can't very well expect her to keep her word when I couldn't keep mine. It would be dishonorable of me, and I don't want to behave dishonorably with another woman."

"I really hate it when you hide behind my sister, Brave."

Brave froze, his glass halfway to his mouth. Both he and Gabriel stared at Julian in stunned silence. Brave had never heard his friend speak with such vehemence.

"Miranda is dead," Julian informed him from between clenched teeth. "Let her be. You weren't the one who made a mess of her life. You weren't the one who killed her." He held up his hand as Brave opened his mouth to speak. "No. I don't want to hear it."

Wisely, Brave closed his mouth.

Julian continued, "You had every right to refuse to help her after the way she treated you. Miranda could have come to me after you rejected her. I would have done everything in my power to help her. There were a number of things that could have been done, but my sister was a foolish girl who believed her life was over because some blackguard used her and rejected her. Miranda alone is to blame for her death, and I am heartily sick of you wallowing in all this unnecessary, ludicrous guilt!" He tossed back the rest of his brandy.

Brave could only gape at his friend. "Julian, I—"

"You would have been miserable married to my sister. I know how much you thought of her, Brave. I loved her dearly, too. I still do, but even I can see her faults. You never would have been happy with her, and neither of you would have loved each other like you both deserved." Rising from his chair, Julian went to the sideboard and poured himself another drink.

Astonished, Brave turned to Gabriel, who simply flashed a rueful smiled and nodded. "He's right, you know. This has gone on long enough. You really must stop blaming yourself."

"And just what would the two of you have me do?" he demanded defensively. His friends—his best friends—had sided against him, and he didn't like it one bit.

"Tell Rachel the truth," Julian suggested. "Tell her that you love her."

Brave stiffened. "I never said I loved her. Besides, I don't know how she feels about me."

"If you don't, then you really are mad," Gabriel remarked.

"That woman loves you. I can see it in the way she looks at you. And any woman brave enough to love a blighter like you deserves to know the feeling's returned."

Brave opened his mouth to respond, but Julian cut him off. "Tell her the truth about why you married her. And not that you-married-her-to-save-her-mother nonsense. Tell her about my sister."

"She knows about your sister," Brave snapped. "I told her about Miranda."

Julian raised a brow. "Did you tell her you married her because of Miranda?"

Leaping out of his chair, Brave slammed his glass down on a table and whirled around to confront his friend.

"What do you want me to tell her? That I married her because I stupidly thought I could make amends for the past by marrying her? That if I helped her it would somehow make up for not helping Miranda?"

"Yes!" Julian cried.

Exhausted, Brave sagged against the back of the chair. "But it doesn't matter now," he said quietly. "That might have been my reason in the beginning, but it's not my reason anymore."

"She needs to know that." Stepping forward, Julian placed a heavy hand on his shoulder. "Brave, you have to be honest. If you don't tell her, this will always be between you, and she'll always doubt your feelings. *You* will always doubt your feelings. And Gabe's right. She deserves better. You both do."

Brave knew when he was beaten. His friends were right. If he and Rachel were to have any kind of future, he was going to have to tell her the truth. He honestly didn't know what he'd do if she rejected him as Miranda had, but he also knew he didn't want to spend the rest of his life wondering what might have been.

Rachel had saved him from the darkness. She'd brought

light back into his life, and when he thought of his perfect match, he no longer thought of Miranda. He thought of Rachel. Julian was right. He and Miranda would have made each other miserable, but Rachel . . . Rachel made him smile. Rachel made him happy, even with all her quirks and faults. And she seemed to like him despite all of his.

"You're right," he announced with a decisive nod. "I have to tell her. I trust the two of you plan to stay on?"

Julian grinned and raised his glass in mock salute. Gabe followed.

"We wouldn't miss it for the world."

"I'm leaving."

Frozen, Brave stood in the doorway between Rachel's room and the dressing room and watched as she tossed clothes into a trunk.

Surely he hadn't heard her correctly. "I beg your pardon?"

She didn't turn. She didn't even pause in her packing. "I'm going to Tullywood to oversee the inventory of Mama's belongings" She sounded so cold, so impersonal. Not like his Rachel at all.

"Obviously Mama isn't in any condition to do it herself, and since she wants it done before she and your mother leave, the task falls upon me."

Something wasn't right. "Surely you don't have to stay there? Can't you travel back and forth each day. It's not very far." Just a little over a mile in fact.

She tossed a pair of stockings into the trunk. "Lord Braven, I have no desire to stay under a roof where I'm not wanted."

Her words were like a boot to the belly. "You think you're not wanted here?"

"I know I'm not." Her voice was sharp and crisp.

"Well you're wrong!" This was ridiculous! He moved toward her, coming up behind her to rest his palms on her shoulders. "Rachel, what the devil is the matter?"

She twisted free of his grip, pushing his hands away with her arm. "I *heard* you. I was coming to invite the three of you to take tea with me and I heard you and your friends talking about why you married me, that it was all because of *her*."

Oh God. Brave's heart stilled. How much had she heard? Obviously not enough or she'd know that he planned to confess all to her. She'd know that Miranda no longer mattered.

"Rachel—"

"I asked you about it before, remember? I asked you if our marriage had anything to do with her, and you said no." She jabbed him in the chest with her finger. He grunted. "You lied to me! It had everything to do with her! God! I can't believe I was so incredibly stupid!"

She turned back to her trunk, but not before Brave saw the tears in her eyes. "Rachel, just let me explain."

She whirled around again. "I don't want to hear it! There's nothing you could say to me right now to make me believe you! Do you know that I was foolish enough to think I was in love with you? And I was even more foolish in hoping that you might someday come to love me! But you're in love with a memory, and I can't compete with that. I don't want to." She sneered, twisting her usually soft features into something harsh and angry.

"You don't understand."

She laughed, a harsh and bitter sound. "Oh, I understand better than you think. You know, if you had been honest with me right from the start, I would have been better prepared. I wouldn't have dared to believe there was anything between us, that you cared for me."

He hated the anguish in her voice. The anger he could handle, but not the pain. "I do care for you!"

"Oh?" Her dark eyes, wet and bright with tears met his. "Tell me, Brave, if you were thinking of Miranda when you married me, did you think of her at other times as well?"

A cold tremor ran down Brave's spine. Was she implying what he thought she was? "What do you mean?"

Rachel's face went white. She didn't want to come out and say it, but he wanted to hear the words on her lips. They'd come too far to hold back now.

"Who were you making love to, Brave? Me or her?"

God, but it still hurt to hear her say it. Did she really think so little of him that she could suspect him of using her in such a way?

"Rachel—"

She held up her hand. He was becoming heartily sick of her cutting him off. "Don't say it. I don't want to hear any more lies right now, Brave. At least I was honest about why I married you. I trusted you, and I feel as though you've betrayed that trust." She shut the lid on the trunk. "I need to be away from you for a few days. I need to think, and I can't think with you so close."

Brave supposed that was a backhanded compliment, but it didn't do much to warm him at the moment. He felt cold, colder than he had in a long time. She'd shut him out, just as he'd been doing to her since the day they were married. He was losing her, and it hurt. It hurt more than Miranda's rejection and suicide combined. It even hurt to breathe.

"How long will you be gone?" He could scarcely hear his own voice.

She shrugged as she stared at the trunk. "As long as it takes."

A voice inside his head screamed at him not to let her go. "You'll send for me if you need anything?"

She nodded. He saw a tear slip down her cheek. "If I need anything."

And Brave knew Rachel would rather go without than admit to needing anything, let alone needing him.

Chapter 19

∞⟩⟨∞

Rachel never thought she'd be so happy—no *relieved*—to be at Tullywood again. The house held so many unpleasant memories that she could scarcely turn a corner without remembering something awful from the years she spent within those walls. But still, she would rather be there than at Wyck's End with the man who had made a complete fool out of her.

She should have known a man like that would never marry someone like her out of the goodness of his heart. She should have known he'd have a reason other than begetting an heir. Any woman could give him children. Only Rachel had been able to offer him penance.

At least David had only wanted her for her body.

"Where do you want this, Lady Braven?"

Rachel looked up from wrapping her mother's porcelain figures. Janie, one of the chambermaids at Tullywood was packing some of her mother's personal items from her dressing table. The girl held a delicate emerald ring in her palm.

It was the ring her father had given her mother the day he proposed. Her parents had known true love. Her father never would have used her mother to replace another woman.

No, her father had been betrothed to another woman while he courted her mother.

"I'll take that, Janie, thank you."

The maid gave her the ring, and Rachel slipped it on her finger. It was cool against her skin, and much more suitable than the large Wycherley sapphire Brave had given her when they married.

Everything about them was so ill suited. So why did it hurt so much to be away from him?

She wasn't angry—not anymore. She'd had twenty-four hours to think about things. Her first thought had been to run as far away from Brave as she could, but she knew that wasn't possible. And even if it were, she didn't want to leave him. Even though he'd lied to her, perhaps even used her, she could not leave him and she couldn't stay angry. Because she loved him. And because she understood what it was like to feel so responsible for something you'd do almost anything to fix it.

No, she didn't approve of his methods; but she certainly couldn't blame him for them.

The look on his face when she'd asked him if he'd been making love to her or Miranda had cut her to the very bone. No matter what other lies he'd told, she knew the answer to that question as surely as she knew her own heart. At the time she'd been too hurt and angry to realize it, but now that she'd had time to go over things in her head she was certain Brave had been telling the truth when he told her he cared about her.

"What about this?" This time it was a cameo Janie held out for inspection. It was the fourth time the girl had asked about a specific piece in the last ten minutes.

"Tell you what," Rachel said, rising to her feet. "Why

don't you finish packing these figurines, and I'll take care of the jewelry?" She should have been the one to pack her mother's personal items to begin with. If she hadn't had her head full of thoughts of her husband and how much she missed him, she wouldn't have assigned Janie to the task.

Switching spots with the maid, Rachel perched herself on the stool in front of her mother's vanity and started sorting through the leftover jewelry. Some pieces her mother would no doubt like to take with her, others would be stored away.

Part of her still felt abandoned by her mother, but another larger part was happy her mother was going to experience such a grand adventure. The past few years had brought her mother so little happiness, so little time out in society. Now, she would accompany the dowager countess to numerous soirees and parties befitting the widow of a baronet. There would be no more whispers behind her back—or very few anyway.

And as for Rachel herself, she would no longer have to face the giggles of the debutantes or the sympathetic remarks from those who remembered her father.

No, she'd only have to face those who guessed that her husband didn't love her. She wasn't sure which was worse.

As she separated her mother's jewelry, Rachel surveyed the barren room. Empty spaces stood out in the dust where knickknacks and trinkets had stood.

"At this rate we'll be finished packing by evening, Janie."

The maid looked up from the trunk of cloth-wrapped figurines. "Will you be leaving then, Lady Braven?"

Rachel shook her head. "No. I won't be leaving for another day or two." She could go. She could return to Wyck's End and have dinner with her mother, Brave, and their three guests instead of eating alone at Tullywood, but she wasn't going to. She needed time alone, time to get used to being on her own, without her mother, and possibly without Brave.

Oh, she had no intention of leaving him. There was no

point to that. She'd promised to give him an heir, and she would keep her promise. But she meant it when she told Belinda that she had no intention of making the best of a bad situation.

She would make her own life as Countess Braven. Now that she knew what was expected of her, she would do what she could to make Brave see that his life hadn't ended when Miranda's had. She would do her best to make him happy. She would be his friend and his lover if he required it. But she would depend on no one but herself for her own happiness. If she was miserable, it would be because she wanted something she couldn't have, or of her own doing.

If she and Brave did have children, she would find happiness in motherhood, and maybe someday Brave would see her for herself and not as a substitute for someone else. And if he didn't . . . well that was his concern.

Perhaps if she kept thinking it, she would eventually believe it. She didn't want to live her life like that. She wanted her husband to love her—*her*. She wanted to earn his love, and if she couldn't, then she didn't want to be with him.

Many *ton* couples lived separate lives; surely she would be able to do so as well.

Staying alone at Tullywood was simply practice. Yes, that was it. It wasn't that she was afraid to face him. He'd had a day to think things over as well. Did he miss her, or was he realizing just what a mistake marrying her had been? Perhaps she wouldn't be welcome at Wyck's End when she did return.

No, she couldn't imagine Brave turning her away. He was too noble for that. No doubt he'd see remaining married to her just another kind of homage to Miranda.

Was it possible to hate a woman one had never met before? It had to be, for Rachel despised Miranda Rexley almost as much as she had despised Sir Henry.

And so she hid at Tullywood, not willing to face the ghost

of her husband's dead love, not wanting to face her husband after that embarrassing scene the day she left. She reacted like a madwoman. Like a woman in love.

In wasn't in her nature to be such a coward. Hadn't she always faced Sir Henry? If he hadn't broken her, surely that said something for the strength of her character. But she hadn't cared about Sir Henry. She hadn't loved him. He'd had no emotional power over her. Brave did. And wounds on the inside sometimes took longer to heal than those on the outside.

She would do what she always did when she ran into adversity. She would fight and plot and find another way around, but no more would she make impulsive decisions. She would think before she acted, because impulse was telling her to run back to Wyck's End and demand to know how Brave felt about her, and that was just asking for trouble.

And so she wasn't going back until the day her mother and Annabelle left for London. They would stay in town for a few weeks to give Marion extra time to heal and purchase clothing befitting her station. Then they would journey on to France and spend the winter somewhere warm. Rachel hoped she might see her mother again before they sailed.

She hoped Gabriel and Julian would be gone by the time she returned. It wasn't that she disliked Brave's friends, but it made her uncomfortable having Miranda's brother in the house. For all she knew, he could be encouraging Brave in this foolish obsession of his. When the time came for her and Brave to discuss their future, she didn't want anyone else adding their opinions.

She was going to have to be honest about her feelings. She was going to have to tell him how she felt. No more lies, no more deceptions. If they were to have any kind of real marriage, that was the way it was going to have to be. And if Brave rejected her . . . well, the next forty or fifty years were going to be somewhat uncomfortable for both of them.

"What do you want me to do with this, my lady?"

Rachel finished packing a delicate wrought-iron brooch and turned to Janie. She held a miniature portrait in her hand. Rachel took it, holding it up to the fading sunlight coming through the window so she could better discern the features.

It was Sir Henry, painted for his marriage to her mother.

A chill slipped down Rachel's spine. Her mother had spent a very uncomfortable number of years with this man. How many more would she have had to endure if Brave hadn't walked into their lives?

Rachel didn't want an uncomfortable marriage. She wanted a real one. She wanted what her parents had had. She deserved no less, and if Balthazar Wycherley wasn't the man who could give it to her then . . . then . . . well, he was just going to *have* to give it to her. It was all or nothing. She would not settle for less.

"Burn it," she said, handing the portrait back to Janie. Her mother was starting a new life; she wanted no reminders of her old one.

As she watched her stepfather's face go up in flames in the fireplace, Rachel decided it was time she took control of her own life as well.

He was a simpleton. Possibly even an idiot.

For only a man with a weak brain would allow his wife to walk away from him. Only a man with some stupid, twisted desire to punish himself would stop himself from going after her out of a sense of honor. He wasn't to blame for Miranda's death. He knew that now. It had taken Julian's anger and a lot of soul-searching to allow himself to believe it. It wasn't his fault, but Rachel's leaving was. And he could attribute it to one thing and one thing only.

Stupidity.

He should have been honest with her when he had the

chance, but he'd been so afraid of her rejecting him that he hadn't seen that he was building a wall between them.

Standing in one of the windows that lined the wall of his study, Brave stared toward the lane, sipped a brandy, and waited for Rachel to return. He'd been waiting since the moment she left two days ago.

The house seemed empty without her in it, even with the servants bustling about their usual chores and his mother and friends milling about. His mother, when she wasn't gazing anxiously at him, was always in Marion's room or one of the parlors discussing their upcoming trip. He could only listen to their plans for so long before his mind drifted. He played billiards with Gabe and Jules or read to occupy the time, but even the company of his friends became tedious after a while. They treated him as though he was made of glass— one wrong move and he'd shatter.

Did they think he was going to drown his sorrows in liquor? Perhaps throw himself into a fit of rage and despair? They were going to be heartily disappointed if they did.

Brave had no desire to dull the pain. He wanted to feel it. He wanted to think about what he had done wrong and wish he had done it differently. He wanted to miss Rachel. He wanted to hope that she would come back to Wyck's End soon.

That she would return to him.

Twice, he'd gone out for a ride, only to turn around when he found himself within a stone's throw of Tullywood. He'd been tempted to ride up to the doors and demand she come home with him. But he didn't. He didn't want to pressure her. So he waited.

If she'd only heard the whole of his conversation with Gabe and Jules, she would have known how his feelings had changed since he first proposed to her. If she'd only let him explain, perhaps she would be with him now. But she'd been too hurt, too angry to listen to anything more he had to say.

After a year and a half of little company other than his

own—and liking it that way—the Earl of Braven found that he craved attention. His wife's attention, anyway. And if she—*when* she came back, he wasn't going to let her go away ever again.

"What the hell are you doing?"

Brave didn't turn. "What does it look like I'm doing?"

Gabriel's boots thudded against the carpet with every impatient step. Brave smiled. He didn't know which one of his friends was more disgusted with him, Gabe or Julian.

"It looks like you're being a complete ass, is what it looks like."

Definitely Gabriel.

"I'm waiting, Gabe. I'm giving her the time she wanted. What would you have me do?"

Gabriel's gray eyes flashed. "Go after her, you stupid fool!"

Brave smiled ruefully. "She doesn't want me to come after her."

The expression on his friend's face was nothing short of stupefied. "What difference does that make?"

"I have to respect her wishes, Gabe." Turning back to the window, Brave squinted at the road, looking for a sign of a carriage—her carriage.

"The only thing you have to do is get the woman you love back in your bed where she belongs."

Brave chuckled. "What do you know of love?" He meant the remark to be teasing, but he regretted the words as soon as they left his mouth.

"Gabe, I—"

His friend cut him off. That had been happening to him a lot lately. "This is one time when I know exactly what I'm talking about, my friend. You know it's been almost eight years since I last saw Lilith."

"I didn't know it had been so long," Brave remarked with sympathy. "It doesn't seem like it's been that long."

"It certainly doesn't feel it." Gabriel stared out the window now as well, but Brave doubted it was the landscape his friend was seeing.

They hadn't spoken much of what had happened between Gabriel and Lilith Mallory over the years. Brave only knew that Gabriel had been one-and-twenty, had loved her, had planned to marry her and that she had disappeared completely. Rumors circulated that her parents had found out about her and Gabriel and had sent her away. Others said Lilith was pregnant by someone else and had fled to the Continent to escape disgrace. Brave didn't know if even Gabriel knew the truth.

"Do you still think about her?"

Gabriel's bitter smile was a dim reflection in the glass. "Every damn day." He turned to face Brave. "That's why you have to go after Rachel, my friend. Go get her. Bring her back to Wyck's End before she disappears on you."

"Rachel's not going to disappear." Brave dismissed the notion with a shake of his head. It was absurd to even think it. Where would she go?

"Does she know how you feel about her?"

His friend's gaze was so intense Brave had difficulty meeting it. "After the way she walked out of here, I doubt it."

"So she doesn't know you love her."

Brave bowed his head. "I never knew for certain myself until she was gone." A part of him had felt as though it had left with her. That part was his heart.

"Well Lilith knew I loved her and I knew she loved me and she still left. You don't think it could happen to you?"

Rachel had said something before she left about being foolish enough to think herself in love with him and she'd left him then. Could she walk away from him completely?

He'd just managed to forgive himself for losing Miranda—a loss that hadn't been his fault. He'd never forgive himself for losing Rachel.

"You really think I should go after her?"

Gabriel nodded, his expression sober. "If you love her, you should go after her and never let her out of your sight again."

Brave's smile was crooked. "Is that what you'd do if you found Lilith again?"

"After all she's put me through," Gabe said with a rough laugh, "Lilith's going to have to find me."

Brave laughed. "Don't ever issue a challenge where a woman is concerned, Gabe. You might find yourself being taken up on it."

Shaking his head, Gabriel turned back to the window. "She's never coming back, Brave. I know that now, but I would hate to see you end up like me just because you thought you were doing the right thing."

Something in his words struck at Brave's heart. For all his bravado and sarcasm, Gabriel was a good man. Brave had never realized in all their years of friendship just how lonely the Earl of Angelwood was.

Brave had had his fill of being lonely.

With a clap on the back, Gabriel steered him in the direction of the door. "I know you'll do whatever is right for you. Now, come see Julian and me off."

With his head full of Rachel, Brave had forgotten that his friends were leaving for London that day.

"I've seen more of you in the last month and a half than I have in the past year," Brave joked, as they left the study.

Gabriel grinned, all of his moroseness apparently forgotten. "And if you're lucky enough to have your lovely wife forgive you, you won't see my shadow darken your door for quite some time. The next time I return to Wyck's End I expect to be an uncle."

The very thought of being a father tightened Brave's gut and made his heart pound. He would like very much to be a father.

"I shall endeavor to meet your expectations," he joked. "Especially since you're leaving this spring for Nova Scotia. I'll have plenty of time to beg Rachel to forgive me."

"Oh, she'll forgive you," Gabriel predicted as they entered the great hall. "Once she realizes how much you love her."

"You make it sound so simple."

"It is." The darker man smiled. "It's just men who make it so difficult."

What convinced Rachel that Sir Henry's nephew was nothing like his predecessor was the reinstatement of Potts as butler. Ever the faithful servant, the aging Potts had been a godsend these last couple of days. Only he and Mrs. Evans, the housekeeper, knew just where everything was, knew how to keep the rest of the staff in line. Some of the servants thought that since Sir Henry had shucked off his mortal coil, they didn't have to do anything or take orders from anyone but the new master. The new master wasn't due to arrive until Rachel had settled her mother's affairs.

But now those affairs were almost settled. Two wagonloads of furniture and trunks had been sent off to Wyck's End. Most of it would be stored until Marion needed it again. Only a few trunks had been set aside for Marion to take with her when she left, and two trunks held the few things Rachel wanted for herself, things she'd brought to Tullywood as a child or things that she had acquired over the years that reminded her of good times and not the bad.

"Everything appears to be in order, my lady," Potts remarked, as Rachel stepped into the foyer.

"Excellent, Potts." She was amazed at how little time it took to pack the entirety of her and her mother's lives at Tullywood. Only their respective bedchambers had any personal touches, any warmth. Other than the few belongings in the attic, those two rooms had been the only ones to inventory and pack.

Everything seemed to be happening very quickly. Mr. Smith had already sold several of Sir Henry's horses and had buyers interested in the rest. That was part of the reason for their meeting that afternoon. He had a bank draft for her mother for the amount of the sales. He had also made arrangements for Sir Henry's personal items to be auctioned off.

How quickly more than a decade of misery could be disposed of.

"Will you be returning to Wyck's End today, Lady Braven?"

Rachel smiled at the thinly veiled curiosity in the old retainer's voice. "Not today, Potts. I have business to attend to in town with Mr. Smith, and the new baronet is coming for dinner this evening. I thought it would be easier for everyone if I showed him the house and introduced him to the staff."

Potts nodded, not bothering to hide his disappointment. "Very well, my lady. Shall I send word to Wyck's End that you'll be returning on the morrow?"

"That won't be necessary." Rachel couldn't keep a hint of sorrow from creeping into her voice. "Tomorrow is the day my mother leaves for London. They'll be expecting me to return before she leaves." In fact she had already received a note from her mother saying she absolutely refused to go anywhere without spending some time with Rachel first. Rachel took the missive not only as an indication that her mother was going to miss her, but as a gentle reminder that Rachel couldn't stay away forever.

"As you wish, my lady. Shall I fetch your cloak and bonnet?"

Rachel nodded. "The rose velvet, please, Potts. And the gray gloves." It was a chilly day, but thankfully clear. Rachel hated it when it was cold and damp. Yorkshire cold had a way of seeping into the bones and staying there for hours.

She looked forward to getting out of the house for a few hours. Tullywood was a lot like that cold in the bones; it lingered long after a person wished it gone.

Glancing around at the polished oak and high windows of the foyer, Rachel realized that it wasn't the house that was so repulsive. It fact, Tullywood was quite nice. It was the man who had owned it that made it such an awful place. With luck, Marcus Westhaver would put an end to his uncle's legacy.

Pott's returned with her garments and draped the fur-lined velvet over Rachel's shoulders as she slipped on her gloves.

"I shall return as soon as possible, Potts," she said, as the butler opened the door for her.

"And if anyone should call, Lady Braven?"

By "anyone" he meant Brave. Rachel didn't have to be a genius to figure that one out.

She smiled gently. "No one's going to call, Potts."

"But if *anyone* does, my lady?"

An exasperated chuckle broke forth from between Rachel's lips. "Ask them to leave a card, Potts. Is there anything else?"

Potts shook his head. "No, my lady."

"Very well. I shall be back shortly."

Huddled deep into her cloak, Rachel stepped out into the frigid afternoon and down the low steps to the drive where her carriage sat waiting. It was one of Brave's carriages. He had several. She doubted he even missed it.

The footman—one of Sir Henry's—opened the door and unfolded the step for her. She was just about to take the hand he offered and climb inside when two men on horseback galloped up the drive.

Now what? Rachel sincerely hoped Mr. Smith wasn't waiting for her because she was in grave danger of being late for their appointment.

As soon as the riders drew close enough, Rachel recognized them as the Earls Angelwood and Wolfram. Her heart lurched against her ribs. Had something happened to Brave?

"I'll just be a moment," she told the footman, and

stepped away from the carriage to greet her visitors. Whatever the two gentlemen had to say, she didn't want the servants overhearing.

"Good day, Lady Braven," they chorused, each with a tip of his stylish beaver hat.

Rachel smiled. Neither of them looked as though they'd come as the bearers of bad news. "Good day, my lords. To what do I owe this honor?"

"We're on our way to London," Gabriel replied as they both dismounted. "We didn't want to leave without saying farewell and thanking you for your hospitality."

"It was hardly my hospitality, Lord Angelwood. I've been absent for most of your visit."

Rachel liked Brave's friends, she truly did, and that made her comfortable in speaking her mind with them. They were protective of her husband. They genuinely cared for him, and that instantly raised her opinion of them right there. They also didn't seem to find her a threat, something Rachel found unusual given their sex and relationship to her husband.

Gabriel smiled. "Your presence was felt every day, I assure you."

He was a charmer, this one. Julian was more serious, more introverted, but no less appealing. Poets were always terribly romantic. Rachel would wager Brave and his friends had broken quite a few hearts when they were younger, and were quite good at it, if the way Brave had broken hers was any indication.

And yet all she wanted to do was have him make her understand so she could forgive him.

"I wish we had the time to get to know you better," Julian told her, stepping closer. "I should like to call you friend as I do Brave."

This coming from Miranda Rexley's brother was almost too much for Rachel to bear. Her throat tightened with emotion. If the warmth of the earl's gaze was as sincere as it looked, Rachel knew he meant it.

"Thank you, my lord." That she could even speak was a miracle.

"Julian," he replied.

"Yes," Gabriel joined it. "There is no need for such propriety between friends. You must call us by our Christian names."

Their offer of friendship, of open acceptance and support was overwhelming. Rachel could only stare and nod dumbly in compliance.

Gabriel glanced at the carriage. "Are you returning to Wyck's End today?"

Rachel caught the hopeful note in his voice and smiled. Everyone wanted to know if she was returning to her husband. Everyone, it seemed, but Brave himself.

"Tomorrow," she replied. "My mother and Annabelle, as you know, are also bound for London."

"So you and Brave will finally have the house to yourselves again." Gabriel's smile was bright. Too bright.

Rachel nodded. "Yes. We will."

Silence stretched among the three of them. Why had they come to see her? Rachel appreciated the sentiment, but she knew they hadn't made a special trip to Tullywood to thank her for hospitality she hadn't extended.

"Go easy on him," Julian spoke softly, finally breaking the quiet. "He was acting out of the kindness of his heart."

Rachel arched a brow. So they'd come to beg for mercy for their friend had they? "Was he?" She didn't bother to hide her doubt, noting with some satisfaction that the Earl of Wolfram actually flushed.

"What Julian is trying to say is that Brave's heart was in the right place," Gabriel suggested, casting a sideways glance at his friend.

"By 'the right place' do you mean with me or with Miranda Rexley, my lord? Because I'm not sure if even Brave knows the answer to that question. If you do, I'd surely love to hear it." She kept her tone light. Brave's friends did not deserve her hostility, nor had they earned the privilege of seeing just how hurt she was.

It was Julian, the poet, the word-bender, who answered, "A heart can start in one place and end in another, Rachel. It does not necessarily mean that one place is better than the other. What matters is how it got there."

She met his golden gaze evenly. "Pretty words, Julian."

Smiling, he took one of her hands in his. "The truth," he told her. "Take it from someone who knows where Brave's heart was when he met you, Rachel. It wasn't in a bad place to begin with."

Rachel was instantly contrite. Of course Julian would consider his sister's memory worthy of such a gesture. How could she have been so insensitive to even mention it?

"But I believe Brave's heart is in a much better place now," he continued in that gentle voice of his. "A place that will appreciate all he has to offer. A place where he can love and be loved as he deserves."

The man was too skilled at saying all the right things, blast it! Rachel's vision blurred with tears as she stared into Julian's earnest gaze.

Gabriel took her other hand. Sniffing, Rachel turned to him.

"I haven't Julian's talent with words, Rachel," he said with a self-deprecating smile. "But I do know that before you came along, Brave believed he had nothing to live for, and now he has you."

"Oh!" Pulling her hands free from theirs, Rachel reached up and dabbed her eyes with the tips of her gloves. "The two of you are awful, truly awful!"

They laughed then, both of them, and each offered her a handkerchief to use instead of her gloves. Rather than choose between them and let one of them off easy, Rachel wiped her eyes on Julian's monogrammed linen and blew her nose in Gabriel's. Each gentleman insisted that she keep the balled-up squares of fabric.

"And now we must depart," Gabriel remarked, once she was feeling more herself again.

Rachel chuckled. "You're a rake, Gabriel, making a lady cry and then running away."

He grinned. "I like to kiss them before I leave them as well." And he brushed a chaste kiss across her cheek.

"I don't normally do either," Julian joked. "But I'll make an exception in this case." Smiling, he leaned forward and kissed the other side of her face.

They said farewell, and Rachel watched them ride away, with a smile, her heart lighter than it had been in the last few days.

"Are you ready to leave now, Lady Braven?" the footman inquired from his position by the carriage.

Oh, Mr. Smith! She was going to be so shamefully late for their meeting!

"Yes, I'm ready!" she cried, scampering up into the carriage. "Please hurry!"

The carriage sped down the drive, and as Rachel was jostled from one side of the seat to the other she silently, joyfully prayed for tomorrow to hurry up and arrive.

"I'm sorry, Lord Braven, but Lady Braven is out at the moment."

"Out?" Brave faced the apple-cheeked butler with barely concealed frustration. "What do you mean, 'out'?"

The older man smiled as though he thought Brave was a complete idiot. "I mean she's not here, my lord."

Brave pinched the bridge of his nose with his thumb and forefinger. "Yes, but where has she gone?"

"She had an appointment in the village with Mr. Smith, Lady Marion's solicitor."

"I know who he is," Brave replied with more brusqueness than he meant to. "How long ago did she leave?"

"Oh, not even a quarter hour ago, my lord."

Damn! She wouldn't be back for some time—possibly even hours—and he had promised to dine with his mother and Marion that evening.

"Would you care to leave your card, my lord?"

His card? For his own wife? Obviously the old man was loose in the attic. "No, that won't be necessary. Just tell her I was here, please." He brushed past the butler and, cramming his hat down on his head, stepped back out into the darkening afternoon.

After all the time it took him to gather his courage and come after her. After he'd labored over just how he was going to beg her forgiveness, she had the audacity to be out? How unfair was that?

Gabe was right. He should have come sooner.

"Begging your pardon, Lord Braven," the old man called from the doorway, "but the countess won't believe me when I tell her you were here if you don't leave a card."

Sighing—either out of frustration or humiliation, Brave wasn't quite sure which—he stopped, turned around, and came back up the few steps to where the aggravating man stood smiling.

"Are you sure just the card will do?" he questioned. "You don't need me to leave some identifying piece of jewelry, do you? Perhaps a lock of hair?"

Pale eyes brightened, round cheeks pinkened as the servant chuckled. "No, no, that won't be necessary. Just the card."

Brave shoved his hand into his inside coat pocket and fished out his calling-card case. It was a good thing he had it with him, or else Lord only knew what he'd have to leave to prove he'd been there.

"Here." He shoved the card under the other man's broad nose.

The old fool took it and chuckled as he read the inscription on it. "I'll give it to her myself, Your Lordship."

Brave didn't even want to know why that statement was said with so much glee. He just wanted to get the hell out of there. He had the uncomfortable feeling that all of Tullywood's servants were watching him from the upstairs windows.

"Thank you, uh . . ."

"Potts, my lord."

It suited him. "Yes, well, thank you." Turning away, Brave walked down the steps, to his horse, waiting patiently in the drive. As he mounted, he looked up at Tullywood's upstairs windows. He didn't see any faces, but several of the curtains were swaying as though someone had just brushed against them.

If he'd known his coming to see his wife was going to be this much of a show, he would have charged admission.

Sighing, he nudged the gelding into motion and trotted down the drive. He missed his wife and wanted her back. He wanted her to love him again—even if he had to beg for it.

Tomorrow couldn't come fast enough.

Chapter 20

Instead of going straight to Brave and demanding to know why he had come to Tullywood the day before, Rachel breezed through the front door of Wyck's End and straight up the stairs to her mother's room.

She wasn't ready just yet to face him. And she still wasn't quite sure she totally believed Potts that he'd been there at all! The aged butler had looked far too smug when he presented Rachel with Brave's card upon her return to Tullywood the previous afternoon.

Maybe he truly had come to see her. Maybe he'd missed her as much as she missed him. From what she'd heard, Brave had been moping around the house like a dejected suitor ever since her departure.

Good. Rachel hadn't been the only miserable one then. It wouldn't hurt him to wonder a little while longer. It was his own stupid fault anyway.

Besides, she only had two hours before her mother went

gallivanting off to London and then to France. She and Brave had the next fifty years to sort things out.

Her mother was rearranging clothing in a trunk when she walked in.

"Are you certain you feel well enough to travel?"

Smiling brightly, her mother closed the trunk and came toward her, her arms outstretched. Each step was carefully taken, but there was no doubt that she was healing quickly. Rachel stepped into the embrace.

"I'm fine," Marion told her with a light squeeze. "Between you and Annabelle, I'll be lucky if I ever make it to the boat. She's already decided that we're going to spend some time at her London town house before we sail. Did you know Balthazar owns his own ship?"

"No, I didn't." The news didn't surprise her, however. From what she'd seen and overheard since their marriage, she'd deduced that her husband was very wealthy, especially since he'd paid Sir Henry ten thousand pounds just to marry her.

Penance was expensive these days.

Funny just how little she cared about his fortune, though. She'd always daydreamed of marrying a wealthy gentleman and being showered in gowns and jewelry, but that was just because she never got anything new unless it was absolutely necessary—not from Sir Henry, anyway. Now that she had the means, those things didn't seem so important.

"Do you have everything you need?"

Her mother nodded. "Yes. Thank you for packing it all for me."

Rachel smiled. It had felt good to take all of her mother's possessions out of the drawers and closets and pack them up. It was like closing a bad book and putting it away on a high shelf, never to be read again.

"You're welcome. Everything else is in storage here, in the west wing of the house. It'll be waiting for you when you come back."

"*If* I come back," Marion replied teasingly. "You never know, I might nab myself some dashing *monsieur* in Paris."

"Make sure he's younger than you," Rachel advised in a similar tone. "That way you can control him."

Her mother giggled. "You sound just like Annabelle."

"You should listen to her. She knows what she's talking about." Frankly, the idea of her mother with a younger man was something Rachel didn't want to dwell on. In fact, the idea of her mother having an affair with anyone made her queasy. Mothers weren't supposed to have lovers.

They sat and talked until the footmen came to collect the last of the luggage. The conversation was purposely kept light. Her mother never mentioned Brave, and neither did Rachel. They talked only of the new life her mother was about to embark upon. It was better that way. Rachel wanted her mother to leave with pleasant thoughts, not worrying about her and Brave.

Rachel helped her mother down the stairs to the foyer where Brave and his mother were waiting.

"Are you ready?" Annabelle asked with a smile as they reached the bottom step.

Her mother positively trembled with excitement. "I am."

Rachel glanced at Brave out of the corner of her eye and caught him watching her with an expression so intense her own knees went weak. God, how she'd missed that somber face!

He stepped forward to say good-bye to her mother, and so Rachel went to Annabelle.

"Have a good journey," she said, and was stunned when the dowager enveloped her in a rosewater-scented embrace.

"Take care of yourself, my dear," Annabelle whispered against her ear. "And take care of my boy."

Rachel blinked back unexpected tears. "I will," she promised.

Her mother-in-law stepped back, holding her at arm's length and staring at her with that same expression Brave wore whenever Rachel thought he was trying to read her mind.

"I know you will." She pulled her close in another quick hug and then turned to say good-bye to her son.

Throat tight, Rachel went back to her mother. "You be careful," she whispered, her voice hoarse. "I don't want to have to come to Paris because you've gotten yourself in trouble with some aristocrat's son."

Marion laughed, her own eyes wet. "I'll be careful." Reaching out, she took Rachel's hand in one of her own and squeezed. "You be happy, you hear? I don't want to have to come back to Yorkshire just because you're being hard on yourself."

It was Rachel's turn to chuckle, but it came out more like a cough around that damn lump in her throat. "I will be. I promise."

Her mother pulled her close in a fierce hug that must have hurt her own ribs, but she didn't show it. "I'm so proud of you," she whispered for Rachel alone.

The tears Rachel had so successfully fought up until that point flowed freely down her cheeks. She couldn't even talk she was so moved.

"Love always wins, dearest," Marion went on in the same quiet tone. "You just have to let it."

Rachel nodded, still too choked up to speak.

Her mother was the first to pull away. She and Annabelle walked to the door with Brave and Rachel following behind. Rachel stood in the door, Brave's hands tentative and warm on her shoulders as she watched a footman help her mother climb gingerly into Annabelle's carriage. The tears continued to fall as the carriage door shut and the vehicle slowly rolled down the drive. Marion and Annabelle waved from the window, two blurry figures that grew steadily out of focus as the carriage drew farther away.

And then they were gone, and she was being steered back inside with a handkerchief pressed into her hand.

She was amassing quite a collection of gentlemen's handkerchiefs.

"Thank you," she murmured, wiping at her face. She was already feeling better. Her mother was off on a grand adventure, and although it had been hard to say good-bye, Rachel couldn't help but be excited for her. And now she and Brave were alone, and they could finally make things right between them.

"I've missed you," he told her when she handed the damp linen back to him. He didn't take it.

"I've missed you, too." Oh, how much!

"You're staying?" His voice rang with hope. Rachel's heart fluttered at the sound of it.

She nodded. "I'm afraid there isn't enough distance in the world that could have made me want to stay away."

His gaze was hesitant, as if he had no more idea of where to start than she did. Part of her wanted to kiss him, hold him, forget all this had ever happened, but there were so many things they needed to discuss.

"We need to talk," he said, so soft she barely heard him.

"Yes."

"Upstairs."

Rachel wasn't sure that was such a good idea, but she had little choice in the matter. Before she could even reply, Brave had swept her up into his arms and was bounding up the stairs in his usual two-at-a-time fashion despite her added weight.

"What are you doing?" she demanded, jostling in his arms as he practically ran down the hall.

"I've had what I want to say to you swimming in my heard since yesterday. If I don't get it out soon, it's going to be garbled beyond comprehension."

He kicked the door of his bedroom open and shut it again in a similar fashion. Unceremoniously, he dumped her on the bed.

Still bouncing on the mattress, Rachel could only stare at him as he paced back and forth across the carpet.

For someone who claimed to have a lot to say, he was certainly silent.

"I'm sorry I never told you the truth about Miranda," he began. It was a good place to start. "Yes, I offered to marry you because of some kind of harebrained notion of making amends."

Rachel wasn't so sure she wanted to hear this right now. She opened her mouth, but Brave cut her off.

"That was before I realized that marrying you was so much more than making up for the past." His eyes were bright as he faced her, as though he was trying to will her to believe him. "Marrying you gave me a chance for a future I never dreamed of being able to obtain. When you asked me about her I had already decided that our marriage was more than just a way to pay for past sins. It was more than me helping you. I felt as though *you* were helping me—and you didn't even know it."

"I wanted to help you," she admitted softly. "I would have done everything I could if you'd only been honest with me."

Sighing, he raked both hands through his hair. "I *was* honest with you. When you asked me about why I married you I was already falling in love with you. *Why* didn't matter anymore."

He'd been falling in love with her? "It mattered to me."

He stared at her, raw emotion in his gaze. "I know."

"It mattered because I would have liked to have known that you were starting to care for me. Instead of thanking God for sending you to us to save my mother and praying that you might someday come to love me, I might have found the courage to tell you how I felt!"

"I'm sorry."

"You should be!" Tears sprang to her eyes, and she didn't care. All the hurt and the hope bubbling inside her boiled over. "I spent nights worrying over how I was ever going to repay you for your kindness! Hours wondering if I was ever going to come close to Miranda in your eyes. I held you up above all other men only to find out that you'd been using me to make peace with some spoiled brat that didn't even deserve you!" The tears spilled over.

Brave looked stunned as she wiped her hands across her cheeks.

"A stupid, cowardly girl who gave no thought to her friends or family but only herself!"—*sniff!*—"An idiot who took her own life to pay back a man who probably never even gave a second thought to her or his child! A . . . a selfish *cow* who would rather die than face the consequences and didn't have enough sense to love you!" She was openly sobbing.

He reached for her. "Rachel, I—"

She grabbed him by the arms, her face wet as tears streamed unheeded from her eyes. "And you felt sorry for her. You felt responsible for it. You probably still feel responsible for it. It makes me so *angry*, Brave! Doesn't it make you angry?"

"What it makes me," he replied, brushing his fingers along her temple, "is thankful beyond measure that you found me, Rachel."

Thankful? He was thankful for her?

He continued, "Because if you hadn't, I would still be lost, blaming myself for something that wasn't my fault and scared that I was doomed to disappoint or destroy everyone I touched."

Sniffing, she arched a brow. "You don't think you disappointed me?"

Brave chuckled, and Rachel was tempted to kick him. She was serious, blast it!

"I know I disappointed you, Rachel." Dropping to the bed beside her, he cupped her face with both hands, forcing her to meet the startling, wonderful honesty of his gaze.

"And I know that by coming back here today you're giving me a chance to make it up to you."

It was tempting to tell him she'd only come back to say good-bye to her mother, but there had been enough lies between them, even little ones.

"But what I realized through all this was that the person I had disappointed the most was myself." His thumbs brushed away the stray tears that trickled down her cheeks. "And I knew that if I let you go without telling you I loved you, I would never, never forgive myself."

More tears, fat and scalding, spilled over her lashes. "I wouldn't forgive you either."

He wiped her cheeks again. "Do you forgive me now?"

Something in his tone made her look up. As her vision cleared, her breath caught at the molten softness of his gaze.

"Yes," she whispered. She'd forgive him anything if he promised to love her and look at her like that for the next fifty years.

A slow smile curved his lips. A smile so sweet and so pure it was heartbreaking just to look upon it. This was her husband's smile—the smile she'd been wanting to see since the night he pulled her from the Wyck.

He loosened the knot of linen at his throat. "Prove it."

Rachel knew what he had in mind and had no desire to stop him. Along with the trickle of desire that pooled low in her belly, spreading heat to her pelvis, was the gut-wrenching happiness that came from knowing she was the reason for that smile. Toeing off her shoes, she kicked the leather slippers across the room. Her fingers then went to the bodice of her gown.

Brave's eyes widened as the wrap-front gown fell open.

"Were you expecting this?" he asked jovially, tossing aside his cravat and yanking his shirt over his head.

Rachel yanked on her sleeves, transfixed by the hard muscles of his chest and abdomen as he unfastened his falls. "I've been expecting this forever."

Standing, he kicked off his boots. "I've been waiting forever for you."

Her heart swelled at his words. "I know."

He flashed her a grin as his hands unbuttoned the front of his trousers. Watching the ripple of muscle across his back as he peeled the soft buckskin down the hard length of his legs, Rachel thought she'd been waiting an eternity just for him to get his clothes off.

She had taken down her hair, shucked off the gown and demi-corset, and was struggling with her shift when he joined her, nude and hard on the bed.

"May I offer some assistance?"

The hard length of his sex was just inches from her hand, and Rachel's mouth went dry at the stark want unfurling in her womb.

"Yes," she croaked.

"I've always wanted to do this." Lifting the hem of the delicate linen, Brave took it in both hands and ripped.

Rachel gasped as the gauzy fabric let go from hem to neck with nothing more than a sharp groan. Laughter bubbled in her chest along with indignation, while shivers of anticipation shook her limbs.

"Brave!"

"I'll buy you another," he promised, pushing her back onto the mattress with the full force of his weight. Bracing himself on his palms, he lay between her thighs, their bodies pressed together from shoulder to groin.

The hard length of him probed the entrance to her body, a delicious nudging that forced her to move against it, trying to take him in.

"Christ," he murmured, shoving himself against her heat. "You're already wet."

Spreading her legs wider, Rachel arched and pushed, gasping as he slid within her.

"I told you," she panted, "I've been waiting for this."

"Me," he told her, with a deep, sweet thrust that made her gasp for breath. "You've been waiting for *me*. Don't ever leave me again."

"N-not even if you ask me to?" Oh God, but he felt good.

"Especially not if I ask you to."

They moved together, neither one of them touching the other for fear of disturbing the acute pleasure of their joined bodies. Pure friction; wet heat that jangled Rachel's senses until she thought she might explode.

It was one of the most erotic experiences of her life. He wouldn't let her touch him, instead, twining their fingers together so all their attention was focused on the spot where their bodies became one. She stared at his beautiful face, watching as passion darkened his eyes to obsidian and tightened his features.

He teased her, slipping into her only so far before pulling almost completely out. Digging her heels into the mattress, she lifted her hips, whimpering for more.

He gave it to her. One fierce plunge pressed her deep into the bed and she wrapped her legs around his thighs to keep him buried to the hilt within her.

"Yes," she whispered, her voice building to a moan. "Oh, Brave, yes!"

Without missing a thrust, he rolled them over so that she rode him. Falling forward, Rachel braced her hands on either side of his head. Her breasts brushed his chest, drawing another hiss of desire as the sensitive nipples tightened even harder. Riding him this way only intensified each sensation. Not only was there the sweet friction of their bodies, but now an ache built within that tiny part of her made for sexual release.

Still he did not touch her. His fists stayed tightly balled as he splayed his arms wide. His eyes shut as his mouth opened with building pleasure.

Rachel quickened the pace, needing the climax as much

as she needed the man himself. The pressure grew and blossomed, then finally flew apart as ripple after ripple shivered through her. Brave's hoarse shout filled the room. She cried out in reply, collapsing on top of him as her muscles refused to support her.

How long they stayed like that, she had no idea. It felt like hours, but time had ceased to exist somewhere along the way.

"I have a surprise for you," he whispered sometime later, when the shadows cast across the room had lengthened to thin specters and Rachel hovered on the cusp of sleep.

How had he known how much she loved surprises?

Propping herself up on her forearm, she gazed down at him with barely concealed excitement. "What is it?"

He flashed her a secretive smile and sat up, swinging his long legs over the side of the bed.

"Where are you going?" A tiny edge of panic crept into her voice, that old fear that he was leaving her raising its head again.

"I just have to get it."

Rachel's heartbeat slowed to its normal pace as she watched him walk naked to where he'd tossed his waistcoat. He fished something out of the pocket and turned back toward the bed.

He was the most incredible thing she'd ever seen. The entire golden length of him was a study in fluid male strength and grace. As he walked toward her, a frisson of desire pooled deep within her. She wanted him again. She wanted him forever.

"Close your eyes," he commanded in a teasing tone.

She did.

"Now hold out your hand."

She did that as well, fighting the urge to peek as she felt something light and cool settle against her palm.

"You can open them now."

She did, the breath catching in her throat as her gaze settled on the object in her hand.

It was the emerald ring her father had given her mother.

As she sat in stunned silence and stared at the delicate piece of jewelry, wondering why her mother had given it to him, Brave tugged the Wycherley sapphire from her other hand.

"Your mother said you'd found it at Tullywood."

Rachel nodded. "I did yes." She met his gaze, unable to hide her curiosity any longer. "Why did she give it to you?"

Brave grinned and sat down on the mattress beside her. "She said that you might need a reminder every once in a while that love isn't always perfect no matter how it might seem it. She also said something about cows and a tree, but I'm afraid the reference was lost on me."

Choking on something that was between a sob and laughter, Rachel wiped at her eyes with her free hand.

"Will you wear it?" Brave asked softly.

She nodded, not trusting her voice at this point.

Tenderly, Brave took the ring from her palm and slid it onto the ring finger of her left hand. It fit perfectly.

His gaze met hers. "I do."

The simple vow was Rachel's undoing. But it wasn't tears that burst forth, it was laughter. Fierce, unrestrained, joyous laughter. She threw her arms around Brave's neck, knocking them both back onto the bed.

Covering his face with feathery kisses, Rachel remembered the rest of what she and her mother had talked about that day Marion told her about her father and his fear of cows. She already knew her husband's fears, just as she was sure he knew hers. But there was one thing she didn't know.

"Brave?" she asked from her position on top of him.

He smiled. "Yes, my love?"

She returned the grin. "What's your favorite color?"

If he was surprised by the question he didn't show it. "Why, Lady Braven, I do believe it's the exact same color as your eyes."

Laughing, she lifted up on her hands as he tried to kiss her. "Don't you want to know mine?"

"I already do," he informed her.

"Oh?" she raised a brow. "What is it?"

"Rose," he replied with a saucy smile. "Not pink, but rose."

He was right, and the fact that he'd known such a trivial detail about her warmed Rachel right to the soles of her feet.

"I love you," he whispered, tracing circles on her back with his fingers.

Rachel's heart swelled with the words. "I know," she replied. And she did. She felt it in her bones just how much he loved her.

"And do you love me?" he asked tentatively, his hands sliding down to cup her bare buttocks, tickling the sensitive flesh just below. She wiggled against him.

He was hard. Smiling seductively, Rachel lifted her hips and reached down to guide him into her. Moaning, she lowered herself until the entire length of him was buried inside her. The expression on Brave's face was one of pure pleasure.

She began to move. "Do you want the impulsive answer, or the long-thought-about one?"

He groaned and raised his hips. "How about both?"

Chuckling, Rachel flexed her internal muscles around him, feeling him pulsate in response.

"Impulsively . . ."

He grabbed her by the waist and thrust upward.

"Yes! Oh, yes!"

He actually laughed. It was a joyful sound and it pierced Rachel's heart with love and happiness. "And the thought-about answer?" he rasped as she churned her pelvis down on his.

Lowering her head, Rachel brushed her lips across his, her breath quickening. "Impulsively, rashly, and forever, Brave. Always and forever."

America Loves Lindsey!
The Timeless Romances of
The New York Times Bestselling Author

PRISONER OF MY DESIRE	0-380-75627-7/$7.99 US/$10.99 Can
ONCE A PRINCESS	0-380-75625-0/$7.99 US/$10.99 Can
WARRIOR'S WOMAN	0-380-75301-4/$7.99 US/$10.99 Can
MAN OF MY DREAMS	0-380-75626-9/$7.50 US/$9.99 Can
SURRENDER MY LOVE	0-380-76256-0/$7.99 US/$10.99 Can
YOU BELONG TO ME	0-380-76258-7/$7.99 US/$10.99 Can
UNTIL FOREVER	0-380-76259-5/$7.99 US/$10.99 Can
LOVE ME FOREVER	0-380-72570-3/$7.99 US/$10.99 Can
SAY YOU LOVE ME	0-380-72571-1/$6.99 US/$8.99 Can
ALL I NEED IS YOU	0-380-76260-9/$6.99 US/$8.99 Can
THE PRESENT	0-380-80438-7/$6.99 US/$9.99 Can
JOINING	0-380-79333-4/$7.50 US/$9.99 Can
THE HEIR	0-380-79334-2/$7.99 US/$10.99 Can
HOME FOR THE HOLIDAYS	0-380-81481-1/$7.99 US/$10.99 Can
HEART OF A WARRIOR	0-380-81479-X/$7.99 US/$10.99 Can

And in Hardcover

THE PURSUIT
0-380-97855-5/$25.95 US/$39.50 Can

···

Available wherever books are sold or please call 1-800-331-3761
to order.   JLA 0402